DIRTY SECRET

CRYSTAL KASWELL

Copyright

This is a work of fiction. Similarities to real people, places, or events are entirely coincidental.

Also by Crystal Kaswell

Dirty Rich

Dirty Deal - Blake

Dirty Boss - Nick

Dirty Husband - Shep

Dirty Desires - Ian

Dirty Wedding - Ty

Dirty Secret - Cam

Inked Hearts

Tempting - Brendon

Hooking Up - Walker

Pretend You're Mine - Ryan

Hating You, Loving You - Dean

Breaking the Rules - Hunter

Losing It - Wes

Accidental Husband - Griffin

The Baby Bargain - Chase

Inked Love

Faking It - Forest

The First Taste - Holden

The Rule Breaker - Oliver

Sinful Serenade

Sing Your Heart Out - Miles

Strum Your Heart Out - Drew

Rock Your Heart Out - Tom

Play Your Heart Out - Pete

Sinful Ever After – series sequel

Just a Taste - Miles's POV

Dangerous Noise

Dangerous Kiss - Ethan

Dangerous Crush – Kit

Dangerous Rock – Joel

Dangerous Fling – Mal

Dangerous Encore - series sequel

Standalones

Broken - Trent & Delilah

Come Undone Trilogy

Come Undone

Come Apart

Come To Me

Sign up for the Crystal Kaswell mailing list

Chapter One

SIENNA

C am cuts through the room with effortless grace. "Sienna." He wraps his fingers around my wrist. "Your sister asked me to walk you out."

My mind blanks.

My senses go into overdrive.

Cameron Hunt's hands are on my body.

His hands.

My body.

Fuck.

I need to keep my cool. "Have you ever heard the word *please*?"

"No." His voice is as strong and decisive as his hand. "She's leaving now."

Right. My sister is leaving, and she asked Cam to walk me out. Because Cam is a tech mogul ten years my senior. He's not interested in an eighteen-year-old college student.

I nod and follow him into the elevator. "Is everything okay?"

"A fight with Ty." He hits the Lobby button. "Nothing serious, but she needs company."

"That's all she said?" The silver doors slide together, leaving us alone together in the tiny space.

"No." Cam turns to me. "She asked me not to fuck you."

My cheeks flush. "And?"

"And?"

"What did you tell her?"

He shoots me a coy look. It's his signature. *Maybe I said I'd fuck you. Maybe I have no interest. Wouldn't you like to know?* "Not tonight."

"Aren't you leaving tomorrow?"

"In the afternoon."

"So maybe you'll fuck me first thing in the morning, before you fly back to London?"

"Anything's possible."

"Really? You'd consider that?"

He shoots me a charming smile. It's easy, relaxed, teasing. "No."

Of course not. My sister will kill him. But why not tease back? "Why not?"

"I'll ruin you for other men."

"You're that good?"

"Better." His smile widens. "I can't do that to you, Sienna. I like you too much."

"You like me too much to fuck me?"

He nods.

I fail to hold a poker face. "Do you really believe that?"

"Of course."

The elevator stops at the lobby. Cam waits for the silver doors to slide open and motions *after you*.

Right. I'm heading home, not flirting with Cam.

Even if he is flirting back.

Even if he is painfully handsome.

Even if he's the object of most of my sexual fantasies.

2

I follow him outside, into the warm, sticky air. Ah, summer in New York. Bright, alive, and humid as hell.

My dress is thin and I'm melting. How is he so cool and collected in a three-piece suit?

How is he so cool and collected all the time? Even now, teasing me about his sexual prowess.

"Do you really think you'd ruin me?" I ask.

"Of course."

"That's such an obnoxious thing to say."

"It's true."

"Then prove it."

He raises a brow. "How should I do that?"

I move closer. Into his space. "Kiss me goodbye."

"What will that prove?"

"No one will ever compare, right? I can test your theory."

He chuckles. "Do you think this challenge is going to work?"

Yes. "Is it not?"

"You should go."

"I know."

His eyes flit to the entrance. The gold lobby. The silver elevator. Then back to me. "What if it's the best kiss of your life? What if you think of it every time you kiss another man? It's not fair to your future husband."

I can't tell if he's teasing, but I like it. "It's not fair to me, to deny me the greatest kiss of my life."

His smile widens. "I suppose not."

"So…" I offer my hand.

He takes it. Places it on his shoulder. "Good night, Sienna."

My fingers curl into his neck. It's different touching him. Intoxicating in a whole new way. "Good night, Cam."

He moves the way he does anything, with equal parts finesse and power.

He presses one hand into the small of my back. Brings the other to my chin.

He pulls my body into his.

Then his eyes close and his lips find mine.

It's soft.

A hint of a kiss.

A second, maybe.

I can barely taste the champagne on his lips.

But, fuck, I feel it everywhere.

My entire body goes light.

The world turns into a perfect, soft, beautiful place.

Cameron Hunt is kissing me.

And, somehow, some way, I'm going to make sure he kisses me again.

Chapter Two

SIENNA

Two Months Later

Thirty seconds on the clock. One–one on the board.

Either I ace this free kick or we call it a tie.

A tie is almost as bad as losing. Maybe worse. It's giving up.

Deep breath. Slow exhale. Eyes on the ball.

I wind up. Kick to my teammate.

The rest of the world falls away as I race onto the field. I don't feel the blazing sun, the humid air, the sweat weighing down my ponytail.

Only the pounding of my feet.

I run toward the goal, but a sweeper blocks me. I dart around her. Signal to Katie.

She kicks to me.

I dribble, wind up, take my shot.

But it's no good. The goalie blocks it.

And that's it. Game over.

My surroundings come back to me quickly. The sticky

air, the deep blue of the Hudson, the noise of the Financial District.

The team captain ready for a chat.

Her boyfriend waiting on the sidelines.

And Cam.

What the fuck?

My breath escapes my body. My cheeks flame. My cool evaporates.

That's actually Cam. Standing on the fake grass in a three-piece suit.

Is he seriously wearing a three-piece suit?

It must be a Hunt requirement.

Handsome. Graceful. In a suit at all times.

Even at the beach, probably.

And, shit, now I'm picturing Cam in a Speedo. Something bright and bold. Red or royal blue.

Every other inch of his dark skin on display. The strong thighs. The defined torso. The tattoos he hides under his jacket.

He nods hello. Looks me over slowly, noting my plain black sports bra and purple shorts.

It's normal practice attire, especially for a hot day, but his gaze still makes my cheeks flush.

I swallow hard, nod hello, pretend I don't care he's here.

We shake hands with the other team. Listen as the captain goes through her usual rundown.

Stay hydrated. Avoid alcohol. Do not, under any circumstances, waste time with boys.

She eyes Cam suspiciously. "Is that a friend of yours, Sienna?" (Friends are unacceptable distractions unless they're fellow soccer players).

"My sister's wedding is in two weeks," I say.

She does nothing to hide her disappointment. How dare my sister marry during soccer season? Why can't she wait until January? Why am I skipping practice to celebrate this milestone?

"Your sister's fiancé is hot," one of my other teammates says. "Does he have any friends? Or a brother maybe?"

"That is his friend." Technically, Cam is Ty's cousin. But he's also Ty's closest confidant. They're friends, business partners, family.

As close as two people can be, really.

"So he's single," she says.

The team captain glares at her. What about *no boys* does she not understand? It's not just boyfriends. It's casual sex, dates, and flirting too.

I get it, honestly. If it was anything but my sister's wedding, I'd choose soccer. But Indigo is my favorite person in the world. I'll do anything for her.

Including keeping my hands off Cam.

Yes, I like him. Yes, he's incredibly hot.

Yes, for the last two months, I've fallen asleep thinking about that kiss.

God, I can taste him now. Smell his soap. Feel his hands.

It's a prime entry in my spank bank, but it's not happening.

The wedding is in two weeks.

Cameron Hunt is officially off-limits. Which is fine by me.

We're friends... friendly. That's all. We text all the time, sure, but it's about the pre-wedding festivities. And a lot about London soccer leagues. Honestly, US men's soccer is a travesty. We dominate the world in women's soccer, but does anyone in the States care?

Okay, we compete on our mile time (we're neck and neck, but I'm running in scorching hot New York weather. He gets the crisp London air). And we talk about the TV shows we're watching. Not that Cam watches a lot of TV.

Mostly, I recap the events of my latest reality TV show, and he tells me they're ridiculous.

And I fall asleep thinking about his smile.

Or sometimes, thinking about his kiss, and his hands, and his lips on other parts of my body.

Ahem.

Like I said, we're friendly. I don't even notice he's here. I certainly don't care that my shorts barely cover my ass. Or that I'm a sweaty mess and he's cool and composed in his suit.

I'm an athlete who works hard. That's better than looking cute or sexy or glamorous.

I repeat this mantra as I jog to Cam, but it doesn't stick in my brain. My blush deepens. Extends to my chest.

I shrug like it's normal post-game flush. Of course, I'm a little red. I'm running around in eighty degree heat.

He offers a water bottle. A grey aluminum adorned with the London Bridge. "Thirsty?"

"Is that really your hello?"

He nods as he hands me the bottle.

The brush of his fingertips sets me on fire. Thank god the aluminum is chilled.

Mmm, cold water. I drink with greedy sips, but my temperature stays high. He's so handsome and close, and did I mention handsome? But seriously, a suit at a soccer game? That's ridiculous. "You look like a drug dealer."

"Do American drug dealers wear suits?"

I nod. "Haven't you see *The Good Wife?*"

He chuckles. "You've seen *The Good Wife?*"

"Why is that funny?"

"It's highbrow for you."

"Oh my god." I push him playfully. My hand against his chest. The soft wool of his suit jacket. "I watch excellent television."

"*Ninety Day Fiancée* is excellent television?"

My lips curl into a smile. He's teasing. I love his teasing. "People have three months to get married or never see each other again! Those are high stakes!"

"I'll consider that."

He smiles that charming smile of his.

My heart beats harder. He's so handsome. And charming. And off-limits.

And not just handsome.

Smoking hot. Sure, it's hard to make out the details of his body in his suit, but I've seen pictures of him in less.

The man is built like a soccer all-star. Tall and strong and incredibly athletic.

Shit, what are we talking about? "What are you doing here?"

"If you want me to go, I will."

No. God no. "I thought you were still in London."

"Flew in today."

Oh.

"Walked here from my hotel."

"Did you fly in the suit or change when you got here?"

"Oh, I never take it off," he says.

"What about showers?"

"Straight out of the suit and into a new one after."

"Sex?"

He smiles *wouldn't you like to know*. "Sienna, you know I can't tell you that. It's all you'll think about."

"Uh-huh." Maybe. Probably. Definitely. "And you're here because…"

"I wanted to see your beautiful face."

My blush deepens, even though I know it's bullshit. "Really?"

He nods *of course*. Motions *and*—"Ty asked me to collect you. We're going to dinner tonight."

Right. It's Friday. With the wedding the Saturday after next, there's a new festivity every day. "Are we going back to your hotel room?"

He shoots me a *nice try*.

"I live in their building! Why would he need you to collect me?"

"Apparently, you're often late to family functions."

That's true, but—"Not everyone runs their own company. Some of us are on other people's schedules."

"Be late. Make Ty wait for once."

"I like the way you think." Okay. I like the way he looks too. The way he dresses. The way he flirts.

I like him.

I want him.

But I can handle my desire for two tiny weeks. Even if I'm spending most of my free time in Cam's presence.

And he's even more handsome today than the last time I saw him.

And I'm already thinking about dragging him to my apartment.

It's only two weeks.

So what if I want him more than I've ever wanted anyone?

How hard can it be to resist him?

Chapter Three

CAM

The last time I was at Ty's flat, the place was sparse, lonely. Now, it's filled with touches of his fiancée: a bookshelf of old movies, a tea set on the dining table, a grand piano in the corner.

He's found a home with her.

I'm happy for him. Sure, I'm a mess when it comes to love and commitment, but I can ignore that for a few weeks.

Ty isn't asking me to deal with my fucked-up thoughts.

He isn't asking me to believe in love.

No, it's much worse than that.

Ty is asking me to keep Sienna company.

Her older sister, his fiancée, is the only family she has left. And Ty being Ty, he's worried Sienna is going to feel like she's losing her best friend.

So, I'm here to keep her entertained.

He trusts me with his future sister-in-law.

But here I am, in his flat, picturing her naked.

There are millions of eligible women in New York City alone. Why am I lusting after the one woman who will destroy my life?

Is my self-destructive streak really that strong?

Fuck. I need a drink.

I find a bottle of gin in the fridge, fill a glass with ice, pour, sip.

It's not red wine, but it's not bad.

Alcohol, cardamom, juniper.

Memories of college parties, bad dates, one-night stands.

The night Ty slipped me my first drink.

It's almost too much. Too familiar. Too close to the wound.

Keys jingle in the front door. Sienna.

She showered and dressed at her flat, the one three flights downstairs. Now she's here.

I swallow another sip of gin. Will it to cool my thoughts. To banish Sienna from my mind.

Instead, my head fills with the image of her in the shower. Naked, dripping wet, her long brown hair sticking to her tan skin.

Fuck.

I'm not this man.

I screw around sometimes, sure, but I'm smart about it. I don't fuck friends or coworkers or friends' exes.

No one taken.

No one who will fuck up my life.

Certainly not the woman my best friend sees as a kid sister.

The door turns. Sienna steps into the main room in a short rust dress. She twirls to show off her outfit.

My gaze goes to her thighs. I'm already picturing the dress five centimeters higher. I'm already imagining her knickers.

Burnt orange. Like her name.

Apparently my cock is a cheesy motherfucker.

She lands. Smooths her skirt. "You like it?"

I'd like it better on the floor. "You clean up nice."

She flips me off.

I take another sip. Focus on the familiar taste. "You look gorgeous."

"Thank you." She crosses the room to me. Sets a gold clutch on the dining table. "I agree."

"Humble."

"Oh, really, Cameron Hunt is giving me lessons on humility?"

My stomach churns at the sound of my full name. No one calls me Cameron. Not anymore. I shrug it off. Find a poker face. My brand of aloof. *Am I teasing or not? Who knows? Certainly not me.*

It's easier with Americans.

They're always more expressive than they believe they are.

And Sienna—

There's so much in her hazel eyes. Curiosity. Desire. Affection.

"Is there something you want to say?" I tease her back.

Her lips curl into a smile. She's wearing makeup today. A soft red on her lips.

I need those lips on mine.

I need them parting with a groan.

I need them wrapped around my cock.

"I know, it must be hard, being so beautiful," she says. "Sometimes, you just need to proclaim it."

"It's painful, yes."

"It's a burden. But you wear it well."

"And you don't?"

Her smile widens. "What are you drinking?"

"Gin."

"Where's mine?"

"Have you ever heard the word *please*?" I copy her tease.

13

"No." She copies my response.

I motion to the fridge.

"You want me to make my own drink?"

"You're not capable?"

"You're not going to say 'no, Sienna, you're eighteen, you can't drink.'"

"You can drink at eighteen in London."

"Damn. I guess that's one for London." She moves into the kitchen. Fills a glass with ice, a shot of gin, an entire bottle of Fever Tree.

"That's a waste of good gin."

"I like it this way."

"You could use cheap shit. You wouldn't know the difference."

"This is what's here."

That's fair.

"Besides, it's good. Try it. You'll like it." She offers her glass.

I set mine on the table. Take hers. It's not overly sweet, but it's more tonic water than gin. "Rubbish."

"It is not." She laughs. "You like it. I can tell."

"How can you tell?"

"Your eyes."

"What about them?"

"Besides their gorgeous dark hue?"

"If you can get past that."

She smiles as she takes her drink back. "I'm learning how to read them."

"You haven't seen me in two months."

"We talk."

"Via text."

"Even so." She takes a long sip. "I'm going to figure you out whether you like it or not."

Chapter Four

CAM

The second Sienna sees her sister, she skips to the table and throws her arms around her.

It's completely out of place at the upscale restaurant, but neither of them care.

Even Ty, master of propriety, greets Sienna with a warm hug. "Is Cam giving you trouble?"

"Oh, you mean how we fucked in your shower?" Sienna teases Ty. "No trouble at all."

He shakes his head *sure you did* as if he isn't bothered by the suggestion.

He is—Ty is protective of everyone in his life, especially Sienna—but he knows better than to show it. Sienna is like me. She fucks with Ty on purpose.

And my friend trusts me. He believes I won't touch her.

I won't. I just need to convince my cock to get on board with the plan.

"Really?" Sienna's sister Indigo plays along. "The shower is slippery. It's difficult. Worth it, but difficult."

"You have an anti-slip mat." Sienna shoots her sister a *please* look.

Indigo blushes *busted.*

Ty plays along with Sienna. "We have handles too. Did you miss those?"

This time, Sienna blushes. It's not quite *busted.* More *dammit, I've lost this round.* "Uh… well… they didn't work for the position." Her brow furrows. "Really? Handles… how do you…? Nevermind."

Indigo laughs as she turns to me. "It's nice to see you, Cam. You're wearing that suit."

"And your dress?" I sit across from her.

"Doesn't she look great? A total boss bride." Sienna motions to her sister's outfit—a long white dress with a very deep v-neck—and sits next to me. "I helped her pick it out."

"And so humble about her skill too." Indigo blows her sister a kiss.

Sienna catches it, holds it to her chest, blows her own back.

They laugh, easy in their close relationship. Easy with their teasing.

For a few minutes, they stay in that state. Indigo and Sienna tease each other about their relative styles. Indigo is always a "boss babe" whereas Sienna has no time for fancy clothes. She's an athlete who lives for comfort. She doesn't have time to stumble in heels, but she makes an effort for dinners with Ty. She doesn't want to look like a total *layabout* next to a guy who wears a designer suit everywhere.

They banter like it's routine—*seriously, Ty, do you ever take that thing off*—then Sienna shifts the conversation to the wedding.

She swoons over the venue, the dress, the honeymoon in the Bahamas. *I want pictures. Lots of pictures. PG ones!*

She doesn't seem upset about the wedding. But maybe she's good at pretending.

I play my part as groomsman. I tease Ty about saving his

strength for the wedding night, packing enough toys for the honeymoon, finding a hotel with particularly thick walls.

When the server drops off a bottle of Pinot, and fills all four of our glasses, I propose a toast. "To Ty. Making men everywhere proud, thinking with his cock."

Indigo blushes as she holds up her glass. "I, uh… Cheers."

Ty shoots me a *fuck off* look, but he's beaming with pride. "You're an arsehole."

"It is what matters, Ty," Sienna says. "That's why I told Indie to marry you."

"Because I think with my cock?" he asks.

"No. I don't think you do. I mean, look at her." Sienna motions to her sister. "She's perfect in every way. Not just the carnal ways."

Indigo taps her glass with Sienna's.

Sienna smiles and turns to Ty. "You… you're not as much with the personality."

"Brutal," I say.

She continues. "But you're rich, hot, and good in bed. That's the total package."

"She likes him. She's just doesn't like to admit it," Indigo says.

Sienna motions *so-so*.

Ty smiles, not bothered by her teasing. "And that's only because I can talk football."

"Absolutely." She taps glasses with him.

He sips his wine and shakes his head *ah, my silly sister-in-law. So odd and so in need of my protection.*

"It's an interesting philosophy on love," Indigo says.

"Not love. Marriage. They're different things." Sienna turns to me. "What do you think, Cam? What's your philosophy on marriage?"

"Don't," I say.

Sienna laughs. "That's pretty clear. But what if you had to do it?"

"Why would I need to get married?" I sip my wine. It's good Pinot. Full-bodied, fruity, strong. A deep berry, without the sweetness.

"Because it's a hypothetical question," she says.

I raise a brow.

"You're that against it?" she asks.

"What's my other option?" I ask.

"Uh… you can never have sex again," she says.

"Let's go to the courthouse right now," I say.

"Me and you?" Her eyes widen with surprise.

"If I have to marry someone," I say. "A cute football player who's obsessed with sex."

Ty shoots me a *tread carefully* look.

"What else is there?" I ask.

"Besides soccer and sex?" she asks. "Coffee?"

"Do you make coffee?" I ask.

"Already asking me to make your coffee?" She shakes her head, *how rude*. "I'm not that kind of wife."

Indigo chuckles. "You have no idea what you're getting into."

I don't.

"I'll make the coffee if you make dinner," I say.

"You do the dishes."

I hold out my hand.

She shakes. "Look at us, negotiating. We're such a great couple already."

"Fuck her over my dead body." Ty tries to sell it as casual, but he doesn't quite get there.

I shrug like I buy his threat as a joke. "Damn. There goes our perfect marriage."

"There's always a catch," Sienna says.

The conversation shifts back to the wedding and Ty and Indigo's happily ever after, but Ty's promise stays in the air.

He'll do anything to protect her.

And he'll destroy anyone who hurts her.

———

BY THE TIME WE FINISH DESSERT, WE'RE THREE BOTTLES OF wine deep, and Sienna is no longer hiding her desire to fuck me.

I should be used to stolen glances. Sure, I haven't seen her in months, but I see the same look in other women's eyes all the time.

Women want to fuck me.

I'm rich, handsome, well-dressed. When I want to turn up the carefree charm, I can.

When I turn it off and let my fucked-up thoughts seep into my behavior—

Women are even more interested when I'm an arsehole. All right, I'm always an arsehole, but when I'm a brooding one, I clean up.

Women see me as a damaged bad boy—a rich one, in a suit, how novel—and they want to tame me. No matter how much I stress that I won't call them after, that I won't want to see them after we part, they take it as a challenge.

No matter how much they claim otherwise, or insist they're fine with a short fling, they believe they'll fix me.

They never do.

It's not possible.

I've been this way for half my life.

No one knows what happened. Only Ty and the older woman who ruined my ability to connect sex and intimacy.

I don't like people after I fuck them now.

I don't know why. I stopped asking why a long time ago.

Sienna deserves better. She's a sweet girl. She needs someone who will hold her, stroke her hair, whisper *I love you.*

That isn't me.

Even if everything was different, that isn't me.

I'll never be what she needs.

I shouldn't even think about it.

But my inhibitions are weak after all that wine. My head fills with images of her in my hotel room.

My tie around her wrists.

Her long legs splayed over the bed.

Her fingers curled into the sheets.

What does she sound like when she comes?

Is it a high-pitched whine?

Or something low and deep?

Breathy?

The server interrupts with the check. I push my dirty thoughts aside for long enough to fight Ty for the right to pay.

We agree to rock-paper-scissors.

He wins.

After he pays, I insist on walking the trio to their building.

We're close to Battery Park, but it's too dark to see the green. I only catch sight of the Hudson. The azure river reflecting the silver moon.

The not quite dark sky. With all the light pollution, the sky never darkens. It stays that perfect soft blue. A perfect contrast to the yellow fluorescent lights and the silver steel.

"Oh no." Sienna shakes her head. "You're one of those people, aren't you?"

"Which people?" I ask.

"Who fall in love with the city."

"I don't know New York well."

The light turns green. She waits for me to walk. Stays in

time with me. Stays four paces behind her sister and Ty. "I could show you around."

It's a good idea. Being in public, far from my hotel room, will make it a lot harder to do something stupid. "Make sure I don't fall in love?"

"I can't control that. But I can show you the ugly parts too. Not just the Empire State Building at night or Central Park in the afternoon."

"I might fall in love anyway."

Her eyes flit to Indigo and Ty. "Aren't you supposed to say something about London is the superior city?"

"How can I judge fairly, when I haven't seen New York?"

"You've been here twice in the time I've known you." She steps onto the sidewalk. "And you're... older."

"Older?"

"Old enough you've been here before."

"Or I was saving myself for you."

"You met me three months ago."

"Even so."

Her eyes meet mine. "You're flirting with me."

I am, and I need to stop, but my judgment is MIA. "I flirt with everyone."

Her cheeks flame. Her eyes fill with envy. It's quick. A second. And then she's back in the game, trying to work out my intentions.

"It doesn't mean anything."

"You pick women up," she says.

"They pick me up."

"When they flirt, you flirt back."

It's a fair point.

"You should be careful," she says. "If you keep flirting with me, I might think you mean it."

"You shouldn't. I don't."

"Then you shouldn't flirt. I know we have this complicated situation." She motions to my cousin. "I respect what a bad idea it is. But if you flirt with me… I might not be able to control myself."

"I'm that irresistible?"

"You know you are." She winks then she turns to her family and follows Ty and Indigo into the modern skyscraper.

Chapter Five

CAM

Always a dutiful sister, Indigo walks Sienna to her place. It's only three flights down the stairs, but Ty assures me they'll be there awhile.

We pour another round—gin on the rocks again—and we settle on the terrace.

It's not the Ty I've known my entire life. It's like the rest of his flat—changed by his fiancée.

The lush plants, the string lights, the view of Manhattan, Brooklyn, the Statue of Liberty—

That's Indigo.

He's different now. Happy in an entirely new way. As if he's transcended normal bliss and found a new plane of it. One off-limits to the rest of us.

We sit.

I raise my glass to toast.

Ty laughs, still drunk and cheerful and thinking of fucking his fiancée. "Have you finally run out of ways to brag for me?"

"Would you prefer I not bring up your ability to make your fiancée come?"

He smiles *you're ridiculous*.

"To you, Ty, thinking with your cock."

He shakes his head *of course* and taps his glass against mine. "Is that really what you think?"

"That's what brought you back to her."

"Maybe."

"And she's more of a freak than you are. It's impressive you found that."

He actually blushes. "Fuck off."

"You're welcome."

He takes a long sip. Sets his glass on the table. Studies me. "You don't fool me, Cam. I've seen the playboy act before."

"What act?"

He shakes his head *it's all bollocks* and takes a sip. "I don't need you happy for me."

"I am."

"You don't—"

"I am, Ty. You're practically my brother." I owe him a lot. Everything. "I'm happy you found someone to fuck."

"Arsehole."

"If I told you I was happy you found someone to love, you'd hug me. But this makes me an arsehole?"

"No. You being an arsehole makes you an arsehole."

"Profound logic."

He takes a long sip. "I'm proud of it."

"If I'm proud you finally admitted what you want."

"Fuck off." He looks away, suddenly shy.

"I am," I say. "It takes strength."

"I said fuck off."

"You're embarrassed."

"You're covering."

"You're still embarrassed," I say.

He shakes his head *you're ridiculous* again, takes a long sip, turns his attention to the city.

Is he so drunk he's desperate to express a profound truth? Or is it something else?

"Is that really what you think of me and Indigo?" His voice is soft. He's treading carefully. "Is that how you see relationships?"

I'm not in the mood. I don't want to discuss my fucked-up head. I'm not taking his bait "You want to fuck her. She wants to fuck you. Why not celebrate that?"

"I love her."

"I know."

"But you really don't understand it." He takes a long sip. "Do you?"

"Is this the conversation you want to have right now?" I ask.

"Why do you think I asked?"

"You know the situation, Ty." I swallow hard. "What else is there to say?"

"Are you sure you can handle this?"

"Your wedding? Of course."

"Keeping Sienna company," he says.

"She's a teenager."

"I'm not worried about her."

He's not worried she wants to fuck me. He's worried I want to fuck her. My shoulders tense.

"I know you, Cam. When your head is a mess, you find someone to fuck."

"Fuck you, Ty."

"And then you hate her and you hate yourself and you try to erase it with someone else."

I say nothing.

"She likes you."

I know. I shouldn't care that she likes me, but I do.

"I see the way you look at her."

"I can control myself." There's no conviction in my voice.

"You're different around younger women. I know it's because of what happened with Winter. But—"

"Fuck you, Ty."

"I don't mean that you'd cross the line."

"It's not the same. She's an adult."

"She's eighteen."

"Not fourteen." My fingers curl into the glass. I should throw the fucking thing at his head. "And I'm not her coach."

"You're supposed to be protecting her."

Fuck him. "Go to hell." I stand.

He grabs my wrist. "I'm sorry."

Ty doesn't say sorry. Is he that drunk? Or does he actually see his error?

How dare he compare me to Winter.

How dare he bring that up.

"I don't care that you're drunk, Ty. You promised—"

"You're right. I'm sorry."

I suck in a shallow breath.

"Sit. Please."

I can't sit. I can't move. I'm frozen. The way I always am when I think of her.

"It's not the same. You're right."

My eyes go to his wrist. "I don't want to fuck you. The Dom thing isn't going to work on me."

He releases my arm.

I sit. Suck the last drop of gin from my glass.

His voice is careful, slow, like I'm a wounded animal, and he's trying to avoid scaring me. "You're already losing your shit."

I am.

"There are two weeks until the wedding and you're already losing your shit."

"I can handle it."

"Are you sure? I can ask someone else." His voice stays soft. "I understand."

"I have it under control," I lie.

He looks at me like he doesn't believe me, but he still offers his hand.

And I still shake.

Chapter Six

SIENNA

U sually, I roll my eyes at Alice's *no boys, no alcohol, no fun* speech.

At the moment, I see her point.

Ugh.

Who invented drinking?

It's fun for a while, sure, but waking up the next day with a headache and a vague recollection of telling your hot friend you'll bone him if he keeps flirting with you?

So much ugh.

I wash my face, tie my running shoes, attempt to look at the sky without squirming.

No good. It's too bright. A second glass of water helps, but not enough. My head continues to throb. My stomach stays queasy.

I didn't listen to Alice, and now I'm paying the price. But that doesn't mean I'm not a team player. I can still make it through my run. It's just a little more painful this way.

I fill the bottle Cam left yesterday, press the cool aluminum to my forehead, take the elevator to the street.

I walk the ten blocks to Battery Park, then I pick up the pace. Jog the loop. Set out for the path along the West side.

He's here.

Cam.

He doesn't stand out the way he did yesterday. He's one of many athletic men in running shorts. Even one of several handsome, tall, Black men in running shorts.

But he's the only one wearing a soccer jersey.

He's the only man who makes my heart race.

Cam and exercise is a dangerous conversation. He's hot in his suit. All sweaty and sleeveless—

He's—

Fuck.

He spots me immediately. Pauses so I can catch up.

I jog to him. "Are you doing hello today?"

He shakes his head. "How's your hangover?"

"How's yours?"

"I'm already on my way back."

"You're on Greenwich Mean Time. It's afternoon to you."

"Uh-huh."

"Yeah huh." I suck another sip of water from the bottle.

He notices. Studies the way my lips wrap around the spout. Traces the cheesy tourist logo with his eyes.

"Want some?" I offer the bottle to him.

"Thanks." His fingers brush mine as he takes it. He swallows. Wipes his mouth with the back of his hand. "How *is* your hangover?"

I motion *a little*.

"You should listen to your sister and take it easy."

"Why does everyone tell me not to drink? No one stops Eve from drinking. She's only a year older than I am."

Eve is Ty's brother's girlfriend. The happy couples are always double dating. And they're often inviting me.

30

Sure, they try to include me in their festivities, but they're in their happy couple worlds. I'm a total fifth wheel.

Even when it's just the girls, me, my sister, and Eve, the two of them have so much in common. They're both boss bitches with edgy hair, epic style, and a deep love of analyzing lyrics.

They don't enjoy reality TV or soccer or sugary coffee drinks.

Sure, Indie watches soccer with me, but only because she loves me. She barely understands the rules.

"Because you're Indigo's sister," Cam says. "Ty sees you as his kid sister."

"Whereas he sees Eve as—"

"The girl his brother is fucking."

"So it's a guy thing?" I'm the sweet, innocent kid sister. She's… the sexpot? What bullshit.

"Ty wants to protect you."

"Is that why you're here?"

He shrugs. *Maybe, maybe not.*

But I'm not stupid. I know he's here because Ty asked.

And there goes my hope he's here to see me in my sports bra and shorts again. Whatever. It's kind of sweet Ty wants someone keeping an eye on me. Annoying, but sweet in a Ty kind of way.

And I can't exactly complain about Cam's company. He's so tall and handsome and sleeveless.

What would his arms feel like around me? Strong and sweaty and safe.

No boys, no alcohol, no fun.

No distractions.

But Cam isn't a boy. He's a man. And even if I tell him to get lost, he's a huge distraction. I might as well work with the situation.

If he's here, he's helping me train.

"I'm going to Chelsea Piers and back," I say. "If you can handle it."

"If *I* can handle it?"

My gaze goes to his shoulders. Bare. I've never seen them bare before. Not in person. They're so strong and broad and in need of my hands. "You are an older man. You may have used up all your stamina."

"I'm older?"

I nod.

"I'm not even thirty."

"Almost thirty."

He chuckles. "Do you think baiting me is going to work?"

Yes. It always does. And I need the challenge. Cam is faster than I am, by fifteen seconds a mile. "Work at what? I'm stating facts. You're older, out of energy. I can run faster."

"You really need to race a man who ran for an hour to win?"

"How do I know you really ran for an hour?" I ask. "You're probably just saying you ran for an hour."

"Okay. If you need the handicap." He smirks *challenge accepted and returned*. "To Chelsea Piers and back. Loser buys coffee."

"You own a tech company."

"So?"

"I'm a broke college student."

"And I'm ordering the most expensive pour over." His smile widens. "Run fast."

My chest warms. My cheeks flame. I'm not sure if I'm angry or charmed, but I know I'm ready to win. "On three or you need a break first?"

"On three."

"You sure? You already ran so much and you are older."

"And taller."

"Heavier." Neither of us is built like a distance runner. They're tall sometimes—tall people have longer legs—but they're incredibly thin.

He's built like a sprinter, the same way I am.

Of course, broad, muscular men are considered the height of hotness. My muscular frame isn't the body type men covet.

But it doesn't seem to deter Cam. He's not exactly shy about checking me out.

And I do have a great ass. Maybe not as great as Cam's, but that's like saying a sport isn't as great as soccer.

It's not possible to compare.

He motions to the edge of a tile. Adopts race position. "On three."

"On three."

He holds out three fingers.

We count down in unison.

I take off the second I finish *one*, spring past a dad pushing a stroller, a couple on a morning walk, two friends sipping coffee.

I don't look back until I round a corner.

Cam's running fast but not full speed. Is he tired or conserving energy?

He is faster than I am, but he's used to running in London weather. It's not as hot as yesterday, but the air is still warm and sticky. It's enough to distract even the most seasoned athlete.

I take my lead for half a mile, then I slow to a speed I can maintain. I focus on my form. My breath. The cool breeze rolling off the Hudson.

I'm too slow. He gains on me.

Cam shoots me a *told you*, then he runs past me.

Fuck. Did he really run for an hour? Where the hell does he get the stamina?

I let him lead until Chelsea Piers. But he's there. Hand on the wall. Waiting.

"Here and back." I struggle through the words.

"I know." His voice is breathy. He's straining too.

It's because of the workout, but it sends my thoughts to the gutter. Beautiful images fill my head.

Cam kissing me.

Wrapping his arms around me.

Pinning me to the wall, sliding my running shorts to my ankles.

Even in my fantasies, we're wearing our sneakers.

I don't even need Alice's warnings. I already eat, breathe, sleep soccer.

"So you…" I uncap my bottle. Suck a sip of water. "You're giving up."

"Taking a break."

"Asshole. You're showing off."

He shrugs. "If I am?"

"I'm buying the most expensive drink on the menu."

"You have the cash for that?"

I flip him off.

He smiles. Waits for me to tap the wall. Then he runs.

Fast.

Faster than he ran here.

I speed until I'm at his pace.

Until I'm gaining on him.

Fuck, he's too fast. But I'm almost there. Two more minutes. I can do that.

My feet press off the ground, my legs burn, my lungs strain.

I go all out. As if I'm chasing the ball. As if winning is the only thing I want.

I catch him.

Gain.

Race past the virtual finish line.

There. I let my bottle drop on the grass. Raise my arms in victory. Double over with a cramp.

A heavy breath breaks up Cam's laugh. It's a strange sound. Sweet and sexy at the same time.

"Come here." He offers his hand.

"Here?"

"I'll help you."

"Help me?" I don't need his help, but I'm not turning down this kind of proximity.

"Yes." He moves into my space.

God, he's so close, so handsome, so sweaty.

I struggle through my next breath. Brush a stray hair behind my ear.

It sticks to my forehead. I'm sweaty too.

It's a hot day. And he's so, so close.

He leans down to meet me. Brings his hand to my wrist. Peels my fingers off the bottle.

Oh.

He steals the water. Sucks liquid from the mouth. Offers it to me.

I swallow with greedy sips. "You owe me coffee."

He nods *I know*. "Now or after you dress?"

"I'm dressed."

He motions to the quiet street. "Pick your poison."

Hmm. Where did I go last weekend? The place with homemade syrups. Yes. That's it. I name the store and head toward it. "I'm not sure they have pour overs."

"They'll make one."

"People do whatever you ask?"

"You doubt it?"

No, actually. "You're not wearing your suit."

"So?"

"You may have less sway in a jersey."

"You really think so?"

"Maybe." No. Not at all. He may not look quite as debonair in his soccer jersey, but he looks just as sexy and powerful.

"You don't."

I nod *I don't.* "Did you let me win?"

"Never," he says.

"You swear?"

"On my honor."

"You don't have any honor," I say.

He chuckles. "On my right hand then."

My eyes flit to said hand. "Is that the one you use?"

"Why else would I offer to swear on it?"

I try to play cool, but my cheeks flush. I'm usually the one teasing about sex. But Cam... he makes me nervous. "I warned you last night."

"I warned you too, Sienna." His voice drops to something equal parts dirty and teasing. "No one will ever compare."

"I survived kissing you."

"Have you kissed anyone else since?"

After too much cheap vodka, and a dare from Katie, I kissed Tony. That didn't compare, but how could it? "Have you?"

"You know I can't tell you that. If I did, you'll be sick with jealousy. If I didn't, it's all you'll think about."

He's right.

It steals my thoughts.

For the entire walk, the question is the only thing on my mind: Is it really possible Cam went two months without kissing someone else?

Is it possible he wants me that badly?

Chapter Seven

SIENNA

The coffee shop is huge by Manhattan standards. A counter at the window, the register on the left, two small booths on the right.

And, in the back, a quiet bathroom with plenty of privacy.

Not that Cam would ever consider sneaking into said bathroom and ordering me to come on his hand.

He has that Hunt presence. He knows how to take control of the room. How to read my body and find exactly the spot I need.

Or maybe it's my overactive imagination. This is my outlet. I'm creative—math is more creative than people think —but I'm not artistic. I can't draw, I can't carry a tune, I don't appreciate fine cinema.

But sex?

My brain buzzes with beautiful images. Flashes of things I've seen in movies or heard from friends.

After all, I don't know. I've never trusted anyone enough.

I've hooked up with guys, sure, but it's never gone much further than fumbling over belt buckles.

Over winter break, at my lab partner's Christmas Eve party, I drank too much Three Buck Chuck and snuck to the roof with the cutest guy on our school's soccer team. It was freezing, even under the blanket, and we were both drunk enough we were sloppy, but it felt good.

Then we were interrupted, and I wanted the warmth of the party inside more than I wanted him.

Was it a lack of trust? My sister's voice in my head, reminding me to use a condom? (Obviously I'm going to use a condom. I'm not an idiot).

Or was it the memory of her crushed after her fling with Ty ended three years ago? (It's a long story).

Maybe that was it. Maybe, deep down, I knew sex would change things.

No matter how much I want to believe I'm able to separate sex and love the way men do, I'm not.

And after Cam kissed me…

No one compares.

"Sienna." Cam presses his hand into my low back, nudging me toward the register.

The barista behind the counter, a cute blonde in a tight pink crop top, shoots him an *I want to fuck you* smile. "Can I help you?" She bats her eyelashes.

It's far too friendly for a New Yorker.

Which can only mean she wants to fuck him. Why else would a New York service professional be nice? We're not nice. We're to the point.

"Yes, thank you." Cam shoots her a dazzling smile.

She nearly topples over from the full force of his charm. "What would you like?"

"Something sweet," he says.

"Sweeter than your smile?" She thrusts her chest in his general direction.

My cheeks flame.

Cam chuckles. "If you have anything that sweet."

"I'm not sure we do," she says. "But I can try."

"You know I'm right here," I say.

Her brow scrunches. "Of course. What would you like, miss?" She doesn't even look at me. She gives Cam a long once-over, not at all shy about staring at his shoulders, chest, hips.

He's hot. I want to look too. But really?

"Seriously?" My temper flares. "I'm right here and you're flirting with him."

"No. I… Uh… I just… want to take his order," she says.

Yeah, I bet.

"What would you like, sir?" Her voice stays breathy. Her gaze stays on his bare shoulders.

"He could be my boyfriend, you know," I say.

"He could be?" she asks. "So he isn't?"

Cam chuckles. "No. It's strictly sexual, right, sweetness?"

Mmm… Cam… using… pet name.

Must bitchslap giggly barista.

Must jump Cam.

Must get ahold of self.

"Sienna," he continues. "What would you like? You need your energy for later."

The barista blushes. "Sorry, I didn't realize… we, uh, we have a large pour over."

"Perfect." He requests a dark roast. Turns to me. "Something sweet for you?"

Him. Touching me. Everywhere. "The spiced mocha, thanks. And the banana toast."

"Make it two," he says.

She nods, accepts his credit card, turns her attention to our drinks.

I fill my bottle at the spigot, take a seat at a booth in the back, will the cold water to lower my temperature.

Of course, it doesn't.

He slides into the seat across from me. Watches as the blonde barista fixes drinks. "You're cute jealous."

"I'm not jealous."

"Really?" He raises a brow *what bullshit.*

"It's just rude of her flirting in front of me. We're together, on a Saturday morning, all sweaty after a workout. It's a girlfriend/boyfriend activity."

"Isn't it more likely we're workout partners?"

The coffee grinder interrupts us. It steals the quiet from the shop.

Most people think quiet is rare in New York City. To a certain extent, that's true. But every neighborhood is quiet sometimes.

And the Financial District is empty all weekend.

My apartment, with its thick walls and its guarded entrance, is quiet all day, every day.

It's not the normal college experience, but I can't complain about having all that space to myself. Even if it comes with strings.

The grind ceases. The barista glances at us. Blushes.

"Still watching her?" he asks.

"No. I just find it curious she assumes we're not together."

"That's not it."

"It's not?"

He nods. "I'm that irresistible." He smiles and the rest of the world disappears. It's only Cam and his effortless charisma.

"Oh my god! That's so obnoxious!"

"Women like obnoxious." He looks to the counter as the barista drops off our drinks. "And I like you jealous."

"I'm not—"

"And denying it too." He smiles. "It's adorable."

God, he really is obnoxious.

And I really do like it.

He smiles, victorious, grabs the drinks, returns with an even more obnoxious smile.

My stomach flutters. He's so handsome. I want to touch him and kiss him and fuck him.

Ahem.

He pours his coffee, holds up his tiny ceramic cup. "To your envy."

"Do you toast at every opportunity?"

"I do."

"It's a lot more fun when you toast to Ty thinking with his cock."

"He's not here."

That's true. "I'm not jealous."

"Okay, to you lying to yourself."

"To me kicking your ass."

"You barely won."

"Barely winning is still winning." I hold up my mug.

He taps his against mine, then he brings it to his lips, groans over his dark roast.

Mmm, that's a beautiful groan. I need it louder and lower and a hell of a lot more.

I try to focus on my drink. Sure, a spiced mocha lacks the sophistication of a plain French press, but it's sugar, spice, chocolate, and coffee. If that isn't heaven, what is?

I take a long sip. Let out a low, deep moan.

He notices. He even watches carefully, but he doesn't say anything. Just sips his black coffee. Like he's so cool and deep and adult ordering a black coffee.

The barista interrupts with our toasts.

Cam motions *I've got it*, moves to the counter, smiles at the blonde.

She flirts openly. Places her hand on his bare forearm. Giggles at something he says.

Blushes.

Ugh.

Gross.

Then she looks at me the way she was looking at Cam, like she's deciding if she wants to fuck me.

She looks back to Cam. Nods tentatively. Grabs a receipt paper and a pen and writes her number.

Huh?

He returns to the table.

"What was that?" I ask.

"I explained the situation."

"What situation is that?"

"It was rude of her flirting in front of you if she wasn't willing to join the two of us."

"What?"

"You don't think?"

Wait, did he—

No.

He wouldn't.

No, he would. Of course he would.

My eyes meet his. I raise a brow.

He nods *of course*.

"You invited her to a threesome?"

"No. It was her idea," he says.

"And you accepted."

"I told her we could all get a drink. Talk about it later," he says.

Oh my god.

"You don't think?" He looks to the barista.

This time, she looks at me, blushes.

"She's not your type?"

"No."

"You don't like blondes?"

"That's it. The hair color. Not that I don't like women."

"I don't want to assume," he says.

"How progressive of you."

He laughs, enjoying this. Enjoying my blush and my nerves. "That's too bad. I would have liked to watch the two of you." He sips his black coffee, completely nonchalant.

"Would Ty approve?"

"He asked me to keep you entertained."

"That would be entertaining," I say.

"Exactly." He struggles to hold a poker face. Breaks with a laugh.

"He would kill you."

"Probably. But only if he found out."

I take my toast. Break it in half. "He'd find out."

"Who would tell him?"

"I don't know. But he always finds out."

"Would you tell him?"

"No. But if he asked, I'm not sure I'd be able to hide it." I take a bite. Savor the salty almond butter, the sweet, soft banana, the perfectly toasted bread. Mmm. What's better than carbs and coffee?

"You really want your brother-in-law to know your sex life?"

"No. But apparently it's of interest to him." I motion to Cam. "Since he sent you to babysit me."

"He's worried about you."

"About me… fucking some guy? He does realize I'm a college student."

"About you feeling left out," Cam says. "With the wedding keeping your sister busy."

Oh.

"Marriage changes things."

43

Yeah. Not going there. I'd rather talk about him fucking blondie.

How would he do it? Would he bend her over the counter, drag her to the bathroom, lay her on this table?

What if it was us, and she was watching, and we were—

"I told him it's ridiculous," he says. "But I couldn't turn down the chance to spend two weeks with the most difficult woman in New York."

"The city or the state?"

"The entire US, I think."

"Thanks."

He dives into his toast. "This is insanely sweet."

"What did you expect me to order?"

He laughs *fair enough*.

"So… you're just hanging out with me?" I ask. "Not trying to cock block me."

"I don't play wingman," he says.

"That's it? Not that Ty wouldn't allow it?"

"I don't care what Ty would allow." He tries to sell it, but he doesn't really get there.

"Really? So we can go back to my place? You can get me off in the shower."

His pupils dilate. "No, Sienna. I can't."

"Because Ty would kill you?"

He shakes his head. "I couldn't do that to you." He looks me in the eyes. "Offer you a taste and deny you a meal."

"Did you just refer to yourself as a meal?"

"I did, didn't I?"

"Yeah. Have some self-respect. Seriously, Cam. I worry about you sometimes."

"It is true."

"There are other meals out there," I say.

"They won't compare. No one will ever compare. I can't do that to you. I can't ruin every fuck of your life that way."

"That's such a bullshit cop out," I say. "Just admit it's because of Ty's instructions."

"No," he says. "I like you too much. I can't hurt you that way."

"You like me too much to fuck me?"

"I do."

"You really believe that?"

"Of course." He says it with conviction.

But I'm not sure I believe him.

Chapter Eight

SIENNA

Cam finishes every sip of his four-cup French Press. He drinks the way he does everything, with effortless grace.

He never seems like he's trying. Even after a five-mile run. It's like he lives and dies by the motto *never let them see you sweat.*

Well, not literally.

He's still all sweaty and sleeveless and tempting.

And we're parting for the next twenty-four hours, give or take. He has work to finish, with Ty, I guess, then we're meeting before dinner Sunday to discuss the joint bachelor/bachelorette party.

It's in exactly one week and we don't have a single hard plan. We've spent the last few weeks trading ideas, from dick shaped straws to custom pornography, but nothing is written in stone.

Honestly, I don't get the point of a bachelor party. Maybe it works for a guy who sees marriage as a prison, but Ty is obsessed with my sister. And she's over the moon. She gets stars in her eyes anytime she hears the words *Ty* or *wedding* or *gown* or *honeymoon.*

She's happy.

He's rich.

It's smart to nail that down.

Sure, it changes things. I guess it's sweet that Ty is worried about me, but I'm fine. I've been through way worse. My dad died when I was a kid. And my mom fell apart after.

Indigo stepped up to take care of us. She made sure there was always food on the table and clean clothes in the closet.

I did what I could, but she insisted I put soccer first.

Back then, with our limited means, soccer was my way out. I was good enough for a full scholarship to a Division I school. Which meant four years to study math and find a grad school program with a generous stipend.

Then Mom died and everything really fell apart.

And, somehow, Ty swooped into her life exactly when she needed him.

She loves him, and she's incredibly satisfied.

Sure, I miss living in the same place, watching reality marathons every Saturday afternoon, grabbing boba tea on the way home after school, being the number one person in her life.

But how can I complain about Ty paying my rent? Okay, yes, it comes with invisible strings. I don't like that.

But a one-bedroom to myself? A closet full of nice clothes? A fridge packed with fresh food?

I eat at the best restaurants in New York City when I'm with them. I can live with a dress code and a little too much lovey dovey talk.

I'm glad Indigo is living her life, finding love, reclaiming her passion for music.

There's no reason to be upset about that change.

There's no reason to throw a party claiming it's a bad thing.

But if she wants a party, she gets a party. I'm not missing the chance to embarrass her. Or Ty.

The man *wears* a poker face. If I can really get him to crack—

That will be something.

I let my thoughts wander on the walk home.

My apartment is clean (ish) and quiet. It's my space. The first thing in my life that's really mine.

Only it's not mine. It's Ty's. I'm a visitor.

And that…

Whatever.

I push the thought aside as I step into the shower. It's a big space, with new stainless steel appliances and perfect water pressure.

Better than I ever expected.

Another perk of luxury.

Is that how Cam sees it? He does wear his suit everywhere. And he did buy the most expensive pour over.

And he certainly enjoys his hundred-dollar-a-glass wine.

Is he comfortable with luxury?

Or does it still feel strange, like he's a visitor in someone else's life?

I close my eyes. Wet my hair. Let water drip down my cheeks, chin, shoulders.

What if he was here, in this warm, wet space with me?

My head fills with beautiful images.

My hand on his chest.

My fingers tracing the tattoo on his shoulders. Those curving black letters. The jagged heart on his chest.

His lips on my neck.

His hand between my legs.

His voice in my ears.

No teasing, no bullshit, just him ordering me to come on his hand.

I slip my hand between my legs. Follow the thread of my thoughts to places I shouldn't go.

I come fast.

Twice.

Then I catch my breath, finishing washing, dress.

Find my sister waiting for me.

Chapter Nine

SIENNA

Indigo is leaning against the kitchen counter in a short black sundress, a takeout coffee cup in her hand.

She has a key.

I have a key to her place too, but I don't usually enter without knocking. There's too high a chance I'll walk in on her and Ty naked.

And I really don't need to see that.

"Iced latte." She offers me the drink.

Mmm. Iced latte. She can stop by to drop off an iced latte anytime.

She can stop by anytime.

That was my policy before Cam showed up. There's no reason for it to change.

"Thanks." I accept the drink with a smile. "You don't have one."

She points to an iced tea on the counter and gives me a slow once-over. An older sister one. Equal parts *I'm your friend and I'm here for you* and *I'm your protector and I'm making sure you don't need protection.* "You look cute."

"This old thing?"

"And you?"

She smiles and does a quick curtsy. "I try."

"Does Ty like it?"

She shoots me a *really* look. "You care if Ty likes it."

"Don't you?"

"Only if we're playing."

Playing what? Indie tries to shield me from her sex life. I don't know details. I'm not sure I want details. "Playing as in role playing?" Okay, I want details.

"If we're meeting for sex."

"You meet for things besides sex?"

"We live together."

"Even so."

She laughs and pulls me into a tight hug. "I hope you never change."

"What about me? I mean, I'm really great, so I'm sure it's a lot of things. But specifically…"

"You have such a strong sense of what matters." She releases me. Takes a long sip of her tea. "Hold on to that."

"You or Ty always object to my marriage criteria." I try my iced latte. Mmm, sweet, sweet caffeine, creamy milk, just enough added sugar. Perfect. "Which is so hypocritical. Since you two are always screwing like rabbits."

"And he's rich."

"Yeah."

She nods *fair*. "It's not about sex."

I raise a brow *really*.

"Not only about sex. It's trust. I, actually… I want to talk to you about that."

Ugh. Not an older sister *be careful* talk. I appreciate her looking out for me, I do. But I've heard this *make sure you trust your sexual partners* lecture enough times.

I don't need the talk. I'm plenty gun-shy.

I hate hesitating. It's not me. It's not comfortable for me. It's not what I want to be.

And now my sister is here to remind me I'm unable to be my badass bold self in this one arena.

Does she know I'm scared? Or does she believe my bark matches my bite?

"Do we have to?" I shrug like I don't care about her lecture.

"Humor me. Please. Let me be an obnoxious, overprotective older sister for ten minutes."

How am I supposed to say no to that? I nod. "You do look good." I take a long sip of my iced coffee. "Chic yet sexy."

"Boss bitch?"

"Totally boss bitch. Expensive."

"I can only be bought for the highest price?"

"No. Like you're the one who buys men for the right price."

"Which men are these?"

"Ones who satisfy you then leave the second you're done with them."

She laughs. "And how much do I spend on these men?"

"I don't know. How much would you spend?"

"I'm not sure I'd hire an escort."

Escort. What a euphemism. As if people are really hiring professionals to escort them on dates.

"I have Ty."

"And he already blows your mind?"

She smiles and drifts into the Love Zone. Hazy eyes, soft expression, intense contentment.

She's happy. I'm happy for her. It's great. I'd say enough already, but I brought this on myself. "Shall we?" I motion to the balcony.

She snaps back to reality, nods, follows me outside.

My balcony isn't nearly as grand as the terrace slash rooftop deck at her and Ty's place. It's a tenth the size, with way cheaper furniture, but it's still a balcony with a view of the Hudson.

It's fucking amazing.

"I don't think I'd want to hire someone," she says. "Not for sex. I wouldn't want to bring money into it."

"What if that was the only way you could be with Ty again?"

"No."

"You're sure?"

She nods. "When he called, I thought he might offer that."

"He might try to pay you for sex?" That's hard to believe. Yes, Ty is obsessed with her. Yes, he's used to getting what he wants. Yes, we were super-broke before he swooped in to save the day... well, the mortgage.

But it's not Ty. He has an over developed sense of right and wrong. He always has to be fair. He always has to win with sportsmanship.

"He wouldn't pay for sex," I say.

"He wouldn't. But it had been three years, and I was used to rich assholes who thought they could buy me. I didn't know what he wanted."

"He did want to fuck you."

"He did." She starts drifting into the Love Zone.

Ugh, no. "Would you have taken money for sex?"

"I don't know. Maybe. If it was him, maybe."

That's harder to believe. Yes, Indie does what it takes to survive, but she's romantic about sex and love. "Really?"

"It would make sense, wouldn't it? This guy, the best fuck of my life, shows up and offers me money for something I want to do anyway. Why wouldn't I take it?"

"It does make sense."

"But I'm not sure. I was scared to be with him again. Scared to lose him again. I didn't realize it consciously, but, deep down, I knew."

"He's that good?" I ask.

"Yes." Her expression gets dreamy. "But it's not because he has a huge dick or nimble fingers."

"It's not?"

She laughs. "Fifty percent of guys are above average size."

"I know how averages work." I take another sip. Try to find a way to phrase the question so she'll answer. "Is he not... noticeably above average?"

"We're not going there."

"You started it."

"Even so."

"He totally is."

Her cheeks flush. "It's not about that. There are guys with huge dicks who are terrible lays."

"And you know from experience?"

"I've had bad sex, yeah."

"Ever with Ty?"

"No."

I raise a brow.

She shakes her head *not going there*. "It's not because of his girth. It's the intimacy, the communication, the trust."

Ugh... this again. "Why do you make sex so unfun?"

She laughs. "Why do you ask for details?"

"Fish swim, birds fly—"

"Sienna Simms asks inappropriate questions about sex."

"And Indigo Simms tries to turn the questions into boring talks about boundaries?"

"Sex is all about boundaries and communication."

"Maybe the kinky sex you and Ty have."

"Definitely the kinky sex me and Ty have." For a

second, she drifts into the Love Zone, then she catches herself, focuses on her tea. "We're good. You know that, right?"

"You and Ty? I am well aware of your healthy sex life."

"We're good everywhere. And I... I'm okay. Do you know that?"

"Of course."

"I'm still here. I'm still your big sister. I know you're a grown-up with your own apartment and everything, but—"

Here it comes.

"I'm still looking out for you."

"I know. I appreciate it."

She slows. Takes a long sip. Looks me over. "You kept me distracted for a while."

"Did I?"

She nods. "But I'm not leaving until we have this conversation."

Ugh.

"I know you and Cam have a certain... flirtation."

"It doesn't mean anything."

"Maybe. Maybe not. It's more than Cam. It's everything."

"So you wouldn't mind if I slept with Cam?"

Her blue eyes fill with surprise. "It's a bad idea."

Obviously.

"He's not just Ty's cousin. They're close. They're business partners. If something happened, it would be messy."

"I know."

"But you're an adult and you can consider consequences like an adult. I trust you with that."

"Why do you make it sound so boring? You should forbid me from kissing him. Tell me you'll never forgive me."

She smiles. "That would encourage you."

Probably.

"I don't really know Cam. I don't know what he wants. But I know you. You're a very appealing person."

"Why does that sound like an accusation?"

"It's not." Her voice softens. "You're my favorite person in the world."

"Before Ty?"

She nods. "You're good company. And Cam... he's human. I'm sure he notices."

"It's hard to miss."

"You're also pretty damn cute."

I feign humility. "Really?"

"And guys, even the good guys... they care about that."

"You don't say?"

She laughs. "Okay. Yes. You know men are shallow. But I'm not sure you realize how appealing you are. You're cute and bawdy and you love sports. Men are going to notice you. They already do."

"I'll use a condom."

"It's not that. Though, yes, you do need to wear a condom. Especially since you have an IUD. It increases your risk of STDs."

"I know."

"You don't need to love someone to fuck them. You don't even need to like them. But you need to trust them."

Okay...

"I know you're tough. But men are bigger and stronger and... there's this Margaret Atwood quote—"

Oh god, she's been hanging out with Ian's girlfriend too much.

"Men are afraid women will laugh at them. Women are afraid men will kill them."

"I know the quote." I hear it nearly every time Ian and Eve show up for a double date plus fifth wheel. It's like Eve thinks we forgot Margaret Atwood exists since we last saw her. Newsflash: she's the most notable Canadian author of all time. Everyone knows she exists.

"It's true about sex too. Most guys are more concerned with embarrassing themselves than making sure you're comfortable."

I'm not sure I see the connection, but I nod anyway. "I'll be careful."

"You promise?"

"I do."

"Thanks." She pulls me into a side hug. "I gave my older sister lecture. Now, I'm done. I swear."

"Uh-huh."

"Really." She holds up three fingers. "Scout's honor."

I laugh. "When were you a scout?"

"Uh, on my love of Amy Winehouse."

"That's a promise I can trust." I take another sip. Turn so I'm facing my sister. "So these guys who are more concerned with not embarrassing themselves... is Ty one of them?"

"God no."

I raise a brow.

Her cheeks flame. "He... uh... He's careful with me. That's all I'll say."

"What if I get you drunk?"

She laughs. "Has that worked before?"

I motion *a little*. "What about Cam?"

"Do I think he's worried about embarrassing himself?"

"Yeah."

"Are we speculating because you want me to think you're going to fuck him? Or because it's fun to gossip about friends?"

"How about both?"

She leans back in her seat. "I don't know. He acts aloof, but I think it's an act."

"And he's secretly as tortured as Ty."

"No. I think he's like you."

"Like me?" I raise a brow.

She nods. "All bravado."

"Did you just call me vanilla?"

"There's nothing wrong with being vanilla."

I shoot her a *really* look.

"What? I can't appreciate the merits of vanilla?"

"I don't know. Can you?"

Her laugh is big and full. "Sometimes. It's nice to mix it up."

"He can't tie you up every single time. That would get old?"

Her laugh gets louder. "It would."

"So to mix it you, you stare into each other's eyes during missionary?"

"Missionary is nice."

"And you like nice?"

Her cheeks flush. "Sometimes. It's intimate. Tender. That's not usually what I want, but sometimes... it feels good, having your body against your lover's body, being close, feeling the weight of them."

"How can someone who's such a freak make sex sound so romantic?"

"Being a freak is romantic. Haven't you seen *The Addams Family*?"

"Of course, that's your idea of romantic."

"It is."

Yeah, it totally is. Morticia and Gomez Addams are totally obsessed with each other. They live to fuck each other and they do it in every conceivable way.

That's the kind of thing I'd usually call romantic.

But now that my sister has really embraced her inner freak—

I tease her about her sex life.

She teases me about reality TV and soccer and my hatred of dressing up for Ty's diners.

And it feels so fucking good, like she's my best friend and I'm hers, like we can tell each other anything.

We can.

Right now, we can.

If I cross the line with Cam—

She's right. I'm an adult. I can appreciate the consequences. She might forgive me if I fuck Cam, but she won't trust me the same way.

She'll see me as the person who came between her husband and his closest friend.

I can't do that.

I can't lose my sister.

Not for sex. Not for lust. Not for anything.

Chapter Ten

CAM

All day, I put out fires at work. It's the usual bollocks. Clients who need hand holding, entrepreneurs over promising, investors with cold feet.

I know how to turn on the charm, and I'm willing to do it for the business, but I'm not usually on client calls. I'm head of finance.

I run numbers, decide where we should invest, work with Ian to determine if a company's secrets will hurt or help us.

We're half venture capital, half corporate espionage. Ty's brother Ian runs the latter. He's former Mi6. It's easy for him to dig dirt, and he's without moral qualms.

Information wants to be free. Why not make it free.

It makes sense for him. His ex-wife kept her affair a secret. He was in the dark for years.

Now, he wants to bring everything to light.

It doesn't take a shrink to put the pieces together.

It doesn't take a shrink to see why I avoid his side of the business.

I understand the burden of secrets. Maybe I should listen to Ty and let go of mine. But I can't.

Sometimes secrets are the only way to survive.

Ty understands that. Not the way I do, but enough.

Enough he doesn't mention the woman who fucked up my head. Not normally.

Now that he sees Sienna as his kid sister, he's concerned.

Look what happened to me, when a woman ten years my senior invited me into her bed. A woman I trusted. A woman who was supposed to protect me.

My football coach.

She was a new teacher. Twenty-four and gorgeous. All the guys on the team talked about how they wanted her. A pretty blonde with light eyes, nice tits, and an intimate knowledge of sports—

What more could a teenage boy want?

I talked the same talk. The same bollocks as all the other boys. I bragged about my experience, about how much girls wanted me, about what I'd do with Winter.

I'd seen porn, I'd seen arty films, I'd read books with sex. I thought I knew what it was like, but I didn't have a fucking clue.

It was all talk. Sure, I fucked myself five times a week, but I wasn't ready to fuck someone else.

Certainly not a football coach ten years my senior.

When Winter took an interest in me—

It seemed normal. I was the star player in my year. Of course, the new coach wanted to spend extra time developing my talent.

At first, it was just football. Then advice on school, friends, girls.

Then, one day, the advice came with a demonstration.

She wanted to show me how to kiss a girl.

How to touch a girl.

How a girl should touch me.

It was important, for my development as a man and an athlete. We worked with our bodies, didn't we?

Wouldn't it help me on the field, if I knew what to do with my body here?

It never occurred to me to say no. Or ask her to stop. Or draw a line somewhere.

Who turns down help from their coach?

What kind of man turns down an attractive woman? Especially one way out of his league?

At the time, it didn't seem all that fucked up. It was against the rules, sure, but what good are rules in the face of love?

That was how I saw it, how she sold it. We had a forbidden love affair.

I couldn't tell anyone.

Who would believe me?

Who would see it as wrong?

I kept it secret for a long time. Then one day, I was pissed at a party, and a friend was challenging me. He didn't believe I had any experience.

It was usual teenage boy talk. None of them had the experience they claimed. I could have shrugged or made up a story or said I had nothing to prove.

Instead, I told him.

I was drunk enough he believed me.

But he wasn't concerned, he didn't call it wrong; he didn't threaten to tell my parents.

He was in awe. How lucky, a gorgeous older woman wanted me. Why couldn't he find that?

Most men say the same when posed with a hypothetical.

A hot older teacher? Of course! Lucky guy.

The friend told someone else and soon it was hot gossip at school.

Then someone told Ty.

He was old enough to know better, to see it for what it was.

I still don't know how he did it, but he stopped her. Somehow, he stopped her.

Or maybe she was done with me. Ready to move on to her next victim.

I don't know. I should have said something. Come forward. Stopped her forever.

But I couldn't. I couldn't be a victim. I couldn't be a topic of debate—

Was he a lucky kid? Or was he raped?

Did he make it all up?

Why would someone like her want someone like him?

I can't even think it.

Ty meant well, bringing her up, reminding me how much it fucked with my head—

But to compare me to her?

Am I that far gone?

Am I really that much of a mess?

AFTER I FINISH WORK, I PUSH MY FUCKED-UP THOUGHTS aside, and prepare for battle: Planning Ty and Indigo's party with Sienna.

We're supposed to do it here, at the office, in the conference room with glass walls and witnesses.

At ten to four, she texts.

Sienna: Can we meet here? My dress is still drying. And I can't be seen in the one I wore Friday. (The horror). Would it kill Ty to go someplace I can wear jeans?

Probably. Ty loves the propriety. For the status and for the extra thrill when he drags his fiancée to a secluded corner.

Tonight, we're meeting at a bright, airy restaurant.

One without secluded corners.

Because he doesn't trust me any longer?

Or because he likes the fucking restaurant?

I don't know. I don't know if I trust myself.

Cam: Fuck Ty. Wear the jeans.

Sienna: I like the dress. Come over. I have coffee and cheap vodka.

Cam: You really know how to convince a guy.

Sienna: It's good coffee.

Coffee at Sienna's flat. It's not a big deal. We're planning a party. We need a place to talk without interruptions.

I can handle going to her place.

I have some self-control.

Not a lot.

But some.

Chapter Eleven

CAM

Sienna opens on the second knock. "A suit, again?"

"Always."

"Did you really wear shorts yesterday?"

"I don't know. Is there proof?"

She smiles and motions *come in.*

I nod *of course* as if it's not a big deal. As if I visit women's flats to plan parties every weekend.

When did I last visit a woman's home?

Hotels are better.

No intimacy.

No closeness. No view into someone's life.

I step into the hallway. Close the door behind me. Look around the space.

The same hardwood floor, high ceilings, and stainless steel of Ty's flat. The same sliding glass door. The same railing on the balcony.

Even the sliver of view—the deep blue of the river, sandwiched between two tall buildings.

Everything else different.

The room is bright, vibrant, alive.

Pure Sienna.

A red couch. A wall adorned in star decals. A white desk in the corner covered in sharpie scribbles.

"Indigo's work." Sienna moves closer to the desk. "Mostly Amy Winehouse lyrics." She traces a line of purple lyrics. "Her favorite."

"You don't like her?"

She motions *a little*. "I like the jazzy vibe, but she's a little… self-destructive, you know?"

Of course, but Sienna doesn't. She really doesn't understand Amy Winehouse's impulse to destroy her life, her relationship, herself.

Sienna is a healthy, functional person.

I'm not.

How could I begin to explain it?

Sometimes you hate yourself so deeply you're driven to destroy yourself. It's alcohol and sex for me.

Other people cut themselves or starve themselves or drug themselves.

Or do stupid shit that burns every bridge around them.

Sienna's eyes flit to me.

She asked a question.

I didn't answer. "Your sister doesn't mind?"

"I think she likes the pain. After Ty left the first time, she was miserable, but she couldn't admit it to herself. She couldn't admit she missed him."

And she hated herself for it.

Sienna doesn't see it. It's completely beyond her understanding.

And I don't know how to explain it. Not with words and not with musical choices.

I need to get the fuck away from this subject.

I turn to Sienna. "Play something you like."

"There's no way you'll like what I like."

"I watched *Ninety Day Fiancée*."

"And you hated it!"

"I still watched it."

She smiles.

My shoulders ease. My stomach settles. I'm not here to dwell in my fucked-up choices. I'm here to plan my best friend's bachelor party.

What's it matter that I can't stop staring at her long legs? Or picturing her shorts on the floor? Or envisioning her coming on my hand?

I have self-control.

I do.

"Okay. Fine. But I'm playing the entire album." She shakes her head *no way you'll like it*, but she stills picks something on her cell.

A peppy pop song fills the room. "Lily Allen?"

She nods.

"You two love your British pop stars."

Her laugh is soft. "Is that why you recognize her?"

"I don't live under a rock."

"So you *do* know who Billie Eilish is?" She laughs. "Ty can never remember. Indie is always explaining it to him. *The pop star with the green hair, with the song—*"

"About blowing some arsehole who doesn't appreciate her?"

Her cheeks flush. "Uh, the snaps. She likes them. And the whisper singing." Her eyes travel down my body. "Is that what the song's about?"

"It's art. Open to interpretation."

"You like art?"

"Who doesn't like art?"

She motions *it's okay*.

"Not everything can be as good as *Ninety Day Fiancée*."

She laughs. "It's a great show. I don't know why you can't appreciate its brilliance."

"Must be some deficiency I have."

She motions to the speaker. "Do you know what this one is about too?"

"This song? No. But there is one about her wishing her boyfriend was a better lay."

"Did I really miss that? Damn, maybe I should be a lyrics person."

"What kind of person are you?"

"I don't know. Indie sits on the couch, listening to an album on repeat, turning over every word. I listen to the song, enjoy it, listen to the next." Her eyes meet mine. "You're a lyrics person, aren't you?"

"I appreciate them."

"Don't tell me you're sitting in your bedroom, crying to sad songs all night?" she asks.

"Only half the night."

"Really?"

"Sometimes."

"Why?"

"Why do you listen to this?"

"Because I like it. It feels right."

"Exactly," I say.

She bites her lip. "So you… what kind of sad songs are we talking here? Amy?"

"Sometimes."

"Adele?"

"Are you going to name British musicians?"

"Until I run out." She nods. "Uh, Muse."

"They're sad?"

"Coldplay! The song where the guy is on the beach in black and white."

"No, not Coldplay," I say.

"Thank god." She studies me for a long moment, deciding whether or not to keep naming artists. She must decide to stop, because she motions to the kitchen. "You want something to drink?"

"Are you going to offer Cabernet?"

"If you brought some." She pulls the fridge open. "I have coffee, water, diet, ginger ale."

"And the cheap vodka?"

"Very cheap." She taps the freezer door. "It's under two bags of peas."

"You're hiding it?"

"I'm not supposed to drink during soccer season."

"You're not following that advice."

"I know." Her expression fills with guilt for a second, then she shakes it off. "But how often does my sister get married? And I'm not drinking on school nights, so…"

"It's Sunday."

She frowns *busted*.

"You don't have to convince me."

"You sure?" She motions to my face. "I see judgment."

"I'm surprised."

She raises a brow.

"You text me every Saturday with your run time."

"I do."

"Three times a week over the summer."

"I want to beat you."

"You want to win," I say. "Always."

"And now I'm giving up my competitive advantage by showing up with a hangover?"

"Are you?"

"I don't drink before games. I promise."

"You really don't have to convince me, Sienna."

"I kind of feel like I do." She moves into the kitchen,

71

pours two glasses of water, brings one to me. "I choose Indie over soccer."

My fingers brush hers as I take the cup. "It's not wrong to prioritize family."

"I got scholarships to a few Division One schools. Full rides. I'm a star player."

"Not to brag?"

"To brag a little." She half-smiles. "But I went to a Division Three school to stay close to her."

"And because you no longer need the scholarship?"

"Yeah." She takes a long sip of water. "So now I can live dangerously." She taps her glass.

"You cannot."

"I can too."

"You don't drink on school nights," I say.

"Game nights."

"Because you want to win."

"Of course I want to win. Who doesn't want to win?" she asks.

"Some people don't care."

She looks at me like I'm crazy.

I chuckle.

"What?"

"You."

"What about me?"

"You don't believe some people don't care about winning."

"No… Indie is like that. I just don't get how they could be that way. How can you do something and not give it your all?"

"Don't ask me."

"You let me win."

Maybe. "I was showing off. Paid the price."

"Uh-huh." She looks to the small couch. The desk chair.

The seats on the balcony. Settles on the couch. "Do you really sit there, listening to sad music?"

"Sometimes."

"What kind of music?"

"Other than British pop stars?"

"If there is anything else," she says. "Sometimes, I think Amy Winehouse created the only two albums in the universe."

A laugh spills from my lips. She's funny. And she's charming too. In this bold, take no shit way.

I like her.

I like her, and I still want to fuck her.

That doesn't happen.

My eyes go to her bare legs. The hem of her shorts. The tight tank top.

What would she say if I ordered her out of her clothes and onto my cock?

Fuck.

I push the thought aside as I sit at the opposite end of the couch. "Grunge."

"The miserable mumbling guys who don't wash their flannel?"

"I can't see their flannel."

She sticks out her tongue *gross*. "Men with guitars, huh?"

"Women too. Hole. Garbage. Sleater-Kinney."

She nods with familiarity. "Indigo and Eve are always talking about Hole." She imitates her sister. "'Courtney Love was a poet. How can anyone think Nirvana is the better band?'"

"She's talented."

"She's not mumbling."

I chuckle.

"What? I don't like to listen to men complaining."

My laugh gets louder.

"What?"

Of course, she plays an album dripping with youth and wit. Of course, she dismisses one of the most popular bands of all time as men complaining. "You're sure of yourself."

"Well, yeah, obviously." She turns toward me. "Do you know what Ty likes?"

"Tying up your sister."

Her cheeks just barely flush. "I was going to say what music Ty likes, but if you have more details…"

"I do."

"Well…" Her hazel eyes fill with excitement. "Cam! Tell me!"

"Do you think that will work?"

"What do you need?" She presses her hands together. "Should I get on my knees and beg?"

Fuck yes. "It won't help your case."

"Want to bet on that?"

No. Come here and come on my hand. Who the fuck cares what Ty likes? What do you like? "No."

She smiles, victorious. "It's relevant. We are planning a bachelor party, aren't we? We have to embarrass them by bringing up their sex life."

"How is that different than every Saturday for you?"

She pushes me playfully. "That's why I need more intel. So I can go further."

"Do I want to know what that means?"

"I'll tell if you will." She moves a little closer. Looks up at me with doe eyes. "Pretty, pretty please, Cam."

Fuck. "You know as much as I do."

She shakes her head. "Men talk."

"Women talk."

"Not the same way."

"Ty isn't—"

"Yes, he is."

She's right. Ty isn't the type of man who brags about his sex life, but when he drinks he forgets to guard the details. And when it's his older brother Ian baiting him to spill—

Ty still craves his older brother's approval.

It used to annoy me, how much Ty worshiped his older brother. I wanted to be his best friend, but I could never trump Ian.

Now-

I'm losing him in a different way.

Sienna continues. "You know something." She shifts off the couch. "Should I grab the cheap vodka and loosen your tongue?"

"You see the bruises on her wrists too," I say. "You tease her about it."

"Yeah, but…"

"He likes to bind her, spank her, threaten her."

"Threaten how?"

"Role play."

Her eyes go wide. She doesn't have that detail.

Fuck. I need to shut my mouth. I'm too eager to impress her, tease her, make her gasp.

"What role play?" she asks.

"You know Ty well at this point?"

"Yeah."

"And you know your sister?"

"Obviously."

"What makes you think he'd stop at one scenario?"

"Fuck, you're right. They probably do everything." She's quiet for a moment, soaking in this new shade, adding it to the image in her head. "Would you?"

"Would I what?"

"Role play."

"You know what I'm going to say."

"Do I?"

"I can't tell you. It's all you'll ever think about."

"Or maybe, if you don't tell me, I'll have to keep imagining every possible scenario. But if you do tell me, I can just imagine the one then move on."

"Maybe," I say. "But I still won't tell you."

"What if I go first? Tell you what I imagine?"

I may as well send Ty a text that says *I'm going to fuck your future sister-in-law. Have a nice wedding and a nice life, since we both know you'll never speak to me again.* "No."

"Because it's all you'll ever think about?"

"Of course." I try to sell it as a joke.

But she doesn't buy it.

Chapter Twelve

CAM

I have to give it to Sienna. She knows exactly what she wants to do with this party.

And the coup d'état: A bondage themed burlesque routine slash strip tease, choreographed to an Amy Winehouse song.

Only—"I don't know where you hire strippers. Do you? You must," she says.

"In the States?"

"Like you've never taken a rich client to a strip club."

"I'm the rich client." And no. I don't go to strip clubs. I'd rather get to the point. Find someone, take her home, get a jump on hating myself and her.

"Okay, like no one's ever taken you to a strip club."

"Not here." I *have* been dragged to some London clubs. I understand the appeal of naked women grinding against poles, even if it's not my thing. But making it a group activity? That, I don't get.

"Maybe we should ask Eve." Her nose scrunches as she says *Eve*. "She used to work at a club, didn't she?"

Ian's girlfriend Eve worked as a cocktail waitress at a strip club when they met, but how does Sienna have that information? "She knows some dancers."

"I'm sure she and Ian can figure it out. Unless you'd rather do it."

"I'll make it happen," I say.

"Do you think we should reserve the club?"

"They won't rent it out on a weekend."

"If you pay enough, they will."

"So kind of you to volunteer my money," I say.

She laughs. "What would it cost?" she asks. "A few thousand dollars? That's nothing to you."

"I appreciate value."

"Then reserve it on Tuesday morning."

"You really see Ty skipping work for that?"

"For his one and only bachelor party?"

That's a fair point. "I have a better idea."

She raises a brow.

"A hotel. Ty and Indigo can use the room after."

"And we can surprise them with an under the bed restraints kit?"

"Thoughtful."

She presses her lips together. "Okay. A hotel. I like it."

"On me."

She looks at me *obviously*.

It is obvious. I have a lot more money than she does. But it's still strange having someone shoot me that look.

It's refreshing.

It's pure Sienna.

Fuck, I really like her.

I swallow hard. "Do you have specific instructions for the dancers?"

"The artist, the bondage theme, just enough embarrassment. Otherwise, they can go crazy."

"No full penetration?"

"Ty would kill all of us."

He would.

"Does that really happen?"

"Do sex workers put on shows for a fee?"

"Yeah, stupid question." She presses her lips together. "Do guys arrange that for bachelor parties?"

"Some."

"Would you?"

"Not my thing."

She motions *go on.*

Shit. I cut off the question—*what is your thing*—before she can ask. "I prefer dick lollipops."

"Really?"

"What's not to like?"

She raises a brow *I think that's obvious.*

"It's candy."

"And you eat candy?" She gives me a slow once-over. Stops on my waist. "I've seen you out of that suit."

"You haven't seen me naked."

"Not yet."

Fuck, I walked into that.

"I've seen enough to know you don't eat candy."

"And you?" I ask.

"What about me?"

"What about you? Really?" My eyes go to her strong shoulders. Her bare stomach. Her long, curvy legs.

Her chest heaves with her inhale. "What about me?"

"You inhale sugar."

"Yeah."

"You still look like a football player."

"What's that mean?" she asks.

It means I need to try harder to avoid her. But I don't. My eyes stay on her thighs.

She stammers. "Uh... my point is, you don't eat candy.

You don't even put sugar in your coffee."

"And?" I ask.

"Do you like men?"

"No."

"So why would you deep throat a lollipop?"

"I'm not going to deep throat it."

Her cheeks flush. "No. Just the tip?"

"Do men still use that line?"

"I don't think so." She blushes. "No one's ever tried it with me."

She's been in a position for it. Been with someone?

Jealousy buzzes through my veins. I hate the thought of her with someone else. Ever.

And especially since she kissed me.

Did it mean nothing to her?

Am I that out of my fucking mind?

I bite my tongue so I won't say something I can't take back.

"They have pussy pops. That might work better for you." Her eyes flit to the bedroom. "But they might inspire Ty so much they go right there."

"In the other room."

"We have multiple rooms?"

"Of course. A suite."

"Of course." She laughs knowingly. "Sometimes I forget I'm surrounded by rich people."

I understand that. I didn't grow up with money. My father was in the military. Like Ty and Ian's father.

We did okay. We were never hungry or on the verge of losing our home, but we were careful with money.

Then Ty and Ian formed their company and asked me to run their London office and—

All of a sudden, I had enough to buy anything and everything.

"You'll get used to it," I say.

"Maybe." She looks to the window. Studies the darkening sky. "Shit, what time is it?"

I check my watch. "Six forty-five."

"We're meeting at seven?"

"Yes." Have I really been here for hours?

"Shit." She slides off the couch. "I hope my dress is dry. Ty picked this place?"

"Yes."

"So everyone is going to look expensive?"

"He will. Your sister will."

"And you look great." Her nose scrunches. "Why do you always look so good?"

"To make your life difficult."

"Now, it makes sense." She smiles and moves toward her bedroom. "I'll be fast."

"You need anything?"

"I don't know. Some vodka and diet maybe…"

"You're nervous?"

"No." She moves into the room. Closes the door. "I just… never mind."

I rise. Take three steps toward her. "Never mind?"

"The suit," she calls from her bedroom, "why do you wear it everywhere? There's no way it's that comfortable."

"Try one. You'll see."

"It's eighty and humid."

"Not today." It's late September. The weather is cooling.

"Tomorrow though."

"Summer wool."

"Uh-huh."

"It's breathable."

"Then why not wear it running?"

"Do you need the handicap?"

She laughs. "I'm flipping you off right now."

"Of course."

I give her space. Piss. Wash up. Find the vodka in her freezer. Pour two shots over ice. Fill both glasses with diet.

The soda does nothing to hide the taste. It's terrible. Like drinking straight rubbing alcohol.

How does anyone drink vodka?

Besides the hidden booze, the fridge is packed with fresh food. Eggs, bread, almond butter, pasta.

Sienna cooks for herself.

She takes care of herself.

She and Indigo have been on their own for a long time. And now it's just her. Yes, her sister is three floors up, and they'll always be sisters, but marriage changes things.

Sienna needs someone.

The image flashes in my mind: Sienna, in my flat, spread out on the couch watching a reality TV marathon as I finish dinner, racing to the table, throwing her arms around me.

Smiling like she's madly in love.

Which is ridiculous.

Wanting to fuck her is one thing.

Wanting to take care of her?

That's out of the fucking question.

"Cam?" Her voice interrupts me. "Can you come here? I need help with the zipper." She taps on the bedroom door. "It's open."

She's inviting me into her bedroom.

No problem.

I do have self-control.

I won't lose my shit.

I move toward the door slowly, rest my hand on the knob, take a deep breath.

Sienna is a friend who needs help with her zipper. That's all it is.

I slip into her room.

It's a small space with a full bed, a TV, a long closet with a mirrored door. The walls are decorated in glow in the dark shooting stars. They're soft against the dim light, the sunset flowing through the windows, the paper lantern string lights.

"Cam?" She motions to her bare back.

Her dress is falling off her shoulders, leaving the long line of her spine on display.

"Cam?" Her voice stays soft. "The zipper."

"Of course." I move closer. Until I'm close enough to touch her.

My fingers brush her lower back.

She lets out a soft groan.

I pull the zipper up a centimeter at a time.

My hand lingers on the nape of her neck. It feels too fucking good touching her. I want to do it again.

I want to do it all fucking night.

Chapter Thirteen

SIENNA

My shoulders relax as I step into the restaurant.

Ty and Indigo are at a four-seat table. Ty's brother Ian and his girlfriend Eve aren't joining us for dinner.

I don't have to nod and smile as Indie and Eve gush over the new artist of the week. *Have you heard the second verse of this song? It's amazing!*

With Cam here, I wouldn't be a total fifth wheel, but it's still a relief, knowing I don't have to compete with Eve's knowledge of music and art and culture and everything that goes way over my head.

"Is it just us today?" I ask as nonchalantly as possible.

"Should we ditch your sister?" Cam's fingers skim my lower back.

My dress is thin. I can feel all the heat of his hand. The pressure. The perfect mix of hardness and softness.

"Grab drinks at the bar. Pretend we don't see them?" he asks.

Yes, let's go back to my place and spend the night in my bed. "No. I mean, uh, Ian and Eve. Are they coming too?" I try to keep my voice casual.

But he finds something in it. "You don't want them here?"

"No... I uh... I'm just wondering."

"I never took you for a liar."

"I'm not lying."

He raises a brow *really*.

It's the same way Ty does it. Ian too, actually. The three of them share so many similarities.

They're family.

This can't happen.

I can't stare at his lips dreaming about kissing him again. Even if they're such beautiful, soft lips. "I'm, uh..."

"You're full of shite?"

Maybe a little. I don't dislike Ian and Eve. They're fun, especially when Ian is riling Ty (honestly, Ty falls for every one of his older brother's traps). I appreciate the company and the increasing size of our family. "It's more that..."

"You despise them?"

"Of course not."

No one would call Ian a nice guy, but he's a good brother. And his girlfriend... she's not really *nice* either, but she's always friendly.

To me.

And to Indigo.

They have a lot in common. Not just the whole dating a Hunt thing. Or the billionaire boyfriend thing.

Cool hair, dramatic fashion sense, love of music and deep thinking, and examining the written word.

They try to include me, really, but they can talk about Garbage for four hours straight. Whereas I tap out around *yeah, I really like that song I'm Only Happy When it Rains.*

"It goes beyond despise, all the way to loathe?" he asks.

"Is loathe really worse than despise?"

"You tell me."

"I don't dislike them."

"But you don't want them here?" He pushes his palm into my lower back. "Are you going to tell me? Or should we sit?"

I don't want to sit. I want to talk with him. I want to feel all the heat of his hand. "There's nothing to tell."

He raises a brow *really*.

"It's not that interesting."

"Then tell me."

That's a pretty good point. "Why?"

"Conversation."

And to keep him here, with me, with his hand on my back. "If you tell me something."

"Nothing to tell."

I copy his *really* expression.

"Okay. My gossip for yours."

"Mine isn't gossip. It's just… a way I feel."

He motions *go on*.

"Yours is gossip?"

He nods. "About Ian and Eve."

"What about them?"

"Ty makes Ian look like a boy scout."

"So… Ian is much better with knots?" I ask.

Cam chuckles. "Wasn't my best metaphor."

"It was a simile, but yeah, I'm not sure either is your strong suit."

His smile widens. "It's about sex. Do I really have to sell you?"

No. I want to know the gossip. And I want to sit with him and talk with him and maybe even tell him my secrets. Just not this one. It's embarrassing. "If you buy me a drink."

"You don't look twenty-one."

"Isn't everyone in the world wrapped around your finger?"

"Only the women."

"You're so obnoxious."

He smiles. "You like it."

"No."

"Yes. But I'll let the lie slide this time."

I flip him off.

He smiles wider. "You're cute angry."

"You're... still obnoxious."

"Which of them do you dislike?" He presses his palm into my lower back to lead me to the bar.

"I didn't agree."

He stops at the bar and holds out his hand. "Mine for yours."

"Plus the drink."

He nods.

I shake.

He turns to the bartender, asks him to fix two aviations. Whatever that is.

The bartender eyes me suspiciously then Cam hands him a hundred-dollar bill and the guy nods *sure, sir, whatever you'd like*.

Cam turns to me. "Is it Ian?"

"He does have that obnoxiousness you have."

"Which you like."

Kind of. "He and Ty have a good rapport. And he knows soccer."

Cam studies my expression. "That's all you talk about? Football?"

"He's like a hundred years old. What else would we have in common?"

"His girlfriend is what, six months older than you?"

"A year," I say.

"She's young though," he says.

"So?"

"You don't approve?"

"No. I don't care." I mean, it's weird that Ian is twice his girlfriend's age, but Ty is almost ten years older than Indigo and they're obviously meant to be. And Cam is way older than I am. I can't really object.

He nods. "You like Ian."

"Sure."

"But not Eve?"

"No." My voice strains. "She's great."

He chuckles. "Yes. You're a big fan."

"She is. Really, really, great."

"And such specificity."

"I can be specific."

He motions go on.

I freeze.

Cam's laugh gets louder. "I guess we found it."

"No, I… she's smart." I need more. "Stylish. Intellectual. Really, very intellectual."

"You appreciate that trait?"

"What's that mean?"

"You don't like art."

"Only the definition of art that doesn't include *Ninety Day Fiancée*."

He smiles. "Is that why you don't like her? Because she's—"

"A snob?"

His smile widens *gotcha*.

Fuck. I might as well write it on my forehead.

The bartender interrupts with our drinks. Light purple liquid in a cocktail glass. A maraschino cherry on each rim. "Two aviations."

He pushes the drinks to us. Heads to the other end of the bar to talk to a pretty redhead in a cream dress.

"This is a hotel, right?" I ask.

"Is that all it is? That she's pretentious?" He ignores my attempt to deflect.

"You think so too?"

"No, but I can see why you would."

"What does that mean?" My cheeks flame.

"You have different taste."

Yes, I'm the lowbrow one who doesn't appreciate lyrics.

"You shouldn't feel bad about it."

Whatever, I'm not talking about it. "Do you think she's a professional?"

"Who?"

I motion to the woman at the end of the bar. She's pretty, as far as I can tell from here, but that's not why I suspect her. It's the short dress (sexy but clearly expensive), the sky high heels (ditto), the perfect retro waves.

It's her smile too. Like she's inviting us to sit and chat and see where it goes.

"Probably." Cam doesn't take my bait. "Is that it?"

"What?"

"You think she's a whore?"

"Why would I think that?"

"Because Ian paid for her virginity."

What?

He...

She...

No.

I try to pick my jaw from the floor. "How much?"

"A lot."

"What's a lot to you?"

"A lot to anyone." He reaches for his drink. "You didn't know?"

90

I shake my head.

"Then I didn't say anything."

"Is that your promised gossip?"

"No, but since you didn't know, I'm counting it."

"Not fair."

"Life isn't fair."

"What if I tell Ty?"

"Tell him what?"

"That you're a huge gossip."

He raises a brow *really*.

"Maybe."

"Bollocks."

"I said maybe. Not yes."

He chuckles as he raises his glass. "To you being full of shit."

"No... I... Whatever, cheers." I tap carefully—these drinks are full and I don't want to waste a drop. The purple hue is way too pretty.

I watch as Cam wraps his lips around his glass. Sips the violet liquid. Swallows.

He's so graceful and sleek and sexy.

And I want to touch him so fucking badly.

And I really, really can't.

I focus on my drink. It tastes like spring. A little sweet, a little tart, a lot herbaceous. It's not my favorite, but it's so pretty I want to savor every drop.

"Is that it?" he asks. "She makes you feel inferior."

"I didn't say that."

"But she does."

My cheeks flame. "No, it's just... she's nice and smart. And she tries to be friendly with me, even though we don't really have much in common. But she and Indigo have so much to talk about. They run off on subjects I don't under-stand even when I'm right there."

He smiles. "You're jealous."

"No." Maybe.

"You are." He laughs. "That's sweet."

"I don't get jealous."

"You almost knocked out the barista because she flirted with me."

"Because it was rude. Not because I was jealous. I wouldn't get jealous over you."

He shakes his head *bullshit.*

"You're hot, sure, but hot guys are a dime a dozen."

He mimes a knife plunging into his stomach. "It's sweet, Sienna, really. Jealous of your sister's friend."

I swallow another sip. Somehow, it's better than the first. Sweeter. More herbal. More promising of a release of inhibitions. "Don't say anything."

"On my honor."

"I thought we agreed you don't have any."

"The right hand then."

My cheeks flush. "You can't lose it twice."

"You want the left? It gets plenty of action."

"With… yourself?"

"With women."

"Oh." Beautiful mental images. Cam's hands on my body. One on my thigh, the other on my ass. Or my chest. Or stomach. Or cheeks.

Anywhere, really.

As long as he's touching me.

"I can't believe he paid for her virginity," I say.

"She was going to sell it to someone else."

Damn. I can't see Eve coming up with the idea. But I guess she was broke. And they can't keep their hands off each other.

Did she want him that much immediately? Or did it come later?

"So he had to stop that?" I ask.

He nods.

"But why?"

"I don't know. But I'm sure he had a good reason. He's never been interested in virgins before."

"Had he paid?"

"Never."

Huh. "He was just that crazy about her?"

He nods.

"What about you?"

"I've never paid for it."

"Do you…" I swallow a sip. "What do you think I could get?"

His pupils dilate. "You're a virgin?"

"Hypothetically."

"Are you?"

"Why do you care?"

"I know men who would pay."

"Ian?"

He chuckles. "Friends from university."

"And you'd set that up?"

"No." He gives me a slow once-over. "You wouldn't do it."

"How do you know?"

"Look me in the eyes," he says. "And tell me you would."

He's right. I wouldn't do it. But not because I think it's wrong. It's more—"I don't need the money."

"It could be a lot. A hundred thousand dollars. A million."

"Is that what Ian paid?"

"Between those two."

"For one night?" I ask.

"A month," he says.

"A lot can happen in a month."

"If it was one night?"

"Maybe. If it was someone I wanted anyway. Someone like you."

He raises a brow. "British?"

"No, uh… a gentleman."

"I'm not a gentleman." His eyes flit to my chest, waist, hips. Then back to my eyes. "I'm not nice. Or soft. Or sweet."

I swallow hard.

"I'm certainly not gentle."

"So you're like Ty—"

"No. I'm like me." For a second, he looks at me like he's considering exactly how he'd fuck me.

Then he turns to the bar and he's picture-perfect cool.

And I'm still on fire.

Chapter Fourteen

SIENNA

At dinner, I focus on my sister, the wedding, hints about the party next weekend. Anything besides Cam's sexual proclivities.

He didn't say anything really. Only that he's not a gentleman. And he's said that before. As a joke. Many times.

I make sure a lady comes first, but I'm no gentleman.

It's just teasing.

Like this. He's teasing.

He thinks he can work me into a frenzy.

Okay, he can.

But I'm not going to take that lying down.

I warned him. If he flirts, I flirt back. And if I flirt back…

I can't kiss him or touch him or fuck him.

But I can make him wish he could fuck me.

———

After dinner, we walk Cam to his hotel room, wish him good night.

Indigo tells Ty she'll meet him at home. Then she kisses him goodbye—kisses him like she's going to fuck him right here—and turns her attention to me.

"Ice cream?" she asks.

"Is anything open this late?"

"I know a place in Little Italy." Her expression is soft. Inviting. "On me."

Sugar and sisterly company. How can I turn that down? "Sure."

She hails the taxi across the street, takes my hand to lead me across the street. Opens the door for me.

"Wow, what a gentleman."

"Gentlewoman." She waits for me to enter. Then she slides in, smooths her incredibly fabulous dress (a silk slip in matte white), crosses her legs.

"You are a gentlewoman now."

The cabbie asks where we're going.

Indie gives him an address and turns to me. "I wasn't before?"

"Not the same way."

"How's that?"

"You're faster with please and thank you. You sound more like you mean it. And this." I motion to the door. "You're seamless now."

"About opening your door?"

"About everything."

She turns over my words. "More like Ty?"

"Basically, yeah."

"But not as beautiful?"

I can't help but chuckle. They really overplay that—she always tells him he looks pretty or beautiful or gorgeous or some other feminine word that fails to describe his chiseled features.

Ty is handsome, period, end of sentence. He's absolutely

not pretty or cute or even beautiful.

He's broad, tall, striking.

"Is it that bad?" Indie teases. "Is he that much prettier than I am?"

"It's pretty bad, yeah."

She smiles. "He is gorgeous."

"Handsome, yes."

"But you prefer the type with boyish charm?"

That's a trap if I've ever heard one. "I don't know if it's boyish charm. But Ty is too serious for me."

She laughs. "You two would be interesting."

"He couldn't handle me."

Her expression gets hazy. She drifts into the Love Zone for a moment. Complete with the *ah, he's so great* sigh. Then she drifts back. "He couldn't. Not the way you mean. Not sexually. I don't really know what interests you, Sienna. But whatever it is, Ty would find a way."

How can she make something so torrid sound so romantic? Gross. "What if I wanted to be dominant?"

"Do you?"

"Hypothetically."

"Maybe."

"He couldn't do it?" I ask.

"He *could* do anything. And he'd try. If he loved you, he would try, but he'd never…"

"Be into it?" I ask.

She nods.

I shake my head. "It's okay. He's too quiet for me."

She laughs. "He is."

"And I'm too loud for him. It works out."

"Plus, he's my fiancé."

"Well, yeah, but if he was my type, forget about it."

"Would you fight for him?" she asks.

"If I wanted him enough." I look her in the eyes. "No offense, Indie, but I could drop you like a hot potato."

"Undoubtedly. But I'm not sure a fistfight would earn you his heart."

"No... but if it could, forget it."

She laughs. "Would you fight for someone else?"

My shoulders tense. The guy who served us carded. I didn't drink at dinner. I'm lucid enough I see the danger zone in front of me.

But then Indie did drink at dinner. Everyone else drank. Even Cam with his irritatingly appealing *look what I have that you don't* grin.

Like he was seconds from offering all these others things he has that I want very, very badly.

Fuck.

What was she asking?

"If I wanted them, yes." I look out the window as if I'm fascinated by the passing buildings. "I'm more focused on soccer."

"Practice tomorrow?"

"Practice all week," I say. "I'm leaving early Friday for your party."

She redirects. "The one you and Cam are planning?"

"Me, Cam, and Ian." I mean, Cam is interfacing with Ian. He's not a part of our planning sessions, but he's involved. Technically.

"Was he there today?"

"Yeah. They double teamed me. It was pretty kinky."

She laughs. "I know what you're doing."

"Do you?"

"Saying something outlandish so I think it's the reason for your blush."

"No. That's me trying to imagine fucking Ty."

"Mm-hmm."

Ah, yes, outside. Are we really passing Chinatown already? Most of the stores are closed, but plenty of restaurants are buzzing.

"You like Cam."

"Sure."

"You *like* like Cam."

"Let's say I do."

"Okay." She holds her ground. Not pushing me to confess or admitting she's concerned. Staying here in this hypothetical.

"He's much older. He lives in London. He's Ty's closest confidant."

She nods *all true*.

"It wouldn't happen."

"Maybe."

"Maybe?"

"Anyone else, I'd agree."

"But we've been flirting too much?" I ask.

"No. Well, yeah, but I don't think that means anything from either of you."

Not necessarily.

She spots the ice cream place as we cross into Little Italy. "Right here. On the corner. Thanks."

The car stops. She presses a stack of bills into the driver's hand. It's exactly how Ty does it. Smooth and seamless, without calling any attention to the exchange of money.

Then she slides out of the car, holds the door open for me, takes my hand.

It's not our usual gelato place. It's a mini chain open across the city.

We used to go to the one in Brooklyn every so often. We even went to this one a few times over the summer, when we explored the neighborhoods around NYU.

But my first thought is still Eve.

This place is her favorite.

Is Indie going without me? Are they sitting and sharing ice cream and gushing over Billie Eilish or some other pop star who's brilliance I fail to understand?

I swallow hard. Cam was right. I'm jealous. It's silly that I'm jealous. Indie is my best friend, yes, but she's also my sister. She'll never be anyone else's sister.

"This place?" I try to stay cool. Like I barely notice it's not our usual Little Italy gelato haunt. "You sure?"

"Yeah. The mint chip is to die for."

That's not her usual flavor either, but hey, it's a hot night. Mint is refreshing. It doesn't necessarily mean anything.

"We can find another place."

"They have coffee ice cream?"

She nods.

"Then I'm good." I force a smile.

She returns a big, authentic *I'm beautiful and madly in love* smile and offers her arm.

I take it and follow her into the small ice cream shop. It's a cute place, with pale yellow walls and an even mix of dairy and non-dairy flavors.

Indie orders the non-dairy mint chip. Says something about how it's the better version.

I nod. Try to think nothing of it. Order the coffee ice cream.

It's not like I'm some dairy die hard. I mean, how weird is it that we drink milk? It's for baby cows. No other species drinks another animal's milk. And people freak the fuck out about human children drinking breast milk into their toddler years.

It's just…

That's what Eve orders.

But maybe it is the best flavor. No big deal. Whatever.

We take our cups to the street. Walk along the increasingly quiet street.

It's a beautiful night. Clear and warm, with a soft breeze.

"Are your shoes comfortable?" I ask.

"No." She laughs. "Are yours?"

I motion *so-so*. "My running shoes will feel like heaven tomorrow."

She smiles *what a Sienna thing to say*. "Good coffee?"

Oh. Right. I haven't tried it.

I take a small bite. Let the rich mix of sugar, cream, and java dissolve on my tongue. Mmm, sweet and robust. "Very good. Yours?"

She nods and takes a bite. "Perfect."

We walk in silence for a few blocks. Soaking up the feel of the city at night. I've never been one of those *New York is the only place worth visiting* New Yorkers, but I still love the view.

Skyscrapers to the north and south. Steel and glass. The soft blue sky dulled by light pollution, but more beautiful for it.

Slowly, we meander to Washington Square Park. It's late, but on a night like this nice, the park is buzzing with a mix of locals and tourists.

We sit at the fountain, facing the mini Arc de Triumph.

(Which is such an NYU freshman from out-of-state thing to do. But no one will recognize me in this outfit, so I allow it).

"You know they closed the park for years to move the fountain," she says.

"So it would be in line with the arch."

"Do you remember how it looked before?" She motions to the east. "It was a few too many feet that way. Or maybe that way." She motions to the west. "We came a few times, when you were a kid."

That's vaguely familiar. "It looks the same."

"It does. It's a subtle change. Easy to miss."

Okay…

"It's the same with growing up." She looks at me. "With you growing up. Changing. You… you're the same as you always were, but you're different too."

"How is that?"

"You're more sure of yourself. You see what you want and you take it."

"I sound like a bitch."

"No. You sound like a man." She smiles. "If you were a man, people would praise you for it."

"But now?"

"I've always admired that about you, Sienna. But it scares me too. Because I can tell you want Cam. And I know you'll do whatever it takes to get what you want."

What happened to her whole *you're an adult who can understand consequences thing?*

I guess, as my older sister, she's supposed to lecture me about stupid decisions.

But I'm not that foolish. "We're just flirting."

"Maybe. But if you're not. If it's more… you can tell me."

"And you'll tell Ty? And he'll kill Cam?"

"No. I'll keep it our secret. I promise."

"But you'll kill Cam?"

"Only if he hurts you."

I'd do the same. I'd ruin Ty if he hurt her again. And he knows that. So I can't really protest. Or complain.

But, somehow, I feel I'm missing something. Some knowledge she has about me or Cam or Ty or the relationship between them.

I don't ask. I know better.

Not during our walk to the subway, our ride back to the Broadway stop, our walk to the apartment building.

Not even when she hugs me goodbye in the elevator. Or when I change into my pajamas, get ready for bed, climb into my sheets.

I have class in the morning. Class all day. Then practice. I don't have time to worry about… anything.

After half an hour of tossing and turning, I get out bed. I find my cell. Text Cam.

Sienna: You're right. I'm jealous.

I expect him to tell me to go back to bed, but he doesn't.

Cam: You admit you're jealous of your sister's friend?

Sienna: No. I'm jealous of the woman you're fucking right now. Of course, of my sister's friend.

Cam: Do you think I'd answer your text if I was fucking someone?

Sienna: You could spare her the horror of no one ever living up to you.

Cam: Considerate of me.

My lips curl into a smile. Everything else fades away.

For one beautiful moment, the only thing in my mind is Cam's mischievous grin. His hearty laugh. The beautiful, perfect image of him in his running shorts.

Then I do something I shouldn't.

Something dangerous.

Sienna: You're not a gentleman. What did you mean by that?

Cam: You know what I mean.

Sienna: What, exactly?

Cam: I can't tell you.

Sienna: Because of Ty?

Cam: Because you'll think of it every time you're with another man.

Sienna: Let's say I do. Say it's the perfect mental image and I replay it again and again. It's so perfect it makes me come like I've never come before.

Cam: Say it does.

Sienna: Why would I deny myself that? Even if it means I compare every other man to you.

Cam: No.

Sienna: Why.

Cam: I'm not going to be the one who fucks with your head.

Sienna: My head is fine.

Cam: And I want it to stay that way.

Sienna: If you don't want me, say that. Don't hide behind this paternalistic bullshit.

Cam: You know I want you. I'm not going to deny it.

Whatever.

Cam: I want you because you're gorgeous and funny and bold. And because it will destroy both of us. Because I've spent the last fifteen years trying to destroy myself and I'm pissed enough to admit it.

Sienna: What if it didn't?

Cam: How could it not? Is that really what you want, Sienna? Do you really want to spend the rest of your life hating your brother-in-law? Resenting your sister? Hating me for letting you make that mistake?

Sienna: It's my mistake to make.

Cam: You didn't answer.

Sienna: You're obnoxious.

Cam: I know.

Sienna: Are you really drunk?

Cam: Yes.

Sienna: Is that why you admitted you want me?

Cam: You already know I want you.

Sienna: I could hear more.

Cam: I'm not going to fuck you.

Sienna: So? We're just texting. You could tell me more. You could tell me exactly how you'd ruin me.

Cam: Can you really handle that?

Chapter Fifteen

CAM

an you really handle it?

It's a ridiculous question. Like asking if she can handle jumping out of a plane or fighting a tiger in hand-to-hand combat.

How is she supposed to answer the question without a frame of reference?

That's not Sienna.

She isn't the type of person who pauses to ask herself *can I handle this?* She isn't the type of person who considers the possibility she can't handle something.

I'm the same.

I thought I could handle everything life threw my way. In a sense, I did. I'm here. I'm successful. I'm holding it together.

But something inside me is broken. Has been broken since the day Winter invited me to her flat.

This isn't the same.

Sienna is an adult. We're flirting.

I'm a great fuck, yes, and she would remember forever.

She'd even be distracted for a while.

Then she'd meet someone else. Someone she loved, who loved her. He'd lack in some way—skill, creativity, stamina, size—but he'd be capable of opening his heart.

Inviting her into it.

Turning sex into making love.

And that would make all the difference in the world.

Making love. How ridiculous. It's something my parents would say.

But then it doesn't need to look like making love. It doesn't need to be soft or slow or tender.

It can be Indigo, trusting Ty enough to let go completely.

They're not soft. They're not slow. They're certainly not tender.

But they're exchanging something every time they fuck. Power. Trust. Intimacy.

I can fake it.

I can tell a woman she's my entire universe.

I can tie her to my bed and ask her to submit.

But not because I'm exchanging trust. I don't have any to give.

Sienna: You're not as intoxicating as you think you are. I kissed you and I'm fine.

That's bullshit. It meant something to her.

I can still taste her cherry lip gloss.

I can still feel her body yielding to mine.

Cam: Have you kissed someone else?

Sienna: Yes.

Jealousy surges through my veins. She's kissed someone. That's all. And I'm ready to find the arsehole and kill him.

I set my cell on the desk. Stand. Rub my sore neck. It's too late, and I've had too much wine.

I need to stop before I do something even more stupid.

I move into the bedroom. Change. Wash up. Ready for bed.

My mobile buzzes against the desk.

Leave it there.

Go to sleep.

Think of anyone else.

I don't. I pick up my cell right away.

A picture message from Sienna. A mirror selfie, from her nose to her toes.

She's in tiny pajamas. That thin black tank top and matching knickers.

One strap falls off her shoulder. Like the top is begging for removal.

Immediately, the image forms in my mind. Me, in her flat. Pushing her top to her waist. Ordering her to take off her knickers.

Demanding she come for my viewing pleasure.

I can ask now. Ask her to fuck herself thinking of me.

Insist she call so I can listen.

Or video so I can watch.

Sienna: I'm not like you, Cam. I'm not a tease. When I want something, I take it. No bullshit. No excuses. It's like the kiss. I know if it left a mark on me. You know if this leaves a mark on you.

It's a dare.

I'm not stupid enough to take it.

I close my eyes. Try to envision my best friend. The night Ty slipped me my first drink, the party where I got too pissed and he carried me home, the look in his eyes when he told me he had Winter transferred.

Then the image slips.

And I'm here, with Sienna.

Her fingers curling into my neck.

Her lips on my lips.

Her body melting into mine.

Another kiss that leaves a mark on me. Then more.

Her knickers in the pocket of my slacks. My hand between her legs. Her groan in my ear.

Dirty.

Depraved.

Tender.

Intimate.

Confusing as fuck.

My mobile buzzes.

The screen flashes with a picture message.

The same as the last, only her tank top is nowhere in sight.

Sienna Simms, topless on my cell phone.

Fuck.

Chapter Sixteen

SIENNA

Light streams through my window. Casts subtle highlights and shadows all over the room.

It's enough I see my reflection.

Light, barely there against the window.

In full detail on the mirror.

My light brown hair brushed behind my shoulders. My feet on the hardwood floor. My tank top three feet away.

The image in front of me is the same as the image I sent Cam—

I'm in only my black panties.

My flush spreads over my body. Cheeks, chin, chest, stomach. All the way to my toes.

Every part of me is on fire.

I did that.

Of course I did that. What else would I do? Let him throw down this *I can't fuck you; I have to save you from my evil sexual powers* bullshit?

No way.

And now…

I can't read Cam. I'm not sure if he's preparing a gentle letdown or wrapping his hand around his cock.

Mm-hmm. What a beautiful image.

Not all that probable.

But more likely than him calling Ty.

Cam isn't a rat. He's not going to tell Ty. Not these details.

But he might say *no, I can't, I'm too fucked up.* Some other bullshit.

Or maybe nothing.

He's not replying.

Okay, it's only been a minute. It doesn't mean anything. Necessarily.

Maybe he's awestruck.

My boobs are just that amazing.

That's possible.

Totally possible.

Finally, my cell buzzes.

Cam: You need to stop.

Sienna: Is that what you want?

He's quiet for a minute. I sit on my bed. Slip under my white comforter.

No matter how hot and humid the weather, I've never slept naked. It's always felt wrong, strange, overly revealing.

Right now, I want to be naked under these sheets. I want to be naked with him. Not just because I want to see him or touch him or fuck him.

All those other implications too.

I want to know him. All of him. In this overwhelming, all-consuming way.

Cam: I can't be what you want.

Sienna: You don't know what I want.

Cam: I do.

Sienna: I didn't ask you to marry me. I didn't ask you for anything.

Cam: You sent me a picture of your tits.

That's true.

Cam: I know you want me. I want you too. But I'm not crossing the line.

Sienna: I didn't ask you to.

Cam: Bollocks.

Sienna: And you aren't doing the same? You're still flirting with me. I warned you too, Cam. If you really mean it, if you just want to be friends, then stop flirting with me.

Cam: Okay.

I wait for him to expand or explain or negotiate some clause that allows him to come over here and fuck me.

But he doesn't.

Chapter Seventeen

SIENNA

After a night of sleeplessly cursing Cam, I greet Monday morning with a glare.

Coffee.

Where is coffee?

Every shop within two blocks of an NYU building is slammed during the fifteen minute break between classes.

Most settle ten minutes after class starts, but I don't have the ten minutes to wait.

I walk a few extra blocks to the San Francisco chain with incredibly overpriced iced coffee.

It's six dollars for twelve ounces, but it's so fucking good. New Orleans style. With chicory, cream, and extra sweetness.

All the good things in the world. Coffee, sugar, and ignoring Cameron Hunt.

I try to push him out of mind as I walk to class, find a spot in my giant lecture hall, take notes on statistics.

And then in my tiny discussion class, the much despised requirement *Writing the Essay*. I try to channel Indigo and her desire to dive into deep intellectual thoughts, at least where music is concerned.

Instead, my head fills with thoughts of Cam.

Him, in his hotel room, dripping wet from a shower, dropping his towel and wrapping his hand around his hard cock.

In my bedroom, backing me up to the wall, pulling my panties to my ankles, ordering me to come for his viewing pleasure.

In Ty and Indigo's apartment, on the couch, the two of us a tangled mass of limbs and groans.

Fuck.

Class ends and I wander to lunch, buy another coffee, find a spot at the park.

It feels different in the day. The sky is a bright blue; the square is humming with students, and Cameron Hunt is officially not happening.

My mind wanders until I'm due in my next class, but I don't head to the lecture hall. I check my cell and find a text from Cam.

Cam: You're jealous of Eve again?

He sent it while I was at lunch.

It's right there, after our... discussion about keeping things platonic.

As if he didn't admit he wants me.

As if I didn't send him a topless pic.

As if everything is normal.

Fine. This is our new normal.

Cam can keep his whole *I have a magic cock so great it ruins women I fuck* bullshit to himself.

We'll stay family friends.

Or whatever.

I don't even care.

Okay. I aspire to not care.

Eventually.

Sienna: Yes. That's why I texted you last night.

Cam: At midnight.

Sienna: Is jealousy limited to daylight hours?

Cam: Was it that pressing?

No. Maybe. I don't know. I wanted to talk to him.

Sienna: Have you ever been jealous?

Cam: Of course.

Sienna: Of who?

Cam: Women I liked. The men who they fucked.

Sienna: I thought you don't fuck women you like.

Cam: I don't.

Sienna: So why are you jealous?

Cam: Because the men offer them something I don't. Love, intimacy, tenderness.

Does he really believe that?

Sienna: And you're not capable?

Cam: I'm not.

Sienna: How can you be sure?

Cam: I've tried.

It's technically an explanation, but it doesn't feel right.

Cam is a caring person. He pretends he doesn't give a shit about anyone or anything, but he's incredibly devoted to Ty.

Cam: Why did you write last night?

Sienna: I felt jealous.

Cam: Of something other than her intellect?

Kind of.

Cam: Her hair maybe?

Sienna: No. I like my style. I appreciate the drama she brings, but I prefer to keep it low-key. Well, as low-key as I can dining out with Ty.

Cam: Can you keep a secret?

Sienna: Of course.

Cam: He sleeps in that suit.

Sienna: He does not.

Cam: No. I'm pretty sure he sleeps naked.

Sienna: He would.

He's quiet for a few minutes.

Cam: It's not her style or her hair. Her boyfriend?

Sienna: Ian? No.

Cam: He's your type. Older. Playful. Handsome.

Because Cam knows I like him?

Is he flirting? I'm not sure.

If he is, it must be accidental. He seems intent on making this whole platonic thing our new normal.

Sienna: No. I'm not interested in him.

Cam: Maybe not Ian specifically, but everything he offers?

Sienna: Kinky sex?

Cam: Have you been to his flat? It's nicer than Ty's.

Sienna: No way. Ty's has the roof terrace. It's way nicer.

Cam: So you have been.

Sienna: And?

Cam: You're not jealous?

Sienna: Wouldn't I be jealous of my sister then?

Cam: Are you?

Sienna: No.

Cam: Never?

Sienna: Never.

Cam: Really? Even when Ty was showering her with gifts and dirty promises?

Sienna: Maybe a little. But Ty's not my type.

Cam: Too quiet?

Sienna: Exactly.

Cam: So it's nothing they have in common. Not their significant others. Or their increased wealth.

My alarm buzzes. Class is starting now. I should go. Listen to my professor explain the inner workings of the human mind.

But I don't.

I grip my cell tighter.

He was right last night. I like him. In all the ways. I want to touch him, yes, but I want this too.

Cam: What happened last night to make you text me?

Sienna: We went for ice cream. But not to our usual place. To Eve's favorite place. And Indie ordered Eve's favorite flavor too. They had pistachio, but she still ordered mint chip. And vegan mint chip.

It sounds so silly written out. Why am I upset about my sister's ice cream preferences?

It's dessert.

It's nothing. Especially compared to next weekend. To her walking down the aisle and forever being a wife first and everything else second.

I swallow another sip of iced coffee, but it doesn't soothe my throat. It's already ragged.

I'm already—

Fuck.

I press my eyelids together. Tell myself not to cry.

Not here, in the middle of Washington Square Park, while texting Cam.

But that only makes it worse.

It's not just Eve.

It's not just his bullshit rejection.

It's everything.

Life is changing.

I want it to change. I want her to make friends and find success and marry the man of her dreams.

But it means losing our reality TV marathons and our tea shop afternoons and everything we built together, out of the ashes of Mom's death.

Cam: They have more in common.

Sienna: Yeah.

Cam: But she's not as charming as you.

Sienna: Sweet talking me?

Cam: No. Eve is charming in her own way. But you're off the charts.

My lips curl into a smile.

Cam: I felt the same way when Ty came home from university for winter break. He made friends on his football team. And the way he described the star player…

Sienna: You were still in high school?

Cam: For another two years.

Right. Ty is thirty-one now. Cam is twenty-nine. Eleven years my senior.

Sure, Ty has nine years on Indie, but she's twenty-two now. It's different.

Cam: I was used to being jealous of Ian. He's always been Ty's idol. But I accepted that. He's older and wiser. And he was never around.

Sienna: Because he was in the military?

Cam: I was over the moon when Ian enlisted. Ty was miserable. He was only twelve. He wasn't ready to be the man of the house.

Their dad was in the military too.

Sienna: Did you care he was miserable?

Cam: Yes. I felt guilty. Even though I was a kid, who didn't quite get the nuance, I knew I wasn't supposed to be happy about my friend's loss. But I was. I got all his attention.

Sienna: And you kept it until he went to college?

Cam: About that.

Sienna: So you were jealous of Ty's new friend?

Cam: Yes. But I didn't realize it at the time.

Sienna: What did you think?

Cam: That this guy was an arsehole.

Sienna: Was he?

Cam: He was a smug braggart.

Sienna: Your territory.

Cam: That's how I know.

I can see it. Young Cam, wanting to impress his cousin, wanting to have all his attention.

Seething when a new friend showed up but hiding it behind his effortless poker face.

Sienna: What happened?

Cam: He went back to school. I stayed home.

Sienna: Is that the end?

Cam: I hated the arsehole until they graduated.

Sienna: Did you go to the same university?

Cam: No.

Sienna: And now Ty lives in New York.

Cam: He's marrying a New Yorker.

Sienna: We're pretty great. You can't blame him.

Cam: No. I can't. I've never seen him this happy. But I still feel the loss of it. I had four years after Ian fled London, where I had Ty all to myself.

Sienna: Wasn't he engaged to someone else?

Cam: Yes, but it wasn't like with Indigo. He was trying to be someone else.

Sienna: So you still felt like you had him to yourself?

Cam: I still took him out. Made him play wingman.

Sienna: He's kind of hot for that.

Cam: But he beckons the serious girls. Then he mentions his fiancée, and they turn to me.

I can see it. The two of them at some crowded London club, sipping gin and tonics, Cam getting handsy with a woman in a short dress.

Ty trying to have an intellectual conversation and tiring of the atmosphere.

Sienna: I guess I'm lucky with Indigo staying here.

Cam: You are. You still have her close.

I really am.

Even with everything changing, she's only three flights up.

His closest confidant is settling on the other side of the Atlantic.

Cam: I'm happy for Ty. Painfully happy. But it's still hard, knowing he's never coming back to London. Knowing he won't be my work partner, my drinking buddy, my football competition.

Sienna: You could move here.

Cam: Never.

Sienna: Is that what Ty said?

Cam: Of course.

Sienna: But he moved here.

Cam: For love. Not because it's the better city. London is.

Sienna: What if you fell in love?

Cam: I won't.

Sienna: Hypothetically.

Cam: I can't imagine a universe where that happens.

Sienna: Really? You're that incapable?

Cam: Yes.

He's not bullshitting. He means it.

I press my cell to my chest. Suck in a deep breath. Try to gain control of my senses.

I'm not sure what we're doing, but I really like talking to Cam.

He understands how I feel. I'm happy for my sister, beyond happy, but I'm scared of everything changing too.

I'm scared of losing her.

Maybe that's the point of a bachelorette party. Maybe it's for the friends and family who don't want life to change.

I want to celebrate her wedding; I want to embarrass the hell out of her.

It's one night in Cam's presence without touching him.

It isn't that difficult.

Is it?

Chapter Eighteen

SIENNA

S occer practice steals my attention. For three hours, I run, dribble, block.

Then, I go home, heat leftover pasta for dinner, shower, try to concentrate on homework, think of Cam.

All week, it's the same.

He occupies my mind from the moment I finish practice to the moment I start my next practice. Sure, I find breaks to listen to my professors or complete math problems or study Psychology.

But he's there, at the back of my mind. And when I actually put my homework away and try to watch TV—

I barely absorb a word.

We text. He sticks with his promise. He doesn't flirt or tease me about sex or hint he'll ruin me for other men.

He doesn't mention his jealousy or other women or Ty's edict.

Instead, we discuss soccer and coffee and *The Good Wife* (he's watching in his hotel room and he's sure I'd never make it past the first episode).

And Ty and Indigo and their party.

And what time I go to sleep.

And why I sleep in too late.

And how I'd much rather have him in bed with me.

Okay, I keep that to myself. And I try to keep my thoughts platonic, really, but every night, I fall asleep thinking of his body against mine.

———

INDIGO'S WEDDING COLORS ARE INK PURPLE AND DARK, DARK blue. Not really my colors—I look better in warm tones.

A few weeks ago, I picked out a purple dress. A flared A-line with a satin skirt and a whole lot of *cute younger sister vibes*.

Perfect for extending an olive branch to Cam, for saying *of course, we're just friends*.

I channel the look as I fix my hair and makeup.

Elegant chignon. Check.

Concealer, blush, brow pencil. Check.

Bronze shadow, brown liner, mascara. Check.

And the finishing touch—

Red lipstick.

Only the lipstick isn't cute or sweet.

It screams of sex. Maybe because the red is bright and attention getting (even if my shade is closer to brick than fire engine).

Maybe because, for the last hundred or so years, movies and TV have associated red with sex. Especially red lips.

It works. I look good.

But it's not enough. I need to look fucking amazing.

I return to my closet. It's no longer Buffalo Exchange and H&M. It's nice, expensive, fancy.

Okay, and a little Buffalo Exchange and H&M.

And this.

The perfect dress.

A violet bodycon with a plunging neckline.

I change. Do away with my bra. Add a gold necklace.

One sure to drive Cam out of his fucking mind.

———

Twenty minutes and one cup of very sweet, very creamy coffee later, I walk into the restaurant

It's a perfect place for Ty. One big, open room with high ceilings and quiet tables.

The bar is on one side, complete with a cute hipster bartender (suspenders, tattoos, blond hair in a fauxhawk).

If Cam wasn't here, this guy would draw my attention.

As it is…

I cross the room and step onto the massive wraparound balcony.

It's cooler tonight. Cool enough I need the jacket I left home.

Then I turn the corner, and see Cam, and I don't feel the cold anymore.

God, he's so handsome. Somehow, more handsome than he was last week.

There's nothing visibly different about his appearance. He has the same dark eyes, short hair, bright smile.

He's wearing a new tie—a royal blue to match the wedding colors—and a different suit. This one is a little darker. Almost black.

His eyes catch mine. Fill with intent.

Desire spreads over his expression. He gives me a quick once-over. Catches himself. Stops.

"Sienna." He offers his hand. "You're just in time."

I take five steps toward him. Shake. "In time for what?"

He motions to the booth behind him. A semi-private space, with sheer curtains and long bench seats.

Eve and Ian are already sitting inside the booth, on one of the three benches surrounding a large, square table.

Tiny string lights illuminate the space. They're twinkling stars against the soft blue sky.

"In time for Cam to explain why he picked a space private enough for an orgy." Ian stands. Moves past his cousin. "You look gorgeous, Sienna."

"Thanks." I hug him hello. Wait for his girlfriend, Eve.

She stands. Smooths her short black dress. Tries to slip past her boyfriend. "Excuse me."

"Excuse you." He makes a show of holding her body against his as she passes.

She shoots him a *you're bad and I don't want you to be good* look and turns to me. "Sienna. Hey." She embraces me with a warm hug. "You do look great. But I was going to start with your abilities, not your looks."

"It's hard to focus on anything besides her beauty, isn't it?" Cam teases.

Eve laughs. "It is. But I'll try." She releases me. "How's soccer? Cam was telling me you're one of the star players."

"We're a division three team. We're not that competitive," I say.

"Us too," she says. "I'm not even sure if we have a football team."

"Of course, you have a football team," Cam says. "You played her team last week."

"American football," Eve says.

"You like football?" I ask.

"Who wouldn't like football?" Ian continues. "It's the world's sport."

"Yes, yes, we know it's called football everywhere else." She laughs. "Do you need to do this routine every time we bring up soccer?"

"I think he does. It's some British guy requirement." I take a deep breath. Exhale slowly.

I'm talking to Eve and it's almost nice. Maybe I'm a little jealous of her rapport with my sister. And she looks amazing with her teal hair in a perfect straight line, her makeup dark and dramatic, her dress somehow punk rock and super sexy at once.

She has an amazing figure too. All hips and ass.

But I…

Whatever.

Ian takes his girlfriend's hand. Leads her back into the booth. "Do you agree, Sienna?"

"That soccer should be called football? And replace American football as the country's sport? Of course, but good luck convincing Americans," I say.

"She's a football player. You don't have to sell her on the sport," Cam says.

"That this is where you invite a woman when you're going to fuck her on the balcony," Ian says.

"I can't say I've ever invited a woman somewhere with the intention of fucking her," I say.

He chuckles. Sits. Pulls his girlfriend into his lap.

She giggles and whispers something dirty in his ear.

He whispers back.

She blushes.

Cam shoots me one of those *god, they're so annoying* looks.

They are. Kind of. They're adorable too. Somehow cuter than my sister and Ty. How is that even possible?

They finish flirting. Turn their attention back to us.

"A man?" Ian asks.

Cam shoots him a *don't* look.

He chuckles. Returns an equally knowing look.

"I have an apartment," I say. "Why do I need a balcony?"

"Exhibitionism," he says.

"Jesus, Ian." Cam clears his throat. "We don't need to hear about your sex life."

"Since when?" he asks.

Eve looks between them. Realizes something.

Probably that Cam is acting weird now that I'm here. Is he? I can't tell. I'm too distracted by his presence.

He's so tall and strong and handsome.

"It's the same thing every time," Cam says. "I need a little novelty."

"Is that the cause for the orgy?" Ian asks.

Cam chuckles. "Am I that obvious?"

"You know I won't share," Ian says.

"You'll watch though," Cam says.

Ian whispers in Eve's ear.

She whispers back. Shakes her head. "Not this time. Sorry, Cam." She sips her drink. No doubt, a gin and tonic. Another inside joke. Something she and Ian share.

I'm the one on the outs.

I'm always the one on the outs.

"This place was Ty's pick, not mine." Cam says.

"You think he's fucked right here?" Ian pats the bench seat.

"Probably." Cam chuckles. "Are you picturing it?"

"Deciding if it's appropriate for the occasion," Ian says.

"It's kind of sweet. Celebrating his wedding at a place he's fucked his fiancée," Eve says.

"Is that really your idea of sweet now?" Ian asks.

"He's corrupted you," Cam says.

"How do you know I wasn't corrupted already?" she asks.

Cam smiles. Looks to Ian. Then me. "You think so too?"

"That Ty and Indigo have had sex here?" I ask.

He nods.

"Probably. This is the kind of place she likes. Nice. Quiet.

With a beautiful view of the city," I say. "But why would they be in a booth for six? It's just two of them."

"More room," Cam says.

"How much room do you really need?" I ask.

"Depends what you're doing." His eyes meet mine. Fill with a dare.

"What would he do that requires this much space?" I ask.

He blinks. Catches himself teasing me. Stops.

"A third," Ian says. "But Ty would never share."

"And you would?" Cam asks.

"Of course not," Ian says. "You wouldn't either."

"I have," he says.

"Two women isn't sharing," Ian says.

"They were fucking each other," Cam says.

"Even so," Ian says.

"Why not?" Eve asks. "Does there have to be another dick involved for it to be sharing?"

"Of course." Ian turns to her.

"So you'd watch me fool around with a woman?" she asks.

"No," he says.

She motions *explain.*

"It's different. I love you," he says.

She melts, but only for a second. "But it would have been fine before you fell in love with me?"

"I was always in love with you," he says. "I just didn't realize it."

She shakes her head.

He nods.

"This isn't about love, Ian. You're so full of shit," Cam says. "It's possession."

"What's wrong with possession?" he asks. "Are you telling me you've never thought of someone as yours?"

"Once," Cam says. "Never again."

Ian's brow furrows. "Who?"

Cam shakes his head *not going there.* "It's not even possession. It's about claiming someone with your dick."

"And what's wrong with that?" Ian asks.

Cam chuckles *of course you'd say that.* "Did you think of your fuck buddies that way?"

Ian shakes his head.

"But Eve?"

Her cheeks flush. "I am right here."

He looks to her. "Do you think of it that way?"

"That Ian's mine?" she asks. "Of course. I know it's not what I'm supposed to say. I'm not supposed to want ownership of his body. But I do."

God, how can she make something so sexy sound so lame?

Is it some kind of older sister skill?

Ian pulls her into another embrace.

Cam frowns. It's not the response he expected.

What did he expect? He isn't here as often as I am, but it's pretty obvious Ian and Eve are crazy about each other.

Finally, they finish making out. (They really do make out a lot for a couple that's been together for a year. Especially with Ian being so much older, but it's sweet in its own way).

Ian turns to Cam. "Not what you wanted to hear?"

Cam shoots him a cutting look.

Eve doesn't notice. "What was it like when you thought someone was yours?"

"Awful," he says.

"Why?" she asks.

Ian wraps his hand around her wrist. It's possessive. A warning.

Does Ian know something I don't? Something about Cam?

"Because it was." Cam shrugs as if he's unaffected, but

his expression stays tense. "You're full of shit, Ian. You pretend it's about intimacy, but it's sex."

"Sometimes they're the same," he says.

"When are they not?" Eve asks. "You don't have to love someone to fuck them, but you're trusting them with your body."

"Men are idiots. The don't always consider that," Ian says.

"Did you have intimacy with your fuck buddies, Ian?" Cam asks.

Ian shoots him a look that screams *shut the fuck up*.

"What? You're the one who fucked them? Keep your trousers zipped next time," Cam says.

Eve clears her throat. Shoots Cam a look of her own.

He is being an asshole. Even by his standards.

I guess the look works, because he shrugs, drops the subject of Ian's past sex life. After his divorce, he ran through a string of one-month arrangements.

It makes sense, in the context of their conversation. A month is long enough for some intimacy. But not long enough to risk hurt feelings when you part.

It's smart.

But not for Cam.

He doesn't like women after he fucks them. That's what he said.

"What do you think, Sienna?" Eve tries to invite me into the conversation. "Is there sex without intimacy?"

"For some people. But I think guys are more attached than they want to believe." I turn to Cam. Study his expression. "I dated this guy junior year for a few months. We didn't have sex. He was saving himself."

"Really?" Eve asks.

"Yeah. He was religious," I say.

Cam's shoulders relax.

I try to maintain a poker face. "We didn't have sex. But we walked all the way up to the line. And after... he was obsessed with me."

"Obsessed how?" Eve asks.

Cam's eyes fix on me.

"He always wanted to talk to me. To know how I was. To tell me how much he missed my lips. How much he wanted to kiss me again. Maybe it wasn't sex—"

"Is this a Bill Clinton definition of sex?" Ian asks.

"She's too young to know that reference," Cam says.

"Everyone knows that reference," I say. When he was caught having an affair with an intern, Bill Clinton suggested a blow job wasn't sex.

Which is silly. It's oral sex. Sex is in the name.

I know what to say. I know how to make Cam jealous. It's already in his eyes. He's trying to hide it, but it's as clear as day.

But I won't.

I'll be honest.

"If anyone participates in another person's orgasm, it's sex," I say.

"So if I call Eve and ask her to take off her knickers and touch herself," Ian says.

"It's called phone sex. It's in the name," Cam says.

"What if it's a text?" I ask.

Cam's eyes meet mine. "Both people are participating."

"Right." My cheeks flush. "So it's sex."

"Not if you can't hear," Ian says. "Where's the fun in that?"

"You don't want to know when I fuck myself?" Eve asks.

"Of course. But I'd prefer to listen," Ian says.

She blushes.

He brings his hand to her cheek.

Boom.

They're making out.

All right, it goes a little slower than that. They stare for about two seconds. Lean for another two seconds.

Then, boom, sucking face.

Like, seriously going at it. Groaning and kissing and putting their hands in totally inappropriate places.

"Will they fuck if we leave?" I ask.

"They'll fuck if we stay." He raises his voice, so both of them will hear. "Ian never tires of bragging about his exhibitionism."

It's really more her exhibitionism, but I don't want to encourage them.

Ian ignores Cam. Or doesn't hear.

I'm not sure which is more alarming.

Cam shakes his head *ridiculous*. Turns to me. "You need a drink."

"I do."

"Keep your trousers zipped, Ian." Cam offers me his hand.

"He can still get her off," I say.

"I can't prevent a woman's orgasm," he says.

I take his hand.

His smile is effortless. The Cam I know well.

The fun loving party animal who teases me.

Only stiffer, slower, not quite himself.

Distracted.

Not by Ian's banter or their make-out session or the occasion.

By how much he wants me.

Chapter Nineteen

CAM

Sienna moves closer as we step into the restaurant. Her bare arm brushes my suit jacket. Her fingers curl into the soft wool.

"This does feel comfortable." Again, she moves closer. "I can see why you wear it all the time."

"Do you want to try it on?" I need the shield, yes, but I'm burning up. She's too fucking close. I want to touch her too fucking badly.

I promised to stop flirting with her.

I can't start now. No matter how badly I want to slide her into my lap, roll her dress to her waist, rub her over her knickers—

Fuck.

My cock stirs.

I thank the genius who invented tailored wool. It's not comfortable in my current state, but it's better than advertising my desire to fuck her.

"Later, maybe," she says. "It's a cool night."

"You're barely wearing anything."

"I'm wearing a dress." She steps to the bar. "Longer than Eve's."

"You're taller," I say. "And she's wearing boots."

"She wears combat boots all the time," she says. "It's some kinky thing with her and Ian."

"He likes her in only the boots."

"I know."

"You object?"

"No. I get it," I say.

"Picture Messi in only his cleats?"

"No." She smiles. "The shin guards and socks too."

Fuck. Now that's in my head. Sienna in her football uniform. Minus the jersey, sports bra, shorts, knickers.

And then it's *her*, and my fucking head hurts.

It's too quiet in here. How can a restaurant be so quiet?

"Cam?" Sienna's fingers curl into my suit jacket. It's soft. Tender, not carnal. "I can order for you, but I don't know anything about wine."

"What did you order?" I ask.

"A Blue Sapphire martini."

"You realize a martini is almost all gin?" I ask.

"Wow, you don't say? Really?" She rolls her eyes. "It's Bombay Sapphire and Blue Curacao. I think I'll be okay."

It sounds revolting, but not in the way she likes. "Is it sweet?"

"It can be," the bartender interrupts. "You want it wet, honey?"

Her eyes light up. "Wet?"

Fuck me.

He smiles. Shoots her a flirty wink. "More vermouth, usually. In this, more Blue Curacao"

"So it will be more blue?" she asks.

"Can't get more blue," he says. "But it will be fruitier, sweeter."

She nods.

"You too, sir?" he asks.

"Yes, Cam. Would you like it wet?" she asks.

"Why not?" I ask.

He turns to make the drinks.

"You realize it's going to be sweet?" She looks up at me. Copies my tone. "Very sweet."

Okay, I'm an arsehole. I deserve that. "Blue for your sister?"

She nods. "I looked up a list online. This one spoke to me."

"Is it the disturbing citrus liqueur or the gin that does it?"

She laughs. "There was one called Something Blue, if that works better for you. It's champagne and Hypnotiq. Something like that."

"Sounds vile."

She laughs. "You know me. I like it sweet."

"The aviation wasn't sweet enough?"

"I want to try this." Her eyes meet mine. "You think they're having sex out there?"

"He's probably got his hand up her skirt."

"Will they stop when we get back?"

"No."

"If Ty shows up?" she asks.

"Maybe. Ian knows he was an arsehole last time Ty was engaged," he says.

"Can he access that information in his current state?"

I chuckle. "Is that what you think of men?"

"Is it wrong?"

Not usually. "We think with our cocks."

"You too?"

"Sometimes."

"What about Ty and his ex-fiancée? Rory?" She says her name like it's a vile odor. "Were they hot and heavy?"

"You don't like her?"

"Of course not. She stole my sister's man."

"That wasn't how it went."

"Indie and Ty spent the summer together, then he left, and he got engaged to Rory." Her nose scrunches in distaste. "How did she not steal my sister's man?"

"People can't be stolen," I say. "But no, they weren't hot and heavy."

She raises a brow.

"Not the way your sister and Ty are."

"They weren't kinky? Or they weren't unable to keep their hands off each other?"

"She was vanilla. He wanted to believe he was a normal guy who liked vanilla and fit into the world of the rich and powerful."

"The opposite of you?" Her red lips press into a smile. "Pretending you're a freak, wishing you were a freak, but secretly super vanilla."

Go to the bathroom and take off your knickers. I'll show you how fucking vanilla I am. I swallow hard. "You read me like a book."

She nods *I know*. "So Ty liked this girl because she was boring and vanilla?"

"Because she was elegant and old money. And, yes, vanilla." I chuckle. "Is it always about sex?"

"Obviously. Look what happened? Vanilla girl, gone. Now, he's marrying Indie. And she's like… what's the opposite of vanilla?"

"Cherry chocolate chip?"

"Wouldn't that make her a virgin?"

"What do you suggest?" I ask.

"Spiced mocha? Something like that."

"Sweet but spicy?"

"Yeah, she's not sweet. And the whole coffee thing…

problematic." She slides onto a bar stool. "I'll have to work-shop it."

A laugh spills from my lips. She's adorable.

I want to make her smile.

And I want to corrupt her.

"Let me know what you settle on." I slide onto the stool next to hers.

She turns toward me. Crosses one leg over the other, pulling her dress up her thighs.

Fuck, I need those thighs against my cheeks. Around my hips. Fighting my hands.

"Do you think they've had enough time?" She motions to the balcony on the other side of the restaurant.

We can't see anything from here—all the semi-private seats have high backs—but I know Ian. He's going to tease her until we return.

"No," I say.

"What do they need? Five minutes?"

"Damn. That's all the stamina he has?"

Her red lips curl into a smile. "I can come in ninety seconds if I want." Her eyes flit to my lips. Chest. Hips. "If he's skilled, he can make her come in ninety seconds."

"No foreplay?"

"What do you call the two of them flirting in front of us?"

She's right about that, but she's wrong about Ian's speed.

Would Sienna get off on being forced to wait?

I'm going to make her wait either way. Even if makes her fucking crazy.

No. I'm not—

Fuck.

The bartender interrupts my dirty thoughts. Drops off our bright blue martinis. "On your tab?"

"Thanks." I wrap my fingers around my glass. Force myself to look Sienna in the eyes.

It doesn't help. Her eyes are on fire.

She wants me.

It's all over her face.

She takes her drink. Holds it up to toast. "To making women come?"

"To making women come." I tap my glass against hers. Watch as she brings her drink to her lips. Sucks the blue liquid from the glass.

"Mmm." She swallows. Licks her lips. "You're going to hate it."

"How do you figure?"

"Too sweet." She takes another sip. Sets her martini on the bar. Waits.

I try the drink. The liqueur is overwhelming. A syrupy sweet citrus.

I should hate it, but I don't.

It's the taste on her lips. And I fucking need that.

Because I'm not tasting them again. This is as close as I'm coming.

"You don't think Ian can do it?" Her eyes meet mine. "Make her come in ninety seconds?"

"He can, but he won't."

"Why not?" I ask.

"He likes to draw it out. Make her wait until she's begging."

"Oh."

"Sometimes he'll make her come. Draw out fucking her."

"How kind of him."

I laugh. "You object?"

"I don't know. I'd have to try it out and see how I feel."

Fuck me. "You haven't?"

"Haven't what?"

Fucked someone. Tell me you've never had anyone inside you. Never come for someone else. Never touched another man. "Drawn it out?"

"With someone else?"

My stomach churns. I shouldn't be jealous. I shouldn't care. I shouldn't keep asking her about sex. "Have you?"

"No." She takes a long sip. Looks at me carefully. "Have you?"

"I've tried it."

"And?"

"It can be fun, making a woman wait. And it can be fun, making a woman come until she can't take it anymore."

The image forms in my mind immediately.

Sienna, rolling the snug violet dress to her waist.

Me, pushing her knickers to her ankles. Ordering her to lie back on the bench and come on my face.

Her thighs against my cheeks.

Her fingers curling into my neck.

Her tugging at my suit jacket. Begging me to undress. Begging me to fuck her.

"Cam?" Her fingers brush my knee. "Should I give you a minute to finish?"

Fuck.

"The bathroom is around the corner. I won't tell anyone what you're doing."

"I wouldn't."

Her fingers brush my knee again. Then higher. Up my thigh.

I grab her wrist reflexively.

She lets out a soft gasp. One I recognize. *Please, do that again. That rough. Rougher.*

My hand looks good around her wrist. Right. Like it needs to stay there as I hold her arms over her head and fuck her.

I force myself to release her.

She pulls her hand to her lap.

Neither of us underline the implications. She was

pushing me, touching me. And I gave my intent away, grabbing her like that.

What the fuck are we talking about?

Sex, you idiot. Are you trying to get in trouble? Or just desperate to destroy everything that matters?

"Do you need a different location?" Her voice drops. "Something more private?"

Say, my hotel room. Or your flat.

"I can tell Ian you left something at your hotel room."

"So I can head out to fuck myself?"

"Yes." Her eyes flit to my cock. Her tongue slides over her lips. "I…"

Whatever she's going to say, I can't handle hearing it. "Sienna—"

"No." She slides off her stool. "We have a deal. I won't flirt if you don't."

Yes.

Her fingers brush my thigh.

This time, I don't move them.

"I'll stop if you will. But I won't do this. I won't play this game where you ask if I like drawing out my orgasms then say my name in that tone that means 'no, we can't, how dare you go there.' It's one of the other. You want to fuck me or you don't. Which is it?"

Chapter Twenty

CAM

There's a correct answer here.

Two letters.

One word.

No.

Hell no.

No fucking way.

Maybe even *I'm sorry, Sienna, but it's not possible.*

It's the right thing to do. She's a teenager. Smart, resilient, stubborn, yes, but still young.

She needs someone capable of intimacy.

For her sake, I should say no.

But every molecule in my body screams yes.

I want her in every way. In any way.

I *like* her. I never liked anyone as much as I like her. Not anyone I've decided to fuck.

But I know how this goes. What happens after. How everything changes.

I try to find a response. Something better than *no fucking way*, but still clear cut, without any ambiguity.

And the resolve I need after, to stop flirting with her. I

can't say *no, I won't fuck you, but I'll keep asking how you fuck yourself.*

I just can't stop myself either.

Her gaze flits to the entrance. Her smile widens.

For a moment, the question hanging in the air disappears. She's a girl at a bar, happy to see her sister.

And I'm a guy who loves her smile.

"Oh my god." Sienna waves to her sister and Ty. "How long were you two fucking?"

She's loud enough three tables look our way. The bartender too. He laughs *how cute.* Shoots me a look. *Is she yours?*

I nod reflexively.

Sienna races to meet her sister.

They embrace. Exchange a few jokes about Ty's outfit— a purple tie, again—and Indigo's short white dress.

"You look fancy. It's really going to clash with our tacky decorations." Sienna claps her hands together. "But uh… your brother and his girlfriend are going at it. So why don't you make sure they've stopped."

Indigo and Ty laugh. Exchange one of those *if only she knew* looks.

Sienna returns to the bar. The happy couple heads to the balcony.

"Can you bring the next round to us?" she asks the bartender. "Or should we wait?"

"Whatever you want, honey," the bartender says.

My shoulders tense.

She notices. Smiles at her victory. "Really? Whatever I want?"

"Anything."

"You won't judge me if I order straight liqueur?"

"Only if you mix different liqueurs."

"So no Blue Curacao and Creme de Violette?"

142

His nose scrunches in distaste. "That's so disgusting I'll be in awe of you for drinking it."

She smiles. "My sister's getting married. Her name is Indigo, so…"

"Ah." He looks to me like he has a new awareness of the situation. "That was her?"

"In the blinding white silk? Yeah." She laughs. "How did you know?"

"You don't look alike," he says.

"No? She's a total boss babe."

"And you're cute as a button."

She looks to me, like she's giving me a chance to step in and tell him to fuck off.

Or prove I'm just fucking around by blessing their potential union.

Sienna moves on. "I was going for hot." She motions to the low neckline of her dress. "Is it not working?"

"It's working." He winks at her. "Do you want the straight liqueur?"

"No. Another Blue Sapphire, please."

"Wetter this time?"

"If you can handle it." She shoots him a dazzling smile. "And one for my friend?"

"Your friend?"

"The groom's best friend." Somehow, she slips *and he's clearly not fucking me* into the four words. "And cousin. Technically."

"Does the groom's best friend want a drink?" the bartender asks.

"Yes, he'll have one." She leans over the bar enough her tits spill into her dress. The thin purple fabric barely contains them. "And if you get off work early, we're having a pretty epic party in the Penthouse."

"Really?"

She nods. "Strippers, cake, dick shaped lollipops."

"A bachelorette?"

"Combined," she says. "Come if you can. But we might ask you to take it all off."

He laughs. "I'll keep that in mind." He gives me one last look, sizing me up, deciding if I'm prepping to hit him, ignore him, ask him to fuck her as I watch. Then he shrugs *I guess he's nothing* and starts mixing drinks.

Sienna turns to the balcony. "I'll see you out there." She shrugs in exactly the same way.

I guess he's nothing.

I deserve it—I'm not being fair to her—but it still makes my stomach drop.

———

I CONSIDER FUCKING MYSELF IN THE SINGLE STALL BATHROOM. I'm that out of my fucking mind.

I don't, but I stand there, trying to talk myself out of inviting Sienna to my hotel room for too long.

Who needs the room?

We can go back to her flat. Or find a private spot on the balcony.

Hell, we can come back here, and I can bend her over the counter and dive between her legs.

All right, I'm officially out of my mind.

I can't talk myself out of wanting her. That's a lost cause. But I keep my trousers zipped.

I wash my hands five times. I repeat *keep it in your pants, arsehole* like my life depends on it.

Then I meet my friends and family at the balcony with a shrug and smile.

I'm here and I'm the same Cam as always. Sure, I might banter a bit, but that's where it ends.

No telling Sienna to fuck herself. No asking what color knickers she's wearing. No fishing for the exact level of her experience.

Maybe she's a virgin.

Maybe she's fucked every guy on the football team.

It doesn't make a difference to me.

Ty greets me with a smile. It's not guilty exactly—the man isn't going to be guilty about fucking his fiancée—but it's clear he knows he's caught.

"You realize you're thirty minutes late?" I ask.

"I do," he says.

"They were having sex," Sienna says. "We all know they were having sex. They basically admitted it."

Indigo blushes.

"Now, we're debating the details." Sienna reaches for her blue martini. Takes a long sip. Lets out a sigh of pleasure.

She's sitting on the bench on the left.

Ian and Eve are on the bench next to that one. Ty and Indigo across from them.

There's really only one place for me to sit—

Next to her.

Keep it in your pants, arsehole.

I slide onto the bench seat. It's my first time really getting inside the booth, and I have to admit Ian is right. This is a place you invite someone to fuck them.

It's the perfect mix of public and private. There's enough risk of getting caught to wind you up, but not so much you need to call your lawyer.

Sienna takes a long sip. Motions to my martini. "I'll drink it if you don't want it."

"How many is that?" Indie asks.

"It's your bachelorette party. Don't worry about me for one night." Sienna's gaze flits to Eve's half-drunk gin and tonic, but she doesn't mention it.

"Smart dodge." Ian raises his glass to toast.

Sienna laughs. "Thanks." She brings her glass to her lips.

They're still that deep, warm shade of red.

I still need them on my lips, neck, cock.

"Now that Cam is here, we can finally crown you." Sienna looks to me. *Ready?*

There's no other implication in it. Not *fuck you for toying with me* or *I'm going to fuck you until you can't walk straight.*

I'm imagining shit.

And I'm done.

My head is officially in the game.

I find my usual carefree smile. "We're not waiting until the room?"

"No. I think now," she says.

Indigo's expression fills with horror.

Ty chuckles.

Ian and Eve share a *this should be interesting* looks.

I pull the duffel from under the bench seat.

She plucks something from them. Stands. Shows off a white sash.

In thick gold script it reads *Super Freak*. The *Super Freak* is crossed out. Replaced with *Bride to Be*.

Indigo laughs. "Oh god."

"Are you suggesting she's no longer a super freak?" I ask.

"Maybe marriage will end their sex life," Eve says. "That's the tired stereotype."

Sienna fights a frown. "I couldn't put *Freak to Be.*"

"You couldn't," Ty says.

"So we'll have to settle for this. Since Indie hides her inner freak." Sienna beams. She shows off the two black sashes. One for Eve, reading *Slay Queen.*

Eve laughs. "It is true."

"There are some other options. But that one felt the most you." She hands Eve the sash.

Eve nods a thanks.

Sienna dons her sash—*Miss Behaving*—and turns to me. "Now, for the gentlemen."

"Are you bringing some?" Ian asks. "I don't see any here."

"You'll have to do for tonight." Sienna takes the last three sashes from the bag. "I admit, I was a little biased with these." She holds out Ty's sash. Deep purple, with silver letters reading *I'm the lucky one.*

He smiles. "It's true."

Indigo sighs, wraps her hand around his neck, leans in to kiss him.

He pulls her body into his. Holds her close. Kisses back with everything she has.

The picture of love.

It makes my stomach turn.

I want to be happy for him. I am happy for him.

I just can't watch this shit.

"Oh my god, you have your whole life for that!" Sienna says. "Tonight is for torturing you. Look more embarrassed." She shakes her head *ridiculous* and offers Ian his sash. The same black with gold letters. *Bad Influence.*

Then mine. *Dancing Diva.*

"How did you know?" I ask.

She laughs as she rises to her tiptoes and places the sash on my shoulders. "How could I not?"

Her fingers brush my neck.

She looks up at me, her light eyes filled with curiosity.

All I want to do is answer it.

Chapter Twenty-One

SIENNA

Cam plays his role as the life of the party. He teases my sister; he banters with his cousin; he debates which London football player would be best as Indigo's second choice (in the event something happens to Ty, she obviously needs to marry an athlete).

It's almost normal.

I almost believe we're just friends.

Only I keep catching him staring.

Studying me. Watching me. Picturing me out of my dress.

His desire is all over his face. I recognize it now. I recognize when his expression gets hazy and his thoughts drift to dirty places.

It's like when Indigo slips into the Love Zone. His version is the Fuck Zone.

I barely notice how much Indigo and Eve talk about fashion or hair or the deep, emotional lyrics of Billie Eilish (and others I don't recognize). I'm too busy watching Cam, trying to place his intentions, deciding whether I want to slap him or mount him.

Both maybe.

After we finish dinner, we head upstairs for dessert.

Ian pulls a room key from his slacks. Opens the hotel door. Motions *after you*. "Should we give Ty and Indigo a few minutes?"

"Only a few?" Cam asks.

"That's all he needs," Ian says.

Cam's eyes flit to me. Search for something.

Yes, it's the same conversation we had, but so what? It's not like he's saying *baby, I'll take my time with you*.

Or is he?

Would he?

I don't know. I have no idea if he likes it fast or slow. Soft or hard. Sweet or—

No. There's no way he likes it sweet. That's not who he is.

"You know Ty doesn't bait this easily." Eve laughs. "You need to work on your routine."

"Vixen, how could you say that?" Ian asks.

She looks up at him with a hazy smile. "The truth is the truth."

"Brutal," he says.

Yeah, they're in love. It's great. I'm over it.

"Cake first. Then you two can try to sneak off to fuck." I don't specify which two people can sneak off to fuck. It could be either couple, really.

Ty and Indie step inside.

Then Ian and Eve.

Cam turns to me, opens his mouth like he's going to say something, stops. "You want to cut the cake?"

"No. I think Ty should."

He chuckles. "That's cruel."

"Thank you."

He offers his arm.

I'm not sure if it's a friendly gesture or a romantic one, but I take his arm anyway.

We move into the penthouse.

It's a huge space, almost as big as Ty's apartment.

On the left of the door, the kitchenette, marble counter, dining table.

On the right, three leather couches around a coffee table, across from a wide-screen TV.

A door to the bathroom. Another to the bedroom.

And two massive windows letting in the soft blue night sky.

With the walls covered in dick shaped string lights, pink balloons, and inappropriate cut-outs, it's the perfect mix of luxe and tacky.

Indigo looks around with wide eyes. Ty smiles, enjoying the horror.

Eve laughs as she takes in the balloons reading *Same Penis Forever* and *Same Vagina Forever*. "I appreciate the equality, but are you sure it's true?"

"You know something I don't?" Ian asks.

"Are you sure they'll never invite someone else?" she asks.

Cam and Ian share a knowing look.

Cam chuckles. "Eve, you have to know something about your brother-in-law."

"We're not married," she says.

"Future brother-in-law," Cam corrects.

She raises a brow *really*.

"Yes, I know Ian claims he'll never get married again, but, what is it you say, Sienna?" He motions for me to step in.

"You need to lock a good thing down," I say.

He chuckles. "Exactly."

"And I'm the good thing he needs to lock down?" Eve asks.

Cam nods.

"Is that really a compliment?" she asks.

"He means it as one," Ian says. "But then he's an idiot."

"And you aren't?" Cam asks.

Ian chuckles *maybe*. "Ty's the only one with brains here."

"Obviously. If he's marrying my sister."

Ian nods *it's true*. "What is it you always say, Cam? To Ty, making men everywhere proud, thinking with his cock?"

"Because he's marrying someone who's also kinky?" Eve's nose scrunches. "Is that really what you reduce their relationship to?"

"You don't like me because I make you come?" He wraps his arms around her.

"Of course. But you're not nearly as clever as Ty." She looks up at him with a smile.

Cam shoots me a *fuck, this again* look.

And, sure enough, bam—

They're making out.

Even Ty shakes his head *really, making out again?* "Have a little restraint."

"Your department," Cam says.

"Not just mine." Ty raises a brow.

Cam laughs.

Mmm. Beautiful mental images. I try to stay here, in the room, celebrating my sister's wedding, and not in a fictional universe where Cam ties me to his bed.

No good.

The image is too enticing.

Cam's tie around my wrists, my dress on the floor, his body over mine, his cock inside me.

Yes.

Now.

Please.

Uh… what.

Right. Cake. "We need to have cake before our next event."

Indigo looks to me. "Our next event?"

"Yes, after the cake and the crowns… the next event." I look to Cam. "Where are the crowns?"

"Part of the next event," he says.

"Oh. Right." I'm here, at the bachelorette party, in a world where Cam is not tying me to his bed. And I don't care. I don't care he's here. Tonight is still my sister's party, and I have a lot planned for the bride and groom. First—"Cake!"

"Are you two coming?" Cam asks Ian and Eve.

They continue making out.

"You think they'll get tired?" I ask.

"At some point," Cam says.

"He's got a lot of stamina for a man his age," Ty says.

Indigo slips her hand around his waist. Whispers something in his ear.

He laughs. Whispers back.

"Dirty talk later. Cake now." I look to Cam. "Have you ever tried this hard to get someone to eat dessert?"

"Not everyone appreciates sugar as much as you do," he says.

Indie laughs. "I'm not sure anyone appreciates sugar as much as you do, Sienna." She releases her fiancé and moves to me. "Let's do it."

Finally! I move into the kitchenette, find the cake in the mini fridge, in a soft pink box reading Cameron Hunt.

I look to him and raise a brow *you checked it?*

He smiles wide.

As if he's not tormented by how much he wants to fuck me.

Or maybe he's not. Maybe he doesn't care.

Whatever. That's fine.

153

This is a time for cake.

Not men.

Especially not handsome British men who play hot and cold and say bullshit like *I like you too much to fuck you.*

They're not even on my mind.

I set the pink box on the counter. Turn to my sister. "Ready?"

Nerves spill over her expression. "Am I?"

"You won't be." This is perfect. No matter how complicated everything else is, this is perfect. "Ty? You should be here for this too."

Cam pulls out his cell. "We have to immortalize the moment."

"Do you?" Ty asks.

"It's our duty." I place my hand on the lid. Focus on my sister and Ty.

She's already standing across from the counter.

He moves next to her. Slips his arm around her waist. "Ready."

She looks at me *would you really?*

I nod. Whatever it is, I would.

Cam slips into the kitchenette. Then he moves closer, into my space.

It's the only place he can really capture Ty and Indigo's expressions, but my body ignores the logic.

He's here.

Next to me.

Then behind me. Right behind me.

He doesn't rub against me on purpose, but I still catch fire from the friction.

Fuck, I want him so badly.

"Okay. Ready," Indigo says.

I try to ignore Cam. Pull the cake box open.

Click, click.

Indigo's jaw drops. Ty lets go of his poker face.

He actually blushes. I think. It's hard to tell with him.

"Oh my god." Indie hides behind her hands.

The cake is perfect. Better than I could ever imagine.

A circle covered in pastel purple frosting. The words *A hard man is good to find* in black letters.

A very erect, very sizeable cake dick next to them.

"It gets better," Cam says.

"How?" Ty chuckles. "That's... fuck. Now, I have to orchestrate your wedding to get you back."

"Repay my genius?" Cam asks.

Ty shakes his head *ridiculous*, looks to Indie, whispers something in her ear.

She blushes. "You think?"

He nods.

She turns to Eve and Ian for a minute. They're no longer making out. Just giving the happy couple enough space to blush over their cake.

I pick up the cake knife. The pastel pink paper plates. Show off their hot pink pussy motif. "Equal embarrassment."

She shakes her head. "Did you?"

"Did I..." I offer her the knife.

"She did, didn't she?" She looks to Ty.

He nods. "Probably. You'll have to—"

"I can't cut a dick in half," she says.

"It's cake," he says.

"But it represents you." She shakes her head. "Never."

What are they talking about? I look to Cam for a clue. Remember, I find him incredibly irritating.

Then he leans in to whisper an answer and I forget everything but how badly I want his lips on my skin.

"She's asking if it comes," he says.

Oh. "Does it?"

"It's filled with white cream frosting."

Oh god. "Your idea?"

"Yes."

"You're smart sometimes."

"Sometimes." He laughs. His usual laugh. The one that usually means *I'm teasing and it's meaningless.*

Now…

I don't know. My thoughts are fuzzy. Gin-tinted.

My inhibitions are fading fast.

I'm *this* close to tugging at his tie and ordering him to put up or shut up. Here. In front of my sister.

Ty nudges Indie.

She shakes her head. "I can't take a knife to it, even if it's cake."

"What would you normally do?" he asks.

"Don't do that. You'll get a yeast infection," I say.

She laughs. "No, I…" She looks to her fiancé. When he nods, yes, she shakes her head *here goes nothing* and she grabs the cake dick.

Sure enough, it squirts white icing.

"Oh my god." She pulls her hand back. Licks the frosting from her fingers.

"Are you really stopping there? Cruel." Ty asks.

"I learned from the best." She smiles.

He wraps his fingers around her wrist. Brings her hand to his mouth. Licks the frosting from her digits.

I try not to think about the implications.

The guys joke about the horror of taking a knife to the cake dick, but they still slice the thing, and dole it onto paper plates.

Cam hands one to me. "Is that enough?"

It's a small square, by my standards. "There isn't any frosting cum. How could it be enough?"

"Go ahead." He motions to the cake dick on the table. "No one's going to stop you."

"No, Cam. I couldn't do that to you. It would be all you'd ever think about." I don't mean to say it with irritation, but I do.

His eyes flare with frustration, but he shakes it off.

Ugh.

Whatever.

Men are the worst. Cake is better. Even phallic cake.

I grab a fork, find a seat on the couch, try to ignore the rest of the festivities.

I need to think. I need to focus on something other than how much Cam's hot and cold bullshit annoys me.

Yes, he's handsome and funny and sexy as hell.

And—

Would it be so bad if I dragged him to the bedroom to mount him?

Fuck it. I leave the cake. Psych myself up in the bathroom.

Tonight is fun. Tonight is for my sister.

Cam doesn't affect me.

I move into the main room with proud posture, but I melt the second I see Cam.

He's so… here. And handsome. And sexy. And hurt.

And ugh.

I send my sister a text—*checking on our drinks*—and I slip out of the room, walk to the elevator bay, hit the call sign.

Finally.

I step into the tiny silver space.

But I don't get air or space or room to breathe.

Cam slips into the elevator after me.

Chapter Twenty-Two

SIENNA

I try to focus on the illuminated *Lounge* button.

The bar isn't the place to check on our drinks, but it's closer than the lobby, and it's got a balcony.

That's air.

Space.

Distance between me and the person making my life difficult.

I take a deep breath. Push an exhale through my teeth. Try to channel an inner calm.

But I don't have any calm.

I'm buzzing.

He's right there. All tall and dark and strong. And I want to touch him so badly. I want to slap him and kiss him and tell him to fuck off and tell him to fuck me.

He steps backward. So he's nearly against the wall.

I stay next to the row of buttons on the right. But I can see him, through the shiny wall.

"Do you need another floor?" I ask.

"What are you doing, Sienna?"

"I need a drink."

"You've had three."

I wrap my fingers around my purse. "I want another."

"You're not twenty-one."

"Are you going to tell on me?"

He doesn't have a comeback. Or maybe he doesn't want to argue. I don't know. Who knows? How could anyone begin to know what the fuck Cameron Hunt wants?

I grip my purse tighter. Focus intently on the illuminated button. A light yellow. Exactly halfway between cream and egg yolk.

Not all that interesting. But better than trying to figure out what his problem is.

I like you. And I don't like people after I fuck them.

Finally, the elevator arrives. The doors slide open.

A handsy couple—seriously, they put Eve and Ian to shame—jumps apart. Shoots us a *you know how it goes* look.

They're both around Cam's age and they're both dressed like him too. In sharp designer suits. Here on business. The business of fucking each other.

He's got a ring.

She doesn't.

Usually, I don't consider the bonds of matrimony.

Today, I'm annoyed. Is this asshole really cheating?

I step out of the elevator. "How's your wife?"

The woman looks away, embarrassed. The guy fumes, but he doesn't say anything to me.

No, he talks to Cam. "What's your girlfriend's problem?"

"I'm guessing it's the ring on your left hand." Cam steps out of the elevator.

"How is it your business?" he, again, asks Cam.

"It's not." Cam looks to the woman. "But you could do better." He ignores the guy. Moves next to me—right next to me—and presses his palm into my lower back. "You're smarter than that."

I shrug.

He nudges me forward. "You know better, Sienna. You can't trust strange men."

"I'm not trusting him."

"You shouldn't challenge him."

Whatever. "He's obviously preoccupied."

"And what if your comment works? And she decides not to fuck him because of it?" Cam leads me into the restaurant. "You think he'll take that well?"

"I think I don't care."

"What if he comes back angry and tries to start a fight?"

"Wow, an angry man at a bar? How could this happen?" I roll my eyes.

"Sienna—"

"We're in a public place."

"The elevator is right there. He could grab you. Keep you there. Hurt you before anyone could stop him."

"There's a security camera."

"So they'll catch the arsehole after he hurts you?"

"I'm not by the elevator anymore. I'm at a restaurant." I motion to the tables. They're not all that busy, but they're busy enough. "And I'm ordering a drink. And what I do is none of your fucking business."

The same bartender is here. The cute hipster guy with the vest.

He recognizes us. Nods hello.

"Would you like something?" I ask.

Cam doesn't reply.

"Suit yourself." I cross the room to the bar.

The cute bartender smiles. "Not enough Sapphire Martinis in the hotel room?"

"Room service won't send Blue Curacao."

He shoots me a winning smile. "Your boyfriend want one too?"

"I don't know." I look to Cam.

His entire face screws with frustration. There's no sign of the carefree party animal who teases his best friend about his penchant for whips and chains.

My stomach twists. Is he this upset?

Is he really worried about that random CEO asshole?

No. Fuck him. He should worry about himself. He should worry about playing hot and cold with me.

"Do you want another martini, Cam?" I ask.

He steps to the bar. Tries to swallow the frustration in his voice. "Sure."

"You closed out," the bartender says.

Cam pulls two bills from the wallet. Slips them into the guy's hand.

"Thanks." The bartender beams. "Right away, sir." He turns. Starts filling a mixer with blue liqueur.

"Sienna." Cam stares down at me.

I stare back at him. "Cameron."

"Don't call me that."

"It's your name."

"I don't like it."

"Then don't say my name in that tone."

"What tone?" he asks.

"Like it means something to you."

"Sienna…" He does exactly that.

"No." I shake my head. "You don't say my name like that." I will the cute bartender to mix faster, but I'm pretty sure Cam tipped well enough he's moving as fast as humanly possible.

"Like what?"

"Like you care about me."

"I do."

Ugh! He's so annoying. I press my palms into the edge of the bar. Tap my nails against the wood. I painted them red last night. A bright red that goes with pretty much any shade of purple.

It's not my color. It's too bright, too cool, too *fuck me now.*

But maybe that's what I need. Maybe I need to paint my entire world red. Take what I want. Fuck who I want. Announce myself as a woman who gets hers.

Everyone knows I make sex jokes. Everyone knows I'm interested.

But they see me as the weird sister. The girl who can't keep her mouth shut. Who just doesn't get manners.

I get them. I just don't appreciate them.

Finally, the bartender finishes. Sets our drinks on the bar. Gushes over Cam's tie and asks if he's from London.

Money changes everything, doesn't it?

I leave them to it. Take my drink to the balcony. To the way too big for two semi-private booth.

It's ours for the night.

The entire balcony is reserved for the night.

Rich men have the world at their fingertips.

I sip my martini slowly. It's not as sweet this time. More gin. Less liqueur. Still good. Maybe even better with all those botanicals.

The first time I tried gin, I thought it tasted like Pine-Sol, but it's not so bad, really. It's almost sweet.

I finish half my drink. Set the glass on a side table. Try to enjoy the view.

It's a beautiful night. Clear and cool and shining with all the lights of the city. But my blood is buzzing.

Cam is infuriating.

And incredibly sexy.

He steps onto the balcony. Looks to me.

It's too dark. I can't make out his expression. I'm concerned. I don't want to be concerned.

He doesn't get to fuck with me like this.

I try to ignore him as he moves closer, but I can't. He's so there.

He stops at the railing. "You were flirting with him."

"So?"

"What if he expects something?"

Seriously? "When did you get overprotective?"

"You're not being smart."

"Because I flirted with the bartender? Or because I told Cheaty McHandsy to fuck off?"

"Both." His voice quiets. "He could hurt you. He's bigger than you. It would be easy for him to overpower you."

"I could hurt him."

"How do you figure?"

"I know this whole watch out for the kid sister thing is new to you, but I'm not a wilting flower. I can hold my own against people who are bigger than I am."

Out of nowhere, he grabs my wrist. Hard enough it hurts. Hard enough to threaten.

He keeps that same pressure as he moves closer. Until he's right behind me. Close enough, no one can see what he's doing.

No one is out here.

No one *can* see.

I should tell him to stop. Or fuck off. Or mind his own fucking business.

But I don't want him to stop. I want him to go. To follow this thread until it unravels completely.

"Cam." My breath is a whisper. A *please*. I'm not sure what we're talking about. Only that I want him.

"It would be easy." He pulls me a little closer. "Trivial."

"What are you—"

"What would you do?" He grabs my other wrist. Holds my hand against his side. "Do you really think you could overpower someone my size?"

"He wasn't your size."

"Sienna—"

"Stop saying my name like it means something."

He doesn't reply.

"I don't know what you're doing. If this is part of the game you're playing with me. But stop it. Stop toying with me."

"Tell me you'll be careful."

"Really? That's what you're doing here? Reminding me men can hurt me?"

"Yes."

"Bullshit."

"I'm worried about you." He pulls me hard. So my body is pressed against his.

A gasp falls from my lips. Fuck. That's intense. And it feels so fucking good. It's wrong it feels so good, but I don't care.

What did he say about possession? I don't remember.

I only know I want it. I want to be his. I want to be claimed.

Even if it does ruin me.

Even if he hates me after.

I swallow hard. "If this is some way to prove you're fucked up, okay, you win. I believe you're fucked up. You never had to convince me of that."

"I could hurt you."

"Probably." He's a few inches taller, a lot bigger, and better trained. "But I could hurt you too."

"No." He slips his arm around my waist. "You could try, but I'd overpower you."

"Cam—"

"Tell me to stop."

"I don't want you to stop."

"You should."

I shake my head. "I don't. But only if you mean it. You don't get to do this. You don't get to warn me about strange men. Or growl when I flirt. Or grab me like you're going to throw me against the wall. Not if you don't want me."

"I want you."

"And that. You don't get to say it. If you want me, take me. Now or never, Cam. Which is it?"

Chapter Twenty-Three

CAM

There's still a right answer.

It's the same fucking answer.

Something mature. Reasonable. Responsible.

I'm supposed to be the adult here. Say *no, of course, you're right. I'm being an arsehole. I can't take you now. Even if everything was different, if you weren't completely off-limits, if claiming you wouldn't fuck up both our lives.*

Even then—

I'm not good for you.

And I care about you.

So, no.

Of course not.

I'm not a monster.

That's what I should say.

But I can't.

There's too much fire in her hazel eyes.

"Sienna." My hand goes to her chin. "You don't know what you're asking."

"I do."

"No. You don't."

"Two hours ago, we were sitting here, teasing my sister about how easily she bruises. I know what I'm asking."

"No." Maybe she has the same dirty desires. Maybe she fantasizes about being hurt. I don't know. But—"It's different when it happens. It changes you."

"Maybe I want to be changed."

"If I start"—I swallow hard—"I can't promise I'll stop."

"Okay."

No. It's not okay. It's never going to be okay. "Sienna."

"If you don't want to do this, fine. But you don't get to use me as an excuse. It's your choice, Cam. I'm saying yes."

"But you don't know. You can't."

"Then show me."

"I might hurt you."

"I want you to hurt me."

Fuck. My balls tighten. I want her every way I can have her. But this—"Have you been with anyone?"

"Will you be jealous if I say yes?"

"Yes."

"My boyfriend last year. We fooled around, but we didn't have sex."

"Fooled around how?" My stomach churns. I am jealous. Painfully jealous.

It's ridiculous.

I try to tell myself it's about love, affection, intimacy. Maybe it is.

But it's about sex too.

About wanting her to be mine and mine alone.

"What do you want me to say?" she asks.

"The truth."

"Above the waist. Nothing serious." She reaches for me.

I grab her wrist. "No."

"I can't touch you?"

"Not now."

"Why not?"

My voice firms. "This only works if you do what I ask."

"Okay."

"Only what I ask."

Her chest heaves with her inhale. "You want me to follow orders?"

"Yes."

Her cheeks flush. "Always? Or now?"

"Both." I bring my hand to the back of her head. Undo the tie in her hair.

The light brown locks fall over her shoulders. "Cam…"

"Yes?"

"You haven't kissed me."

"I know."

"Will you?" She reaches for me, but this time it's tentative. Slow. Like she's trying to pet a wounded animal. She brings her hand almost all the way to my chest. "Please."

I wrap my fingers around her wrist. Bring her hand to my neck.

Her fingers curl into my skin. Her body melts into mine.

She looks up at me for a minute, then her eyes flutter closed.

Mine follow.

Slowly, I bring my lips to hers.

She tastes like gin and liqueur and Sienna. There's something that's just her. Something I recognize.

Something I need in a way I've never needed anything.

I bring my hand to her lower back. Pull her closer as I kiss her harder.

Her lips part. My tongue slips into her mouth. Dances with hers.

It's strange, kissing her like this. Intimate in a way I barely recognize. Terrifying all the way to my bones.

Maybe I'm full of shit. Maybe I'm not afraid of hurting her. Maybe I'm afraid of hurting myself.

I pull back with a sigh.

Her eyes flutter open. Meet mine. Fill with all the trust in the world.

Too much. More than I deserve. More than I've earned.

"Cam." Her voice is yielding. All the softness under the brash, headstrong girl who demands what she wants.

"Yes?" I run my fingers over her shoulder blade.

She shudders. "You're a good kisser."

"I am?"

"Yeah."

Fuck, that's not what I expected her to say. "Thank you."

"Sure." She looks up at me, equal parts nervous and needy. "I've never... I... I know you can't promise, but I want you to know that I've never done this."

"Never kissed someone?"

"Fucked someone."

"I'm not going to fuck you."

"Oh." She deflates. "Why not?"

A laugh spills from my lips. "Because."

"Because..."

"I don't have a condom."

"I do."

Fuck me. "Even so."

"Then why?"

"Because I want to make you wait." I bring my hand to the strap of her dress. The fabric is smooth, slick, some synthetic I need on the floor. But one thing at a time. "No more questions."

"Why—"

"Or I won't make you come. Your choice."

Her eyes fill with drive. That's the Sienna I know. The one who rises to every single occasion.

"What are you wearing under this?" I hook two fingers under the strap.

She shudders. "It would be easier to show you."

"Answer anyway."

"Underwear."

"A bra?"

"No."

"Knickers?"

"Yes."

"What color?"

Her eyes fix on mine. Look for something. "I don't remember."

"Really?"

"Really." Her fingers go to the hem of her dress. "I'd have to check."

"No." I grab her wrist. "Not yet."

"Okay."

Not here. No one is supposed to come onto the balcony, but I don't trust the restaurant security. Especially with the bartender so keen on Sienna.

We need privacy.

So I'm the only one who sees her.

I don't want anyone else to see her.

I release her. "Move into the booth."

She nods. Grabs her drink. Slips past the sheer curtains.

It's the same space we were in an hour ago. Only our friends and family are upstairs, celebrating the promise of forever.

And we're here, about to cross a line that can't be uncrossed.

"This is all I'm offering you, Sienna." I finish my drink. Set the glass on the table.

"This, right now? Or sex?"

"Sex."

"Okay."

"Okay?"

She nods. "You've warned me sufficiently. Honestly, I'm not sure anyone could live up to your hype."

"My hype?"

"How you're so fucked up and you'll fuck me up."

"I might."

"Okay." She brings her drink to her lips. Takes a long sip. "You might fuck me up. I might fuck you up."

No. She will fuck me up. But I can't begin to explain that to her. I can barely understand it myself. "I might hate you tomorrow."

"Will you fuck me anyway?"

"Maybe."

"Maybe?"

"Yes. Maybe."

She takes another sip. "Take it or leave it?"

I move closer. "I'll give you what I want to give you. Take what I want to take. As soft or hard as I want. Understand?"

Her eyes light up. "I think so."

"You think so?"

"I think about it. You tearing off my clothes or pinning me to the wall or holding me down as you fuck me."

My balls tighten.

"What if it's too much?"

"You want a safe word?"

She nods.

I can do that. "Pick a word."

She looks up at me. "Sweeper."

My laugh breaks the tension. "Okay. Sweeper." I bring my hand to her hip. Nudge her softly. "No more questions now. You do what I say, or I stop."

"Yes." Her voice softens. That same yielding tone. Like she's desperate for me to take her, bend her, break her.

"Step back."

She does.

I push her dress off her shoulders.

The slick purple fabric falls to her waist. Reveals her breasts.

Fuck. "Gorgeous."

"Thank you." Her chest heaves with her inhale.

"Who's seen you like this?"

She shudders as I trace her collarbone. "I don't know. A lot of fellow soccer players over the years. I haven't kept track."

"Men?"

"A guy I dated junior year. And then two last year. I was going to sleep with one of them, but we were interrupted."

"You wanted him?"

"Yes, but not the way I want you." Her eyes fill with fire.

"Who else?"

"Three guys at a party. My friend dared me to flash them."

"And you never back down from a dare?"

She nods.

"How did you feel when they saw you?"

"Exposed."

"Did it turn you on?"

"Yes."

"Does this?"

She nods.

My cock stirs as I trace her collarbone. "You want me to touch you properly?"

"Please." She looks up at me expectantly, like she'll die if I don't touch her properly, like she's desperate to beg for more.

Sienna is brash and headstrong. There isn't an obedient bone in her body. That's what I like about her.

But here—

Here, I need her playing by my rules. I need to make sure she can do that.

"Not yet." I bring my other hand to her hip. Pull her closer. So she can feel how hard I am.

She groans as my cock brushes her stomach. "Please."

I reply by bringing my lips to hers.

The kiss she returns is hard and hungry. Then I slip my tongue into her mouth, and she yields.

Her body melts into mine.

Her groans vibrate down my neck.

It makes me dizzy.

The affection. The intimacy.

The control.

I bring my hand to her breast. Run my thumb over her nipple.

She pulls back with a sigh. "Cam."

I watch pleasure spill over her expression. It's so fucking beautiful and it's only the beginning.

It's different with her, terrifying and thrilling in equal measure.

I tease her with my slow circles.

Back and forth.

Up and down.

Softer.

Harder.

Until she yelps.

Enough, she yelps.

Harder.

Her eyes press together. Her lips part with a groan.

Harder.

"Fuck." She reaches for me. Finds the cuff of my jacket. "Cam. Fuck."

I move to her other breast. Tease her until her groan is

equal parts pain and pleasure. Then I push her dress off her hips.

The fabric falls to the floor.

She steps out of it. Looks up at me, waiting for instruction.

"Turn around," I say.

She does.

Fuck, I need her naked. I need to see every fucking centimeter of her body. "Take off your knickers."

She brings her hands to her hips. Slides the soft black fabric to her ankles.

"The shoes."

She steps out of her shiny wedges.

She's naked. For me.

Mine.

No. That's a ridiculous thought. There's no fucking way she'll ever be mine. Not anywhere else.

But here—

Here, I can take her.

"Bend over. Touch the floor," I say.

She does.

I move closer. Until our bodies are aligned. Until she can feel my cock against her cunt.

My slacks and boxers are in the way.

It's too much. I need her skin against mine.

But not yet.

Not until I can handle it.

"Cam." She pushes into her hands, so her cunt rubs against my cock.

Even with all the fabric between us, it's divine. I need more. I need to touch her, taste her, fuck her.

I'm as impatient as she is. More even.

"You fuck yourself with toys?" I run my fingers over the flesh of her arse.

"Yes."

"Your fingers?"

"Sometimes." She gasps as I move my fingers closer and closer.

Closer. "But no one else?"

"No one."

"I'll be the first?"

"Yes."

Without warning, I slip two fingers inside her.

She gasps as I stretch her.

She's wet. Ready.

Still, I move slowly as I push my fingers deeper.

Deeper.

Until she gasps.

Then I pull them back and do it again.

Softly to start.

Then harder.

Harder.

Hard enough her nails dig into her ankles.

She gasps as I release her. "Fuck. Cam." It's a plea for more. And a curse for stopping. "Please."

"No." I bring my fingers to my lips. Fuck, she tastes good. Like honey and Sienna. "Stand up."

Slowly, she rises.

"Sit on the bench."

She moves around the low table. Sits on the bench on the left. The one where we sat a few hours ago.

How can everything change in two hours?

Either I'm out of my mind or I've finally found it.

I'm not sure.

I don't care.

I don't care about anything but making her come.

"Spread your legs," I say.

She parts her thighs.

I place my body between her legs. Lower myself to my knees.

Then, I take her hands, place one on my shoulder, curl the other around the back of my neck.

I bring my lips to the inside of her knee. Kiss her gently. Then harder.

Then it's my palms against her thighs. I push her legs into the bench seat. Hold her in place as I bring my mouth to her cunt.

I brush my lip against her clit.

"Fuck." Her nails curl into my neck. "Cam."

"Say my name when you come." I sink my nails into her thighs. "Exactly like that."

She nods a yes and watches as I dive between her legs.

I lick her slowly, tasting every fucking part of her.

Then I bring my mouth to her clit. Test her with soft flicks of my tongue. Hard ones.

Slow. Fast. Back and forth. Zigzag.

There. I find the spot she needs me.

I don't tease her.

I pin her to the bench seat and I flick my tongue against her, again and again, harder and harder, until she gasps and tugs at my jacket.

There.

She's exactly where I need her.

So fucking close.

And I need that. I need to savor every bit of her pleasure.

I pin her harder. Push my nails into her flesh.

"Cam." It falls off her lips, equal parts blessing and curse. "Fuck."

I savor the anticipation in her hazel eyes for a moment, then I bring my mouth to her clit, and I lick her exactly how she needs me.

Again and again.

Until she's digging her nails into my skin, groaning my name, coming against my lips.

I lick her through her orgasm.

Then I release her. Stand. Wipe my mouth with the back of my hand.

She looks up at me, her eyes hazy with pleasure. "Fuck." Her fingers brush my trousers. "Can I?"

"Not now."

"But—"

"What did I say?"

"You give me what you want to give me." She presses her lips together. "And you don't want to give me that?"

"Not yet."

"So later?"

"Later." I find her dress. Slide her knickers into my pocket. "We're going to be missed."

"Oh. Right. We're uh…" She looks around the booth like she can't remember why we're here. "At the party."

I nod. Offer her my hand.

She takes it. Lets me pull her up. Wraps her arms around me. "I kind of like this."

"Kind of?"

She smiles. "Me naked. You in your suit."

"Me too." I hold up her dress. "But you'll probably want this."

She nods. Lets me help her into it. "My panties?"

"You're not getting them back."

"This is a short dress."

"And I'm going to spend the entire night dreaming about rolling it to your waist."

"Oh. Good."

Fuck, she's adorable. It's wrong how adorable she is.

"You promise you'll fuck me later?"

"No."

Her lip corners turn down. "Why not?"

"Because I said so."

"That's not a reason."

"Take it or leave it."

She pouts, but she still takes my hand.

Chapter Twenty-Four

SIENNA

H oly shit.

It's the only response I have to the situation, and it's not enough. It doesn't begin to describe the magnitude.

I smooth my dress. Step into the elevator. Push the button for the Penthouse.

My eyes go to Cam.

He's standing there, in the elevator bay, his gorgeous brown eyes wild and contained at once.

"Are you coming?" I lick my lips. They taste like him. Like gin and sugar and Cam.

My new favorite flavor.

Even if it's just this. Or just tonight. Or just the time he's here.

Even if it fucks up everything—

He'll always be the first man who made me come. And I'll always love the taste of gin and sugar and citrus.

Blue Sapphires forever.

"Later." His voice drips with intention. No, he isn't taking the elevator to the room yet. No, he isn't going to fuck me yet.

But later.

Later is such a beautiful word.

"How much later?" Impatience drips into my voice. I don't want to wait. I want more. I'm satisfied, but still, I want more.

How is that possible?

How can I be in two states at once? How can he be wild and contained?

These are opposites. In need and needy. Uncaged and controlled. But they're both true.

Cam smirks. It would be annoying on anyone else. It would have been annoying an hour ago. But now, it screams *I know I'm good at making you come and I'm going to do it again.*

"As much as I want." He nods as the elevator doors slide together.

And then I'm alone in the tiny space. It's not big enough for the anticipation coursing through me.

Three drinks and I'm still nervous. For more. For later.

For my sister's party.

Fuck, my panties are in his pocket. We might as well scream *yeah, we're totally fucking.* It's stupid and reckless and perfect.

The car rises. I fix my purse. My hair. My lipstick.

There. I look presentable. And not *just fucked*. Not that I was fucked. I just—

Ding. The elevator arrives. I turn the corner. Walk the few dozen feet to our room. Pull the key from my bag.

Click, click.

I slip inside.

The same decorations adorn the room. Dick shaped string lights. Teasing balloons. Silly cutouts.

Ty and Indigo sharing cake.

Ian and Eve… totally noticing I rolled in here after a very long absence.

He raises as if to say *I know something is going on here. I'll find the details whether you offer them or not, so you may as well save us all some time and offer them.*

I shrug.

Eve studies me carefully. She's looking for something, but I'm not sure what it is. And she tries to convey something to me, but I'm not sure what that is either.

She smiles, whispers something in her boyfriend's ear, releases him. "Champagne?" she asks no one in particular. "Room service just dropped it off."

When no one answers, I say, "Sure. Need some help?"

"Thanks." She motions *after you.*

I try to move normally, but without my underwear, every step is illicit. I feel every brush of my dress, every blow of the air conditioner, every move of every muscle.

And every single sensation screams *Cameron Hunt is going to fuck me.*

By the time I'm at the table, I'm on fire.

Eve meets me there. Leans close enough to whisper. "Your zipper—"

Shit.

"Can I?" she asks.

"Yeah."

She rights it.

"It's not—"

"None of my business."

That's not true. Not at all. Cam was right. She and Ian are going to get married. The only person who doesn't seem to realize that is Ian. And maybe her too.

Even if they eschew the legal formalities, they're so clearly in love, and so strangely right for each other. They're in this for the long haul. Ty is going to be her brother-in-law too.

And this is going to be complicated.

For a second, my shoulders tense. Then the air-conditioning blows my dress against my thighs, and I only care about fucking Cam tonight.

Nothing else matters.

"Vixen, are you trying to tease me?" Ian sends *I'm going to fuck you* glances her way.

"You really need new material." Ty chuckles.

Indie does the same. "She deserves to tease you for once." Ian laughs.

Eve blows him, and my sister, a kiss. She makes a show of hiking her dress up her thigh and grabs the bottle of champagne.

I pick up the other.

The door clicks open.

Cam enters right as the bottle *pops*.

Foam spills from the lip. I bring it to my mouth. Suck the champagne from the glass.

Cam watches from the door. He's too far away. I can't tell what's in his eyes. Only that I need it.

I push it aside as Eve and I fill flutes and hand them to the attendees. Once everyone is with drink, we meet at the table.

Ty raises his glass. "Let me guess. To Ty thinking with his cock?"

"Get some new material, Ty. Honestly." Cam rolls his eyes as if he hasn't made the joke a million times.

Everyone laughs.

Cam looks to me. "To the female orgasm."

My cheeks flush. But I don't think anyone notices. I'm pretty sure everyone here is blushing. Maybe even Cam.

We clink glasses. Drink. Laugh.

Cam moves closer. Close enough, his hand brushes my hip. My lower back. My waist. He looks to the bride and groom. Then to Ian. "It's time."

"Already?" Ian asks.

Cam nods. Looks to me. "Are you ready for our next activity?"

Yes. Take me into the bedroom, throw me against the wall, fuck me until I'm screaming.

But that isn't.

We have—

Oh my god. This is—

Fuck.

I'm not sure which is more exciting—

No, that's bullshit. Cam fucking me is a lot more exciting than our next piece of torture, but this is amazing.

"All right, victims take their seats." Ian leads her to the love seat.

Cam does the same with Ty.

The guys bust out the love rope.

"I'm sure you're familiar with this." Cam ties my sister and my future brother-in-law to the couch with a big, loose, not all that constraining knot.

Then he ties their arms together.

"Trapped together forever. Better get used to it." Ian tries to sell the horror of it, but he's smiling way too wide.

Cam shoots me a conspiratorial grin.

My chest warms. My stomach flutters. My thighs shake. We're in on this together. The four of us, really—

Cam and I came up with the idea. Then Ian arranged details. And Eve asked a friend who worked at Devil's Point.

But it still feels like ours. Like some dirty secret that belongs only to me and Cam.

Or maybe that's my panties in his pocket.

Probably my panties in his pocket.

I move behind the couch, next to Cam.

I'm too close—it's obvious I'm trying to get closer—but I can't bear to move away. It feels too good being near him.

Cam looks to Ian and Eve. "Who wants to do the honors?"

"I will." Eve smiles and moves to the door. For a moment, the room goes dark.

Then the door bursts open.

The lights turn on.

An Amy Winehouse house cover fills the room.

Two dancers skip inside. A man in tuxedo print shorts and a woman in a tight lace one-piece that screams *horny bride*.

They saunter around the room, slowly circling the couch, teasing the bride and groom, almost but never quite touching.

Then the guy sets the female dancer on the table. He picks up the furry handcuffs hidden under a gift bag and ties her hands behind her back.

Spreads her legs.

Feigns performing oral sex.

(They usually do actual sex acts, but that seemed a little crass. And, well, let's add that to the list of things I don't get about bachelor parties. Why would I want to watch other people have sex next to my sister? Weird).

The song shifts to a remix of the wedding march. An electronica version Eve found, with a female vocalist groaning *here comes the bride* with enough breathiness we all know which version of *comes* she means.

The performers go through an acrobatic routine of positions and acts.

Him tying her.

Untying her.

Her tying him.

Then, the two of them, tied together, in a giant sash that reads *matrimony*.

It's hilarious and weird and super sexy too.

Then they finish. Take a bow. Blow kisses to their adoring audience.

My sister is laughing, but she's bright red. And Ty... I think he's blushing, but I can never tell.

"The champagne room is over there." I motion to the bedroom. "If you want a private dance."

The female dancer perks. She knows private dance means extra tips.

Indie starts to shake her head, but Ty whispers something in her ear.

And they...

Say yes.

"One dance," Indie says. "If you'll be so kind..." She motions to her restraints.

"Maybe we should make the suite the champagne room." Cam shoots his cousin a look. "So you two can enjoy it after."

Ty whispers something in Indie's ear.

She nods.

"Britney will untie you," Eve says. "If you treat her right."

The female dancer, Britney I guess, nods. "I'll be gentle. I promise." She smiles. Flicks her long blond hair behind her back.

She's pretty. Short and curvy, with the kind of hot girl next door look guys adore.

But then maybe I don't know anything about guys.

My sister couldn't be less girl next door if she tried. And Eve has a banging body, sure, but there's nothing low-maintenance or easy about her style.

And I...

Fuck, am I really the picture of "girl next door" here? I'm not an easygoing person, but I love sports, I wear sneakers everywhere, and I live in my ponytail.

How am I the normal one here?

I turn to my sister. "Can I trust you with the dancers?" I shoot her a look. *It's okay if this is too much.*

She gets it. Nods *it's fine.* "One set. Then I'm going to fuck my fiancé." She kisses Ty. Then she turns to the dancers. "If that works for you, Britney."

"You're going to fuck me?" Ty asks.

"You have a problem with that?" She laughs.

"I'm going to fuck you," he says.

"Yes, yes, you're very dominant and kinky. We saw the routine." I find my purse. Grab the half-full bottle of champagne. "See you Sunday, Indie." I blow my sister a kiss. "Take care of her Ty, okay?"

"Always," he says.

Cam and Ian exchange their own banter. Finish. Leave with us.

I try to keep a few feet between me and Cam, but, fuck, I want to touch him so badly.

"Can we trust them alone?" Cam asks.

"You really think Ty would share?" Ian asks.

"She wants someone to watch," Cam says.

"Even so." Ian pulls his girlfriend closer.

"Maybe he'll watch her and the dancer," Cam says.

"Or maybe the dancer will watch the two of them," Ian says.

"I don't think so," I say, though I don't really know. I hear a bit from Indie, but, of course, Ty only spills to his male friends.

"Britney is very persuasive." Eve laughs at a memory. "But I can't imagine Ty sharing." She looks at Ian. "Would you?"

"Fuck you in front of the dancer?" he asks. "I don't know. Beg me. See if you can convince me."

"I don't want to." She leads us into the elevator.

He shoots her one of those couple looks. *I know you and I know that's bullshit.*

"Not with someone I know. And not that close," she says. "You know… God, you're infuriating sometimes."

"Only sometimes?" He offers his hand.

She takes it.

"How can a thirty-seven-year-old man act so much like a seventeen-year-old?" Cam asks.

"Do you need tips on stamina?" Ian asks. "I'm sorry, Cam. It happens to everyone, eventually."

"Were you really more insatiable once upon a time?" Eve asks her boyfriend.

"Never more than when I'm with you," he says.

"Sweet talker," Cam says.

"It does sound like bullshit. Sweet. But bullshit," I say.

But they're already in their own world. Not making out, thankfully, but teasing each other as the elevator makes its way to the lobby.

God, Cam is so close.

Two feet.

Right there.

I want to touch him so badly, but Eve and Ian are also two feet away. I have to wait. How long could an elevator ride possibly take? There are only five floors to go.

Four.

Three.

Two.

One.

There. The doors open. I step out first. Then Cam. Then Eve and Ian.

Ian and Cam trade a few barbs about Ty.

"Should I walk you to your hotel?" Ian asks.

Cam shakes his head. "It's in the wrong direction. Go. Fuck each other."

Eve just barely blushes. "Thanks, Cam. I'll see you soon." She kisses him goodbye.

On the cheek. But it still makes my veins buzz with jealousy.

I hug them both goodbye. Watch them leave.

Then it's just me and Cam. And six blocks to my apartment.

I follow him outside.

It's a beautiful night. Cool air, soft blue sky, quiet streets.

"Are you cold?" he asks.

I shake my head.

But he still undoes the button of his suit jacket and slides the soft wool over my shoulders.

I slip my arms into the sleeves. "How do I look?"

"Dapper. It suits you." His fingers brush my neck as he adjusts the collar. He looks down at me like he's going to kiss me.

Then he does.

His eyes flutter closed and his lips find mine.

He kisses me like he's claiming me.

This time, I'm pretty sure he is.

So when I pull back, I look up at him, and I say, "It's later."

"It is."

"My apartment is close."

"My hotel room is closer."

Chapter Twenty-Five

SIENNA

I s it possible to die from desire?

The female equivalent of blue balls, maybe.

Technically, it's only three blocks to Cam's hotel room. They're short blocks, without lights. There's no reason why this walk should feel a million miles long.

But with his palm on my lower back, only the thin fabric of my dress between his hand on my skin, it does.

Finally, we arrive. From the outside, the hotel resembles the one we left. Steel, glass, grey adornments, tall windows glowing with soft yellow lights.

But it's not any other building.

It's Cam's hotel.

It's the place where he's going to fuck me.

He hasn't promised that. He's very explicitly not promised.

But he...

I...

Fuck.

He pushes me a little harder. Not enough to hurt or force

or even move me in one direction. Only enough to say *I have you*.

He does.

I'm not sure he realizes how much he has me.

I'm not sure I can accept how much he has me.

This isn't smart. Not given the circumstance. Not given who he is.

A man eleven years my senior, with the power to crush me, physically, practically, emotionally.

He's more or less promised he'll leave me in ruins.

And, of course, I took that as a challenge.

Am I stupid, reckless, brave?

I'm not sure I care. My judgment is on vacation. Dulled by the potent mix of alcohol and desire.

Let's face it. I'm not all that cautious at the best of times. I rush into things. But not with men. Never with men.

Something always stops me.

I haven't been with anyone, really.

Until Cam.

And he—

Fuck, I'm in so far over my head it's not even funny.

And I still don't care.

Cam leads me through the hotel's luxe lobby. It's old money trying to look modern. Marble floors, gold accents, sleek leather couches that stand out like sore thumbs.

It's not Cam. He enjoys the finer things—I don't know wine, but I've seen the price of his bottles on the bill—but he's like me. New to this.

Not as new—he's worked with Ty and Ian for most of his adult life—but new enough. He grew up middle class. Both his parents worked. They still do.

But that's all I know about them. A father in the military. A mother with a nursing degree. And I only know that because Ty's mentioned it.

I don't know about his friends or his apartment or his life in London.

I don't know how he'll tell this story.

You won't believe the night I had with this virgin.

Or *I felt every fucking piece of her pouring into every fucking piece of me.*

No. That isn't him. It's not even me. It must be some of Indie's influence. Or even Eve's. I don't have a poetic bone in my body.

Neither of us do.

And this—

Fuck is all I have and it's still not enough.

Cam whisks me inside the open elevator, slides his key into the slot, pushes the button for his floor.

The penthouse. "Is that why you needed another hotel for the party?"

"There are four suites on the top floor."

"But you couldn't do this across the hall."

Something flares in his eyes. Some realization. Then it fades into that perfect, pure desire. "I couldn't do what?"

It's a dare and I'm going to answer it.

I sit on the safety bar and slide my dress up my thighs.

One inch.

Two.

Three.

Almost—

His eyes follow my hands. "Are you daring me, sweetness?"

Sweetness. Fuck, that sounds good on his lips. It's not a romantic pet name, not really, but that only makes me crave it more. "Yes."

He takes a step toward me. "You think I won't fuck you right here?"

"You won't."

His eyes flit to the display. We're halfway up the building. There isn't time for sex, but there's time to tease.

I pull my dress another inch. "We both know you won't."

"You're sure?"

I nod.

In one quick movement, he closes the distance between us. He brings his hand to my thigh. Pushes hard enough my leg hits the cold metal bar.

His other hand goes to my cheek. He tilts my head, bringing us eye to eye.

God, there's so much desire in his dark eyes. I can barely take it.

"You have no fucking idea what I'm capable of." Without warning, he presses his palm against me. "No fucking idea."

I wrap my legs around his hips.

He slips two fingers inside me. Pushes deep and hard. Hard enough it hurts. But fuck it hurts so good.

"Cam," I breathe.

"I *am* going to ruin you, Sienna." He pushes deeper.

Fuck. My eyes flutter closed. That's intense. Too intense. But somehow, still not enough.

"Fuck, I want to ruin you." He brings his lips to mine.

His kiss is hard, hungry, completely unyielding.

I want all of it. Him commanding me, moving me, destroying me.

How can I want that so badly? Everywhere else in my life, I stay in control. I win, I accomplish, I achieve.

I don't let anyone tell me what to do or think or wear.

I certainly don't consider men's opinions of me.

But this is different.

He isn't taking. We're exchanging something.

Cam pushes his fingers deeper.

Then he pulls back and drives into me again. Slowly. So I feel every inch.

Again.

Again.

The elevator dings. The doors slide open. Cam stays pressed against me, his lips on my lips, his fingers inside me.

He pulls back slowly. Brings his fingers to his lips. Licks the taste of me from them.

Then he helps me down, rights my dress, guides me into the hallway.

Somehow, I walk the fifteen feet to his door.

Cam unlocks the room and leads me inside.

In one swift motion, he pushes the door closed and pins me to the wall.

The lights of the city stream through the window. That perfect soft blue. The tiny squares of yellow. The silver of the moon.

Even though the rest of the room is dark, I can tell it's huge. I'm not sure if it's the air or the distance between the door and window or some sense I have of Cam.

Maybe he's right. Maybe I have no idea what he's capable of. Maybe I have no idea who he is.

But I want to know. I want to know him in every way I can.

He brings his hand to my cheek, strokes my temple with his finger.

For a moment, he's soft, gentle, sweet.

Then his hand goes to my hip. He holds me in place as he rocks into me. So I feel his pelvis against mine.

He's hard.

And I want that. I want it so fucking badly.

"Please." It falls off my lips. I don't say please. Not normally. But I'm ready to drop to my knees and beg if that's what it takes. Whatever it takes.

"Please?" He pushes my dress up my thigh.

"Fuck me."

"How?" He pushes my dress higher. "Here?" He pushes his hand into my hip, pinning me to the wall.

Not hard enough to hurt. Only hard enough to threaten hurt.

Will he hurt me? Does he want to?

Do I want him to?

I don't know. My thoughts are fuzzy. I'm too overwhelmed by desire. I want to fuck him in every way, every place, every position.

"Your back against the wall. Your thighs around my hips." He pushes my dress a little higher. Until it's at the apex of my thighs. "Or should I turn you around? Slam you into the wall." He brings his hand to the back of my neck. "Bind your wrists behind your back so you can't do anything but take me?"

"Yes."

"Or should I take you to the bed? Lay you on your back. Fuck you like a gentleman?"

"What does that mean?"

"I don't know. I've never tried it."

"Would you?"

"Is that what you want?" He runs his fingers down my neck. Over my collarbone. To the neckline of my dress. "Do you want it soft and slow?" He pushes the dress aside, so my breast spills from the fabric.

"No."

"Good." He cups me with his palm. Runs his thumb over my nipple.

Softly.

Then harder.

Hard enough it hurts.

My eyes close. My head falls back. My lips part with a sigh.

What do I want?

More. The other details are irrelevant.

He rolls my nipple between his thumb and index finger.

It's hard. Rough. Painful.

Fucking perfect.

"Cam," I breathe.

"You've been teasing me." He does it again. "Do you have any idea what that does to me?"

I shake my head.

He takes my hand. Brings it to his cock.

I cup him over his slacks. Fuck, that feels good. I want more. But when I run my palm against him, he grabs my wrist.

Hard. Way past hard enough to threaten. Hard enough to stop me.

It shouldn't make my sex clench, but it does.

I'm out of my fucking mind.

"What did I say, sweetness?" He takes my hand and pulls it over my head. "This only works if you follow my orders." He does the same with my other arm. "Understand?"

Not completely. Not why. And not why it makes me shake. But I can do what he's asking. I really want to do what he's asking. "Yes."

"Good." He pins my wrists to the wall. Kisses me hard. Releases me. "Take off your clothes."

I nod.

He steps back. Watches intently as I slide his suit jacket off my shoulders. There's no place to hang it, so I let it fall on the floor.

I step out of my shoes and pull my dress over my head.

It's not as seamless as I'd like. I don't have the grace he does. But his eyes stay glued to me.

He stays tuned to me.

He's different than he's been before. The pretenses are gone. The bullshit is somewhere else.

It's just the two of us.

Me, in his hotel room, completely naked.

Him in all his clothes, but without something else. The shield he hides behind.

"Beautiful." His voice is an octave deeper. A tone I've never heard before tonight.

A tone that makes me shake.

"Turn around." His voice stays firm. Demanding.

My body obeys for me. I turn before I realize I'm doing it.

His fingers skim my hip. My ass. My lower back. He traces a line up my spine, then all the way down it.

Around my hip.

To the apex of my thigh.

He holds his hand there as he moves closer. Brings his body against mine, his cock against my ass, his stomach against my back, his lips on my neck.

He kisses me gently.

Then harder.

"Keep your hands at your sides." He scrapes his teeth against my neck. "And watch."

Before I can ask what he means—it's too dark to see a thing—he flips the switch.

The room illuminates instantly.

My eyes go to the full-length mirror.

The reflection of my body against his. My light brown hair falling over my shoulders and chest.

His hand, between my legs, so fucking close to where it needs to be.

Me, completely naked.

Him, still in his suit and tie.

Fuck. I'm on fire.

He holds me in place, one hand on my hip, my ass against his pelvis, as he brings his fingers to my clit.

He works me with long, slow strokes.

They're patient. Too patient.

"Please," I breathe.

"Please?" He scrapes his teeth against my neck again.

"Fuck me. Please."

"Not yet."

My body whines. "Please."

"Ask again and the answer will be no."

Fuck. I'm so desperate to be filled. I don't even understand it. What it means. How it will feel. But I know I need it. I need him inside me.

"Watch." He rocks into me again.

His cock grinds against my ass.

His nails dig into my hip.

His fingers glide over my clit.

Slow, steady strokes.

I watch him work me.

It's strange. I've never watched myself masturbate. I've never looked closely. But there's something about seeing his hand against me—

It's intense. I can barely keep my eyes open.

Then he brings his free hand to my chest, and I have to close my eyes.

He stops. Waits.

I suck a breath through my teeth. Push an exhale through my nose. No begging, no matter how badly I want him inside me.

I can't risk him stopping.

He needs to fuck me.

My eyes flutter open.

I watch Cam toy with my nipple. I watch him run his teeth over my neck. I watch him rub me.

He stays behind me, pressed against me, his cock hard

against my ass, his slacks and boxers the only thing between us.

He holds me there as he works me, his thumb against my nipple, his fingers on my clit.

Those slow, steady strokes.

Then faster.

Faster.

There—

"Fuck. Don't stop." I breathe. "Please don't stop."

He stays at that same perfect pressure as he works me again and again.

And again.

He pushes me all the way to the brink.

My sex winds tighter and tighter.

Until I'm so taut it hurts.

Then he pushes me over the edge.

With the next stroke of his fingers, I come. My sex pulses. I groan his name. I force my eyes open.

So I can watch him work me through my orgasm.

Pleasure spills through my pelvis, down my thighs, up my torso, all the way to my fingers and toes.

Every part of me is awake and alive and every parts want him.

I'm satisfied and in need at the same time.

The more he gives, the more I want to take.

How is that possible?

Cam's fingers brush my hip. "Can you stand?"

"Kind of."

"Go to the bedroom. Sit on the bed. Wait."

"Wait?"

He nods.

"For what?"

"For me to decide you've waited long enough."

Chapter Twenty-Six

CAM

I t's official.

I'm out of my fucking mind.

I'm not so far gone, I don't realize it. I still know I'm out of my fucking mind.

But I don't give a fuck.

Sienna is behind the plain white door, sitting on the bed, waiting for me. For whatever I want to give her.

If she was someone else, if this was something else—

I can't even imagine that. She isn't someone else. This isn't something else.

She's Sienna. The sassy loudmouth who gives as hard as she takes.

And this is—

I'm not sure what this is, but it's different. I care about her. I trust her.

I trust her more than I've trusted anyone in a long fucking time.

And now I'm here, risking that to get off.

I wash up in the bathroom in the hall. To make her wait. And get ahold of myself.

Yes, I'm going to fuck her.

Yes, I'm going to push her.

But it can't be the way it is with other women. I'm not sure I can stay in control with her, but I have to try.

She's brave and bold and strong, yes.

But she's never done this before. I don't want to hurt her. I won't forgive myself if I hurt her. This is already—

Fuck, I really am out of my fucking mind.

No bollocks, no excuses, no explanations.

I'm risking everything that matters in my life, and hers, and I don't give a fuck.

I take a deep breath. Shrug my shoulders. Move toward the bedroom.

The hum of the air-conditioning fills the space. I can't hear Sienna through the door. I can't tell if she's wound with fear or anticipation.

Both maybe.

I push the handle.

She lets out a gasp. It fills the space, then the air-conditioning drowns the sound of her breath.

I step inside. Push the door closed behind me.

My shoulders tense as it clicks. I'm the one on edge here. I'm the one who's terrified.

Sex is new to her.

But it's something she understands. Something she wants.

This, fucking someone I want to see tomorrow, is incomprehensible.

"Cam." Her chest heaves with her inhale.

Sienna Simms, sitting on my bed, naked, waiting, ready.

I flick the switch. The main lights turn on. The shaded ones on both sides of the bed.

It's not the lighting I'd choose for this—I'd want the bright light of day, so I could see every fucking detail—but she's just as gorgeous in the soft yellow glow.

"Stand up." I try to find the right tone. Firm enough to demand. Soft enough to invite her.

Sienna looks up at me, her hazel eyes filled with equal parts nerves and desire.

She's scared.

I need to be careful with her.

How the fuck am I supposed to be careful with her?

She pushes off the bed. Stands at the foot of it.

"Turn around," I say.

She does it slowly.

Fuck, she's perfect. Long and lean with strong shoulders and lush thighs. Thighs I need against my cheeks again.

She meets my gaze. "You're cruel. Making me wait so long."

"Get used to it." I pull a condom from my dresser.

Her eyes light up. Her fingers dig into her thighs.

She wants me that badly.

I take a deep breath, so I stay in control, so I don't push her too hard or too fast. "You fuck yourself thinking of me."

She nods.

"What do you imagine?"

"Everything." She runs her fingers through her long hair. "The two of us alone in my bedroom. Sometimes the one I had in Brooklyn. Sometimes the one I have now. My new bed is bigger, big enough for two."

"Your old bed?"

"It was a twin. But I don't imagine that would stop you."

"No."

Her lips curl into a soft smile. For a second, the tension in the room fades. My shoulders soften. My chest eases.

Then she takes a step toward me, and I lose every degree of cool.

"Stay there." I try to keep my voice even, but my nerves

betray me. "You need to follow my orders, sweetness. Do what I say, when I say it. Or I'll stop."

A whine falls from her lips. "Please."

"Please?" I let my voice drop to a teasing tone. *You know what happens when you dare me.*

"Please don't stop. I know I'm not supposed to ask, but—"

"I'll let it go this time. But only this time."

She nods, attentive, obedient.

So much unlike the Sienna I know, and so similar at once. She's brash and headstrong and ready to conquer any challenge.

This is another challenge.

Is that why she's interested? Or does she get off on following orders?

I'm not sure, but I'm going to find out.

"How do I fuck you?" I move closer. "In your fantasies?"

"Sometimes it's gentle. Your body over mine. My arms around your neck, my legs around your hips, the two of us kissing. Sometimes, it's hard or rough. Your hand on my throat. My arms tied over my head. You throwing me on the bed and ordering me to take whatever you're going to give."

Where the fuck did she get all those ideas? "Which makes you come the fastest?"

"I don't know. They're all fuzzy. Like a daydream, an image I've seen in a movie, a story I've heard from a friend." She's careful not to mention her sister or her future brother-in-law.

But it fills the air anyway.

The reason why we shouldn't do this.

The reason we're both ignoring.

We're both out of our fucking minds, but she's got a good excuse. She's eighteen.

I'm older, wiser, more experienced, more responsible.

Sworn to protect her.

And I'm here. Deciding how I'm going to fuck her. Trying to find the thing she wants the most.

"When did you last fuck yourself?" I ask.

"Last night."

"Where?"

"My bed."

"What did you imagine?"

"You," she says. "I thought about tonight. The two of us at the party, sneaking off to a private space. You pinning me to the wall and sliding your hand between my leg. Or pushing me to my knees and ordering me to suck you off."

"Don't tempt me."

She smiles, victorious. "It's the truth."

"Is that when you came?"

"Yes."

Fuck. "And now." I take another step toward her. "What do you want?"

"I want you to fuck me."

"How?"

"You've been daring me. How much you'll fuck me up. How hard or rough or kinky it will be. Like that."

"You want it rough?"

"Yes."

I can't offer her that. Not the way she's asking. I won't stay in control. I'm barely staying in control now. "Not the first time."

"But… a second time?"

"Maybe."

"Maybe?"

"What did I say about asking me the same thing twice?"

Her chest heaves. "It means the answer is no?"

I nod. "I'm not warning you again. Understand?"

"Yes."

"Stay there." I close the distance between us.

She stays glued to me. Every fucking molecule of her body tuned to every one of mine. There's no other way to explain it.

I'm the only thing in her universe. The only thing she's ever needed. The only thing she could ever need.

It's fucking perfect.

I wrap my fingers around her wrist gently. "Turn around."

She does.

I undo the knot of my tie, pull her wrists behind her back, bind them together.

Then I wrap my arm around her waist. Hold her body against mine, her back against my chest, her arse against my pelvis.

She whines as her hands brush my cock. "Cam."

There's too much fabric between us. I need her touching me. I absolutely can't handle her touching me. Maybe in some other universe, but not in this one.

"Can I say it?" She wiggles her fingers, trying to feel more of me.

I grab her wrists hard.

She gasps. "Can I ask you to fuck me now?"

"Yes."

She lets out a soft sigh. "Please. Please fuck me."

Without warning, I push her onto the bed.

She falls face first. Groans as she turns her chin. To the window. Then to the mirror.

I don't have to tell her to watch, but I do it anyway. "Keep your eyes on me."

She nods into the gold sheets. This hotel is trying so fucking hard to look expensive.

Usually, I don't like the faux luxury, but Sienna looks so

fucking beautiful splayed over the comforter, her long hair falling over her cheeks, her eyes fixed on me.

I want more of her.

Every centimeter of her body against every centimeter of mine.

But there's no universe where I can handle that. I can barely handle this.

Without warning, I slip a finger inside her.

She's already wet. There's no resistance when I push deeper.

Slip another finger inside her.

I stretch her gently.

Then harder.

Hard enough she groans. "Fuck."

This is going to hurt. There's no way around that, but I can make it easier for her.

If I stay in control.

I need to stay in control.

I push deeper.

She lets out another groan.

I knot my hand in her hair. Tug hard enough she yelps.

"Watch." I push her thighs apart to give her a better view. Then I pull my hand back and plunge my fingers inside her again.

Fuck, that's a beautiful sight. I need more and I need it now.

There's no patience in my veins.

I push deeper. Until she groans.

Then I pull back and do it again.

Her expression gets hazy. Her eyes fill with the perfect mix of pain and pleasure.

I need that. I need it more than I've ever needed anything.

I have to close my eyes. So I won't push her too hard, too fast. So I won't hurt her.

I drive into her again.

Again.

Until her low, deep groan fills the room.

"Cam," she breathes. "Please." Her hips rock to meet me. "Please fuck me."

Fuck, that's the best thing I've ever heard.

"Please. I need you inside me." Her fingers dig into her palms.

She's splayed on the bed, bound, forced to take whatever I want to give her. And she's begging me to fuck her.

No wonder I'm out of my mind. This is heaven.

I stretch her one last time. Then I pull my hands back. Push her thighs apart. Find the condom in my trousers.

She watches as I unzip my slacks. Tear the wrapper. Slide the rubber over my cock.

Her eyes go wide. "You're…"

"Take a deep breath."

She sucks an inhale through her teeth.

It's not enough. She's tense again. I need to ease her. This isn't the kind of pain I want for her.

I push her thighs apart. Dig my nails into her skin.

I hold her there, pinned to the bed, as I tease her.

She gasps as my cock brushes her cunt. "Fuck. Cam." There's no fear in her voice. No nerves. Only pure desire. "Please."

I tease her again and again. Until I can't take it anymore.

Then I drive inside her with one hard thrust.

She feels like heaven. Sweet and soft and thoroughly mine.

I stay there for a moment. Give her time to get used to the pressure. To the feeling of our bodies joining.

Then I push deeper.

Her nails dig into her palm. "Fuck."

I pin her thighs to the bed, pull back, drive into her again.

She lets out a soft gasp. "Cam." Her breath hitches. "Fuck."

She's on the verge of what she can take.

I need to push her to take more. "Watch." I drive into her again. "Or I'll stop."

Her eyes open instantly.

I study her expression. The need in her eyes, the part of her lips, the softness of her brow.

Every part of her tuned to every part of me.

I savor the sight of her for a moment, then I fill her with a steady thrust.

Slow to start.

Then faster.

Harder.

Hard enough her groans fade together.

Her lids get heavy.

Her nails leave red marks on her palms.

And I lose it. Forget all about fucking control.

I hold her in place and I drive into her again and again.

Until her groans fill the room.

Fuck.

I pull her back, so I can bring my hand to her clit.

I rub her with my thumb and I fill her with hard, deep thrusts.

I fuck her.

There's no other way to explain.

There's nothing else I want. There's nothing else in my universe.

Only Sienna's body against mine. Her brimming with more bliss than she can take.

I go too hard, too deep, too fast.

But that only makes her groan louder.

She comes quickly, groaning my name as she pulses around me. As she pulls me further and deeper.

It's too much to take.

With my next thrust, I come. I dig my nails into her thigh, groaning her name as I work through my orgasm.

Fuck.

When I'm finished, I pull back. Take care of the condom. Unbind her.

She sits up with a hazy expression.

Her eyes fix on me. Her lips curl into a soft smile.

She climbs up the bed. Stands. Wraps her arms around me.

It shouldn't be strange, holding her after I've fucked her.

It shouldn't steal every ounce of my breath.

But it does.

It really fucking does.

Chapter Twenty-Seven

CAM

I expect to feel relief when Sienna excuses herself to clean up.

But I don't.

I want to be there, in the narrow space, my body pressed against hers, the two of us warm and wet and wrapped in each other.

It's a pipe dream but it's a new one.

She showers without a word. Emerges from the bathroom clean and wet, terry-cloth robe draped over her shoulders.

It's cinched at the waist, but just barely.

She doesn't wear a lot of makeup, but she still looks younger without it. Smaller. More in need of protection.

It's ridiculous. She's an athlete. Tall, powerful, strong.

Stronger than I am in every way but one.

How can I be obsessed with that single way? She's faster than most men. She can get away from someone who wants to hurt her.

She can fight back.

She won't need to fight back. There's no one out there trying to hurt her. She doesn't go to dangerous corners of the city.

And I—

Fuck, I need to get ahold of myself.

Tonight.

This is only tonight.

"Do you have anything to eat?" She brushes her wet hair behind her ears. "I'm starving and exhausted."

"I can order something."

"This late?"

I nod.

"Hmm…" Her brow furrows with concentration. "No. I think I'll go to bed." She moves into the main room. Pulls her cell from her purse. Taps out a text. "But you owe me breakfast."

"Of course."

She sets her cell down.

I bring her a glass of water. Ask her to drink.

She looks at me like I'm silly, but she still does it. "What do you think happened with the dancers?"

"Did they have an orgy?"

She nods.

"Ty wouldn't."

"Would you?"

"It's never appealed to me."

"But you've had a threesome?"

I nod.

"Why?"

"Do I really need to explain why?"

"Was that all it was?" She finishes her last sip. "Extra tits and ass?"

No. It was like every fucking thing I've tried. An attempt to feel what everyone says they feel after sex.

Even the most womanizing arseholes in the world feel something. A thrill, a sense of pride, a satisfaction.

No matter how well I perform, how many times I make a woman come, I feel the same after: empty, worn, used.

It's ridiculous. I'm the arsehole using women to get out of my head. Where the fuck do I get off feeling like they used me?

I don't know. It's not what happens. But it's the same every time.

Only right now…

I don't want to sleep on the couch. I don't want to leave before Sienna wakes. I don't want to put a wall between us.

I don't hate her.

"Cam?" She stretches her arms over her head as she lets out a yawn. "Was there something else?"

"It's complicated."

She nods *uh-huh, sure.*

"I thought it would excite me."

"Did it not?"

It did. That's not exactly right. "I thought that excitement would change things. I thought I'd feel differently after."

"But you still hated yourself after?"

I nod.

"And now?" Her eyes meet mine. "Is this different?"

"I don't know."

"Oh." She picks up her glass. "Do you hate me?"

"Not yet."

"But maybe later?"

"Maybe."

"Okay." She does nothing to hide the disappointment in her voice. "I think I might hate you in the morning. When I wake up with a massive hangover. Who's idea was it to have all those sugary drinks?"

"Yours."

"Dammit. I was afraid of that." She smiles. Rises to her tiptoes. Presses her lips to mine.

It's soft, but I feel it in my bones.

"One more of these. Then I'm going to bed." She kisses me again. "Can I wear something of yours?"

"What do you have in mind?"

"A t-shirt and boxers would be great. Do you even own a t-shirt?"

My lips curl into a smile. "I brought a few."

"Really?"

"Second drawer on the right."

She moves into the bedroom and checks the drawer. "Ah." She pulls out a plain white v-neck. "I bet you look good in this."

"I look good in everything."

"I hate to ruin it."

"I hate to see you put on clothes."

"Does this help?" She slips the robe off her shoulders. Does a quick spin. Lands with a smile.

Fuck, she's adorable. It warms me everywhere.

And sends blood back to my cock. I need to fuck her again. I need to teach her everything.

But not now.

Now, I need to put her to bed.

I take the shirt. Pull it over her shoulders.

"I don't suppose you'll return my underwear?" she asks.

"Never." But I do pull a pair of boxers from the dresser and help her into them.

She cops a pose, hip cocked, arms folded. "Do I make a good Cam?"

"Excellent."

"What should I say? Something about how I'm the greatest lover in the world and no one can ever compare?"

She climbs under the gold spread and shoots me a cocky grin. "Baby, you have no idea what a great fuck I am. I'll ruin you forever. No one else will ever be enough."

"No. They won't."

Chapter Twenty-Eight

CAM

Sunlight streams through the window. It bounces off the gold comforter to cast the room in a soft glow.

And there's Sienna, asleep, in my fucking t-shirt.

Calm.

At peace.

Beautiful.

I don't feel a single shred of resentment in my chest.

I give it time to grow as I wash, dress, fix coffee in the cheap machine.

But it doesn't.

I'm not empty or angry or used.

I don't hate her.

I don't want to leave.

No, it's much, much worse.

I still like her.

I still need more.

I need to teach her everything.

One night isn't enough. We can have the weekend.

But that's all.

Two days that stay our dirty secret.

Chapter Twenty-Nine

SIENNA

Mmm. The room is warm. The perfect soft feeling of the sun on my skin.

I blink my eyes open. Wait for my brain to curse the illumination or the hum of the air conditioner or the dryness in my mouth.

But I'm okay.

I'm not excited to run six miles, but my head is easy, my stomach is calm, my chest is light.

Then I remember last night and my entire body is buzzing.

I rise slowly. Stretch my arms over my head. Check for signs of wear.

My thighs are sore. The usual *wow, I haven't worked that muscle in a while* sensation. And my sex is—

Well, I feel like I was fucked. There's no other way to explain it.

Dirty thoughts fill my head as I wash in the bathroom. Even here, in this small space, there are so many places Cam can fuck me.

In the shower.

Against the wall.

On the counter.

I want them all. I really do.

But he hasn't promised anything. I can't get too excited.

Okay, that's a lost cause. And it's not like dirty thoughts ever killed anyone. If it was possible to die of sexual frustration, I would have kicked the bucket last night.

I find the hotel's disposable toothbrush and toothpaste, wash my face with warm water, adjust my pajamas. Cam's t-shirt is thick, the way men's t-shirts are, but my breasts still show through the light fabric.

Will it drive him crazy?

I need to drive him crazy, so he doesn't say anything ridiculous like *that was fun, but it was enough. Here's some cash for coffee. Bye.*

No. I need to prepare myself for any response.

Yes, I want to encourage the right response, but I agreed to his terms. I need to honor them.

If he really does want to say goodbye—

I don't have to like it, but I do have to respect it. And I really, really need to get the fuck out of here before I lose it.

I need to hold it together until after the wedding.

Until Ty and Indie leave on their honeymoon.

That's more than a week away.

Deep breath.

Slow exhale.

Maximum chill.

I follow the smell of coffee into the main room. It looks different in the light of day. More ornate. Less Cam.

Gold wallpaper with a Fleur de lis print, cream couch and carpet, sheer curtains, big cherry desk.

Cam sitting behind a laptop, already in his suit.

"Is it really that comfortable?" I ask.

"It is." He smiles.

My heart thuds against my chest. He's even more handsome today. How is that possible? "Or are you wearing it to tease me?"

"Likely."

I roll my shoulders back. Lift my chest. "I can tease you back."

"I hope you do."

My lips curl into a smile. "I smell coffee. Tell me there's coffee."

"How's your head?"

I motion *okay*.

"You should eat something."

"Do you have something?"

"I was waiting for you."

My eyes go to the clock. It's late, by his standards. "Aren't you hungry?"

"I'm a patient man." His voice drops to a teasing tone. So I know he means sex. So I know he's daring me.

Does that mean this isn't over? God, I hope it isn't over. "Oh. So, uh… did you want to have breakfast then?"

He nods. "I just ordered."

"Oh. Thanks."

"There is coffee." He motions to the coffee maker on the TV stand. "But you have a latte coming."

Mmm. A latte. That's way better than hotel drip. "Thanks." I adjust my t-shirt. "Do you need to do more work?"

"A little."

"On Saturday?"

He nods.

"Really? With the wedding next weekend?" I bite my tongue. I shouldn't remind him of the wedding. I don't even want to think about it. But it's there. Without the potent mix of alcohol and need in my veins, I'm...

Well, I'm not considering leaving. Or turning down any additional sex. Or suggesting we end this.

I'm more aware of the realities of the situation, but I still can't bring myself to care. It feels too good, watching him smile.

It's different than his usual smile. Fuller. Realer. More personal.

"Ian and I are trying to make sure nothing interrupts Ty," he says. "It's not easy. We have specific roles. Neither of us can do Ty's job."

"What is his job?"

Cam chuckles. "Give me five minutes to finish this. Then we'll talk."

"Sure." I distract myself by checking my cell. I have a few soccer reminders. A teammate defying our captain's orders, inviting people to the party she's throwing tonight. Another looking for a training partner, so she can spend the entire day running. Which I should really... "Do you know when breakfast is coming?"

"Soon."

"Oh."

He looks up from his laptop. "You need to be somewhere?"

"I should run."

"Go. I can order again."

"Oh." I press my lips together. "You want me... to come back after I run?"

"I want you to stay here, but I'm not going to stop you from training."

My chest warms. He wants me to stay here. Hell yes.

"We can run tonight if you'd like."

"Tonight?"

He nods. "It's the same temperature all day here, but it will feel cooler in the dark."

"We could do the afternoon too. The weather's in the sixties today."

He raises a brow.

"Put it in Google if you want Celsius."

"Aren't you a math major?"

"Math. Not Chemistry. I don't need to know anything about temperature systems."

"Can't give it to me in Kelvins?"

Kelvins… that's zero as absolute zero. And you add… something. Two-seventy, I think. It's been awhile since AP Chem. "Or tonight. Tonight is good too."

He nods *of course* in that matter-of-fact way. Like it's totally obvious we're going to train together tonight.

I decline both offers from my teammates. Send my sister a text claiming a need to study.

It's true. I have a test on Monday. I really should study.

But I can't bring myself to leave this perfect, warm space.

It's late morning. The curtains are drawn. The room is light. And the city is Cam's backdrop.

Bright blue sky, dark river, yellow sun, the silver tinted steel and glass of nearby buildings.

Maybe I'm turning into my sister. I feel a sudden need to verbalize my appreciation of the view, to drag Cam to the Empire State Building and walk around Central Park.

What would appeal most? Nature? Architecture? Modern art?

Soccer fields, maybe. Or shopping. A small coffee shop with great French Roast. An only in New York store in the Village. Maybe the rice pudding place. Or the cereal themed soft serve. The ice cream shop with chiffon yellow walls.

A walk to Washington Square Park, down to Alphabet

City, to an Indian restaurant with enough string lights to make a casino jealous.

A knock on the door interrupts my train of thought. Someone outside calls, "room service."

I stand reflexively.

Cam shakes his head. "I'll get it."

"I can."

"Sit. I don't want the bellboy staring at your tits."

My cheeks flush. He's overprotective. Jealous even. I shouldn't like it, but I do.

Cam moves across the room with his usual seamless grace, no sign of hangover or exhaustion.

He thanks the room service guy, wheels the cart into the space, presents a ceramic cup brimming with milky coffee.

Then he holds it up, out of reach, teasing me.

My lips curl into a smile. "I'll knock that out of your hand."

"You won't get to drink it."

"But I'll ruin your suit."

He smiles. "So I have to take it off?"

I nod *exactly*, jump from my seat, feign an attempt to knock the drink from his hand.

"I have others."

"How many did you bring?"

"Three."

"Sounds excessive."

"One for work. One for the ceremony. One for leisure."

"A suit for leisure?"

He nods.

"Is it really that comfortable?"

Cam hands me the drink. "What did you think last night?"

"About you fucking me?"

His pupils dilate.

"I liked it."

"The jacket."

"It was comfortable. But not really in the realm of you fucking me."

Pride spills over his expression.

It makes me warm everywhere.

I want to earn that expression again. I want his pride in every way I can have it.

Fuck, I really like him. Way more than one night, one time. Way more than one weekend or one fling before a wedding.

Way too much, given the circumstance.

And I still don't care.

I take a long sip of my latte. It's not great coffee, but across from him, it's rich, creamy perfection.

A sigh falls from my lips.

Cam's eyes glue to me. "Sweetness, don't tempt me."

Mmm. He's still using the pet name. Fuck, I want him using that pet name. "Tempt you how?"

"To spill that drink all over your shirt as I throw you on the couch."

"I'm okay with that." I take another sip. Let out a loud groan. Fuck, this hits the spot. And the way he watches me, like he's going to die if he doesn't make me come—

I really like it.

I draw it out as long as I can, savoring sips as he watches intently.

He waits patiently until I'm finished with the drink, then he takes the mug from my hands and pulls me into a slow, deep kiss.

His tongue slides into my mouth. Dances with mine.

Fuck, he's a good kisser. How is he such a good kisser?

When he pulls back, I'm shaking.

"I went easy on you last night," he says. "I won't do it this time."

"There's a this time?"

He nods. "I want you here all weekend."

All weekend.

"I want to teach you as much as I can."

Chapter Thirty

SIENNA

I *want to teach you as much as I can.*

My chest warms. My stomach flutters. My knees buckle. "All weekend?"

He nods. "Only the weekend."

"On Monday, I turn into a pumpkin, and we forget this ever happened?"

"Wouldn't it be your carriage that turns into a pumpkin?"

"Uh…" I motion in the general direction of my shoes. "My wedges turn into little pumpkins."

"Can you do that?"

Maybe. "So… I see you at the wedding, say hey, dance a little… like nothing happened?"

He nods.

"I don't know. I can say goodbye on Sunday night." I can't like it, but I can do it. "But I'm not sure what we'll look like to other people. I…" I swallow hard. "I really want to touch you."

"I know."

My sex clenches. "Do you want to touch me?"

"I want to bury myself in you."

Mmm. Yes. Now. "But you're confident you can carry on as if nothing happened?"

"No," he admits. "I'm not sure."

"Well… maybe we'll have to practice."

"Practice not trying to fuck each other?"

I nod. "Not right now. But later. After we say goodbye to this part of our relationship." Or maybe before. In case not touching leads to a lot of touching.

"Can you do that? Say goodbye?"

No. Maybe. I don't know. "I think so. Can you?"

His brow furrows, but he nods. "It's the only thing that makes sense."

Right. "So, uh… Midnight Sunday? Or when I leave Monday morning?"

"Monday morning."

Monday morning I turn into a pumpkin. "I don't have clothes."

"I can get you clothes."

I can stop by my place. But not with Cam. We might run into Ty and Indigo. My sister might stop by to talk, or check on me, or help me study. We spend a lot of time together.

"But I'd rather you stay naked."

"All weekend?"

He nods.

"You'd really have a lot to live up to keeping me naked all weekend."

He smiles as he brings breakfast to the table and sits across from me. "Eat. You need your strength."

Fuck. "You talk big talk."

"Did I not meet your expectations?"

He met them and invented new ones. It was everything I wanted and a lot of things I didn't know I wanted.

It was… easy.

This is easy.

I expected him to push me out the door. Tactfully, yes, but clearly enough I got the point.

But he's here, with enough food for a family of five, and lots of coffee, and he's teasing me about how thoroughly he's going to fuck me after breakfast.

"Better than my expectations." In every way. "But with all this food... you're really setting the bar high. Are you sure you can deliver?"

He smiles. "I should punish you for your smart mouth."

"You should." My knees press together. Why do I want that? I don't know, but I do. I want him to spank me and call me a bad girl. And I want him to whisper *I need you* as he fucks me. "But you won't."

"I won't?"

"You like it."

His smile shifts into something I recognize. The look Ty often has. *I'm caught and I'm proud of it.*

Maybe that should remind me of how stupid this is, or encourage me to call a halt, but we've already arranged that. Sure, I don't want to say goodbye to him in forty-eight hours. Well, I don't want to say goodbye to this version of him.

But he's right. It's the only thing that makes sense.

Even if he wasn't Ty's closest confidant, he has an entire life in London. I'm already too distracted by my sister's wedding and my soccer season to make friends at school. I can't add a long-distance boyfriend to that.

He doesn't want to be a long-distance boyfriend.

It doesn't make sense.

I'm not romantic and artistic the way my sister is. I follow my head, not my heart.

"Where are you going, sweetness?" He leans back in his chair. Brings his mug to his lips.

Fuck, how is he so sexy sitting here, drinking coffee? I

want to toss breakfast aside and mount him. "You're too appealing. It's not fair."

"I am?"

I nod. "I'm at a distinct disadvantage."

"At…"

"Teasing you."

"Because I'm too sexy?"

"Yeah."

"And you?" His eyes flit to my chest. My thighs. "Sitting here in my clothes with a *teach me everything* look in your eyes?"

"I have a look?"

"It drives me crazy."

"You have a look too."

"So eat your breakfast."

I pour syrup on my pancakes. "And you'll fuck me?"

"Maybe."

"Maybe?"

He raises a brow. *Are you really going to make me repeat myself.*

Right. "If I ask again, the answer is no?" Does he really mean that?

"You're on the line."

"For how long though… this morning or all weekend?"

"Ask again and you'll find out."

"I think that's an empty threat."

He raises a brow, but it's softer this time. More teasing. "If you want to find out…"

"That would punish you too."

"Even so."

Mmm. Mean. "Do you have that much restraint?"

He chuckles. "Are you daring me, sweetness? You really want to do that?"

No. God no. I'm not daring him not to fuck me.

Maybe he's bluffing. Who cares? As long as he fucks me, he can bluff all he wants.

I need to mount him now, but he won't fuck me until after breakfast.

I know him well enough to know that.

This meal is going to kill me. Maybe conversation is enough distraction I'll survive.

"You were working earlier?" I slice my pancake with my fork. Bring the sliver to my lips. Mmm, sweet, sweet carbs. Maple syrup, chocolate chips, coffee. This is heaven.

"I was."

"What do you do?"

He chuckles. "Me personally? Or Ty and Ian's company?"

"They have multiple, don't they?"

"This one is their bread and butter."

"The one you…"

"I'm head of Finance in Europe."

I take another bite. "What does that mean?"

"I'm the CFO."

"That's another way of saying the same thing."

He laughs and takes a bite of his toast. "I keep track of the top-level financial decisions. If we should work with a new company. If we should invest. What we can charge for information."

"Is that what the company does? Corporate espionages?"

"That's not the most charitable reading."

"Isn't that what you do?"

"Partially." He finishes his toast. "We have two main departments. Consulting and venture capital."

Venture capital. That's when rich people invest money in new business in exchange for a share. "Which do you run? Probably investing? That's more financial."

He nods.

"You studied math in school?"

"I did."

"So I could have your job one day?"

He smiles. "Are you coming after it?"

"Maybe. It pays pretty well."

"Is that what drives you?"

"Honestly?"

He sets his mug on the table. "You can always be honest with me."

"Even if it hurts?"

"Especially if it hurts."

"What if I want to tell you last night wasn't that great?"

"That wouldn't be honest." His voice is teasing, confident, but there's hurt in his eyes.

"How do you know?"

"I know." His eyes flit to my thighs.

Fuck. "What if it's... painful in a different way?"

"Always."

"Even in five years when we're..."

"Family friends?"

"Yeah." I try to find comfort in my latte, but there isn't any. I hate the idea of us being reduced to family friends, but that's the future. It makes sense.

"Always, Sienna."

"I wouldn't feel like I earned it," I say. "If I got a job through Ty. I'm sure you're good at it, but—"

"Don't apologize for your opinion. I just asked for it."

Right.

"It's not you, Sienna. I like you the way you are."

"A tactless bitch?"

"Forthright."

My lips curl into a smile. "I wasn't just sucking up. I do think you're good at the job. If you weren't, Ty would fire you."

"Even though I'm family?"

"Definitely. He doesn't deal with incompetence."

He smiles. "True."

"It's weird, isn't it? Having rich family? Four months ago, I wasn't sure if we'd make our mortgage payment. Now, we're subletting our place in Brooklyn and Ty is paying my rent."

"He cares about you."

"Maybe. But it's so he has more time to fuck Indie."

"How long does it take to get to your old place?"

"From Ty's apartment? Half an hour on the subway, give or take."

"That's an hour round trip. A lot of time to fuck her."

"I do appreciate it," I say.

"I appreciate the job."

"And the money?"

He nods.

"But it's weird… like there are invisible strings."

"I know what you mean."

"Do you think about striking out on your own?" I ask.

"Sometimes. But I like being on a team."

"Once a soccer player, always a soccer player?"

"Something like that." He takes a long sip of his coffee. "It's a strange company, but we have our roles. I handle finance in Europe. Ian is head of information."

"What a euphemism."

Cam chuckles. "It is."

"And Ty?"

"He's our chief operations officer. All the practicalities of running a business. Negotiating, managing, laying down the law."

"That sounds like Ty." My eyes stay on him. "But you… I'd never peg you as a math guy."

"Why is that?"

"I don't know. You seem too playful for that."

"Do I really have to tell you how creative math can be?"

No. Of course not. And then the playfulness… it's part him. And it's part front. "True." I take another bite. "Could I do your job?"

"Maybe. You'd charm the pants off stuffy business men."

My cheeks flush.

"But not all of them would respond to your frankness."

"Rich guys don't like hearing they're wrong." And especially not from women.

He nods.

"How do you do it?"

"You doubt my ability to turn on the charm?"

No. Of course not. He's painfully charming. "I think it's harder for you to turn it off."

"It is."

"Why is that?"

"Practice keeping people out." His eyes stay on mine. "I don't offer trust to many people."

Mmm, earning his trust. I want that as much as I want his body. The same need but entirety different. "I understand that."

"Do you?"

"Yeah. I mean, I don't like to hold things back. It makes me feel… dishonest, but full disclosure invites its own problems."

"Most people can't handle the truth."

"Tell me about it."

"I hope you don't change. I love how forthright you are."

"Thanks." My chest warms. "What else do you like about me?"

"Your humility."

I chuckle. "Oh yeah, that's one of your best traits too."

"I know." He pours another cup of coffee. "You're determined. You're funny. You're fucking gorgeous."

"Is that all it is?"

"It doesn't hurt."

"You either. I mean, you're very handsome. You might not have realized it, with all your humility."

He nods *of course*.

"I really enjoy looking at you."

"I noticed." Intent slips into his voice.

"Right. Those times. And other times. But I also like you. That you challenge me. Dare me. Tease me. And you care, even if you hide it. You care that I'm okay."

"So it's all about you?"

"That is what I said, isn't it?"

He smiles. "You did."

"It's how you make me feel."

"Go on…" His voice dips to something flirty.

It's an invitation and, god, I want to take it.

We have the entire weekend together.

And he likes me.

It's a big deal for him. I'm not sure why—he's way too old to fawn over a crush—but I don't care either. I want to soak in the soft warmth of it. I want to scream it from the mountaintops.

Cam likes me.

Sure, we only have two days as lovers, but after…

We can stay confidants. We can talk about our weeks and our friends and maybe even our new lovers.

No. Not our new lovers, but something. I can't lose him completely. I don't even want to lose this.

Maybe I have to accept it one day. But not today. Not this weekend.

I'm enjoying it. Every second. No matter what happens later.

Life is short. Fuck now. That's what I tell Indie. It's good advice for me too.

Fuck now, talk now, love now.

Not that love is on the table.

Just…

Better to focus on the fucking.

"And this…" I finish my second pancake. "You don't like people after you fuck them. Not normally. But you still like me."

"I do."

"Do you keep fucking people, even though you don't like them?"

"Sometimes."

"Isn't that… weird?"

"I'm used to it."

"So you…" I try to find a way to ask what I want to know. "Do you trust the people you fuck?"

"No." He finishes his coffee.

"Is that why you stay in control?"

"Part of it."

"What's the other part?"

"I like things that way." He sets his mug on the desk. "Is that a problem?"

"No."

"Good." Intent slips back into his voice.

My toes curl. "I like things that way too. I just… want to check in."

"That's responsible."

"Thanks." I think. "You need to be the one leading?"

"Yes."

"Always? Or can I touch you sometimes?"

"You can come here and sit on my lap."

"But could I do it if you hadn't offered?"

"That was an invitation."

Oh. My heartbeat picks up. "Right." I rise. Smooth my shirt.

He motions *come here*.

I do.

His hands go to my hips. "You can do this." He pulls me into his lap. Then he takes my hand and brings it to his neck. "You can kiss me." His eyes flutter closed. His lips find mine.

It's a soft kiss, but I still feel it in my toes.

He pulls back with a sigh. "You can move closer. Sit on my lap. Touch me when we're dressed."

"When we're not?"

"Then I lead."

"Always?"

"Until I say otherwise." There's hesitation in his voice. Because he doesn't trust me? Or because he doesn't trust himself?

Or maybe this is just what he likes. Maybe there's no deeper explanation.

"Is that a problem?" He hooks his fingers in my shorts.

I shake my head.

"Good." His posture shifts. Into the demanding, in control version of Cam I saw last night. "I've been thinking about fucking you all morning."

Chapter Thirty-One

SIENNA

I've been thinking about fucking you all morning.

He pulls me closer. So our bodies are pressed together.

His hand goes to my cheek. His thumb brushes my bottom lip. "I'm in a generous mood."

Mmm.

"Tell me what you want." He slips his thumb into my mouth. "I'll consider giving it to you."

Fuck, he tastes good. Like salt and Cam. I'm not sure why I want this, but I do. There's some primal part of me taking over. Some part desperate to have him in my mouth. To have him everywhere.

He catches my bottom lip as he pulls his hand back. "Should I fuck you here?" He slips his hands under my t-shirt. Cups my breasts. Draws circles around my nipples. "Or like this."

Mmm. Fuck.

"Maybe I should toy with you until you can't take it anymore."

"Cam."

"Is that a yes, sweetness?"

I can't ask him to stop, but I'm not sure I can survive teasing. "You might kill me."

"Good." He brings one hand to my hip and pulls my body into his, so I can feel his cock against my sex.

He's already hard. And fuck, that feels so good.

I press my thighs against him.

He responds by pinching my nipple.

"Fuck."

"You like when it hurts."

I nod, even though it's not a question.

"Is that what you want, sweetness?" He does it again. "Should I torture you as I fuck you?" Then harder.

I let out a groan.

"Tell me what you want." He brings his lips to my neck. "Or you get what I want. And I want to make you beg for mercy."

Fuck.

He knots his hand in my hair. Pulls me into a hard, deep kiss.

Mmm. I'm already losing conscious thought. I want him. In every way. But this is an offer. I need to take it. Or he might do something horrible like not fuck me. "I want you inside me."

"In your pretty mouth?" He runs his thumb over my lip again. "In your sweet cunt?" He shifts his lips, so I feel his cock against me. "Or maybe in that gorgeous arse?"

"Would you?"

"Yes."

"Now?"

"Yes."

Why do I want that? I've never even thought about it before, but now I need it. I need to have him every way I can. "Can I say all?"

"No."

"Here." I rock my hips against him, so my sex is against his cock. Fuck, that pressure is divine. I need more. I need all of it. "But I want to taste you too."

"Greedy girl."

That's the perfect way to say it. I am greedy. I want every fucking drop of him. "And later—I want all of it later."

Pride fills his expression. It's so much like before, but so different too. Somehow, it's completely dirty.

"Will you?"

"Maybe."

"But—"

"You know what happens if you finish that sentence."

Right. No. Not that. Anything but that. I nod.

The softness in his expression fades. He shifts into that other version of Cam. "Stand up."

I do.

"Take off your clothes."

I pull my shirt over my head. Pushes my boxers, his boxers, to my feet and kick them aside.

"Fuck." He looks me up and down, slowly, savoring every inch. "Fucking gorgeous."

My chest flames. "Thank you."

"Come here."

I take a step toward him.

He cups my hip with his hand. "Here."

I'm standing in front of him. Right in front of him. My knees are inches from his.

And he's sitting there, cool and confident, looking up at me like he's deciding what he's going to do with me.

Fuck.

He keeps one hand on my hip. Slips the other between my legs.

He presses his palm against me. "You're wet."

I nod.

"You get wet when you think about it hard and rough?"

I nod.

"Do you think you're ready for that?" Without warning, he slips two fingers inside me.

Fuck. My eyes close. My hands go to his shoulders. My toes curl.

That's intense. Intense in a good way, but really fucking intense.

He pushes deeper.

Deeper.

"Fuck," I breathe.

"You have no fucking idea." He pulls his fingers back and drives them into me again. "How hard and rough I want it." He does it again. "How badly I want to split you in half."

"Please."

"No." His voice is firm, direct, final.

It makes me shake. I don't know why it makes me shake, but it does.

He drives his fingers into me again. "You're not ready."

"But—"

"I said no." He does it again.

My fingers dig into his suit jacket.

"I'll give you whatever the fuck I want to give you." He drives into me with those same hard, steady strokes as he brings his hand to my chest. "When I decide you're ready."

I try to hold his gaze, but his dark eyes are too intense. I have to look to his shoulders, his tie, the bright light streaming through the window.

The light hint of our reflection.

Me naked, him clothed.

It winds me tighter.

I try to feel everything. The intense pressure of his hand inside me. The soft brush of his thumb against my chest. Those perfect slow circles. So light I can barely feel them.

It's like last night. The pressure stays intense, but the discomfort fades to pleasure. It's not the same as him inside me, but it's still so fucking good.

He winds me tighter and tighter.

Until I'm so taut, I'm sure I'll break.

Then he brings his thumb to my clit and rubs me exactly where I need him.

I come fast and hard.

My world goes white. Nothing but the blinding light of the sun outside, the steady sound of his breath, the sweet pressure of his hand on my skin.

He works me through my orgasm. Then he releases me. Looks up at me, once again deciding what he's going to do with me. "Turn around."

I do.

"Give me your hands."

I put my arms behind my back.

He cinches something around them. Something soft and smooth. His orange tie.

I yelp as he tests the restraints.

Fuck. I like him binding me. I like it too much.

He moves behind me, so I can feel his cock against my ass. "I wanted to do this yesterday." He pushes his palm against my lower back, leading me into the hallway, to the spot in front of the mirror.

"Why didn't you?" I ask.

"I didn't have a condom."

"I did."

"You prepared?"

Okay. Maybe I prepared for the possibility. "I wanted to be safe. Just in case."

"In case I fucked you?"

"Yes."

"Did you think I would?"

"No. Maybe. I don't know. Better to have it if you did."

"Greedy."

"For you, yes."

He lets out a soft groan.

My sex clenches. Already, I need him again. I need *that* again. His groan, his need, his bliss.

He wraps his arm around my waist. Turns me, so I'm facing the wall. "This is going to hurt." There's no threat in his voice. It's a matter-of-fact statement.

This is going to hurt. And that sets me on fire.

He pushes me against the wall. Hard enough I have to turn my head.

With my arms behind my back, I can barely balance. I have to trust him to keep me upright.

He holds me in place as he shifts back, unzips his slacks, rolls the condom over his cock.

Without warning, he drives into me.

No teasing. No warm up. One hard, deep, perfect thrust.

Fuck.

The pressure is intense. Almost too much to take.

But still, I want more.

He holds my body against his as he drives into me again. Harder.

Then harder.

Then hard enough my cheek bumps against the wall.

It does hurt, but the force of it—

Fuck. Why does that set me on fire? Why don't I care?

He does it again.

My cheek bumps the wall again.

Again—

"Fuck." It hurts too much. In a bad way. A *my forehead isn't made for this* way.

But I don't want to ask him to stop.

I don't want him to stop.

I like him rough and commanding.

I bite my lip. Try to take it.

He rocks into me again.

My eyes close. My breath hitches.

Again.

A yelp falls from my lips.

He stops immediately.

My shoulders fall with relief. "I…"

"Like this." Gently, he undoes the binding on my wrists, then brings my hands to the wall, over my head. "Keep them there."

I nod.

His hands return to my hips. He holds me in place for a moment, then he drives into me, hard and deep.

Even with my hands on the wall, I nearly hit the plaster. It's intense. Rough.

But only in a good way.

In such a fucking good way.

I arch my back, my pelvis against his for leverage.

He rocks into me again.

Again.

My body stretches to take him.

The pressure fades to pleasure. Still intense, but in the best possible way.

I dig my fingers into the wall.

He rocks into me again and again.

Those same deep, hard strokes.

My gaze goes to the mirror.

I watch the perfect mix of bliss and control bleed over his expression.

I need that.

Him coming, him groaning my name, him under

my spell.

His breaths run together. Drift into low groans.

His nails scrape my skin.

I rock my hips to meet him. I'm close too. So fucking close. So desperately in need of release.

"Please." I arch my back. "Cam. Please."

He doesn't ask what I mean. He brings his thumb to my clit. Works me with those perfect circles as he drives into me.

Again.

And again.

And again.

Fuck.

I watch him fill me one more time, then I let my eyes close. My world goes white as I come. It's different than before. Faster, harder, more intense.

My body pulses around him, pulling him closer and deeper.

Pulling us together.

I groan his name as I come.

He works me through my orgasm. Then he brings both hands to my hips and he fucks me.

Those same hard, deep strokes, but faster. Again and again.

Until he's there.

I watch as his brow furrows, as his nails dig into my skin, as his shoulder tense and release.

He drives into me as he comes. I can see it in his posture. Feel it in the way he pulses inside me.

It feels so fucking good. But still, I want more. His flesh against mine. No clothes.

No barriers.

No end date.

Some of that is possible. Maybe just the first. But even

that, the thought of every inch of his body against every inch of mine—

I really fucking want it.

He finishes, untangles our bodies, takes care of the condom.

Then he scoops me into his arms, carries me to the couch, runs his fingers through my hair as I catch my breath.

We don't stay there for long. Only a few minutes.

But I still feel like he's mine.

Like I'm his.

Like the entire fucking world is perfect.

Chapter Thirty-Two

CAM

"I can't wear this." Sienna holds her short purple dress against her body.

"Stay naked."

"Are you going to fuck me again?"

"Eventually."

"Now?"

"No."

"Then no deal." She pulls the dress over her head. Checks her reflection in the bedroom mirror. The one she was staring at when I fucked her last night.

She remembers. It's in her eyes. In the flush of her cheeks. The heave of her chest.

I don't usually care if a woman remembers me. With Sienna, I need it. I need to know I'll be in her head, forever.

It's all I can have. The spot as her first. As the man who introduced her to sex.

Usually, I avoid the responsibility. I don't want to fuck someone up the way I was fucked up.

"I want to show you New York, but I'm reasonable." She smooths the dress. Turns to check out her arse.

Or maybe that's me.

That dress is short and she's not wearing anything under it.

"I'll stay here all day if you make it worth my while." She shoots me a coy look. "And I'll stay naked."

"Answer is still no."

She makes a show of pouting. "Then I'm going to show you New York. At least, a few New York highlights." She steps into her wedges. "What do you like?"

"Fucking you."

She smiles. "Besides that?"

"There's no besides that." I motion *come here*. When she does, I wrap my arms around her. Pull her into a slow, deep kiss.

She groans against my lips. "Cam." Her hand slips under my jacket. Her fingers dig into the fabric of my shirt. "You just said you wouldn't."

"Not now."

"Could you?"

"Could I?"

She looks up at me. "Could you go again so fast?"

A laugh spills from my lips.

"What?" Her brow furrows. "What's funny?"

"You, asking that."

She shrugs *if you say so*. Steps backward. Finds her purse. "It's a perfectly reasonable question."

"It is."

"Then why is it funny?"

My laugh gets louder. Fuller.

"That's just cruel." She shakes her head, but she's smiling. "Okay. Fine. Laugh. I'm going to find clothes. And then I'm going to take you somewhere that will make you fall in love with the city."

"I'll buy you something."

"An entire outfit?"

I nod.

"I can change at my apartment."

"No."

"Because of Ty?"

Yes. If he sees her walking into her apartment in last night's clothes, he'll get ideas. And he'll ask me first.

I can keep this to myself. But if he asks point-blank?

My poker face isn't that good.

But why focus on that? "I want to buy you something."

"Is this some rich guy kink?"

"If that's how you see me buying you lingerie."

Her eyes light up. "Oh. Okay. I accept your offer." She holds out her hand. "So let's go. I need more coffee."

"You had two."

"One and a half." She motions *let's go*. "Unless... you are ready to go. Right here, right now."

Again, I laugh.

This time, she folds her arms. "What is so funny?"

I offer my hand. When she takes it, I grab my wallet and room key, move to the door. "Most women don't ask."

"Why not?"

"I don't know, but they don't."

"Because men get upset? They don't want to accept their physical limitations?"

My laugh gets louder.

"What? That's what happens!"

"That's why I'm laughing."

"Oh. Good." Her fingers curl into my jacket. "So that's what's funny? That men are idiots?"

"More or less."

"And you...?"

"Do I accept my physical limitations?" I open the door for her.

She moves into the hallway. "Do you?"

"Usually." I lead her toward the elevator.

"Not always?"

"Sometimes, a proud woman dares me, and I see if I can make it happen."

"Could you go again so fast?"

"It's been twenty minutes."

"I said *so fast!*"

I laugh all the way to the elevator.

She steps inside. "Is it really that funny?"

"Yes." I hit the button for the ground floor then I bring my hands to her hips. Lift her. Set her on the railing.

"It's mean laughing at me."

"I know." I bring my lips to hers.

She tugs at my jacket as she kisses back.

Fuck, she tastes good. Like coffee and sugar and Sienna.

I want to be here forever, in this tiny space, only the two of us, and all the desire between us.

No complications. No confusion. No fucked-up thoughts in my head.

But that isn't the case.

Even if she weren't Indigo's sister, even if Ty wouldn't kill me if he found out, even if she weren't a teenager with her entire life ahead of her—

I'm a mess.

She's not.

The elevator dings. The doors slide open.

But, still, I kiss her like there's no tomorrow.

Someone clears their throat.

She pulls back. "Shit."

I help her down. Nod to the older couple standing in the lobby with takeout coffees in their hands.

Sienna offers them an apologetic shrug and follows me to

the street. She stops in front of a black town car. "Don't tell me."

"Of course."

"Overkill."

It is. But then I can't risk spending a lot of time outside in her sister's neighborhood either.

We have two days together if we keep this our secret.

I need every minute of them.

————

Sienna's eyes go wide as she steps out of the car. She surveys her surroundings, carefully, deciding if they're up to her standards.

We're at a quiet shop in midtown. A boutique run by a friend of mine. A friend who owes me a favor.

It's not quite Sienna—mostly lingerie, mostly ornate and impractical—but I'm greedy. I want to see her in sheer lace.

Then out of it.

Sienna studies a mesh bodysuit. She picks it up. Holds the sheer fabric against her frame. "This would be your idea of dressing me."

"Of course."

She smiles. "We could have stayed in the hotel."

"I thought you needed coffee."

"I do! Where is it?"

I chuckle.

"What?" She shoots me that same *what could possibly be so funny* look.

"You're a very demanding woman."

"Did you just realize that?"

"People don't usually take that tone with me."

"I can't believe I ever thought you were the down-to-

Earth Hunt." This time, she laughs at me in that playful *I really do like how ridiculous you are* way. "You're very difficult."

"Of course."

"And you act so normal, like you can't believe how fussy Ty is."

"He's not fussy."

"Maybe not compared to you." She shakes her head *ridiculous*. "Let me guess? You bought the shop so you could fuck me here."

I raise a brow.

"Hmm. You didn't buy the shop, but…" She moves to a rack of pink lingerie. Dismisses it and moves onto a red bra and pant set. "You're going to fuck me here anyway?"

"No."

"No?" She pouts. "Why do you like saying no so much?"

"Why do you keep asking questions you know the answer to?"

Again, she makes a show of pouting. "Okay, fine, but you're the one who has to watch my lingerie show way over there, with your hands to yourself."

"I do?"

She nods *hell yes*. "It's only fair." She grabs the red set. "Stay there and don't distract me."

"Distract you how?"

"Like that." She motions to my face. "That look that screams *I'm going to think about you naked in the dressing room*."

"Would you prefer I not think about you naked in the dressing room?"

"Oh my god, Cam! You know what I mean!"

I smile.

She folds her arms.

It's adorable. I want to take her now.

I want to slip her panties to her ankles and pull her into my waist.

I want to fuck her face-to-face, soft and slow, so I can see every bit of pleasure in her expression.

It's not what I do.

But I want it with every molecule of my body.

Sienna picks out half a dozen lingerie items. She shoots me a *get real, you call this clothes* look as she grabs a pair of jeans and a t-shirt and she moves into the dressing room.

I still consider inviting myself into the space.

Ordering her out of her dress.

Onto her knees.

Against the wall.

Sienna steps out of the dressing room in only the red knickers. "What do you think? Does it suit me?"

"I think you're begging for punishment."

"If I am?" Her lips curl into a smile.

I want to give it to her, I do, but I'm not sure I can stay in control. "No."

"No? Just no."

Fuck, I want to bend her over my lap, slide those knickers to her ankles, scold her for teasing me. For asking me to risk everything. "Not yet. You're not ready for it."

"How do you know?"

"I know."

She studies my expression for a moment, then she nods, accepting my answer. "Well... I am here. In lingerie." Her gaze flit to the curtain behind us. Enough privacy no one will know it's us.

But if anyone walks by the store—

They'll see what's going on.

"And I think I'm keeping this one." She reaches behind her back. "But I need to take it off if I want to try others." She unhooks her bra. Slides it off her shoulders.

Her eyes meet mine as she brings her hands to her hips. Pushes her knickers to her ankles.

Fuck.

She takes a single step toward me. Stops. Waits.

She's careful with me.

I should be the one careful with her. I shouldn't need her so careful with me.

But I do.

I really fucking do.

"Try it," I say. "Show me."

She nods and slips into the dressing room. A few moments later, she returns in a sheer one-piece in the perfect shade of champagne.

She spins, showing off her lush arse. "Should I try another?"

"You daring me, sweetness?"

She nods.

I motion *come here*. When she does, I wrap my fingers around her wrist. Bring her hand to my cock.

She cups me over my slacks.

I pull her into a slow, deep kiss.

It's soft, intense, enough to make me dizzy.

My head is already a mess. I can't handle her touching me. Not yet.

Maybe soon.

But not yet.

So I back her up to the couch, I lay her on the cushions, I pull her knickers to her ankles. And I lick her until she comes on my face.

It's heaven.

But it's not enough.

Nothing is going to be enough.

Chapter Thirty-Three

CAM

fter she's finished with her selections, Sienna pulls back the curtain. Motions to her new attire—a pair of blue jeans and a tight white tank top. She pulls the strap aside to show off a sheer red bra.

Then she holds out an entire stack of underwear.

She's not upset.

Why the fuck would she be upset about coming on my face?

I need to get ahold of myself. That is possible. There's no universe where this is easy, but there's some universe where it's possible.

"Are we just taking it?" Her eyes go to the register. "Or is your friend going to show up?"

"Let me."

She raises a brow, but she still hands me the stack of lingerie. "You're going to ring it up?"

"You don't see me as a shop boy?"

"Actually… yes. I can see you selling women lingerie. Or shoes. Purses. Anything where you turn on that Cam charm."

"I worked at a department store for a few months." I move to the register. Ring up everything she picked, and a few surprises.

"Really?"

I nod.

"You did well?"

"I did."

"Why only a few months?"

"I slept with a coworker." I wrap the lingerie in tissue paper. Slip it into one of the store's discreet silver bags.

"Did you hate her after?" She says it without judgment.

But my shoulders still tense. "I didn't want to be around her anymore, but she had another idea."

"She couldn't get enough?"

"Yes." I finish paying.

"Was that it? She wanted more and you didn't?"

"She thought the sex meant something to me."

"Didn't it?"

"Not the way she hoped." It meant I didn't want to look at her anymore. I couldn't stand to be around her, to be around anyone who'd seen me so vulnerable. "I was young. I didn't know how to communicate my intentions. I told her it was casual, but…"

"She didn't realize it was the end of the line."

"How could she?"

Sienna nods. She looks at me curiously. "Did you realize it then?"

"No."

"That must have been confusing."

"It was."

She motions to the door *shall we*. "And that happens with everyone? Every woman you've been with?"

"Usually."

"Do you think it will happen with me?"

"I hope not."

Her lips press together. "Okay. Well, uh… I hope that doesn't happen also. Uh… should, we, uh… should we drop off the lingerie somewhere?"

"I have the car."

"And then we should go somewhere." The fear stays in her voice. She tries to push it away. To push the entire subject away.

Or maybe I'm seeing what I want to see. Maybe it doesn't matter to her.

If she was someone else, I'd be relieved. But the thought of Sienna only wanting a weekend of sex makes my stomach turn.

It's ridiculous. I made the offer; I set the limits; I controlled the entire conversation.

And here I am, upset she agreed to my terms.

Ty is right. I'm an arsehole.

But I'm not dwelling on that. I'm not dwelling, period. I'm enjoying my time her.

Sienna follows me outside. Soaks in the sight of Midtown. The silver skyscrapers, the yellow cabs, the tourists and locals rushing around. "How can you not love New York? Look at it!" She motions to a man with a cart selling pretzels and hot dogs. "It's so alive."

"Hot dogs?"

She nods.

"When did you last eat a hot dog?"

Her laugh dissolves the tension in her shoulders. "You can't insult hot dogs in America. Sure, they're disgusting, but we're proud of them for some reason. It's the same with baseball. Everyone who likes it admits it's boring, but it's as American as apple pie."

"Your favorite among the options?"

"Well, yeah, it's dessert. The only sport better than dessert is soccer." She looks up at me, invitation in her eyes.

This time, it's not sexual. It's like she's inviting me to forget I might hate her.

She accepts it and she's still here.

Maybe it is okay.

Or maybe I'm officially out of my fucking mind.

No, there's no maybe there. I'm crazy.

And I'm crazy about her.

Already.

But I meant what I said this morning. There's no universe where Sienna and I have a future.

This is the only thing that makes sense.

We have a weekend together. I have a weekend to savor my time with her.

I'm not spending any more of it worrying about the future.

I'm enjoying every fucking drop of her.

———

SIENNA SQUEEZES MY HAND AS SHE LEADS ME DOWN FIFTH Avenue. "We need caffeine and this place is perfect. It's like you, like your entire family. Incredibly extra."

"Isn't *extra* last year's slang?"

"Are you seriously correcting my language?"

"If you're dated."

She smiles. "Okay, what would you call it?"

Extra, meaning more than expected or over the top, like Ian wearing a fuchsia tie to match his girlfriend's teal hair, or Sienna showing up to dinner in her football jersey, or me bringing three suits on vacation—

It's the perfect word.

But I still need to tease her. "You're the young one."

"You don't even know! You're so full of it." She shakes her head *ridiculous* and marches forward. "You should be proud of me for using it. Eve's the one who pointed it out. She said something about how Ian and the shop were both so extra." She barely stops herself from rolling her eyes.

"You object to her passion for her boyfriend?"

"They could have some self-control."

"Could you?"

"I have." She looks up at me. "Haven't I?"

"If we didn't have to keep this secret?"

"I don't know. Maybe." She moves closer. "We don't have to keep it secret here. And I haven't jumped you yet."

"Yet?"

She nods, rises to her tiptoes, brings her lips to mine.

Fuck, she tastes good, like Sienna.

"Mmm. What are we talking about?" She pulls back with a sigh.

"Caffeine."

"Right. This place. It's actually, uh, Eve's favorite. Well, her sister's favorite. I do appreciate that she's good to her sister."

"Your enthusiasm is contagious."

She flips me off. Then she smiles, takes my hand, leads me south.

"Did she first take you here?"

"No, I've been a few times. One of the girls at Rick's liked it. Sometimes, I'd bring her a drink if I was visiting Indigo."

The bar where her sister worked, smiling at rich arse-holes for tips. Was that Sienna's fate too?

"Did you ever go to a place like that?" she asks. "Where it's all 'distinguished gentlemen' buying overpriced cocktails served by pretty girls?"

"I've been everywhere that sells alcohol."

"It doesn't seem like your scene. But maybe the places in London are different. Rick's is like... you've seen *Casablanca*?"

"I don't live in a cave."

"That's where he got the name. Rick's Cafe Americano is the bar in *Casablanca*."

"The owner isn't named Rick?"

"He is. And he sometimes even calls himself Big Dick."

"He does not."

She nods *he does*. "One of the girls at the bar said she uh... had experience that would suggest otherwise."

"She fucked him?"

"I think she gave him a hand job for better shifts."

Fuck, that turned fast. I shouldn't be surprised. A lot of rich men are entitled arseholes. A lot of poor men are entitled arseholes.

It's usually men abusing their positions of power.

When it's women, attractive, young women—

People rarely see it in those terms.

"Cam?" She tugs at my suit jacket absentminded. "You there?"

"Yeah."

"You really need that caffeine, huh?"

"Did he ever ask you?"

Her brow furrows. "What?" She's not even thinking it. She's already past it.

"The owner. Did he ask you for sexual favors?"

She looks at me funny. "Are you jealous or mad?"

"Both."

"No. He wanted me to work there. He'd bring it up every time I visited Indie. And, uh, there were other guys who asked. Who propositioned me. Or offered money." Her voice softens. "I considered it a few times."

My stomach churns.

"There were attractive men who offered. Men I wanted

anyway. And we were always short on cash. But I... I don't know. I couldn't do it."

"There's no shame in that."

"I guess not." She looks up at me. "I just... I sound like Indie."

"Your sister, who's about to be set for life?"

"She signed a prenup."

That's surprising. Ty is old-fashioned when it comes to love and marriage. He's not the type to ask for a prenup.

Even though it's the smart thing to do.

Even though his older brother is divorced.

"How much does she get?" I ask.

"A lot."

"So... maybe she's not such a bad role model."

Sienna smiles. "You sound like me now."

"You're wise."

"I try. I just... I love Indie. I love that she's a musician with all this passion and drive to follow her heart, but I always thought... I'm an athlete. I do what it takes to win. Whatever it takes to win."

"You're upset you couldn't bring yourself to fuck a rich arsehole for money?"

"It sounds ridiculous like that."

I shoot her a knowing look.

"Okay, yes, it's a little ridiculous, but... only a little. For most of the history of Western civilization, fucking a rich asshole has been most women's best bet. Well... marrying a rich asshole."

My lips curl into a smile.

Her cheeks flush. "What?"

"That's something Eve would say."

Her brow furrows. "Maybe she's infecting my brain."

"You agree with her."

She swats me playfully.

I pull her closer. Follow her around the corner.

There it is; a matcha shop in shades of bubble gum pink and forest green, palm tree print and Cha Cha albums everywhere.

She leads me inside the warm, crowded shop. Points to the pink on green menu. One column of matcha drinks and one of coffee.

"You drink tea?" I ask.

"If it's sweet and full of caffeine, I drink it."

"It's sweet enough for you?"

"Mean."

My laugh eases the tension in my shoulders, but not by enough.

"It's sweet with the macadamia milk. You'll like it. And even if you don't, we're at this super extra matcha shop. You have to get the matcha."

"What does your nemesis order?"

"She's not my nemesis." She clears her throat. "I just don't like being a fifth wheel."

"And…"

"Well… she's kind of obnoxious sometimes."

"Is that right?"

"Yes! Does she have to talk about gender roles all the time?"

My lips curl into a smile. Her blush steals my attention. She's adorable jealous. What else matters?

"You can admit it's a little annoying how much she talks about it?"

"And when you talk about football?"

"You think I'm obnoxious? I can't believe this."

"It's all right to have different interests."

"She could talk about it less."

"Whereas you never bring up football?"

"That's different," she says. "Everyone else wants to talk

about football."

"And when she brings up gender roles?"

"I bet you can't remember her last point," she says.

"Every detail."

Envy flares in her eyes again. She catches herself and turns to the line.

The person at the register finishes. Sienna moves forward. Orders for both of us.

She lets me pay, moves to the pickup area, tries to shake off her blush. "What did she say?"

"Something about Bond."

"The movies?"

"The very famous film franchise, yes. You're familiar?"

"Of course I'm familiar. I just don't care. A suave British guy in a suit. Like I need more of that in my life."

I chuckle. "Uh-huh."

"You know, before I met you, most of my experience with rich guys in suits was watching assholes try to pick up Indie at Rick's. So I wasn't really all that interested in seeing more in my off time."

"How long did she work there?"

"A few years. She worked at a different bar when she first met Ty. Though I suppose you've heard that story."

I nod.

"It was a good job. And good for her. Guys fall all over her when she goes full ice queen. And... she never told me, not directly, but I know men offered her money for sex too."

"Did she take it?"

"She says she didn't, but... I don't know. I don't think she would. We were never that desperate, and she..."

"Is romantic?"

Sienna nods. "I..."

"There's no shame in not wanting to take money for sex."

Her brow furrows. "I guess."

"I'm glad you didn't."

"So you could be my first?"

"Yes." I slip my hand in the back pocket of her jeans. It feels good touching her, but it's not enough. I need to say this too. "I'm glad I'm the person introducing you to sex. I can't trust anyone else to do it." I can barely trust myself to do it.

Her eyes meet mine. "Yeah?"

"Yeah." I bring my hand to her cheek. "I'll always be your first."

She leans into my touch.

I pull her into a soft, slow kiss.

Someone nearby *awws*. Someone else whispers.

The barista calls our drinks. Sienna blushes as she pulls back, but she stays on her *more caffeine* mission. She grabs the drinks and leads me out of the shop, onto the bright street.

Midtown is bustling, loud, alive.

It would be easy to let this go, pretend as if I only care because I'm possessive.

As if it's normal I want to possess her.

But I want to tell her this. Not all of it, not here, not now, but soon.

Really fucking soon.

Chapter Thirty-Four

SIENNA

I s there such a thing as a perfect day?

It's four and I'm already over the moon.

Between the morning session, the fantastic new shoes I bought at the only in New York eight story Macy's, a lunch of proper New York pizza, and the view from the Empire State Building—

Okay, maybe the day would be better with more *activity*, but I kind of like him making me wait.

I want him so badly I'm going to explode.

It's wonderful.

Horrible.

Thrilling and bright and alive.

Sure, I'm wound a little tighter than I prefer, but the want feels so fucking good. Like the fourth quarter of a soccer game.

Or the final minute.

My desire to have him is overwhelming my other senses.

And now—

I've waited long enough. I want to kick the winning goal.

But I'm pretty sure it's not happening here, at this Dutch

cafe in the Village. According to Cam, the place is a pretty accurate recreation of cafes in the Netherlands (he studied in Amsterdam for a year in college and he's always wanted to see if New York had anything to offer in the stroopwafel department).

It's not the kind of place I imagine him—framed Van Gogh prints adorn the baby pink walls—but he's completely in his element demonstrating proper stroopwafel eating technique.

Between his suit and the tiny chairs, he looks like a dad invited to his daughter's tea party.

Too big and too well dressed and completely and totally enthusiastic.

Oh god. Cam. Holding a baby.

Mmm.

Why am I picturing this? I don't even know if I want kids. Or if he wants kids.

He doesn't want to get married, so why would he want to have kids?

And why am I considering this?

It's a no-fly zone. It's so far past the fly zone.

It's just I want to fuck him again. To feel him come inside me.

That's it.

Sex.

Not domesticity.

Really hot, dirty, raunchy rough sex.

And we're talking about, uh...

Something. Something that isn't how much I want to drag him to the bathroom.

I try to find the thread of our conversation, but I'm distracted by his forearms. He gave me his suit jacket (it's cold in a tank top) and he rolled his sleeves to his elbows for the stroopwafel festivities.

So his gorgeous strong forearms are there, on the table, all sexy and visible and begging for my hands.

And the tattoos. Did I mention the tattoos?

Black ink on dark skin.

I can barely make out the letters of the Latin quote on his forearm, but I can.

fortes fortuna adiuvat

Fortune favors the bold.

Very Cam.

Very hot.

Very lickable.

He sets my stroopwafel on my mug of coffee. The steam melts the caramel and softens the cookie. The caramel seeps into the drink. Sweetens it.

His hand skims my knee.

Mmm.

Yes.

Here.

Now.

More.

All.

"Where are you going, sweetness?" he asks.

"Now."

"Now?"

I motion to the bathroom.

He shakes his head.

"Why not?"

"Because I said so."

"If you're going to torture me, you should entertain me."

"How's that?" He slides his hand up my thigh.

My eyes flutter closed.

"Like this?" He presses his palm against me, over my jeans.

"Cam. Please…"

"Right here?"

No. The cafe isn't crowded, but it's not private either. I shake my head.

He pulls his hand away.

"Mean."

"Always."

I suck a breath through my teeth. Try to find a single coherent thought. "Conversation. You should talk to me if you're not going to fuck me."

"About…"

Uh… Forearms. Hands. Lips. Shoulders.

Must touch him.

Must kiss him.

Must mount him.

"What you do for fun." For example, fucking me or thinking about fucking me or fucking himself.

"I work too much. I don't have time for fun."

Or… things that aren't sex. Must think about something other than sex. "What about soccer?"

"That's it."

"That's all you do? Work and soccer?"

"I read." He pulls the stroopwafel from his cup and takes a bite.

"You read?"

"Is it that surprising?"

Talking. Not mounting. Yes, I can do that. I even like doing that. "Not if I picture you reading in bed."

"Naked?"

"You're always naked when I picture you."

He smiles. "You too."

Mmm. "What do you read?"

"Mysteries."

"Mysteries, really?" I can see that.

He nods. "I'm a sucker for secrets."

"Secrets or uncovering the truth?"

"Two sides of the same coin."

That's true. "I watch them sometimes. On TV." For a second, I feel insecure about my more lowbrow tastes, then I catch sight of his smile.

He's teasing.

He's teasing because he likes me.

"You're watching *Sherlock*?" he asks.

"Too slow."

"Of course."

"An hour and a half is too long for an episode. That's an entire movie!"

"You're impatient."

"I can be patient."

He smiles. "You can wait, but you can't do it patiently."

"I've been waiting since… a long time."

"Since I made you come at the lingerie shop?"

"That was a long time ago."

His smile widens. "Four and a half hours."

"See. An eternity."

He breaks his stroopwafel in two and offers half to me.

"Thanks." Mmm, it's perfect. Soft on one side, crunchy on the other, cookie and caramel and sweetness. "Does that mean soon?"

"What soon?"

"Cam!"

His eyes meet mine. "You know what I'm going to say."

"Maybe. Maybe not?"

He nods.

"I should do the same to you." I take another bite. Let the delicious cookie caramel hybrid dissolve on my tongue. "Maybe I'll fuck you tonight. Maybe I won't. I'll see how I feel."

"Really?"

"Yeah. Really." I finish the cookie, fold my arms, try to cop his in-control posture. "I enjoy making you wait."

"I enjoy waiting."

"Ugh, you're ruining it."

"You're full of shite."

"I had you going?"

He shakes his head.

"For a minute?"

"Not a second."

I make a show of pouting.

He leans across the table to press his lips to mine.

Mmm, he takes like coffee and sugar and Cam.

He pulls back with a heady sigh. "Soon."

"Really?"

"I like how eager you are."

"I'm just… uh…" Very eager. "Honest about what I want."

"I like that about you."

"And I… uh… when you say soon, you mean…"

Again, he smiles. "Soon to anyone."

Okay, I can live with that. Maybe. In theory. But only if I do something besides stare at his beautiful forearms. "Are you going to actually eat that stroopwafel?"

"Do you want it?"

"Well, yeah, it's a cookie. But it's sweet. Even for me."

He takes a bite and offers the rest to me. "It is, but it's familiar. Like home."

"That's how I feel about the Royal Milk Tea at Boba Stop. Indie and I went there every day, after school, when she walked me home. Well, all spring. During soccer season, I got home after she was at work. And it was too late for tea."

"Too late for tea?"

"I know my limits."

He raises a brow.

"Usually." Sometimes.

He picks up his spoon. Stirs his coffee.

"Did you like Amsterdam?"

"I did."

"For the Absinthe or the uhh… art."

"Van Gogh Museum?"

Right. That explains the prints.

"Both."

"You like art?"

He lets out a hearty laugh.

"What?"

"Isn't *Ninety Day Fiancée* high art?"

"Yes."

"So don't you like art?"

"If it includes excellent reality TV content."

"But not visual art?"

"It's okay. I mean—" I point to a print of a famous painting. Flowers in a vase. All swirly and yellow. "It's flowers. Am I supposed to be moved?"

His smile widens.

"What?"

"Art is like anything. More interesting the more you know about it."

"And you're going to tell me things about it?"

"Later. If we go to the MoMa. After this maybe."

My lips curl into a frown. "You're teasing, right?"

He shrugs *am I?*

"What, uh, what else did you like about Amsterdam."

"The music scene."

"You like EDM? Really?"

"I can't?"

"I thought you liked mumbling grunge guys."

He chuckles. "I do."

"And, usually the guys who like EDM are tools who want to tell you how great ecstasy is."

"You've met these guys?"

I nod. "Mostly older brothers of friends, usually visiting from some school in California or one of those states that's all desert."

Again, he chuckles.

"What?"

"You're not worried about hurting my feelings."

"Of course not." Not with this.

"I told you a hobby and you called me a tool."

"It's a hobby for tools. But I was surprised because you're not a tool. And you're not… well, if all you do is work and play soccer, you don't really have that club going druggie personality."

"I don't."

"Are you offended?"

"No." He smiles. "Just thinking about how much I like you."

"Oh." My cheeks flush. "Because I insulted you?"

"Because you told me what you thought. And that was more important to you than tact." He takes a long sip of his coffee. "It feels good, being in a room full of people dancing. Even without the ecstasy—"

"Have you done it?"

"A few times. It's like everyone says. You feel all this love and connection with the people around you, with the entire world."

That doesn't sound like Cam.

"It's strange. I liked it while it was happening, but after I didn't understand it."

"I guess everyone experiments in college." I could call this an experiment, but I won't. That's selling it short.

He nods. "Back then, I needed loud distractions like a

room of packed strangers. I couldn't be alone with my thoughts. I couldn't handle it."

"Was there a reason?"

"I didn't like myself."

"Do you now?"

"Sometimes."

I take a long sip. "Because of sex?"

He pauses. Studies me. "Yes." His eyes meet mine. "I'm glad you didn't fuck strange men for money, Sienna. Not just because I'm glad to be your first, though I am."

My blush deepens.

"Because I don't want shit to fuck with your head."

So he… had sex for money? That can't be right. "Have you?"

"No. But my first experience with sex was fucked up. It fucked me up. I'm still… I still don't know how to connect sex and intimacy."

"Usually, you hate people after?"

"Yes." His voice softens. "I still like you."

"Oh."

"I… you're fucking with my head."

"I warned you."

"I'm glad. But it's… new. I still don't know how to handle it."

He doesn't know how to handle how much he likes me.

Fuck.

We need to go now.

Here.

Did I mention now?

"I haven't kissed anyone since July," he says. "I haven't touched anyone since I kissed you. I tried, but I couldn't. I couldn't stop thinking about you."

"Oh."

"Have you?"

"There was a guy at a party. I was drunk. It didn't mean anything, but I did… I thought of you immediately. Of how he'd never compare."

"That was all?" he asks. "A kiss."

I nod.

"What was it like?"

"A dare at a party."

"And you always take dares?"

"Mostly."

"How would you prefer it?"

"I don't know. I couldn't really think of anyone but you."

"If it had been me?"

"At some party?"

He nods.

Mmm. Cam at a party. "Are you wearing your suit?"

"I never take it off."

"What about this?" My fingers brush his forearms.

"It's not off."

"The running jersey?"

"Prove it."

Mmm. Sassy Cam. Yes. More. Now. "I don't know. I, uh, I know a lot of older people think it's not sexy if a guy asks if he can kiss you, but I like the way you do it. Like you're daring me."

"Older?" He points to his chest.

"Are guys asking to kiss you?"

"Not often."

"Do you think it's sexy?" I run my fingers over my cup. "When a woman asks?"

"It depends how she asks." He places his hand on my forearm, looks into my eyes, lowers his voice. "If she says, Cam, I want to kiss you. And she leans in close and looks at me like she'll die if I don't touch her."

Mmm.

"I'm glad you asked me to kiss you. I was terrified."

He was? He always seems so strong and in control. "It didn't show."

"I know."

"You're not supposed to say that."

"Why? I do."

My lips curl into a smile. "It, uh, I do think it's sexy, that you ask what I want. Other guys aren't like that. Even guys my age, who claim they're all about the new rules for sex."

"There are new rules?"

"Enthusiastic consent."

"And they object?"

"They complain women won't tell them what they want. Or that talking kills the mood. But, uh, I think when you..."

"You like dirty talk, sweetness?"

Mmm. "Yes."

"You like when I order you to take off your knickers and sit on my cock?"

Fuck. "Now?"

He chuckles. "No."

"But..."

"Not here."

"So now, but somewhere else."

"Soon." His eyes meet mine. His lips curl into a smile. "I'm having too much fun torturing you."

God, he's so mean and I like it so much. "I, uh, what was I saying?"

"How you want to sit on my cock."

"Cam!"

"You were."

"You think I won't do it right now?"

"I do." His voice drops to a dare. "I know you won't do it now."

Fuck, he's right. I won't do it here. "I just… I was saying something."

"You were."

About… sex… and… something. Oh. Other people. That's a way to keep from mounting him. Talking about other people who I want much less than I want Cam. "I've wanted people. I've wanted to have sex just to experience it. But I've never trusted anyone enough. Or wanted them enough to get over the lack of trust."

"Which is it?"

"Huh?"

"Do you want me or trust me?"

"Both." I take another sip of coffee. Mmm, sweet, sweet caramel and cinnamon. "Did you think it was sexy when I asked?"

"Very."

"Why?"

"It takes confidence to ask a question with a yes or no answer," he says. "It takes strength to take a no in stride."

That is what happened, isn't it? "Is that why you love saying no?"

"I love torturing you."

"Is that what you've been thinking about all summer, torturing me?"

"Mostly."

If it's really been two months—"Have you had an STD test?"

His pupils dilate. "You want me to fuck you bareback?"

"Are you safe?"

"Yes."

"I have an IUD. It's basically foolproof."

"Nothing is foolproof."

"This is close."

"Maybe."

"Really?"

"Do you really want to ask again, sweetness?"

I shake my head. "But you have my permission."

He half-smiles. "Ten minutes ago, you tried to claim you're patient."

"I'm being very patient. I could be on my knees under the table."

"You'll hurt yourself."

"Then in the bathroom."

He shakes his head. "Your first experience in a bathroom? No."

"Why not?"

"Because I said so."

"Where would you consider acceptable?" I ask.

"Wherever I decide."

I pout.

He smiles. "Would you really do it here?"

"Maybe."

"Bollocks."

Okay, it's bullshit, but—"I would in the bathroom."

Again, he shakes his head.

"The limo. Or your hotel room. A hotel room nearby. Or a dressing room."

"You could wait until we got back to my hotel room?"

Maybe. "Yes."

"Say it."

"Say what?"

"Say, Cam, take me back to the hotel room and fuck my pretty mouth."

My cheeks flush.

"You can't say it." His smile widens. "Bold, brash Sienna Simms can't admit she wants to suck me off."

My cheeks flush. "Cam!"

"Is it not true?"

"I… uh…" My blush deepens. "So Amsterdam."

"Say it. You might get what you want."

"Here?"

"No."

"Soon?"

He nods. "It's up to you." His voice is a dare. "Say it and get what you want. Or ask about Van Gogh and… we can go to the MoMa. Your call."

Chapter Thirty-Five

SIENNA

*ay it and get what you want. Or ask about Van Gogh and...
we can go to the MoMa.*

Sex or a museum?

An art museum?

A modern art museum?

What an obvious choice.

Of course, sex with Cam is the clear winner in any face-off. Even against soccer.

Would I rather get sweaty on the field or in his bedroom? Duh.

No wonder Alice tells us to stay away from boys all season. If he asked, I'd skip practice all week to sweat my ass off in his bed.

I want him.

And I want this. Not just because I want to try it, because I want to know how.

Because it's Cam and I trust him and I want him and I really fucking like him.

I've had chances with other guys. Make out sessions that

could have gone further. Guys who hinted, or asked, or took my hand and put it on their dick.

Over their pants, but still.

I know where it is. I don't need them to put it there.

They don't do it the way Cam does, slowly and carefully, like he's the one offering me the privilege of touching them.

They're rushed and clumsy and desperate for any kind of action.

Don't get me wrong. Sometimes, it feels good to brush against a hard-on. But I never understood why other women were so enthusiastic about the event. The first time Katie blew her boyfriend, she couldn't shut up about it.

Which was annoying—she's always bragging about sex—but also curious. What's so great about getting a guy off?

Sure, I wanted to have sex; I wanted to experience all of it. I even contemplated sex with random guys.

But I never once considered blowing them.

No way. No thanks. Uh-uh.

Now, with Cam—

Fuck, I want it so badly.

Like what I've read in books. His hands in my hair, his cock in my mouth, his groan filling the space.

And what I've seen in movies. The positions of bodies. Women kneeling before men in their thrones, or crawling up their bodies in bed, or bending over the back seat of a car.

The full range of experience in porn. From the soft, slow savoring to the aggressive face-fucking.

Whatever it is, I want it.

As long as I get him in my mouth.

As long as I get to touch him.

As long as I make him come.

But I have to say it.

Why can't I say it?

He's right. I'm bold, brash Sienna Simms. I claim what I want. I shout it from the fucking mountaintops.

I can claim this.

I can do it verbally.

Eventually.

Cam's eyes stay on me as he waits. Unlike me, he's incredibly patient.

No, it's worse.

He enjoys waiting.

He enjoys torturing me.

Okay, I enjoy it too. But in a much more *oh my god it needs to happen now* way.

Whereas he savors every single second of my anticipation.

God, he's so sexy staring at me like he's going to mount me.

Why is he so sexy?

It's not fair.

"I do." I take a long sip of my coffee. As if that's the only thing keeping me here. As if that's the only reason why I'm not currently under the table.

Okay, he's right. The table is way too low. I'd hurt myself.

And I don't want it like that anyway.

I want him looking at me.

I want to be able to see him. To see the bliss spread over his expression. To hear my name fall from his lips.

It sounds so good on his lips.

"You do?" He raises a brow, inviting me to elaborate.

"I do want that."

"To go to the MoMA?"

"Cam!"

"It's a great museum. Only in New York."

"Have you really not been?"

"Not recently."

"Oh my god."

He motions *go on*. "We can see *The Starry Night*."

That's a Van Gogh painting. The famous one with the city and the stars. There's a print on the wall to our right.

"Should I check the special exhibit?" He pulls out his cell. "Or if we should go to the Met instead?"

A whine falls from my lips.

"That is what you're saying, isn't it, Sienna?" He tries to hold a poker face, but he breaks with a smile. "You do… want to go a museum?"

I shake my head.

"You want to go for a run? You missed this morning."

Again, I shake my head.

"Hmm… what could it be then? The Sienna I know isn't shy about asking for what she wants. And I just told her how sexy it is."

Okay, I can say this. "In the limo."

Again, he raises a brow.

"I'll say it there."

"Say what?"

"I do want to… do that with you."

"Are we talking about the museum again?"

My cheeks flush.

His smile widens. "In the limo. If you say it." He finishes his coffee then he leans across the table and kisses me. He grabs the check, motions *one minute*, and heads to the register.

I take a deep breath. Try to find my confidence.

I do want to suck him off.

A lot.

Just thinking about it, my entire body is buzzing.

It's harder to say the words stone-cold sober. But he's right. I'm not shy. I'm not afraid to ask for what I want.

What's the worst he'll say?

No.

God, he'd say no just to torture me. He really would.

But not now. He already promised. And I, uh.

Yes. I can.

I open my cell camera and fix my lipstick. The red-pink shade that screams *I'm a woman who gets what I want and I want this makeup on your cock.*

Okay, maybe it only says the first part.

But I can say the rest.

At least… in text.

I tap out the words.

Sienna: I want to suck you off.

Then I hit send.

A moment later, Cam shoots me a coy look. He smiles *of course* and taps a reply.

Cam: You still have to say it.

Sienna: Once we're alone.

Cam: I already called the driver. He'll be here in five. I'll meet you outside.

Okay. Five minutes to say it. To meet Cam outside.

That's a lot of time for preparation.

I gather my stuff, use the bathroom, consider taking off my panties, decide against it.

I want him to see my lingerie. The lingerie he bought me. The lingerie I'm wearing for him.

I want him to take it off.

And I—

I apply another coat of lipstick. Pop a breath mint. Head outside.

The limo arrives early. The driver opens the door for me. Nods a hello and motions for me to slip inside.

The touch of luxury doesn't feel as strange as it usually does. It feels right.

Of course, I'm going to touch him in a limo. That's my life now. Or at least, my weekend.

A weekend of fucking a hot, rich guy who adores me. Who I adore.

That's my usual criteria. Hot, rich, good in bed. And he loves soccer.

And he likes me.

And I like him.

A lot.

Maybe even more.

Maybe everything.

But definitely enough I want to taste him.

I set my purse on the bench seat. Smooth my jeans.

A few moments later, Cam slips inside.

The door closes behind him.

The space darkens. No strange purple mood lighting or disco balls or cheesy music. Just the afternoon light streaming in through the tinted windows.

"To the MoMA?" he teases.

I growl.

He smiles. "Music."

Yes, music. "Something sexy."

"What meets your criteria?"

"What you think is sexy."

He nods, attaches his cell to the sound system, plays a pulsing EDM song. It's not what I'd normally think of as sexy, but it's super hot.

"Did you have a playlist ready?"

"What do you think I do when I'm listening to music in my hotel room?"

"When you're not crying?"

He nods.

"You're making playlists."

"For different moods."

"Have you used this with someone else?"

"Never."

"Oh. Good."

He motions to the window. "Should I tell him to drive to the MoMa?"

"If there's enough time."

He shrugs *is there*.

"I don't care where we go after this." I move closer. So my thigh is pressed against his. "As long we can do this."

"This…"

I bring my hand almost all the way to his thigh.

He wraps his fingers around my wrist. Holds my hand there.

"I want to touch you." I take a deep breath. Find all my confidence. "I want to suck you off."

His pupils dilate.

"Here. Now. Will you show me how?"

Chapter Thirty-Six

SIENNA

For a long moment, Cam stays there on the precipice, his expression intense, his attention on me.

Then he places my hand on his thigh. "Follow my instructions."

"Only your instructions?"

He nods. "I don't want to hurt you."

Is that all it is? I don't know. But I can't really object. "I like taking orders from you."

"Do you, sweetness?" The hesitation drops from his voice and his posture.

I didn't even realize it was there, but now it's clear he's uncaged. Like last night, but different.

He trusts me more.

Trusts himself more, maybe.

His fingers brush my knee over my jeans. "You get off on following orders?"

"Yes," I breathe.

"Take this off." His fingers brush his suit jacket, the one I'm wearing around my shoulders.

It's too big for me, but it feels good, wearing his clothes.

Of course, it feels better, watching his expression brighten as I slip out of them.

"The tank top too." His voice stays firm. Demanding and yielding at once. Restrained and wild at once.

He makes me feel that way too.

Free and contained.

Like I have so much need I'll die if I don't fill it.

I pull my tank over my head and drop it on the floor.

He looks me over carefully, savoring every inch of my skin. Then he takes my hand and brings it up his thigh.

Closer and closer.

Until I can feel his hard-on through his slacks.

"Fuck." It falls from my lips. "Please."

"Please?" His voice is a dare.

"Can I touch you now? Please."

"Not yet." He brushes my hair behind my shoulders. "I want to take my time with you."

Mmm.

He brings his hand to my cheek. Runs his thumb over my temple. Over my jaw. Along my bottom lip. "You have any idea how much your lipstick drives me crazy?"

I shake my head.

He slips his thumb between my lips.

I don't wait for instructions. I suck on his digit. It feels so fucking good having him in my mouth, even though it's only the pad of his thumb against my tongue.

"I've been dreaming about seeing your pretty lips wrapped around my cock." He pulls his thumb from my mouth. Brings his hand to the strap of my bra. "And this. I've wanted to see you in this all fucking day."

Mmm. Yes. "I want you to see me in this." The bra is see-through red mesh. It makes me feel like a sex goddess on its own. With him staring at me like he'll die if he doesn't touch me?

Maybe I was wrong, and it is possible to die from desire.

I'm pretty sure I'm a goner.

His eyes flit to the mirror across from us. The entire limo is mirrored walls. "Can you see it sweetness? Can you see how much you drive me out of my mind." He pulls me closer.

My eyes go to our reflection. I look hot as hell in the lingerie, my nipples showing through the sheer fabric, my skin flushed, my lips red-pink.

But that's not what winds me tighter.

It's the intensity in his eyes.

"Take it off." His drops another octave.

I turn to him. Watch his expression change as I undo the hook of the bra and slip it off my shoulders.

"Fuck. Beautiful." He brings his hand to my chest and runs his thumb over my nipple. The right, then the left. "You drive me out of my mind, Sienna."

"You too."

"Have you imagined this?"

"Yes."

"How does it go?"

"Sometimes, like this. I'm topless in a car. Or we're both dressed in a stopped elevator, racing the clock. Or I'm completely naked, and you're standing, and ordering me onto my knees."

"Greedy."

"When it comes to you."

A groan falls from his lips. "Do you know how I imagine it?"

He pictures me. If it was anyone else, I'd be annoyed, but knowing Cam thinks of me sucking him off—

Fuck, I really might come from anticipation.

Is that possible?

Right now, I'm wound so tight.

He cups my breast and rolls my nipple between his thumb and forefinger. "Like this. Halfway out of your clothes, completely tuned to me, your pretty red lips wrapped around my cock."

Fuck yes.

"Are you ready for that, sweetness?"

"Yes," I breathe.

"Unzip me."

I nearly topple from the mix of anticipation and relief. We're really doing this. Finally. But we're only starting.

And I—

I need him so badly.

And I'm in so far over my head.

"I've never." Suddenly, I'm all thumbs. I fumble over his zipper.

"I won't be gentle."

Fuck. There. I get his zipper down.

He pushes his boxers out of the way.

His cock springs from the fabric.

He's bigger up close. More enticing. And more intimidating. That's a lot to fit in my mouth.

"Wrap your hand around me." His fingers curl around my wrist. "Like this."

I do. He feels so good against my palm. His skin is so soft, but he's so fucking hard. How can both be true?

How can this man be so full of contradictions?

"Like this to start." He guides my hand over his cock, from his based to his tip, then back again. "But harder."

I grip him tighter.

He guides me through another stoke.

His eyes flutter closed. For a moment, pleasure spreads over his expression, then his eyes blink open and fix on me.

"Harder?"

"Perfect."

The praise makes my sex clench. It's absurd, and I don't give a fuck.

He guides my hand to his base. "Keep it there. So you don't gag." He releases my arm and brings his hand to the back of my head. "I meant it, Sienna. I won't be gentle."

"I don't want you to."

"You want it rough, sweetness?"

My cheeks flush. "Yes."

"You want me to fuck your pretty mouth?"

"Yes."

"Good girl."

Fuck. My entire body hums. I shouldn't like the compliment so much—it's praise for a small animal, not a person— but I do.

"I've got you." His fingers curl into my hair. "And you're going to do exactly what I say."

"Yes."

He pulls my head into his lap. It's not gentle, exactly, but it's not rough either. He's leading, not pushing.

My lips brush his tip. Soft skin over hard flesh. It's so much like kissing him, but so different too.

"Try it. Test me." His fingers curl into my hair. "See what you like."

What I like? I don't care what I like. I want to see what he likes. But then I guess that is what I like.

I brush my lips against his tip again. Then along his shaft.

He shudders.

This time, I'm the one teasing him. And, fuck, I like winding him tighter.

I do it again, as softly as I can.

A groan falls from his lips.

Again and again.

Until his hand knots in my hair. "Lips around your teeth."

I slide my lips over my teeth.

He pulls me onto his cock. There's no other way to explain it.

My lips slide around his tip.

I swirl my tongue around him reflexively. I want to taste him, test him, see what makes him groan.

His fingers curl into my hair as I flick my tongue against his tip. The top. Then the bottom.

Hard and fast.

Soft and slow.

He gives me a moment to explore him.

Then his grip tightens and his voice drops. "Press your tongue against me."

I do.

"Stay like that. I'll guide you."

I groan a yes against him.

His thighs shake.

It's strange, being in this position, taking orders, but in the best possible way.

Cam is in my mouth.

It's every fucking thing.

His palm goes to the back of my head. Slowly, he guides my mouth over him. From his tip, down his shaft, to where my hand is wrapped around him.

It's deep.

Almost too deep.

Then too deep.

I pull back as I gag. All the way back. Off him. Almost upright.

For a second, I worry I'm doing it wrong, that I can't handle it the way he likes.

Then he looks at me like he's going to consume me and

he brings his hand to my cheek. "Not so deep."

"It's…"

"Next time. I'll order you onto your knees and fuck your pretty mouth."

Mmm. Next time. Yes, there needs to be a next time.

"This time, like this."

"This is good?"

"Perfect." He takes my hand, guides it a little higher. "Keep it there."

I run my thumb over him then tighten my grip.

He lets out a soft groan.

Mmm, I want to do this all day. I want to test him and tease him and toy with him.

But I want this more.

For him to guide me, take me, use me even.

I'm not sure why that's so fucking hot but it is.

"You ready, sweetness?" His fingers curl into my hair again.

"Yes." I run my thumb along him again. "I want to taste you. I want you to come in my mouth."

His pupils dilate. "Good girl."

Mmm.

He pulls me into his lap again.

I slide my lips over my teeth and take him into my mouth. For a second, I stay there, savoring the pressure of his flesh against mine.

Then I press my tongue against his base and I go along for the ride.

He pushes his hand into the back of my head, guiding me over him. With my hand a little higher, I can take all of him.

He starts slowly.

Then he pushes harder.

He guides me again and again. Until I have the rhythm

on my own and I start to lead.

His hand knots in my hair. The other goes to my chest.

He toys with my nipples as I take him.

Every brush sends pleasure through my body. It feels so fucking good, taking him as he teases me.

A beautiful cycle of pleasure.

And me, driving him crazy, pushing him to the edge.

I run my mouth over him with that same speed, the same pressure.

Again and again.

Until he lets out a low, deep groan. "Fuck, Sienna." He pushes me harder.

Faster.

I take him again.

Harder.

Deeper.

His thighs shake.

His breaths run together.

His cock pulses against my lips.

He groans my name as he comes. He pulls me over him as he spills into my mouth.

Warm and sticky and a little sweet.

I just barely manage to swallow.

He tugs at my hair, letting out another groan of appreciation. This beautiful sound that means I'm his entire fucking universe.

Then he pulls me up, wipes my lips with his thumb, helps me into my clothes.

"Good?" I smooth my tank top.

"You couldn't tell?"

"I still want to hear it."

"Fucking perfect." He pulls me into a slow, deep kiss.

And, once again, I'm somehow completely satisfied and entirely in need at once.

Chapter Thirty-Seven

SIENNA

Cam gives me two minutes to catch my breath, then he pulls me into his lap, rolls my jeans to my ankles, rubs me until I come.

"Fucking beautiful," he purrs as I groan his name.

It is. I understand his obsession with my bliss now. It feels fucking good making him come.

I want to do it again.

Now.

Forever.

Also now.

Did I mention now?

"Could you?" I run my fingers over his neck.

"Could I what?"

"Go again."

He chuckles. The same chuckle from earlier. *You're ridiculous and I like it.* "I really like you, Sienna."

"That isn't an answer."

He pulls me into a long, slow kiss.

"Also not an answer."

"Are you complaining?"

"No," I murmur into his lips. "I just…"

"No." He helps me into my jeans. "Not yet."

"But in… thirty minutes?"

Again, he chuckles. "Usually, about that."

"Can I set the clock?"

"Tonight. If you have the energy."

"You promise?"

"What do you think?"

"That really sounded like a promise."

He smiles. "If you convince me."

Mmm. Yes. Okay. I can work with that.

Again, I fix my clothes, check my hair, shoot him a wink as I reapply my lipstick.

When the car stops, I have no idea where we are and I don't care. I want to stay in this perfect small space forever.

But the driver opens the door and offers his hand.

Uh… I should probably wash my hands first. "I've got it."

Cam catches my meaning right away. He motions something to the driver—some rich guy code—and helps me out of the limo.

And we're the last place I expect.

We're actually at the MoMA.

God help me.

Chapter Thirty-Eight

SIENNA

"**A**rt?" My nose scrunches. "Really?"

"I know it's no *Ninety Day Fiancée*."

"Obviously."

He chuckles. "But there are paintings you'll like."

"Really?"

"Really." He presses his palm into my lower back to lead me into the space.

Mmm. I'm not sure I can turn down anything that includes that steady, reassuring gesture.

After we wash up in the bathroom (separately, tragically), he shows me around the museum.

For a museum supposedly devoted to modern art, there's a lot I recognize. Not just that guy who paints an entire canvas blue (he's at the Met, apparently). A sculpture garden, realistic self-portraits, impressionist work.

Usually, I don't get it. It's some bushes and the sky only all swirly.

But Cam explains the movement to me. (He knows a lot about art). It started as a small movement of artists, mostly in a single neighborhood in Paris, reacting to the previous realistic movement.

They wanted to create something new. To capture their unique point of view of the world instead of a literal reading of it.

And isn't that the point of art? Even if it's *Ninety Day Fiancée*.

It entertains, yes.

But it also expresses a world view, whether it's a big blue canvas, a graphic novel, a reality TV show, or a swirling painting of cypress trees.

Impressionists wanted to create the sensation of viewing something rather than recreating it line for line or hue for hue. They made big advances in paint and color theory. And the reason why Van Gogh painted those bright yellow sunflowers everyone knows is that the medication treating his mental illness changed the way he saw yellow.

His story isn't one of an artist's madness or darkness turning into art. Not completely.

It's also of healing creating art.

The yellow sunflowers.

All the paintings he made in the institution.

I don't know a lot about the guy besides the swirling colors and the whole chopping off his ear thing, but after a semester in Amsterdam (and an art history class on Impressionism), Cam knows everything.

His voice changes when he explains Van Gogh's supposed descent into darkness. It's something he's thought about a lot.

Something meaningful to him.

Because of how he hated himself?

How his first experience with sex was fucked up?

I'm not sure. I don't ask.

Instead, I let him talk about art and artists and

Amsterdam and how he wants to show me the neighborhood in Paris that housed the impressionists and the rest of the city too.

Is that really possible?

I'm not sure, but I let myself believe it anyway.

We stop in front of the crown jewel of the museum.

The Starry Night.

I've seen a thousand prints. On walls, t-shirts, mouse pads, screensavers. None of them do the painting justice.

There's an energy to the paint strokes. Somehow frenetic and calm at once.

Like a dream.

Like this weekend.

We stay in that state all night.

As we grab dinner at a hole in the wall restaurant with amazing Kung Pao.

As we walk to the ice cream shop with the chiffon yellow walls and I tell him about Eve and Indigo and how scared I am of losing my sister or life changing.

I want the world for her; I do.

But I miss the home we used to have too.

He orders the non-dairy mint chip to tease me, but when I try it, I have to admit, it's really fucking good.

We walk up to Washington Square Park, and I show him around campus, the outside at least. I show him where I get coffee, where I study, where I break for lunch most days.

He smiles as he imagines me there, imagines my life, and maybe where he'd fit into it.

Or maybe that's me.

I don't mention it, but I let my thoughts wander. I let myself consider how Cam could fit into my every day.

Would I live with him one day in some grand apartment in the Financial District? Or maybe a modern loft? A charming place in the Village, near school?

I'm here for the next four years, but after that... I don't know. I always imagined myself staying in New York City, but then I never considered falling for a handsome British billionaire.

Would he live here for me? For four years?

Forever?

Would I leave my sister and move to London?

She'd have plenty of reason to visit, but it's still strange to imagine. In all my many visions of my life, I always prioritized staying near her. Even when my only option was a Division I soccer scholarship, I planned to attend the university closest to New York City. (My life would have been so much easier if Columbia offered me a full ride).

And now...

I guess this is how it works. Growing up. Changing.

For her. For me.

For Cam too.

After a long talk at the fountain in Washington Square Park, we take the car to his hotel room, and he guides me to the bedroom, strips me out of my clothes, binds my arms over my head, and he fucks me.

He's still firm and in control, but it's a little softer, a little slower, a little more of him yielding to me.

I finally understand how Indie talks about sex.

It's really good like this too. Special in a different way. Intimate in a different way.

But not as fun as him ordering me out of my clothes.

After, he runs a bath, helps me clean, puts me to bed.

It's all softness, all tenderness, all love.

Well, something like it.

Not what I expect.

Better.

So much better.

Chapter Thirty-Nine

CAM

I t should feel wrong, climbing into bed next to Sienna—
At the very least, it should feel temporary.

But it doesn't.

I love the feel of her body against mine. I love the sight of her long limbs tangled in the white sheets, her hair falling over the pillow, her chest rising and falling with her slow, steady breaths.

I fall asleep quickly. Wake rested and refreshed and ready to torture her as much as possible.

I wash, dress, finish some necessary work, make an excuse for why I can't see Ty.

She wakes a little later. Emerges from the bedroom with tired eyes and an adorable yawn. "Why did you let me sleep?"

"You looked tired."

"But..." She tugs at the sheer t-shirt covering her torso. "We could have had sex."

I shake my head.

"Why not?"

"You need your energy."

"You know, you really talk big." She lets out another yawn. "You're setting yourself up to fail."

"Have I not lived up to your expectations?"

She tries to shrug *maybe, maybe not* but it only lasts a few seconds. She smiles wide, her entire expression bright and warm. "You have an entire day. Are you really going to spend it making me come?"

"What do you think I'm going to say?"

"Yes, Sienna, I dream about your bliss. It's all I want in the world."

"Most of it."

She moves closer. "So…"

"I enjoy making you wait."

She makes a show of pouting but it's as short-lived as her shrug. She crosses the room and wraps her arms around me.

I pull her into a soft, slow kiss.

It's sweet, gentle, romantic.

There's nothing carnal about it. Sure, I want her. I want to throw her against the wall and fuck her until she's screaming my name.

But I want to claim her like this too. Not just her body but her head and her heart.

Mine, mine, mine.

It echoes through my head like a whisper. Like a memory.

I haven't wanted that in fifteen years, but right now, I do.

Of course, I want more; it's the one woman I can't have. That must be why I want more.

I can't have it. So it's safe to want. It's safe to want to offer my heart to someone entirely off-limits, because I can't.

I can tell myself it's the circumstance or loyalty or duty or anything but my inability to love.

She pulls back with a sigh and a smile. "I'm awake and alert now."

"What do you mean?" I play dumb.

"We could have sex now."

"You're supposed to play along."

"I just told you I'm going to make you wait."

Again, she makes a show of pouting. "Wouldn't it be more fun for everyone if we had sex right now?"

I'm considering it. We only have the day. Why waste hours making her wait when I could have her again and again? "No."

"Just no?"

"Maybe after breakfast."

"Breakfast?"

"The meal that starts the day."

"Shit." Her brow screws. "Indie and I are supposed to have brunch. We do it every Sunday." Her eyes go to the clock. "She's supposed to stop by my apartment in ten minutes. I can tell her I'm on a run, but…"

If her sister shows up at her apartment to find it empty, she'll start asking questions.

"I, uh, I can meet her there." She finds her cell and taps a text to her sister.

"Do you need help?"

"No. I don't think so." Her phone buzzes in her hand. She glances at the screen. Lets out a sigh. "Okay, she's fine to meet me there. So I'm good." She kisses me again. "It should only be a few hours. I'd cancel, but…"

It would be suspicious. "Go, be with your sister." That's what I want for her. I want her to keep her best friend.

"Are you sure?"

"Positive."

"Will you promise to fuck me after?"

"What do you think?"

She brings her fingers to her lip corners and pulls them into an over the top frown.

"If you're going to be this cute about it, I'm going to keep torturing you."

"You're going to do it anyway." She pulls me into another slow, deep kiss. "You don't fool me."

"Are you sure?"

"Are you sure you won't promise?"

"Ask again and you'll get your answer."

She laughs and shakes her head. "I think that's a bluff, but I'm not going to risk it."

She moves into the bedroom, dresses in yesterday's tank and jeans, slips her essentials into her pocket, and kisses me goodbye.

Then she leaves and the room isn't the same without her.

Chapter Forty

SIENNA

When we were kids, Mom made breakfast every day. If Dad was home, that meant eggs, bacon, and toast. A manly breakfast that promised strength.

Why bacon is manly, I'm not sure, but it is. And my dad was a firefighter. He had odd hours. I was too young to keep track of his schedule.

So when I woke up to the smell of bacon and coffee, I knew he was home. I knew we'd go play at the park or jam out to old records (I didn't appreciate the nuance, sure, but I liked to dance) or watch a movie on the couch.

I knew everything was okay. I didn't even understand why it was okay, but I had that sense of safety.

When he died, the breakfasts stopped. Not just the feast Mom made when Dad was home. The faster, easier eggs and toast. Or crock pot oatmeal. Or, sometimes, if we were lucky, pancakes or French toast.

It was me and Indie and cold cereal—she's really not much of a cook—until I was old enough to fix breakfast and I brought back the tradition.

No full feasts, but eggs and toast, and on the weekends, something delicious and sweet.

When we lived in Brooklyn, we sat together every Sunday, for a fancy, at home brunch just for us. And when she moved in with Ty (unofficially then officially), we switched to a restaurant with really good French toast.

Since she can't cook and my apartment is too small to host and we don't need Ty intruding on our girl time.

Although I do consider it sometimes. Ty is a fantastic cook, and he even makes freaking amazing cinnamon roll French toast and while sugar isn't as great as girl time, it's very tempting early in the morning (okay, yes, we brunch at eleven o'clock) or after a run.

Most Sundays, I get up early to run, arrive fresh from the shower.

So, naturally, Indigo looks at me funny when I stroll into brunch with dry hair, in a tank and jeans and wedges way too cute for this time of morning.

"You look cute today." She greets me with a hug. "Running late getting dressed?"

"It's my last chance to show up the bride."

There. The change of topic sends her straight to Love Land. For a moment, she stares at the bright blue sky, no doubt imagining a vaguely phallic cloud is her fiancé's dick—

And now I'm imagining it's Cam's dick.

It's kind of an ill-shaped dick, being a cloud and all, but it still sends my thoughts to dirty places.

The feel of his hands in my hair.

The taste of him in my mouth.

The sweet pressure of him inside me.

I've always been obsessed with sex, but I've never been obsessed with dick. On its own, a dick is just a dick.

But attached to a sexy as fuck man like Cam.

Mmm…

Would he send me nudes if I asked?

Full-length ones?

With his face and his shoulders and his chest and his hand wrapped around his cock?

At least the lower abs? Or the thighs?

God, he has nice thighs. I haven't seen enough of them. He's always partially dressed. Every time we've fooled around, he's kept most of his clothes on.

I don't mind. If anything, it's really, really hot. But it's kind of strange I saw him more undressed on our run.

And I want him naked.

I just do. I want to see him and touch him and feel him and feel every inch of his skin against every inch of mine.

"Sienna?" Indie taps me on the shoulder. "You okay?"

Shit, I'm the one in the Love Zone. Or the Fuck Zone. Whatever the zone is called, I'm the one spacing out thinking about my man.

Even if he's only my man for another twenty-two hours.

Not that I'm counting.

What if I skip class Monday? Will he call in sick to work and spend the day with me?

Until soccer practice, at least?

Or maybe I can come back after practice, have dinner in his hotel room, fall asleep in his bed, wake up and push our date to Tuesday morning.

Or skip practice.

If that's what it takes.

Whatever it takes to fuck him again and again.

"Sienna?" she asks again.

Shit. "I missed my alarm." I take my seat at the cozy table. This place is a hidden gem on an easy to miss side street. It's small enough it's crowded with office workers Monday to Friday, but on weekends, it's calmer. Not calm enough to break free of its size. But reasonable for a New York City restaurant.

The tables are close together; the space is humming with conversation; the servers are quick and to the point.

And the coffee—

Mmm, the coffee.

Like an angel from heaven, the server appears, drops off waters, asks what we'd like.

We order our usual breakfasts and drinks. A latte with an extra shot for me. A black tea for Indie. Apparently, the brand they use here is second tier.

Not bad. Not great.

Good enough, considering the quality of the food and the difficulty of finding good tea anywhere other than a specialty shop.

The server jots our order and disappears with a nod. Unlike the blonde barista who clearly wanted to bone Ty, she's neither friendly nor flirty. She's to the point.

"You skipped your run?" She takes a long sip of her water. Leans into her seat, casual, relaxed, not at all suspicious I'm fucking Cam.

"I'll run later. It's supposed to be nice today." Or I'll get my work out in a much more fun way. There's time to run all week. I can skip one weekend.

My sister looks at me curiously. Is there suspicion in her eyes? Or am I imagining things.

"You look cute today. Not in white for once."

She laughs, and the furrow of her brow relaxes. "It's a little exhausting being bridal for three weeks straight."

"But you wear it well."

She swats *oh stop*.

It's almost normal, except for her getting married and thus wearing bright white every single night.

But right now, sitting at brunch, at a cafe that's actually in my price range, with my sister in her usual black jeans, black tank top, leather jacket getup—

Sure, the jacket is now real leather and her boots are now several hundred dollars instead of several dozen, and her purse is way more expensive than her old H&M one (but not into several-thousand-dollar designer)—

This is almost how things used to be. If I squint, we're back in Brooklyn and nothing has changed except for our dire need to make the mortgage payment.

And then I stop squinting and I see it. Her boots and purse and smile and my wedges and lingerie and sense of having recently been fucked and really wanting to fuck again.

Things are changing.

It's just how life happens.

But… maybe that's okay. "Will you promise me something?"

"Will you tell me why you missed your alarm and showed up in wedges?"

Uh… "I was out last night."

"Out…"

"With Katie. You remember Katie? Well, she needed help cramming for her Chem test, and even though it's basically AP Chemistry, which I took like two years ago, I offered to help. And she lives in Jersey with her parents. I'm not even sure how she makes it to soccer practice every day. And we were so late I fell asleep there and I had to take the train in this morning."

"You don't have to make something up," she says.

"I'm not." That happened. It was a few weeks ago, but it happened.

"You're an adult now, Sienna. I respect that. And I know you respect that being an adult means you're responsible for the consequences of your actions."

Uh-huh.

"You can stay out late at a party. If it means you have a hangover and you miss your run... that's not the end of the world. And if it means you're late to class and you miss an important test and your GPA falls... that's also not the end of the world. It's your mistake to make."

Right. I was at a party. "You got me. We weren't studying. We were at a party."

"In Jersey?" Her nose scrunches.

Why would any New Yorker go to Jersey? It's a serious step down. But it explains why I'm being secretive. "Well, there were supposed to be a lot of hot Princeton guys there."

"Were there?"

"The entire soccer team."

This time, her nose scrunches for a different reason. An older sister *oh god, please tell me you didn't gang bang the soccer team.*

"Don't worry, I only fucked one soccer player."

Her eyes go wide.

"Kidding." Sorta. "I didn't screw any Princeton players. But I had a lot of fun talking and I lost track of time and it was too late to make the train."

"Why didn't you Uber?"

"My phone died."

"And hers?"

I shrug like I didn't think of that. "We stayed with her parents."

Unlike my possible party going, or even sleeping with strange men, this fills my sister's face with concern. "Be careful without your phone. If there's an emergency—"

"I was with a friend."

"Yeah, but..."

The server interrupts with our drinks. She's fast, and not at all concerned with offering us privacy. She's in and out and clearly listening for a few feet. Then she moves onto another table like we don't exist.

312

I take a long sip of my coffee. Let the sweet, sweet caffeine rouse my senses. But I'm already awake and alert from all the desire racing through my veins.

"I'm sorry. You're a grownup. It's your business." She breaks open her bag of tea and places it in the clean ceramic pot. "It's bad enough Ty is… has he said anything to you?"

My danger alarm flashes. "About what?"

"Nothing. Forget I said anything."

He's worried about Cam. About me and Cam. Did he notice us leaving at the party or was he too lost in Love Land?

"Seriously, forget it. I love Ty, but he's so overprotective sometimes."

Okay, perfect, we're moving away from the topic of me hypothetically fucking Cam. I need to stay away from it. To keep her in Love Land, or at least Lust Land. "I can't believe you guys asked the dancers to stay."

That distracts her. Mostly. "It was only one dance."

"But they were grinding on you?"

"Maybe."

"Maybe? You're dropping a juicy detail like maybe and leaving it there?"

She smiles. "There's my sex-crazed kid sister."

"I'm not crazed." I'm so crazed. More crazed than ever. I need to mount Cam right now. Like right now. "I just find the subject matter interesting." I take another sip of my coffee. "Was it only one dance?"

"I think they call it a set. Three songs."

"And…"

"And… after, we made use of those under the bed restraints you left for us. That was very thoughtful."

"My idea."

"Very sweet. A little weird, but sweet." She shakes her head *you're ridiculous*. "Is that what you want to hear?"

Kind of. "Did you tell Eve?"

"Tell her what?"

"The details?"

She looks at me funny. "Why would I?"

"You're friends. Friends talk."

"Sure, I talk to her. Sometimes, I talk to her about sex. But she's not nearly as nosy as you are."

Right. There's no reason to be jealous. And I'm not even jealous. I just… whatever. I have more important things on my mind.

Like drinking this latte.

And eating my delicious French toast.

And fucking Cam.

And asking this—

"You didn't hear my request," I say.

She nods *shoot*.

"Will you promise we'll always get brunch? Every Sunday, as long as we're close enough. And when we're not, we'll call or Skype or text. Every Sunday."

"Of course." She smiles and holds out her hand. "I promise."

I shake.

Then I sip my coffee and eat my syrupy French toast and fall into a perfect morning with my sister.

The sister whose wedding I'm definitely not ruining.

No matter how badly that hurts.

———

AFTER MY SECOND LATTE, I SNEAK TO THE BATHROOM AND check my texts from Cam.

He's already had a busy morning. A run and a shower, then breakfast (naked, he's sad I missed it), and now he's at the office.

Sienna: Is that your excuse for wearing a suit?

Cam: It's not my fault you weren't here when I was naked.

Sienna: How can I know you were naked? Is there photographic evidence?

Cam: There might be.

Oh my god. My thighs shudder. My breath catches.

Photos of Cam naked.

Yes. Please. Now.

Sienna: Will you send them?

Cam: If you earn them.

Sienna: How do I do that?

Cam: I haven't decided yet.

Fuck.

Sienna: I sent you a picture.

Cam: I didn't ask you to.

Right. I probably should have waited on that. I mean, he was totally daring me, and he didn't seem all that upset, but now that I know more about Cam and his limits—

I kind of crossed the line there.

Sienna: I'm sorry. I should have asked.

Cam: I doubt other men would mind.

Sienna: I don't care about other men.

Cam: Next time, warn me first. I don't want to accidentally show a colleague your tits.

Mmm. Yes.

Cam: I don't want anyone else to see you.

Sienna: Are you trying to kill me?

Cam: Yes.

Sienna: It's working.

Cam: I know.

Sienna: If I send a picture now? Will that help?

Cam: Aren't you with your sister?

Sienna: In the bathroom.

Cam: Go be with your sister.

Sienna: Does that mean you don't want a picture?

Cam: Of course I want a picture.

Sienna: You're alone?

Cam: I'm the only one in the office.

Sienna: I wish I was there with you.

Cam: Me too.

Sienna: I can go after breakfast. Meet you there.

After I pick up a few things at home. And change into clean clothes.

Cam: I'm not sure. What would we do here? It would be boring if you watched me work.

Sienna: You could fuck me on your desk.

Cam: Could I?

Sienna: Or the conference table. The couch. Against one of those big glass walls.

Anywhere, really.

Yes.

So much yes.

Cam: I could. If you convinced me.

I need to clinch this deal.

So I roll my tank top to my waist, and I reapply my lipstick, and I angle my phone just right.

There.

I send Cam a picture of my sheer lingerie.

And then another one.

He replies quickly.

Cam: Are you tempting me, sweetness?

Sienna: If I am?

Cam: I'm going to have to get you back for that.

Sienna: Go on.

He sends the address.

Cam: Be here by two. Without your knickers.

Chapter Forty-One

CAM

I visit our New York office once a quarter, give or take. Usually, I only stay a few days. Usually, those days are filled with work.

There's no time to imagine fucking someone on my desk.

Right now, my head is flush with images.

There are so many places I can fuck Sienna.

The single stall bathroom at the end of the hall.

The conference room in the middle of the space.

And here, in my office, on the desk or the couch or against the wall.

I try to finish my work, but my concentration is shite. How the fuck am I supposed to think about numbers when her tits are on my cell screen?

After half an hour of struggling through a spreadsheet—one that should take me five minutes—I give up on work.

I let my head fill with images of her.

Hard and fast.

Soft and slow.

Rough.

Tender.

Intimate.

Whether I imagine her naked or dressed, bent over my lap, or staring into my eyes, it's intimate.

Am I really capable of that?

It's been a long time since I've even considered it, but I meant what I said yesterday; it's different with her.

I care about her.

I trust her.

I don't trust myself with her, not completely, but enough to give her what she wants.

If she still wants it rough—

Somehow, that's scarier than soft and slow. That's scarier than the two of us naked, pressed together, whispering I love you in each other's ears.

That image is hazy. A scene from a film.

The last time I told a woman I loved her—

It was Winter.

It was a sick love, one based on lies and manipulation, but it felt real to me.

Every molecule of my body craved every one of hers. And she used that like a weapon. She wielded *I love you* every time she didn't get what she wanted.

If I mentioned a friend who asked questions.

If I couldn't sneak away to see her.

If I wasn't sure I wanted to try something.

I love you, Cameron. Don't you love me? This is what people in love do. This is what love is. You love me enough to do this for me, don't you?

Did she mean it?

That's the sick thing. I think she did. I think, deep down, she really believed she loved me.

She really believed she was teaching me how to love.

I guess she was right. She taught me love was a weapon. One to avoid at all costs, whether on offense or defense.

And that tangled with sex.

For the last decade and a half, I haven't been able to fuck a woman without losing some part of myself.

Until Sienna.

It's terrifying. But there's plenty of time to consider that tomorrow.

Or next week.

After the wedding.

After I set her free, to find someone who won't fuck up her family, to find someone who can share every part of himself with her.

Sure, the thought of her with another man makes me sick, but—

No sense in dwelling on it today.

She's due here in twenty minutes. I need to prepare.

I need to make sure I'm reading her right.

I finish work, clean up, send her a text.

Cam: You still want it rough, sweetness?

She replies a few minutes later.

Sienna: Yes.

Cam: Can you handle that?

Sienna: I'm not sure, but I want to try.

Cam: Two. My office. Nothing under your clothes.

Sienna: Or…

I could threaten to punish her, but it's too tangled in my head. I don't trust myself to stay within her limits.

But this—

I can do this.

Cam: Or I won't fuck you.

———

AT FIVE TO TWO, THE LIFT DOORS SLIDE OPEN. FOOTSTEPS move into the hallway. They're fast, nervous.

Flat shoes, or at least ones with long soles.

Sienna turns the corner.

She's gorgeous in a fresh pair of jeans and a soft cream camisole. Silk. Something I bought her at the lingerie shop? Or something of hers?

I don't usually imagine her in silk. Sienna is an athlete. She lives in comfortable, sturdy fabrics, not ones that need dry cleaning.

But the sight of the smooth top clinging to her tits sends my senses into overdrive.

I'm already on edge. I need her so fucking badly, need this so fucking badly.

How the fuck am I going to stay in control?

How can I do anything but give her what she wants?

She turns the corner, moves straight to my office—it's the only one with a light on—stops in front of the door.

She looks at me through the glass walls.

I nod *come in*.

She turns the knob and presses the door closed behind her. "Cam." Her breath hitches as she leans against the glass. "Hi."

"You're early."

"Is that a problem?"

"No." Maybe one day I'll make it a threat. *Show up at two on the dot or I'll punish you.* Maybe one day I'll pull her over my lap and spank her.

It's fucking tempting.

But not today.

A voice in my head reminds me we only have today, but I push it aside. I don't want to be stuck in my fucked-up past or imagining a future without her.

I want to be here, with Sienna, in this beautiful moment.

Teasing her.

Torturing her.

Making her come.

"You changed." I stand. Check my desk one more time. It's set up for this. For her.

She looks up at me. "Was I not supposed to?"

"Did I buy you that?"

"No." Her chest rises with her inhale. The silk clings to her nipples. She's keyed up too. She's on the edge too. "I bought it when I was shopping with Indie. I don't remember."

"You like silk?"

"I've never worn it before." Her fingers curl into the glass. "Do you like it?"

"You care if I like it?"

She nods. "I want to drive you crazy."

"You do."

"Right now?" Her eyes fix on mine.

I move around the desk. Lean against the sturdy cherry surface. Motion *come here*.

She moves with soft steps. She's nervous.

Should I use that to push her? Or should I ease her into this?

I try to be careful with women, to set limits, find theirs, make sure we're both clear on what's happening.

I don't want to fuck them up.

But I don't want them enough for it to cloud my judgment.

With Sienna—

I can't tell where I'm reading her and where I'm letting my desire overwhelm me.

I want her so fucking badly.

She crosses the space. Stands there, so fucking close to touching me, but so far too.

She's in a different pair of shoes. One that brings us eye to eye. And her hazel eyes are filled with a beautiful mix of desire, need, nerves, trust, affection.

I wrap my hand around her wrist gently. "This is what you do to me, sweetness." Slowly, I bring her hand to my cock.

Over my slacks.

She gasps as she curls her hand around me.

I test her by tightening my grip.

She lets out a soft groan. This is what she wants. Rough.

I want to give it to her.

I want to give her everything.

"You think you can get away with that?" I bring my hand to her cheek. Run my thumb over her temple.

Her expression gets hazy.

"You think you can tempt me like this?" I run my thumb over her chin. "And not give me what I want?"

"What do you want?"

I pull her body into mine, so she's pressed against my hard-on.

Her hips rock against me.

I pull her closer.

She gasps.

"You think you know what you're getting into?" I catch her bottom lip with my thumb. "You have no fucking idea."

She wraps her lips around the pad of my thumb, sucks hard, releases me. She's daring me.

Daring me to test her limits.

This is what she wants.

And I'm going to give it to her.

"I want to know." She looks up at me, proud and defiant. "I want everything you'll give me."

I bring my hand to her chest, pressing the smooth silk against her hard nipple. "You followed my orders?

She nods.

"Good girl," I purr.

She lets out a soft groan.

I toy with her, running my fingers over the smooth fabric. Slow circles to start. Then faster.

Harder.

Softer.

There. She shudders. Grabs onto my suit jacket. "Fuck."

I hold her body against mine with one hand. Use the other to toy with her. Again and again, until she's shaking.

Then I move to her other breast and I tease her mercilessly.

Her eyes close. Her breath hitches. Her fingers dig into my jacket.

Finally, I push the straps off her shoulders.

The loose top falls to her hips, then off them, all the way to the ground.

She kicks it aside. Looks at me with that same proud posture. She's not patient, but she's willing to wait, just to prove she can.

I bring my hand to her cheek again, and I trace a line down her chin. Slowly, I run my fingers down her neck, over her collarbones, between her breasts.

She shudders as my fingers brush her stomach.

The waist of her jeans.

I undo the button and the zipper, peel the denim just enough to check she's not wearing knickers.

She groans as I press my palm against her, over the denim. Again, I rub her through the material.

I rub her until her groans run together.

Until need fills her expression. Then impatience.

She hates waiting, but she loves it too, and she's not about to let me win the war of patience.

Of course, this is how I win. By having her exactly where I want her.

Giving her exactly what she wants.

Am I this far out of my fucking mind?

I haven't done this in a decade and a half. No matter how drunk and stupid I was, I always used a rubber.

Always.

And now—

Fuck, the thought of her flesh against mine threatens to derail me.

Soon.

But not yet.

Exactly like she wants.

I slip my leg between hers, bring my hands to her ass, pull her body over mine, so my thigh rubs against her cunt.

The denim and slacks in the way, but close. Really fucking close.

Her eyes flutter closed.

Her fingers curl into her palms.

She looks so beautiful on the edge, but I need more. I need everything.

I toy with her again and again, then I push off the table, pull her into my arms, swap our positions.

So she's against the desk and I'm in front of her.

Sienna stares at me for a second, then her eyes flutter closed, and she moves closer.

Almost all the way to kissing me, but not quite.

I leave her there for a moment, then I bring my hand to the back of her head, and I pull her into a hard, deep kiss.

I rock my hips, pinning her to the desk as I claim her mouth. She tastes so fucking good, like sugar and Sienna.

She pulls back with a sigh.

"Stay where you are." I pin her with my hips as I do away with my suit jacket.

My red tie.

She looks up at me expectantly, like she's not sure if she wants to ask me to take the rest of my clothes off or fuck her now or bind her wrists.

All of the above maybe.

But first, this.

I leave the tie on the desk, take her hand, bring it to my chest, to the first button on my shirt.

She slides onto the desk, looks up at me as she undoes the buttons, one at a time.

Her fingers brush my shoulder, collarbone, chest. "I've wanted to touch you for so long." She traces the lines of the broken heart tattooed to my chest. "I haven't seen this. It's beautiful."

She moves slowly, all intimacy, all tenderness.

Not the rough scene I imagined.

Soft and sweet, like she's desperate for every part of me.

Fuck. My eyes flutter closed as she runs her fingers over my skin.

She explores me slowly, like she's trying to savor every single sensation, like she's lost in the feeling of my skin against hers.

Or maybe that's me.

The intimacy of her touch overwhelms me.

It's been a long time since anyone has handled me this way. I've been with plenty of women, women who wanted me, who touched me.

But never like this.

Not even close to this.

"Can I?" Her voice is just as soft and yielding. "Cam?" Her fingers brush my shirt. "Can I?"

She wants to take it off.

I'm not sure I can handle it, but I nod anyway.

She pushes it off my shoulders. I let it fall to the ground, behind me.

I bring my hand to her cheek, stare into her eyes one more time, soak up this moment of intimacy.

Then I give her what she needs.

I take her hands, curl them around the desk. "Keep them there."

She nods.

I push her jeans to her ankles. I bend, peel the fabric from her feet.

So she's sitting on the desk, completely naked.

Fuck, I want to capture this image, stay with it forever. But I need more. I need all of her.

"Lie back."

She looks up at me, all that desire in her gorgeous hazel eyes.

"Spread your legs."

She does.

I slip two fingers inside her. She's already wet, but I push deeper, to make sure she's ready.

A little harder.

A little deeper.

Her eyes flutter closed. Her head falls to one side.

I work her one more time, then I raise her legs, hold them against my chest.

She's not bound, but she's at my mercy.

I look down at her. "Hands stay on the desk. Or I stop."

She nods with understanding.

I unzip my slacks. Let them fall to my ankles.

Then I bring our bodies together.

Closer.

Closer.

She groans as my cock brushes her cunt. "Fuck, Cam."

The last hint of stubbornness disappears from her expression. She doesn't care about winning or outlasting me or proving she's patient.

Only about our bodies joining.

"Fuck me." Her fingers dig into the desk. "Please."

I push into her slowly, savoring every sweet second.

She feels so fucking good. Soft and warm and mine.

Nothing in the way.

My flesh against hers.

All that trust flowing between us.

It's overwhelming.

I stay there for a second, then I pull back and I drive into her.

She shakes against the desk. She bounces. Lands on the leather mat—I prepared for this—with a soft impact. Lets out a soft groan. An *I want more groan*.

So I hold her in place and I drive into her again.

A little faster.

A little harder.

Her eyelids fall together.

Her brow softens.

Her thighs shake.

I find the rhythm she needs and I drive into her again and again.

She feels so fucking good too. It's almost too much to take.

No, it is.

I pull back.

She whines as our bodies separate. "Cam. Please." Her heels dig into my chest. "Please, fuck me."

I need to give her that.

I really fucking need to give her that.

And I need to come with her.

"Touch yourself." I dig my nail into her calf. Softly.

Then hard enough her groan is equal parts pain and pleasure.

"My hands—"

I told her to keep them there. "Which do you use?"

"The right."

"Keep the left on the desk."

She nods, slips her hand between her legs immediately. There isn't a single shred of patience in her posture.

She's desperate to come.

Desperate for me.

It's so fucking beautiful.

It's everything.

I watch her wind herself tighter, watch pleasure spill over her expression until she's so fucking close.

Then I dig my nails into her thighs, and I drive into her.

I fuck her with steady thrusts.

Hard and deep, so I feel all of her, and she feels all of me.

Her head falls back as she rubs herself.

Her groans deepen. Her breath hitches.

She's close.

And I need that.

I really fucking need that.

"Look at me, sweetness." I scratch her again.

Her eyes burst open. "Fuck." She sucks in a deep breath and looks up at me.

For a moment, our eyes meet, and she sees everything inside me.

And I see everything inside her.

Then I drive into her again, and it pushes her over the edge.

Her eyes close, her nails scrape the desk, her heels dig into my chest.

She groans my name as she comes, pulsing around me, pulling me closer.

It pushes me over the edge.

I thrust through my orgasm, spilling inside her, claiming her as mine.

She is.

Maybe not for long.

But for now.

Chapter Forty-Two

SIENNA

After Cam cleans me up, and helps me into my clothes, we go uptown, to the fucking Met.

Another art museum and I love every second.

We hold hands and eat hot dogs in Central Park and walk around the reservoir. We talk about where Cam would live in New York City.

A fancy, old penthouse on the Upper East Side?

Some new construction in the gentrifying Hell's Kitchen.

Or maybe somewhere like Ty? A big Financial District palace.

A house way out in Queens.

A loft in the Village.

I can see him anywhere, everywhere. But I like picturing him living near a park. Any park, as long as it has a lawn, and he can get up early to run. Or reserve the field for a game.

We eat dinner at a fancy Italian place and walk through Times Square—everyone has to see it once—and make our way to the bar where Indie used to work.

He orders something sweet for me.

It's perfect, exactly what I want. I drink every sip.

The bartender recognizes me.

I fill her in on my sister's life—mostly the whole marrying a billionaire thing. She swoons over the story then she asks if Mr. Tall, Handsome, and British is mine and I say yes.

It's true for tonight.

And that's true enough for now.

At the hotel, I undress and shower and find a fancy silk robe waiting for me. Burnt orange, of course. Cam hates to be cheesy but it looks damn good on me.

And, well, I can't really complain about him draping me in silk.

We stay up late watching *Casablanca* and talking about the movie and my how my parents loved it and how it used to feel like home.

How it still does.

But it doesn't too, because Mom and Dad are gone, and everything is changing.

Everything is always changing.

And then he strips me out of his robe, and pulls me into his lap, and we fuck face-to-face, him watching bliss spread over my expression, me savoring the feeling of my hands on his skin.

It's intense in an entirely different way.

When he puts me to bed, he lies there with me, his body cradling mine, his breath warming my neck, his hands in my hair.

And I fall asleep content, safe, completely at peace.

It's not forever.

But right now, it's really fucking good.

Chapter Forty-Three

SIENNA

I rouse as someone shifts off the bed.

"Sleep in." Cam presses his lips to my forehead. Pulls the covers to my chest. "I have to work."

"What time is it?" My sleepy brain struggles to keep up with events. He's leaving for work. That means something.

"Early. You have two hours until your first class."

Oh. Class.

Monday morning class.

Which means—

This is it.

I'm a pumpkin again. Or my shoes are pumpkins. Someone is a pumpkin.

"Is this goodbye?" My eyes blink open. Fix on him.

He's so handsome in the morning light.

All tall and broad and shirtless.

Mmm, Cam's shoulders. Cam's chest. Cam's chiseled torso.

I want to trace the lines forever.

But this is it. Goodbye.

I expect him to protest, say something about how we'll always be friends, but he doesn't.

He nods. "I'll miss you."

"You have to say a proper goodbye."

"I do?"

"Yeah. Hold on. Let me brush my teeth."

His eyes go to his watch.

"I'll be fast. I promise."

He nods *go ahead.*

I rush to the bathroom, pee, wash, brush my teeth, meet him in the main room.

He's already in his suit, even the jacket.

And I'm naked. "Well, that's not fair."

"And you torturing me is?"

Am I really the one torturing him? He's incredibly yummy in his suit, but I'm not going to waste time arguing.

I move closer.

He meets me halfway. One hand goes to my lower back. The other goes to my chin.

He tilts my head so we're eye to eye, then he pulls me into a slow, deep kiss.

It's not like our other kisses. It's still intense and hot as hell, but there's a sadness to it too.

We both know this is goodbye.

Our last kiss.

Our last chance to consume each other.

He claims me with his kiss, his finger curling into my skin, his tongue swirling around mine.

Then he pulls back with a heady sigh and he looks at me like he loves me and he says goodbye. "I'll miss you too."

I don't know what to say, so I nod, and I watch him leave, and I savor my hour in his hotel room.

The silk robe, the room service breakfast, the smell of his suit jacket.

The present he left on the table.

Then I pack, and I go back to my apartment to shower and dress and get ready for school, and I turn back into a pumpkin.

Chapter Forty-Four

SIENNA

N o matter how hard I try to concentrate on math or lunch or conversation with Alice, I drift back to Cam.

His dark eyes, his intense voice, his sweet smile.

His hard body against mine.

His soft skin against my palm.

His deep groan in my ear.

Between classes, I open the present he left me.

Cuff links. Tiny silver circles engraved with his initials.

I read the tiny card—black ink on cream stock—again and again.

You look more dapper in a suit than I do. And I like thinking of you in something of mine, something secret.

Wear them well.

XO Cam

There's no way to explain these.

They mark me as his. Yes, they're small and easy to miss, but anyone who looks closely will see.

I belong to him.

Maybe not anymore. Not the way I did yesterday. But a part of me still does, a part of me always will.

And now… a part of him will always belong to me.

It's more than the cufflinks. It's something else, something I can't see or touch or taste. Some ephemeral quality like love or trust or devotion.

Not what I usually crave.

But with him…

I want all of it.

————

SOCCER PRACTICE MANAGES TO STEAL MY ATTENTION. FOR the first time all day, I focus on something other than Cam.

I run, I dribble, I kick ass in our scrimmage.

And then I head home, shower, try to find distraction in my homework. When that fails, I climb the floors to Ty and Indigo's place. They're busy, hosting Ty's mom, and some other friends from London, but it's nice being another person at the party.

I stick with Mrs. Hunt, mostly talking about London and embarrassing stories about Ty. She has plenty—no big surprise, he was as exact and restrained as a kid—and I manage to enjoy the evening.

This is what matters. My sister, my family, her new family.

It makes sense ending this thing with Cam.

It's all that makes sense.

But no matter how much I repeat the mantra, I keep drifting back to Love Land. I trace his cufflinks and crave his touch and dream about his lips.

And I wake up empty and lonely and completely uncertain of how to square these two truths.

My sister is the most important person in my life. I can't

risk ruining her wedding or her family or her husband's closet friendship.

And I can't stand being away from Cam.

I repeat the mantra all day. Every time my thoughts turn to Cam. To his dark eyes or his soft smile or that sound he makes when he comes.

It doesn't make sense.

This is what makes sense.

And we're smart people. Logical people who do what makes sense.

I need time to get over it, to find another guy who sets me on fire, to put the Atlantic Ocean between us.

Or another focus for my energy. Something more engaging than Psychology 101 lectures.

So when my phone buzzes with a possible distraction, I size the opportunity.

Eve: Hey Sienna, I hope I'm not interrupting your school work. I'd love to ask a favor when you have a second.

Sienna: Shoot.

Eve: I want to buy your sister a wedding present, but I'm not sure where to start.

Sienna: You hang out a lot. You know her well.

Eve: Not as well as you do.

My fingers brush my phone case. It's almost like she's trying to smooth things over, but nothing needs smoothing.

Is my jealousy as obvious as Cam suggests? Or did he talk to her and suggest this?

No. I'm reading into things.

Cam and I are back to family friends.

Eve wants help with my sister's gift.

There are no ulterior motives.

Sienna: Do you have something in mind?

Eve: A friend of mine has an indie lingerie shop in Alphabet City. Or is that too much for Ty too?

Sienna: Kind of. But she'll like it.

Eve: I'm taking the afternoon off tomorrow to shop. How about I buy you dinner after?

Sienna: Make it coffee first and we have a deal.

Eve: Done.

Sienna: One at that shop around the corner from your place? The one with the New Orleans style cold brew.

Eve: It's a date.

Chapter Forty-Five

SIENNA

Even though I arrive early, Eve beats me to the coffee shop. She's sitting at a table in the back, sipping a milky iced coffee, reading something on her Kindle.

She's in her usual *punk rock badass* getup—combat boots, short black dress, leather jacket—and her makeup and hair are on point.

But she doesn't look like an evil intellectual bitch stealing all my sister's attention.

She looks like a young woman who doesn't really care what other people think of her. Or at least one rebelling against what people expect her to do.

What with the short teal hair and the wine lips and the *I'll kick your head in* boots.

It's kind of cool, even if it's so incredibly extra. Or maybe because it is.

Her eyes light up as she spots me. She waves, slips her Kindle into her purse, slides off the seat.

She moves like a New Yorker, with quick steps and an innate understanding of her surroundings.

"Hey!" She offers me a hug. When I accept, she squeezes me tightly, motions to the line. "What are you having?"

In her lightly heeled boots, we're the same height, and we're about the same size, but we're built very differently.

I'm all shoulders and muscle. She's all hips and ass.

And she really has a lot of tattoos. Ian is obsessed with the quote from *The Handmaid's Tale* on her forearm. The first time, it was cute. After a hundred stares…

I usually roll my eyes. But it is cool. A Latin quote on a ribbon, surrounded by lush flowers.

nolite te bastardes carborundorum

Don't let the bastards grind you down. I've heard Ian tease her enough times to know that. And I'm literate enough I know the book is basically a feminist manifesto.

I always thought she was… I don't know, making a point, trying to make me feel less than.

But she's not. She's just trying to be her. And her tattoo really is gorgeous. And it's her too.

I'm almost jealous. She's so brave to face the needle that many times.

And she's so sure of who she is. Sure enough to mark her skin forever.

Usually, I feel confident, sure of myself, like I know exactly who I am and what I want.

Right now—

Fuck, I miss Cam.

"I have to warn you." Eve motions to her tattoo, to me staring at her tattoo. "If you ask about it, I might not be able to stop gushing."

"Huh?"

"The book. I'm sure I've gone off on it around you at some point. Ian is always baiting me."

Yes, he loves pushing her to talk about her favorite book.

As a way to tease her. And because he loves to sit there, watching her talk, absorbing every ounce of her enthusiasm.

He really loves her. All of her.

They're kind of obnoxious sometimes with their constant making out, but I have to admit I'm in awe of the passion.

And totally not thinking about what it would be like if it was me and Cam. And what tattoo I would get that would get him teasing me every day.

Something about soccer. Or *Ninety Day Fiancée* (it's really a great show). Or my love of sugar.

Or a Blue Sapphire martini.

"Yeah," I say. "But I was thinking more about the needle. How much does it hurt?"

"You don't have any?"

"I never really wanted one."

"It's a needle on your skin. It hurts, but some spots worse than others." She turns over her arm. Shows off the EKG line on her wrist. "The lines closer to the palm were brutal, but the ones here"—she traces a flower on her forearm—"they're not so bad."

"Was that the most painful spot?"

"No. The ribs. Or maybe the hips." She draws a line on her hipbone, over her dress. "That was brutal."

"You have a tattoo there?"

"I have tattoos a lot of places."

"How did you get so many in such a short time?"

"A friend who started doing them when I was sixteen."

The person in front of us finishes ordering. The barista calls us forward.

I'm not sure what I want—my head is still screaming *Cam, Cam, Cam*—so I order my usual New Orleans style cold brew. The barista asks Eve if she wants another. She says yes, whips out her credit card, swipes.

She's not as seamless as Indie. Not even close to as seamless as Ty or Ian or Cam.

She's almost… awkward. Not the vision I have of her as the girl who somehow belongs to this world and shines as an outsider at once.

She's new to it too.

She's like me, really. She grew up in Brooklyn without all that much.

And now she has everything. Money and security and the love of a man who makes her come.

I swallow the jealousy that rises in my stomach. It's not even about my sister this time.

It's Cam.

I want his love. I want his lust. I want his everything.

Most of all, I want that to make sense, but it doesn't.

It can't.

We move aside, to the pickup area of the tiny shop. Eve takes another sip of her milky drink then offers one to me. "Cold brew with almond milk."

"You're having a second?"

She nods. "I didn't sleep well last night."

"Boyfriend… distractions?"

"Kind of." She offers the cup again. "You sure you don't want a sip?"

"I need it pretty sweet."

She smiles *fair enough*, takes the last sip, tosses the drink. "Have you ever wanted a tattoo?"

"When Indie got her first one, I thought it was really cool. I wanted to be more like her, get my own. I told her and she freaked out. Even after she got a second and a third and a fourth. Such hypocrisy, huh?"

Eve smiles. "What did she say?"

"To wait until I turned eighteen. And then, if I thought

of a design I wanted, try it out for a few weeks before I get it. But I haven't wanted anything enough."

"It's not for everyone."

"Maybe." Instantly, my thoughts go to Cam. The broken heart on his chest. The feel of the ink on his skin. The lines are raised. Just barely, but they are. It's like I'm tracing some part of his soul.

"I know a good artist if you change your mind."

"Weren't you scared?"

"The first, I was. Of the permanence. And the needle. It hurts. It hurts a lot, but after a few pricks, your body starts releasing all these endorphins and it still hurts, but it's kind of a high too."

"Like… pain during sex."

She shoots me a curious look. "Sort of."

The barista calls our drinks. After Eve grabs hers, she motions to the door *shall we*. I nod and follow her onto the street.

I button my coat, try to hold in all my warmth, but it's a lost cause. Between the cold drink and the dull ache in my chest, I'm completely lacking energy.

How am I supposed to make it to practice?

How am I going to run sprints like this?

How can I do anything else? Cam occupying my thoughts during class is one thing. Cam keeping me from soccer is another. That's a line I can't cross. It's just… wrong.

She sips her cold brew. Lets out a soft sigh of pleasure. The one that means *sweet, sweet caffeine*.

"Don't you drink tea?" I ask.

She laughs. "Usually."

"But you got a coffee? Because you're tired?"

"And because there's no good tea at that place."

Indie says the same thing about most coffee shops. But she still goes for coffee with me. She still sits and sips a mediocre black tea as I groan over my latte. "We could have gone somewhere else."

"Next time." Eve smiles. "I needed the extra caffeine today." She holds out her arm to hail a cab. "Are you still thinking lingerie works? My friend's shop is open for another few hours."

She's going to a local designer. That's so her.

For a second, it annoys me. Why does she think she's so special and important?

But that's ridiculous. Local shops are what make the city great. Especially artists and designers. We're supposed to be the fashion capital of the US.

Sure, I don't get fashion, but I can appreciate it's our thing.

And where else would we go? La Perla is expensive. Victoria's Secret is disgustingly pink.

A local shop is perfect for my sister.

"Definitely," I say.

"Perfect." She points to the cab that stops in front of us. Opens the door for me. Motions *after you*.

I slide inside.

She slides after, instructs the driver, pulls the door closed.

And we're off, heading to an area of the city with terrible subway coverage. It makes more sense to take a cab, but it doesn't really strike me as Eve either.

Maybe I don't know her that well.

Maybe I should stop making assumptions.

Maybe I should focus on anything that isn't Cameron Hunt.

"How's the coffee?" she asks.

"Sweet."

"Too sweet?"

"I'm not sure that's in my vocabulary."

"I wouldn't peg you as someone with a sweet tooth."

"Because I'm an athlete?"

She shakes her head. "Because you're tough."

"Really? Everyone thinks I look nice."

"Sure, you look like someone who will give me directions. But when you turn on that fire, the way you do when you talk about sports—you look like you'll destroy anyone in your way."

That's probably true.

"Whereas I have a resting bitch face." She laughs. "But it's nice in its own way. People don't mess with me."

"What about guys who are into tough babes?"

"Nothing stops them."

"You probably got that a lot. At your old job. I know Indie did and that place wasn't…"

"A strip club?"

"It was supposed to be refined."

"Devil's Point was not trying to be refined. The most popular dancers were playing up blonde bimbo stereotypes."

"Like Britney?"

"Yeah. She's usually in a schoolgirl skirt and pigtails. Guys eat it up. But the owner wanted a lot of different types of women, so he could cater to all tastes. He hired me because he didn't have any 'punk bitches.' He thought I'd start dancing after a few weeks, when I saw the dancers were making four or five times what I was."

"Why didn't you?"

"I don't know. I thought I'd be able to do it. I thought I was the kind of person who did what it takes, even if it took touching strange men. But I couldn't get past it. The men at the club acted like twenty dollars bought them carte blanche."

"Did it?"

"Not exactly. But, well… let me demonstrate. Try to touch me and I'll stop you."

"Try to touch you?"

She laughs. "It doesn't have to be sexual."

Okay… I reach for her shoulder.

She grabs my arm and says, "don't" in a firm voice. "That's how I want to stop you. I can trust you to take it, because you're a uh—"

"Tactless bitch?"

"You appreciate directness."

I nod.

"But if you were a guy, or my boss, I might have to be a little softer." She cops a gentle voice. "'Please don't.' Or 'not right now.'"

"Of course."

"But the way dancers have to do it… do it again."

Okay. I reach for her shoulder again.

This time, she doesn't stop me. She lets my hand graze her shoulder. Then she giggles as she gently takes my wrist and moves my hand to my side. "Not yet, sweetie."

"They have to politely ask the guys not to grope them?"

"Basically."

No wonder she always wants to talk about dismantling the patriarchy. I've seen plenty of guys act like creeps. I saw a lot of guys hit on Indie at Rick's, but everyone was dressed. "Indie had to do the same thing, at Rick's, but with requests for sex. Never… so direct." I swallow another sip. "I can't imagine you putting up with that?"

"The punk bitch thing bought me a little latitude."

"But you still had to smile when guys asked if they could fuck you?"

"Or tried to grab my ass. But mostly, I was behind the bar, so it was a lot of pretending I didn't mind guys were talking to my boobs."

"But not always?"

"Not always," she says.

"Is that where you met Ian?" I ask.

"Kind of."

"Kind of?"

"It's a long story," she says. "And I'm sure you're sick of us."

A laugh spills from my lips. I motion *a little*.

"Were we obnoxious at the party?"

"I hate to be the one to break this to you, Eve, but the two of you are always obnoxious."

She laughs too. "Will you forgive me?"

"Maybe… let's hear your case."

"You have looked at him."

"A persuasive argument, but I'm mostly immune to Hunt charms," I say. "After so many dinners with Ty."

She raises a brow *are you*.

I blush. "I, uh, he is handsome. I'll concede that point."

"You don't think he's sexy?"

"Not so sexy I'd be totally unable to control myself."

"Fair." She laughs. "Completely fair."

"It's kind of amazing you two are that… hungry after a year."

She nods. "It's not the same as it was at first. I don't have that desperate need to consume every ounce of experience."

That's exactly how it feels.

"But I… well, I still need him. I need his love and his touch and his support. And, lately, with Ty's wedding… I can tell it brings up memories. I can tell when he's tensing and I just…"

"Want to relieve that tension?"

"I want him to feel something else, but yes." She looks at me. "It's not always about sex."

"Says the girl who makes out with her boyfriend every time I see her."

She nods *busted*.

"Does it bother you that he's upset about his ex-wife?"

"No."

"That he doesn't want to get married again?"

She shakes her head. "I never wanted to marry."

"Really? But he's so rich. And handsome. You have to lock that down."

She laughs. "It's the practical thing to do."

"Yeah, even with a prenup. I bet he'll offer a lot."

Her laugh gets louder. "Do you really believe that, Sienna?"

"That he'll offer you a lot in the prenup? Of course. He's crazy about you. You two are the only people who don't think you'll get married."

The car slows to a stop.

"No. Do you really believe the practicalities are all that matters?" She gets out. Holds the door open for me. Waits until I'm focused on the edgy lingerie store to spring. "Or has that changed since Friday night?"

"Huh?"

"You and Cam disappeared together."

Ahem.

"It's none of my business. I told myself I wouldn't ask, but there's something about you today, something different. What happened with the two of you?"

Chapter Forty-Six

SIENNA

What happened with the two of you?

My heart thuds against my chest. My fingers glide over the slick plastic. Somehow, I manage to hold my drink. I even take a sip.

The cold brew fails to lower my temperature. Why am I in this coat? It's hot. It's way too hot.

"You don't have to tell me," Eve says. "Really."

"But you…" I don't know where to start. Will she tell Ty directly or go through Ian? Or maybe straight to my sister. "It's nothing."

"Okay." She motions to the shop *after you*.

Somehow, I move into the cozy space. It's the size of my apartment, with a tiny dressing stall in the back and a lot of fabric. Lace, mesh, chiffon, silk. This place has it all. In every color of the rainbow and a whole lot of black.

Does Indie want something in black? Or maybe dark blue, deep teal, ink purple?

Something as bold as she is.

Will she even care about the lingerie after my news ruins her wedding?

"Sienna." Eve puts her hand on my shoulder. "I won't say anything. I promise."

"But—"

"Pretend I didn't ask."

"But—"

"It's none of my business."

But... I look for a place to put my drink, but there's nowhere.

Eve takes it. She helps me out of my coat, hangs it on the rack, sets the drinks... somewhere.

I think the room might be spinning. It's not as steady as it should be. But why would it be steady, when—

She grabs my hands. "Sienna, look at me."

Her eyes are green. A grey-green. And they're not lined in black like I suspected. Her makeup is a dark grey with a metallic sheen.

"I'm not going to tell anyone."

"Your boyfriend?"

"No."

"Won't he ask?"

"Yes. You two were gone for half an hour. It was hard to miss."

Oh.

"He won't say anything."

"Are you sure?"

"It's his job, guarding secrets. And... believe me, he acts like it."

"Oh." For a moment, my stomach settles, then I remember everything Cam told me about her and Ian. "But, uh, well... I know a lot about you."

"Me?"

"And Ian. Your... arrangement."

"Oh." Her cheeks flush. "Did Indie tell you?"

"You told her?"

"Some of it."

"No. Cam. Indie wouldn't... she's never said anything about you that would be a secret."

"Oh. I guess... I'll talk to Ian. I'll make sure he's quiet. Don't worry."

"Don't worry about him possibly telling his brother I slept with Cam?"

"You slept with him?"

Shit.

"Sorry. Still none of my business." She picks her jaw off the floor. "But, uh... Ian doesn't think you slept with him."

"No?"

"No. He doesn't think it went that far."

"Oh."

"But he wouldn't tell Ty either way. Cam is his friend too."

I motion *a little*.

"Okay, sure, his loyalty is with his brother, but he's good with secrets. Trust me."

Maybe. "Are you sure?"

"I am."

"Swear on something important to you."

"I swear on *The Handmaid's Tale*."

"How does that hurt you?"

"On my tattoo then." She taps her arm. "Ian won't say anything. I won't say anything. I swear on my tattoo. And my hatred of the patriarchy."

That does sound like a firm promise from her. "Okay."

"You want to sit down?"

"Maybe."

She guides me to a chair. Places my coffee in my hands. "We can leave it at that."

"Okay."

"Or... If you want to talk about it, you can talk to me. I won't say anything."

"What?"

"You and Indigo are really close. You tell each other everything."

Does she really think that? "Not about guys. You probably know more about her and Ty than I do."

"Maybe, but not from her. From Ty. He talks when he drinks, especially when Ian baits him. And Ian always baits him."

That's true.

"If you need someone to someone to talk to, I'm here."

"Oh. Thanks."

"Sure." She takes a spot on the floor next to me. Sips her coffee. "What did Cam tell you about me and Ian?"

"He bought your virginity for a lot of money."

Her smile is soft. Inviting. "More than half a million dollars. But it wasn't technically my virginity. I could say no at any point. He was going to pay me even if I never touched him."

"That's pretty BS. No offense, but we both know he bought your virginity."

Her lips curl into a knowing smile.

"What?"

"I like you, Sienna."

"You do?"

She nods. "I like that you say *you're fucking wrong, no offense.* I know you don't mean offense. You're just... straightforward."

"Usually."

"I know you don't like me."

I swallow a sip of my coffee. "I..."

"It's okay. You don't have to like me."

"I don't not like you."

She raises a brow *really*.

"It's just… you and Indie are always talking about Garbage or Hole or whatever and you're so smart and worldly and you have all these ideas about things I don't begin to understand. But she does. And she wants to understand them. And talk to you about them. And listen to Billie Eilish or whatever."

She laughs.

"What?"

"I'm sorry. It's not funny you're… jealous?"

My blush deepens.

"But we totally disagree about Billie Eilish's brilliance."

"You do?" Which of them likes her?

She nods. "You're right. I love talking to your sister. We're already close friends and we connect in a lot of ways, including music."

"Cool hair?"

"And cool hair. And even old movies." She laughs. "But she loses me when she starts to talk about melody. And I lose her when I talk about literature."

"Really?"

"Really. We're friends, good friends even, but she's always going to be your older sister."

"Maybe."

"Maybe? Is she going to stop being your sister?"

I nod. "If she finds out I fucked Cam."

She laughs. "She won't."

"She'll be disappointed."

"Maybe, but she'll get over it."

I shake my head.

She stands. "I won't argue. She's your sister. You know her better. But I'm an older sister too, and my sister did a lot worse to me and I still love her more than anything."

"What did she do?"

"I can't say. It's hers. But it's bad. It's weird to call it bad. It's probably selfish, thinking about my feelings in this situation, but... she hurt me. She hurt me deeply, and I didn't know if I'd ever forgive her."

It's hard to imagine anything coming between Eve and her sister. They're incredibly close. They're twins. But there's an edge to Eve's voice. Whatever it is, it did hurt her deeply. Deeply enough, it still causes her pain.

"Besides, Indigo is much sweeter than I am."

"Maybe."

She offers her hand. "You want to look? Or you want to sit a little longer?"

"I can look. Just... slowly." I take her hand. Let her help me up. Follow her to the wall on the right, the one filled with black silk. "This is really her."

"Ty must like silk. She has a lot of it."

"Have you worn silk?"

"Yeah, okay, I see your point. It's very..."

"Sensual?"

"Yeah." My cheeks flush at the memory of Cam rubbing me over my silk camisole. And then I remember that he's not mine and he won't be mine and my stomach sinks.

"Are you okay?"

No, but I need to finish this, so I can go home and hug his cufflinks by myself. "I'm surprised you let Ian dress you. You know, with your..." What was it she said? "Hatred of the patriarchy?"

"Am I that much of a broken record?"

"No... sometimes." And Cam was right. "I'm probably just as bad with talking about soccer all the time."

"It all sounds the same to me." She nods.

"But, uh, it is cool that you're so passionate. I don't always get the nuance, but I appreciate the commitment."

"Thanks."

"So I'm surprised you let Ian dress you."

"It was part of our agreement at first."

"Really?"

She nods. "And… what was I going to do, turn down half a million dollars?"

"Did you think about it?"

"Of course. I was scared."

"Even though you wanted him?"

"Because I wanted him. He's… intense. I was afraid I'd fall in love with him. But, of course, I wasn't going to let something silly like that talk me out of paying my college tuition."

"Yeah."

"I didn't really get him at first," she says. "He was teasing me when he was dressing me. Because he knew the idea I had of him."

"I can see that." Well, I can see Cam doing it. "Plus, he gets to picture you naked in the dressing room."

She laughs. "And he didn't want me to feel under-dressed. Though—" She flips her teal hair. "I'm not sure I ever blend in."

"Would you want to?"

"Sometimes. Not usually." She dismisses a slip as *too similar*. Studies a bodysuit with a deep v-neck. "Do you?"

"I don't usually think about it. I like to look cute, but unless I'm dressing up, I'm all about comfortable."

"Dressing up to appeal to someone?"

My cheeks flush. And my stomach sinks again. I want Cam. I can't have Cam. It doesn't make sense.

She holds up a lace bodysuit. "This would be cute on you."

"Maybe."

"With your shoulders and the halter neck? Definitely."

I glance at the price tag. Sure, it would be cute, but it's

really not in my budget, and I'm not really in the mood to try on lingerie. "I don't know."

"On me?"

"No way."

"On… Cam?"

"No, we, uh… it was a temporary thing."

"And it's…"

"Over."

"Oh." Her eyes go wide. "I'm sorry. That's hard."

"Yeah."

"Fuck lingerie. And fuck men, right?"

"No, it's okay." Maybe I will feel better if I try it on. Maybe I'll be able to focus on how much I want to fuck Cam and turn that into wanting to fuck, period. Or maybe I'll feel badass and hot and ready to find a new guy to make me forget Cam.

That's a theoretical possibility.

Technically.

"I'll try it," I say.

She hands me the bodysuit. "Should I try something too?"

"No offense, Eve, but I really don't care if I see you in lingerie or not."

She chuckles. "Being able to see my hip tattoo isn't doing it for you?"

"Not so much."

"I guess we're not meant to be."

I force a smile. She's trying to cheer me up. And not even in an obnoxious way. In a gentle way.

She's actually… not the worst.

I move into the tiny space. Shift out of my boots, socks, jeans, sweater, top, bra.

I pull the bodysuit on, over my panty.

My hands go to my phone reflexively. I snap a picture. Pull up my messages with Cam.

Remember, we agreed this is over.

I should do the smart thing and put my phone away.

But I don't.

I hit send.

Chapter Forty-Seven

SIENNA

Fuck.

I change into my clothes and bring the lingerie to the counter.

Yes, I'm going to buy it. Sure it's way too expensive, but, hey, I'm buying it for me.

I'm taking pictures for me.

Not for Cam.

Especially not when I didn't warn him first. I mean, technically, I'm not naked, but still.

I grab my cell. Try to find a reply.

Sienna: Sorry. Meant to warn you first. Finding a wedding present for my sister. Thought I might buy something for myself too and wanted your thoughts. Take care.

Right. That's a normal thing to send to Cam.

My ex-lover?

Ex-boyfriend?

Man, I have to pretend I don't want him because he's my future brother-in-law's business partner.

I shove my cell into my pocket.

It buzzes with a reply. His reply.

Is he going to tell me he's so hard from the sight of my lace-covered tits he wants me to come to his hotel room for one last time?

Or is he going to tell me to stop?

Or threaten to cut me off completely if I do this again?

Thankfully, Eve decided to try on some piece of lingerie. She's still in the dressing room.

I find my coffee—it's on the display ledge in front—and take greedy sips.

She emerges, fully dressed, holding a teal and black bra and panty set (obviously for her) and a mesh black one piece. "You think Indie will like this one?"

"Will Ian wear a fuchsia tie to match your hair?"

"Are we that bad?"

I try to smile and laugh, like I'm teasing her and not dreading the message on my phone.

Whatever it says, the situation stays the same.

We can't do this.

"You're way worse," I say.

She laughs, but it's short-lived. She can tell I'm upset.

And I don't want her telling I'm upset. We're not friends yet. "I should really get going. I have soccer practice."

"You're going back to NYU?"

No.

"Wherever you're going, I'll ride with you. I'm heading back home, so it's on the way."

I'm not sure NYU is really on the way to her apartment, but I'm going home anyway.

Maybe I'll skip practice. I can't break down in front of my teammates.

But I can't stomach the thought of an entire night without the distraction of running fast and working hard.

I have to see Cam soon.

At dinner Friday.

Then at the wedding.

After that, who knows?

"Give me five," Eve says. "Then we'll go."

I bite my lip.

"On me." She moves to the counter. "You don't have to talk if you don't want to."

"Okay."

She offers that same soft smile. The gentle one that screams *I know you; I need to handle you with kid gloves.*

But it's not like I can object. I'm pretty sure I'm going to crack at the seams.

I move outside. Finish my drink. Toss it in the nearest trashcan.

Eve emerges with a wrapped gift box. Black with a deep purple bow. Not at all bridal. Very much my sister.

The reason why I need to get the fuck over this.

Whatever Cam says, I need to reply with something sensible. No, or I can't, or oops, I meant to send that to the captain of the guy's soccer team.

What is it people say? Sometimes you have to be cruel to be kind. Maybe I need to be cruel. Or maybe I need to make him jealous, so he comes to his senses.

"Where are you headed?" she asks without implication.

But I still feel an accusation. *You're trying to get away to see Cam, aren't you?* "Home. I have to study before practice."

"I'll call a car. Ride with you."

"Isn't your school uptown?"

"I took the afternoon off."

"Are you missing class?"

"One." She pulls out her cell and summons a rideshare. "Five minutes."

Right. Five minutes. Then, what, ten minutes to the Financial District? Too much time with my thoughts. Too much time keeping a poker face.

She doesn't push. Or ask for details. Or do anything but make wedding small talk. Something about my dress. She doesn't want to upstage me or Indie and she's afraid her dress is too dramatic.

The car comes. We keep talking about the wedding. I try to describe my dress, but I can't even remember the color at the moment.

My head is a mess.

Eve lets the quiet fall. Once we cross Houston, we ride in silence. I expect the short drive to feel awkward, but it doesn't. It passes in a blink and then we're at my apartment building.

Ty and Indigo's apartment building.

Eve helps me out of the car. Thanks the driver. Leads me to the door. "I'll walk you up."

"I'm fine."

"I know, but I'm hoping to get a look at your dress. To make sure mine doesn't clash."

It's an excuse, so I can save face. Usually, I hate that kind of thing, but I nod *okay* and I lead her up to my apartment.

———

I MAKE IT ALL THE WAY TO MY BEDROOM, TO THE DRESS proudly displayed on the hanger above the mirror—

As if it's saying *this is the most important thing I will ever wear, because it's for my sister's wedding, and what could matter more than that.*

I sit on my bed, watch Eve study the dress, try to take in the description of hers.

Then I pull out my cell and I see his message.

Cam: I'm sorry, Sienna. I can't.

And I fall apart.

"Sienna." Eve moves to the bed. Motions *can I?* When I

nod an okay, she sits next to me, offers her shoulder. "You don't have to talk about it, but if you want to…" She mimes zipping her lips. "I promise. Really."

"You're sure?"

"Positive."

I start at the beginning.

And I tell her everything.

———

ONCE I FINISH, EVE FIXES TEA WITH HONEY, BRINGS TWO mugs to the bedroom, hands one to me.

It's good. Soothing and familiar. Something Mom made when I was sick. When I was a kid. And even when I was older. She wasn't all that present after Dad died, but she had her moments.

I don't usually think about it. Why dwell on painful things? She's gone and she's not coming back.

My sister stepped up and did what it took. She sacrificed for me. She protected me.

Now this.

"Thanks." I take another sip. Let the warm liquid soothe my sore throat. "I… I can't do anything that would hurt her."

She nods with understanding.

"And this is the only thing that makes sense. We had time together. It's over. We're both moving on."

"Maybe."

"What do you mean maybe?"

"I can't argue with your logic. It doesn't make sense for you to be with Cam. It's complicated and messy and likely to cause trouble with the most important people in your life."

"Not very encouraging."

She smiles. "It makes sense to end it now if it's just sex.

Or just a crush. Or just… a learning experience with an older man." Her voice softens. "But not if you love him."

"What?"

"Do you love him?"

"No." Maybe.

"Are you sure?"

I shake my head.

"Maybe that doesn't change anything for you. Maybe it still doesn't make sense. Love isn't always enough. And, honestly, I have no idea how he feels. I haven't seen him since Friday. But what if he loves you too?"

"I don't—"

"Hypothetically then. What if you're in love? What if he understands you in a way no one else does? Do you really want to deny yourself that chance?"

It's the opposite logic he used with me. He was teasing, sure, but it still feels familiar. "Indie will disown me."

"She won't."

"Ty will kill him. And then I'll be responsible for him going to jail. And Indie—"

"If Ty kills Cam, that blood is on Ty's hands, not yours. But he won't."

"Are you sure?"

"I am."

I'm not, but I'm not going to argue either. There are plenty of more salient points. "I'll ruin the wedding."

"I'm not saying you should stand up in the middle of the ceremony. Maybe wait until after. Or talk to him… today, so you both have time to figure it out."

"Today?"

"He's at work, isn't he?"

I have no idea.

"He's at work, at the office five blocks away."

"Ty's at work."

"And Cam is capable of walking here. Or meeting you somewhere private."

Maybe.

"It's your life, Sienna. I can't tell you what to do. I don't want to, and you wouldn't listen anyway."

"Hey."

She laughs. "If this is really what makes sense to you, do it. But don't discount your feelings for him."

"But he doesn't... It's not the same for him."

"Maybe. Maybe you're right and it won't work. Maybe he doesn't love you. But what will you regret more in five years? Not telling him how you feel? Or telling him?"

Chapter Forty-Eight

SIENNA

fter Eve leaves, I fix more tea, and I watch *Ninety Day Fiancée*, and I pick myself up enough I make it to practice.

Running clears my head.

And my team losing our scrimmage (against players technically on our team but still) sharpens my thoughts.

Eve is right.

I'm right. Or I was right, when I was teasing Cam about his kiss ruining me.

I owe it to myself to try.

I send him a text as I move into the subway station.

Sienna: Can we talk in person? Please. We can meet at a bar or restaurant if you want. It doesn't have to be private.

He doesn't reply until I'm home, showered, dressed in the orange robe he left me.

Cam: Twenty-third floor of my hotel. Nine.

Okay. It's not in his room, but it's in his hotel.

And—

I'm not going to fuck him. I mean, I wouldn't turn it down. But I'm going for this.

To tell him how I feel.

I…

I can do that.

Sienna: Sure.

Less than three hours to find my nerve.

I can totally do that.

Chapter Forty-Nine

SIENNA

I can do this.

I can do this.

Oh god, can I do this?

The elevator doors slide open. The gold wallpaper comes into view. The same wallpaper as the one in Cam's room.

The bar isn't trying quite as hard to look expensive, but it's still trying pretty damn hard. It's a lot like Rick's actually. Trying to look classy and distinguished, but not quite hitting the mark.

I smooth my dress, reapply my lipstick, check my text from Cam.

Instructions to meet him on the patio, at one of the private booths.

It's cold tonight. And I'm not wearing a lot of clothes. My *I want to look like I belong here and I know you want to fuck me but I'm not pressing the issue* gold fit and flare dress isn't the warmest.

Deep breath.

Slow exhale.

I head straight to the balcony. Then I see him and my steps slow.

Cam is sitting in a booth in the back, in his usual suit and tie, strong and confident and in control and still clearly miserable.

He spots me. Nods a *hello*. Waits.

Okay, he's not getting out to hug me. That's fair. I don't like it, but it's far.

We're over.

So.

Uh.

No problem.

I move past a happy couple in a booth. Two friends sharing a pitcher of something lime green.

An empty booth.

To Cam.

The space is halfway between a chain restaurant booth and the decadent *this is a place to fuck, complete with sheer curtains* spot where everyone met the night of the bachelorette party.

Where he laid me on the bench seat and ate me out.

Not that I'm imagining it.

That much.

I move into the space, take the seat across from him.

It feels more private inside. More like we're in our own world.

And look, we have our own sheer curtains. "Should I?" My fingers brush the soft fabric.

I want to be alone with him.

I want to see the lights of the city.

I want this to make sense.

He shakes his head. "The server is coming back."

"Oh."

"Do you want something to eat?"

No. I was starving when I finished practice, but the

second I sent the text, my stomach went topsy-turvy. I'm not sure I'll keep anything down. "I'm too nervous."

"Did you have dinner?"

I shake my head.

His eyes go to the half-finished bottle of wine on the table. To his full glass.

He's been drinking. He's nervous too.

"I'll order something sweet," he says.

"Not too sweet."

"That's a category for you?"

"It's just... something plain would be easier on my stomach."

He nods *one minute*, slides out of the booth, heads inside to the bar.

So he isn't waiting for the server. He's just... something.

There are already glasses of water here too. I take one, drink half of it, fix my lipstick again.

Something to distract me from the wait.

But it's not enough. I slip out of the booth, find the bathroom, try a pep talk in the mirror.

I can do this.

I can do this.

I lost once today. I'm not losing again.

There.

More lipstick. Maybe it helps. Probably not.

I meet him at the booth.

He's already in his seat. And there's already food here. A pretzel appetizer.

"It's not a hot dog, but..." He motions to the small tray of mustard.

It smells amazing, like bread and salt. My appetite returns full force. I grab a piece, dip it in mustard, take a big bite.

Mmm, it's honey mustard. Sweet and a little spicy and so many carbs.

My stomach feels better immediately.

"Can I have some of that wine?" I ask.

"If you eat more."

"Kind of bossy."

"You're the one asking me to commit a misdemeanor."

I guess that's fair. "Like you'd get caught."

"Even so."

I nod *fine* and sit at the booth.

He waits for me to eat another wedge of pretzel, then he pours a glass of wine. "It's dry."

Right. He likes those deep, full-bodied reds. They're complex. I guess that's what you say, but they're not sweet.

I take a long sip. Just barely stop my lips from puckering.

He laughs. "I can order something else."

"No. That's okay." I drink half the glass in three sips.

Again, he chuckles. "That was a hundred-dollar glass."

"And I enjoyed it." I finish the rest. "Well, now, I enjoyed it."

He doesn't offer to pour me another. Already, I want the loss of inhibitions, but it's better to do this lucid.

"I, uh, I guess I'll just say it." I take a deep breath and push out a slow exhale. "I… I, uh, I really like you, Cam. A lot. Maybe more, I'm not sure. I've never loved anyone before."

His eyes glue to me.

"I know we made this agreement. It's what makes sense. That's what I've been telling myself. That I can't mess up things between you and Ty."

"It wouldn't be your fault, Sienna."

"Right. You made your choices. But I made mine too, and I knew this would be… complicated."

He nods.

"It's more logical to end it there. To say goodbye and avoid you for the next week and then over the holidays. And every time I see you for a while. That makes sense."

"It does."

"And I'll honor that, if it's what you want. But it's not what I want anymore. I don't know how it will work. I don't know how to make it not fucked up, but I... I want to be with you. All the way."

"You live in New York."

"And you live in London. And that's another way it's complicated. I'll miss you all the time and I'll have jet lag when I fly to London and back in a weekend and it will be hard but I... I'm going to miss you either way."

"Sienna..."

No, no, no. That's the *Sienna, we can't* tone.

"I care about you."

"But—"

"I do. I care deeply. Maybe it's more. I don't know either. I haven't loved anyone in fifteen years."

Since he was fourteen? That's awfully young to fall in love, but, stranger, it's awfully young for a first love to fuck with his head that much.

But then his first experience with sex was fucked up.

And he has all these limits.

And he needs me to be careful with him.

"You've fucked with my head, Sienna. And it's a good thing for me, but it's confusing, and it's going to be confusing for a long time. Even if everything was different, if you weren't eighteen—"

"Ian is sixteen years older than Eve."

"Even if your sister wasn't marrying Ty and we didn't live thousands of miles apart... I'm not ready." His eyes meet mine. "I'm not ready to be with someone. Not the way you deserve."

"But—"

"I'm sorry, Sienna. I wish I had another answer for you. I wish things were different, but they're not."

"But why?"

His eyes stay fixed on mine.

"Why aren't you ready? Why can't you be with someone? Why can't we figure it out together?"

"I have to do it alone."

"Are you sure?"

"No." He takes a deep breath. Lets out a slow exhale. "I've wanted to tell you this. For selfish reasons. Because I wanted to tell someone. I wanted you to know and look at me the same way. I wanted to have all your understanding."

"I want that too."

"I've never told anyone else. Not like this. And I... I'll tell you if you're ready to hear it."

"I don't understand."

"This is a big secret, the kind that sometimes feels like a burden, and I don't want to put that on you if you can't take it."

"I can."

"You can't tell anyone. Not your sister or—"

"Ty?"

"Ty knows. Not because I told him, but... it has to be between us."

I nod.

"And it won't change my answer. I'm still saying no."

"You're scared?"

"Terrified."

"I... I do promise, to keep it ours, but if you don't want to tell me—"

"I do. Just give me a minute."

I nod *okay*.

He refills both our glasses, but he doesn't drink his. "I was like you growing up. A football player. A good one. Always best in my year."

Okay.

"Coaches took an interest in me. I didn't think anything of it when my high school coach did the same."

I press my palms into the bench. I need to listen to him. To let him talk and not jump to ugly conclusions. And not put him in a position where he's apologizing for making me feel bad, apologizing for his pain.

I hated when my parents died and people looked at me like *please, tell me what to say* expecting me to apologize for making them feel awkward.

"She was a new teacher. Twenty-four, blonde, gorgeous. All the boys on the team talked about how much they wanted her. Or the things they would do to her if she gave them a chance," he says. "It was bollocks. They didn't have a clue. I didn't have a clue, but I played along anyway. Bragged about moves I'd seen in porn and how I knew exactly how to make a woman come."

"And she took an interest?"

He nods. "At first, it was normal. Extra training or talking plays after practice. Then, it was more, but still what I expected from a teacher. Help with homework, advice on family or university. Then I told her about a girl who liked me, and she asked if I knew how to kiss."

Oh no.

"I'd kissed a few girls, but I didn't know, not really. So she offered to show me."

I bite my tongue.

"That was it for a few weeks. Practice kissing. And then my coach, Winter, asked if I knew what happened after kissing. I knew it wasn't usual for her to show me. I knew she was crossing some line. But she was beautiful and experienced, and what kind of man would I be to turn that down? I should trust someone older and wiser, someone tasked with building my talent."

"Did you want to be with her?"

"I was just a kid. I wasn't ready to have sex. But I never said no. It never occurred to me that I could."

That's awful.

"I knew it had to be a secret. I knew people would see it was wrong. But at the time... I thought we were in love. I thought we were misunderstood."

"Oh."

"That's the sick thing. Under everything else, I loved her, but that became my idea of love. And it tangled with sex and now..." His gaze shifts to the city skyline. "I've spent half my life running from it." He's quiet for a moment, then he turns to me. "You changed that. Forced me to face it."

"Is that a good thing?"

He nods. "But it's terrifying too."

"I'm sorry. Not about the two of us having sex. And I'm not sorry I have feelings for you. But I'm sorry you went through that."

"Thank you."

"And I do... I really appreciate you trusting me with that. I..." I've never really been ashamed of anything. Certainly not anything sexual, but I can see that in his eyes. It's so unlike the Cam I know and so strong too. "I know it's a big deal."

He nods. "I'm not telling you as an excuse, Sienna. I just—"

"Want me to know and look at you the same?"

"Yes."

"Am I?" I try to stare into his eyes the way I did an hour ago. With all that need and affection.

But I must not get there, because he looks away. "No."

"It's not... I still think you're incredibly sexy."

"Is that what matters?"

"That's part of it, isn't it?"

He nods.

"And I... I still care about you. But I... I understand now, I guess. I understand certain things you've done. And why... why you believe this won't work."

"I haven't convinced you?"

"No... I think..." I think I'm sure I'm in love with him. But I can't say that now. Not after what he told me about this woman who abused him. And how she turned the word into something awful.

One day.

But not today.

I take a deep breath. "Are you sure this is what you need?"

"No."

"But you're asking for it anyway?"

"Yes."

I don't like it, but I understand it. "Okay." I slide out of the booth, hold my purse, wrap my arms around my chest. "I guess... this is goodbye again."

"I'll miss you."

"I'll miss you too."

He slides out of the booth, stiff, uncomfortable. But he still pulls me into a soft, slow kiss.

It's not like Monday morning.

There's no heat in it. Only trust and affection.

I pull back with a sigh. "I guess I'll see you Friday."

"Are you walking home?"

"It's only a few blocks."

"You're shivering."

I shake my head.

He slips his suit jacket from his shoulders anyway. "I meant to leave this for you." He hangs it over my shoulders.

To wear with the cufflinks.

He pulls me into another soft, slow kiss, then he whispers goodbye, and I leave the restaurant, walk back to my apartment, fall apart alone.

Chapter Fifty

CAM

I stay late at the bar, finish the bottle of wine, order a plate of pasta.

I expect to feel sick over my confession.

Or to feel naked, used, vulnerable.

But I don't.

I'm lighter.

Freer.

I trust her with this.

I trust her with anything.

———

BACK AT MY HOTEL, I TOSS AND TURN. IT'S NOT THE UNEASY sleep I expected. There's no pit in my stomach or dread in my chest.

Only that ache in my heart. The empty space she's carved for herself.

Around three a.m., I give up on sleep. I sit on the couch, turn on the TV, find something to numb my thoughts.

A reality TV marathon.

Strangers move into a house to find love, but really all they do is fuck each other.

It's the kind of thing Sienna watches.

It's terrible, of course.

But the antics of the idiots on the cast still make me smile. I imagine her here, next to me, explaining why the show is actually brilliant, demanding coffee, asking if I'll fuck her again.

It's still confusing.

And tangled.

It's going to take a long time to figure it out.

But maybe it's possible—

Maybe it's possible I'll be able to say *I love you* without my throat closing.

———

MY THOUGHTS STAY FUZZY. EVEN AS IAN AND I ARRANGE final details at the rehearsal dinner venue—the groom's family is supposed to pay, and there's no way we're letting Ty's mother cover the cost.

We convince the waiter to take our card, fight over who has the right to pay, rock paper scissors as a final decider.

He wins, like always.

How the fuck does he always win? The man is practically clairvoyant. I guess that's why he's a former spy.

We order wings, set up decorations, pass out gifts.

One by one, people filter in.

Friends from work.

Family from London.

Sienna and Indigo's cousins from New Jersey.

Sienna in a short red dress and gold heels, her hair pulled behind her ears, her long legs on display.

She's wearing my suit jacket over her dress. Even my cuff-links. It fits her better than it did the other night.

Did she already have it altered?

Or am I seeing what I want to see?

Her eyes catch mine. Her lips curl into a sad smile.

I nod hello.

She nods back and returns to her sister.

Indigo steals everyone else's attention. She's gorgeous in her bright white dress, but I can't keep my eyes off Sienna.

She looks beautiful, hurt, angry, sad.

Then she turns to her sister and her lips curl into a big, authentic smile. She teases Indie about something. Teases Ty.

The three of them laugh. She forces Ty to introduce her to a friend of his. Flirts just enough to make him growl.

Her eyes flit to me. So I know it's for my benefit. Or so I know she's moved on. Or maybe just to say hi.

I don't fucking know.

It doesn't matter.

I stick with Ian, even though Eve keeps shooting me loaded glances. He takes up the mantle as the life of the party, offering embarrassing stories about Ty through cocktails and dinner, standing to toast over dessert.

He raises a glass of champagne. "To true love."

Everyone toasts, drinks, laughs.

Ian looks to me. "Anything to add?"

Fuck, my head hurts. But I know how to play my role. I stand. Look to Ty. To my cousin, my closest confidant, the person who's done everything for me.

And to the love of his life. The woman who lights up his sky. Who will do anything to protect her family. To protect her sister.

This is fucked up, yes, but it doesn't have to stay that way.

Sienna and I can be friends. We can pretend this never happened. No matter how much it kills me.

I give my toast. "To Ty, making men everywhere proud thinking with his—"

Indigo cuts me off. "We know."

"Too much for polite company?" I toast to Ty's mom.

She laughs. "You turn fifty and everyone thinks you forget what sex is."

Indigo blushes.

"You know the rest." I raise my glass to both of them. "I'm proud of you." I mean it. I'm proud of him. Not just for finding someone who likes what he likes. For finding someone who loves him, all of him, the dark and the light.

Chapter Fifty-One

SIENNA

It's incredibly painful watching Cam from afar, but I manage.

This is what he wants.

And I respect what he wants.

Even after I have one too many Blue Sapphires and walk my sister to the elevator and hug my future brother-in-law goodbye.

I say goodbye to friends and family. Wait for the room to clear.

Then I return to the table to collect my purse, head to the elevator, prepare for a deep, deep sleep.

One with some *why can't I have him* dreams, but still the sleep of total and complete exhaustion.

I step into the elevator.

The doors slide together.

At the last minute, someone stops them.

Cam.

My heartbeat picks up. My stomach flutters.

He slips inside.

Like when we first kissed.

Well, kissed for real.

He's so tall and handsome and broad and hurt.

And offering something to me?

"You forgot this." He hands me the suit jacket. His suit jacket.

"Thanks." I slip it over my shoulders.

"It looks good on you."

"I had it altered. Is that okay?"

"It's yours."

"Yeah, but... I was kind of hoping to give it back to you one day." It's still oversized, but in a more intentional way.

"Don't." He hits the button for the lobby and turns to me.

The car descends. "Yeah?"

"It would break my heart."

Words rise up in my throat. I try to swallow them. It's not the time, and it's not the place. "Really?"

"Irrevocably."

And then the words spill from my lips. I can't stop them. "I love you."

Surprise spreads over his face.

"I'm not saying it to convince you of anything. I... I'm not trying to convince you of anything, Cam. I just... I wanted to say it. It's selfish, I know, but I... I had to say it. In case I don't see you tomorrow."

"You think I'd miss the wedding?"

"I don't know. Probably not. But anything can happen."

He nods *true*.

My heart thuds against my chest. "So, I, uh, don't say anything... if you have something to say. Tell me after the wedding. I want to believe it's good news for a day. Okay?"

The elevator stops at the lobby. The doors slide open.

I take a deep breath.

He motions *after you*.

I step into the lobby. Look at him for a response.
He mimes zipping his lips.
God, he's so adorable and so Cam and so handsome.
And I really fucking love him.
Whatever happens, I know that.

Chapter Fifty-Two

CAM

All night, Sienna's words echo through my head.

I love you.

I'm not trying to convince you of anything.

I just had to say it.

Just in case.

Anything can happen.

She's right. The world can change in an instant. She's lost both her parents. She knows that better than anyone.

And I—

I'm not ready to be what she needs.

I'm just not.

But maybe that's not permanent.

Maybe it's a problem with a solution.

———

Saturday is filled with wedding prep. The time passes quickly. When I arrive at Ty's, I fall into it completely.

Like so many grooms before him, Ty is a nervous wreck.

Of course, Ty being a nervous wreck means a slight crack in his facade.

Ian offers champagne, but Ty refuses him. He wants to remember everything.

"You need something," Ian says. "Or you're going to burst the second you see her."

"Go fuck yourself." I motion to the bedroom. "Take the edge off."

He flips me off.

Ian chuckles. "It's not bad advice."

"Think about what you want to do to her tonight."

"That's going to make him more antsy."

"But it's a good anticipation."

Ty shakes his head. "You're both arseholes."

"No argument here," Ian says. "But we are the arseholes you've got. So…" He offers the bottle again.

Ty shakes his head again.

He's not drinking. And he's not giving in to any of our baiting.

I need to up my game. "What are you scared of?"

He looks at me like I've sprouted horns.

"What?"

"That was sincere."

"I'm capable."

Ian and Ty exchange a *not really* look.

I flip both of them off. "You want to mock me or you want to get married today?"

"Can I not do both?" Ty's shoulders fall with his laugh.

This is helping. And this is where I excel.

So I step into my role as shit stirring life of the party. I make Ty laugh until he forgets why he's scared.

Ian joins with his own mocking stories. We tease each other about anything and everything on the way to the limo, the ride to the venue, the elevator up to the roof.

Then Ty steps onto the aisle and his nerves return.

Of course he's nervous.

He's marrying the woman he loves.

His entire life is changing. Of course, it's terrifying, even if it's what he wants.

Love is terrifying.

We take our places.

Me and Ian in the front row, on the groom's side.

Ty's mother walks him down the aisle.

The music swells.

The second Ty sees his bride, he calms. The rest of the world slips away. It's just the two of them.

She looks gorgeous in her sleek white dress, but I don't watch her.

I watch Sienna.

She's the one walking her sister down the aisle. Since their parents are gone, Indie wanted Sienna to "give her away."

Sienna is beaming, as proud as any father ever has been. She even kisses Indigo on the cheek before she takes her seat.

I try to keep my eyes off her, to watch my best friend marry the love of his life, but I fail.

Instead, I watch Sienna watch her sister marry the love of *her* life.

I watch joy spread over her face.

I feel every fucking ounce of it, hold it close, claim it as mine.

———

AFTER WE TAKE PICTURES (THANKFULLY, I'M NOT TOUCHING Sienna in any of them), I slip into my role as life of the party.

We eat, toast, cut the cake.

The room fills with *As Time Goes By*. Ty and Indigo take

their first dance. It's a simple waltz, but they still draw the attention of the entire room.

Watching them still makes my thoughts fuzzy.

Then I spot Sienna watching and I give up on clarity. She's gorgeous in her purple dress, and more, she's ecstatic.

I want that for her.

Maybe more than I want anything.

She doesn't catch me watching, so I stay at the bar, drink too much wine, accept a family member's offer to dance. For a dozen songs, I sway with aunts and family friends.

Then the song shifts to an EDM mix of an Amy Winehouse song and someone taps me on the shoulder.

Ty's mother. "You still owe this one a dance." She steps back.

And there's Sienna, standing on the dance floor in a gorgeous purple dress, her cheeks flushed, her eyes on fire. "Mrs. Hunt, it's really not necessary."

"Nonsense. You're both excellent dancers." She pushes Sienna toward me.

I offer my hand.

Sienna accepts. "Of course."

I bring one hand to her waist. Pull her closer. As close as I can with everyone watching.

"Hey." She looks up at me. "You look handsome."

"You too."

"Handsome, really?"

"Really."

She smiles. "Is this our joke? Like with Indie calling Ty beautiful?"

"I'm game if you are."

"Deal."

Fuck, it feels so good being this close to her, seeing her smile, smelling her shampoo.

She loves me.

Is that really possible?

It's still beyond my comprehension.

The song shifts to something slower.

I pull her closer.

She rests her head against my chest, sways with me through the entire song, then she pulls back and kisses me on the cheek. "Will I see you tomorrow?"

I don't know. I can't do this here, but I can't leave without talking to her either. "You know where to find me."

She nods *I do* and accepts a friend's offer to dance.

I stay as long as I can, but the atmosphere of love and togetherness overwhelms me. It's too fucking confusing.

I find Ian. Tell him goodbye. Make him promise to send Ty and Indigo to their hotel suite in style.

He convinces me to have one drink for the road. Champagne, of course. It is a wedding.

I finish a glass, then I slip out of the room quietly, move into the lift.

But right before the doors close, Sienna slips inside.

Chapter Fifty-Three

SIENNA

"Hey." I smooth my dress, but it does nothing to soothe me. I'm nervous. Way too nervous.

"Are you leaving?"

"No. I wanted to walk you out. If that's okay."

He nods.

"And, uh... I know it's after the wedding, but—"

"You're not leaving yet."

"If I was?"

His lips curl into a half-smile. "You should stay for the last dance."

"If I revised my previous statement... and was okay with hearing a response now. I mean, if you're ready to give one."

"Are you?"

Am I? What if he says *no, I'm sorry, I meant never*? Can I really go back to the wedding and smile for my sister?

Or will I burst into tears and confess everything and totally ruin the night?

"Yes." The words spill from my lips. "If you have something to say, I can hear it now. I can hear it later too. If that's what you want. I... I just wanted to walk you out."

His eyes fix on me.

"And tell you… I can wait."

"You can wait?"

"For you. If you need time to figure out what you want. Or if you love me. Or if you're capable of loving me. I can wait."

"You're eighteen. You should be having fun."

"I'll have fun."

His brows furrow.

"I'm supposed to avoid boys during the soccer season anyway. That's our team captain's edict."

"And you've really stuck to it so far."

"I know. So I, uh, I have some catching up to do on that."

He half-smiles.

"And I have classes and friends and new friends to make. So I… it would definitely work for me to wait."

"Really?"

I nod. "I'm capable. Maybe I won't patiently, but patience is overrated."

He smiles.

"And I… please, Cam. If you don't want me, okay. If you'll feel too much pressure having me on the hook, okay. But don't say no because you think it's what's best for me. This is what I want. I want to wait. Because I want you. And I love you. And I can figure the rest out."

"You might be waiting a long time."

My chest warms. "I can do that."

"Months?"

I nod.

"Years?"

"I don't know, Cam. I think so. I can't promise I'll feel the same way in two years, but, right now, I know I love you, and I want to wait if that's what you need. Anything could happen, but right now—"

He cuts me off with his lips.
I mumble against his mouth.
He kisses me like he's claiming me.
This time, he is.

Chapter Fifty-Four

SIENNA

Waiting is torture.

The first week is the hardest.

Cam is still in New York. He's still honoring his promise to Ty to watch me until my sister returns from the honeymoon.

Every night, after practice, I show him a new sight in the city. Or take him to a fancy restaurant way out of my price range.

After he teases me about my love of dessert, and eats half my chocolate cake, he walks me home.

When he kisses me goodbye, every molecule in my body begs for him.

But we're not having sex. Not until he figures this out.

Only kissing.

And even that—

Only while he's here.

When the happy couple returns, I take Cam to the airport (well, ride in his limo with him) and I kiss him goodbye at the terminal. It's like something out of a movie. Like he's going to war.

In a way, he is.

He flies back to London and I go to my life and everything gets so much harder and so much easier with him on the other side of the Atlantic.

I can't give into my temptation to mount him, but I miss his touch and his laugh and his smile and even the smell of his soap.

We still talk, but it's more like before. Not platonic, but not sexual either.

We text about run times and TV (we're finally watching *The Good Wife* together, and he's totally wrong. It's not too high brow for me. I mean, it's no *Ninety Day Fiancée*, but it moves fast and it's full of hot guys in suits).

We text about lunch and coffee and school and soccer and work.

I don't ask if he's ready. I don't ask if he fucks himself thinking of me. I don't even send him pictures of me in lingerie.

Instead, I send evidence I'm living my life. Post practice selfies, photos at parties, delicious French toast brunches with Indie, Ty overdressed at a soccer game or a coffee shop or a fast-food restaurant.

The man walks into Dunkin' Donuts like he's the regional manager.

And even a few nights with Eve. We're not best friends or anything, but we both like live music and Indian food and trading college stories.

I even learn to appreciate her deep thinking and her love of dissecting literature. It's not what I do, but it's cool she's able to find so much in a book or a song or a movie.

She comes to some of my games and cheers me on and takes me out for drinks when we lose. (Well, back to her and Ian's place, for very fancy gin and tonics).

And I tell her about Cam and how I'm waiting and how I miss him and love him and need him.

She's gracious enough not to say *I told you so* (but we both know she's thinking it).

I make friends, I play, I study.

I live my life. Not waiting for Cam, exactly, but still in this state of limbo.

His pictures are the highlight of my day.

London tourist attractions, work meetings, sweaty post-run selfies (so yummy, seriously), favorite coffee shops, new restaurants, pub nights with friends.

The decorations in the waiting room of his therapist's office.

His Halloween costume. (He goes as Ian, which basically means a suit, but with a hot pink tie. Supposedly, it's a hit at the office, but I don't buy it).

(I go as a unicorn, of course).

I celebrate my birthday with friends.

He sends me a rainbow cake (dick shaped, of course) and a new suit jacket, a thicker one for cooler weather, already tailored to fit me.

I send him pictures of the changing leaves.

He stays in London for Thanksgiving. He's not ready yet. He doesn't trust himself with me.

He knows, as soon as he sees me, he's going to fuck me senseless.

And that makes the waiting such beautiful agony.

Chapter Fifty-Five

CAM

After four months avoiding the subject of sex with Sienna, I'm on my way to New York. It's my first time leaving London since I kissed her.

And the first time I'm asking myself *can I handle fucking her* and really considering the answer.

I think about it all the time, but it's always hypothetical. Will I be ready when I see her... sometime in the future.

Only I'm seeing her tonight.

I'm not sure I'm ready, but I'm in a fucking frenzy anyway.

I need to see her.

I need to touch her.

I need to kiss her.

After that, I'm not sure.

But I really fucking need to kiss her.

———

After a bad night of sleep and a long day of meetings, I get ready for our company's holiday party.

I finish dressing; I arrive early; I mingle.

I play my part as life of the party—it's not like Ty can do it. I tease, I laugh, I fill champagne glasses.

The second Sienna enters, my calm evaporates.

She and Indigo are arm in arm, and they're dressed to complement each other.

Indigo in a silver gown (as Sienna would say, it's a total boss bitch look). Sienna in a short gold dress and matching tights, her lips the perfect shade of red, my suit jacket hanging on her shoulders.

The same cufflinks.

Her eyes meet mine. Brighten. She nearly runs to me, but she stops herself.

She sneaks a text—*thirty minutes, then you're mine*—and suffers through Indigo's meet and greets. Then Ty's.

He beams every time he introduces Indigo as his wife.

I was wrong. He is lighting up the party. Not with the kind of energy I bring, but with his own.

He's still over the moon.

He's still the picture of love and devotion.

It doesn't make my stomach drop.

It doesn't make my throat close.

I'm happy for him. Happy for Indigo.

Happy, period.

After Sienna does the rounds with her sister, she finds Eve at the bar. After ten minutes sipping their drinks—something bright green for Sienna, a gin and tonic for Eve—they turn to me.

"Cam!" Eve waves as if she just noticed I arrived. "Hey, I haven't seen you in forever."

Sienna stares at me like she's going to rip my clothes off, but she stays where she is.

"Are you going to make us walk over there?" Eve waves to me again. "Look at our shoes."

"Does he have to look to know you're wearing combat boots?" Sienna laughs.

Eve does too. "How else will he know my laces are silver?"

"And Ian's still wearing a bright pink tie." She nudges her friend, finishes her drink, looks to me.

Immediately, desire overtakes her expression. Her pupils dilate. Her tongue slides over her lips. Her fingers dig into her glass.

"Yes, we're hilarious. I agree," Eve says. "Like Cam with his whole thing about calling soccer football. Like we don't know it's called football everywhere else."

"If you knew, you'd call it football," I say.

Eve whispers something in Sienna's ear.

Sienna whispers back.

They're good friends now. If that's the case, anything is possible.

This is possible.

Fuck, it needs to be possible.

Eve nods and looks to me. "Okay, if you insist, we'll come over there." She leads Sienna to me. Moves to the side, so she's blocking us from view. "Oh no, I just realized, I have to ask Ty and Indigo a very long, complicated question that will distract them for the next two minutes. Damn." She snaps with faux disappointment. "Make use of the time."

Sienna mouths *thank you.*

Eve turns and moves in the direction of her brother-in-law.

Sienna's fingers brush my suit jacket. "You look handsome."

"You too."

"I want to touch you so badly. But I know… not here." She doesn't add *and maybe not at all, if that's what you want,* but it's in the air.

It's not what I want, but it might be what I need.

I want to be there, I do, but I'm already overwhelmed by her presence. "Get your coat. Meet me at your place."

"Are you sure?"

Is she asking because Ty might catch us? Or because she wants to know I'm ready to fuck her? Either way, the answer is the same. "No. But I can't wait another second. I need to kiss you. After that, I'm not sure, but I need to kiss you."

"Okay."

"I'll go first. Wait five minutes, then leave."

"Hold on." She pulls something from her purse. A tiny key attached to a sleek silver key ring. One with my initials. "I figured... just in case."

"You always prepare, sweetness?"

"For you, yeah." She slips the key into my pocket. Runs her fingers over my wrist. "I missed you."

"I missed you too."

Her cheek brushes mine as she pulls away. She takes a step backward, surveys the room, nods *now*, and heads to the coat check.

I take the stairs to the lobby, then I walk to her building, let myself into her flat, ask myself if I'm ready.

The answer is the same.

I don't know.

I only know I need her.

I really fucking need her.

Chapter Fifty-Six

CAM

Sienna's flat still screams of her. No, it's even more her. More vibrant and alive.

Christmas lights, lyrics scribbled on the desk in hot pink and bright orange, coats hanging on a rack by the door, a bottle of my favorite wine on the counter.

Her footsteps steal my attention. She unlocks the door quietly, slips inside, presses it closed.

She gives me a long, slow once-over, then she follows my gaze to the wine. "I stole it from Ty."

"You stole it?"

She nods. "He bought two dozen bottles. He won't miss this one."

"You could have said you bought it."

"Why would I blow a grand on a bottle of wine?" She shakes her head *no way*. "Some of us aren't made of money."

"Then what are you doing in that designer jacket?"

Her lips curl into a coy smile. "This old thing." She tugs at the sides of the blazer, spins, lands on her toes. "Some guy gave it to me."

"Some guy?"

"Yeah. I think his name was… Hunter or something."

"Hunter or something?"

"Yeah. Something like that." She moves closer. "Maybe, uh… maybe Hunt."

"Some guy with the same last name as your brother-in-law?"

"Yeah, I think they're related." She takes another step toward me. Another. "Pretty fucked up, huh? He's technically my cousin."

"Is he?"

"Cousin-in-law, I guess. Is that a thing?"

"I've never heard of it."

"Yeah. Me either." She stops at the bottle. "You want some?"

"One glass." I'm terrified, but I want to feel this.

"Now?" Her fingers brush the bottle. "Or after?"

"After?"

"Well…" Her eyes fix on me. "After whatever you're ready to do."

"Come here."

"Now?"

I nod *now*.

"The same rules as always?"

"Yes."

Her eyes light up. "You're going to fuck me."

"Sweetness, if it's the same rules as always, what do you think I'm going to say to that?"

"Maybe, uh… 'yes, Sienna, I've spent the last four months fucking myself to you every night. I can't deny how much I want you.'"

"I did."

"Me too." She picks up the bottle opener and offers it to me. "I fucked myself to you almost every night."

"Almost?"

"Sometimes, I was too tired," she admits.

"You didn't say anything."

"Should I have?"

"No." I'm not glad she didn't, exactly, but it was what I needed. "You were perfect."

"I *was* perfect?" Her fingers brush mine as she hands me the bottle opener. "Do you know how much self-control it's taking not jumping you right now? Not demanding an answer? Not demanding you fuck me or leave?" Her fingers brush my wrist. "It's killing me."

"It's killing me too."

"You never show it."

"I know." I open the bottle, pour two glasses, hand one to her.

Again, her hand brushes mine. This time, she doesn't fight her sigh. "You said you needed to kiss me."

"I do."

"And you're all the way over there."

"I know."

"So…"

"I told you to come here," I say.

"You don't want wine first?"

I shake my head.

She swallows half her glass in one sip, sets the thing on the counter.

"That's a waste of good wine." I set my glass next to hers.

"What about this?" She downs the rest then she closes the distance between us.

Her eyes meet mine. For a moment, they study me, then they flutter closed and her lips find mine.

Her kiss is overwhelming.

Soft, sweet, tender.

Wine and Sienna.

I pull her closer, kiss her harder.

Her lips part to make way for my tongue.

Her groan vibrates down my throat.

When she pulls back, I'm shaking.

"Fuck." Her fingers dig into my chest. "You need to tell me, Cam. If you can't handle more, you need to tell me, because I'm going to lose control if I kiss you again."

"You're going to lose control?"

"Maybe. I don't know. I miss you so fucking much."

"I miss you too." It feels good, being this close to her.

Not complicated, not messy, not loaded.

Right.

"Has it really been four months?" she asks.

I nod.

"Are you going to come fast?"

My laugh breaks the tension in my chest. "Did you just ask that?"

"It's a fair question."

Again, I laugh.

"What? You haven't had sex in four months. It would be normal if you were quick. I don't mind."

"I haven't said I'll fuck you."

"Yeah, but if you do. We can... thirty minutes, right? We can go again in thirty minutes."

"If I'm not ready in thirty minutes?"

"It's been four months. You will be."

My laugh gets louder.

She makes a show of pouting. "Okay, if you're not, I have the vibrator you sent me. All three of them."

That might have been overkill. But this... It's such a Sienna reply. *I love you.* It almost forms on my tongue. It's so fucking close, but that's not a place I'm ready to go.

It's too loaded, too messy, too hard.

But this—

I can do this.

I wasn't sure two minutes ago, but now that's she's asked that—

Now, I'm sure.

"I am." My fingers curl into her lower back. "But you're right. It's been four months. It might be too much. I might need to stop. If you can't—"

"I can. I just… might need you to tell me twice."

"You're not going to follow orders, sweetness?"

"Cam." Her voice drops to a whine. "No teasing. If you're not—"

I cut her off with a kiss.

She groans against my lips.

I take her into my arms, carry her to the bedroom. Her bedroom.

Lit only by the twinkling string lights and the soft blue glow of the sky outside. It's perfect. It's her.

I lay her on the bed.

She looks up at me with a hazy expression. "I really fucking missed you."

"I know." I do away with my suit jacket. "Clothes off."

"All of them?"

"All of them."

She slips out of her shoes first. Slowly, she rolls her tights to her ankles. Then the suit jacket.

The gold dress.

She's wearing the red lingerie under it.

The lingerie I bought her.

"Sweetness." The sight of her steals my breath. Not because she's gorgeous, though she is.

Because she's mine.

She's known it all this time.

She's trusted it all this time.

Sienna looks up at me as she does away with her bra. Then her knickers.

She's naked on her bed, ready, waiting, buzzing with anticipation.

Her need fills the room. It overwhelms me. But not in a way that sends my head to ugly places.

It fills me with pride.

Affection.

Desire.

My feelings for her are overwhelming, but this—

This makes sense.

She watches as I do away with my jacket and tie.

Then my shoes and socks.

My shirt.

My slacks.

Her eyes go wide as I slip out of my boxers. "Fuck." Her chest heaves. "I've never seen you naked before. Not all the way."

"I know."

"You... fuck."

"Spread your legs, sweetness."

She nods and does as she's told.

I pull her to the edge of the bed and drop to my knees between her legs.

She's right. I'm keyed up. I'm going to come fast.

I need to make her come first.

I really fucking need to make her come.

"I've been dreaming about this for four months." I press the heels of my hands into her thighs, pinning her legs to the bed.

She groans as I bring my mouth to her clit.

I take a moment to savor the taste of her. Take another to tease her.

Then I go to the spot she needs.

I lick her with steady strokes.

Slowly to start.

Then faster.

Faster.

There.

"Fuck." Her thighs fight my hands. Her fingers dig into the sheets.

I release one of her legs. Take her hand. Bring it to my shoulder.

"Fuck, Cam." Her fingers dig into my shoulders. "Fuck me. Please."

"This first." I press my lips to her inner thigh, then I work her exactly how she needs me.

Hard.

Fast.

Steady.

Her touch firms.

Her thighs shake.

Her groans run together.

With the next flick of my tongue, she comes. She groans my name as she pulses against my mouth.

She gets wetter, sweeter, even more in need.

I'm not sure how it's possible. She wants more the more she comes. She's fucking greedy and I fucking love it.

I work her through her orgasm, then I stand, climb onto the bed, place my body over hers.

She wraps her legs around my waist. Looks up at me as if to say *are you sure?*

Slowly, I bring our bodies together.

My tip brushes her cunt.

Her eyes flutter closed. Her lips part with a groan.

"Fuck, Cam. Please." She wraps her arms around me. "Please fuck me."

I tease her one more time, then I drive into her.

She feels good. Warm and soft and mine.

More than before. More than anyone ever has.

It's overwhelming.

I stay there for a moment, savoring the feel of her.

Her nails dig into my back. Hard. Then softer. "Is it okay?"

"Yes."

"You're sure?"

"Positive."

"Then fuck me already."

A laugh spills from my lips. "You're perfect, you know that?"

"Yes, I'm perfect. Fuck me."

I love you. It almost forms on my tongue again. But still, it's too much.

Still, this is as much as I can take.

I can't say it. I can barely think it.

But I can show her.

I bring my lips to hers. She's not shy about kissing back. And I'm not shy about claiming her mouth as I drive into her.

Soft and slow to start.

Than harder.

Deeper.

The two of us, locked together, breathing together, hearts beating together.

Making love.

Fucking.

Sex.

Whatever I call it, it's the same.

She's mine.

And I'm hers.

I drive into her again and again.

Her nails dig into my skin.

Her thighs squeeze my hips.

Her groans vibrate down my throat.

Pleasure winds inside me quickly. I'm too keyed up. I need her too badly.

With my next thrust, I come.

I groan her name as I spill inside her.

She rocks her hips to meet me, taking me deeper, pulling me closer.

When I'm finished, I untangle our bodies.

She nestles into my chest, pulls the blanket over us.

For a moment, we lie together, still locked together, breathing together, hearts beating together.

And then she says the perfect thing. "You think thirty minutes is going to happen?"

I laugh.

"I still don't see the humor in this question."

"I know."

"If it's not, you do have a hand."

"Do I?"

"Two. Last time I checked."

I hold up my right hand. Then my left. "I see two."

"Hmm."

"I can use one now."

"No. Later."

"It could be now and later."

"Well, if you insist."

I'm not about to deny her.

Chapter Fifty-Seven

SIENNA

I f this isn't heaven, I don't know what is.

Every inch of his body against every inch of mine.

As he fucked me. And now, the two of us, lying in my bed, a few days before Christmas, a bottle of wine waiting for us.

Cam asking if I had dinner.

When I admit, no, I was too busy getting ready for the party (and too nervous to eat, not knowing how seeing Cam again after four months would go), he asks if I want to order Chinese.

"Does that go with your wine?" I ask.

"It's not a traditional pairing, but it works." He rises to grab his cell. Naked. Very, very naked.

Mmm. I mumble an agreement as I look over every inch of his skin.

"Kung Pao?"

Like we had on our first dinner in Chinatown. Perfect.

He orders on his phone, all tall and beautiful and naked, then he puts his cell down and motions *come here*.

"It's only been twenty minutes. Are you really ready?"

A laugh spills from his lips. "Fuck, Sienna. Are you trying to kill me?"

"So that's a no?"

"Follow me."

"So it's a yes?"

He shrugs *who knows*, motions *follow me* again, heads to the bathroom, runs the shower.

My shower isn't big enough for two, really, but I'm not passing up this opportunity. I grab the waterproof lube (water really does wash the natural lubrication away) and follow him into the bathroom.

He helps me into the tiny shower.

He presses every inch of his body against every inch of mine.

Then he kisses me, soft and slow.

And, uh, it happens. His cock presses against my stomach, all hard and ready and begging for my hands.

I motion to the lube on the shelf.

He smiles. "Always prepared."

"For you."

He kisses me again, then he turns me around, brings my hands to the wall, makes me wait as he slides the lube over his cock.

He holds me in place as he fucks me.

Soft and slow, like before, every inch of him against every inch of me.

He brings his hand to my clit, makes me come twice.

The second time, with him.

He stays pressed against me for a long moment, then he pries our bodies apart, helps me clean.

And I do the same for him.

After, we dry, and he dresses in his suit (it's all he has), and I don my favorite burnt orange robe.

The delivery arrives just in time.

Cam motions *I'll get it* and shoots me a look that screams *no one else is seeing you in that*.

He opens the door.

But it's not our food.

It's my sister.

And Ty.

Chapter Fifty-Eight

SIENNA

"**O**h. Uh... You forgot your scarf, Sienna." Indie's voice fills with surprise. "And, now that we've dropped it off, we'll be going."

Ty doesn't say anything.

Cam doesn't say anything.

Indie doesn't say anything.

Fuck.

I move into the main room. Then the hallway.

My eyes go to my sister. I don't know what to make of her expression. There's surprise in it, yes, but there's something else too.

And Ty—

Fuck, the man holds a poker face.

"Do you want to come in?" I ask. "Or do you guys need to go downstairs to have a fist fight or something?"

"Baby, you knew this was a possibility." Indie wraps her hand around Ty's wrist. "Let's talk in the morning, after, uh..."

Ty stares daggers at his cousin.

Indie stills. She's scared of what her husband is capable of.

I am too.

Ty is intimidating under normal circumstances. With this?

Is that simmering rage in his dark eyes? Or is he...

Uh...

I don't have a more realistic option than simmering rage.

I move into the hallway. Next to Cam. Maybe Ty wants to punch out his cousin. If he does—

I won't win the fight against machismo, but I can keep him from knocking out my boyfriend in my apartment.

Well, Cam isn't necessarily my boyfriend.

And Ty pays for this apartment.

But, uh—

Deep breath.

Slow exhale.

All the calm logic in the world.

"Ty, I appreciate your concern. And I appreciate you looking out for me. I know you're about to punch Cam because you think he hurt me," I say.

Ty's jaw cricks.

"And... if that's what you have to do, fine. I won't tell you how to handle your relationship with Cam. But you're not punching him in my apartment."

He doesn't pull rank as payer of the rent. He just stands and stares.

"And you're wrong. Cam hasn't hurt me. Not even in the normal way, the way you hurt Indigo three years ago." It's been agony, waiting for him to be ready, but a good agony. Like when he teases me again and again and—

Not sharing that with my brother-in-law.

"I'm an adult. I decide who I date, who I fuck, who I love. And I love him. So I'm going to have to ask you not to

420

hurt him." I pull my robe tighter. It's really not helping my case, but here we are. "Please."

Ty stares at me with that expert poker face. "You love him?"

"Yes. And we… we were planning to tell you soon. But, uh, it's a long story. And I—"

"Wanted to fuck her first?" Ty addressees his cousin.

My cheeks flame with anger. "Hey, if you have an issue with Cam breaking his promise not to fuck me, that's between the two of you. But he's been working really hard on his issues." I stare back at him, no longer concerned with his ability to destroy me, or put a hit out on my boyfriend, or ruin my relationship with my sister. "Don't take that tone with him."

I guess Ty realizes he's being an asshole, because he softens. He turns to Cam, like we're not here. "Is that true?"

"Since I got back to London," he says.

"And you love her?" Ty asks.

"I do," Cam says.

He loves me.

Holy fuck.

My heart jumps into my throat. I open my mouth to speak, but I'm tongue tied.

Cam loves me.

And Ty might throw him off the roof.

And Cam loves me.

"So, uh, we'll talk about this tomorrow," Indie says. "Right, baby? We're going to let them unpack this revelation, and if you want to kill Cam, you can do it tomorrow."

"You won't hold it against me?" Ty asks her.

"If you kill him? Yeah, I like Cam. And he's my sister's boyfriend now." She looks to me *we are so talking about this later*. "And who would have thought Sienna would stick with one guy for months."

Ty actually chuckles. "That's true."

"And someone on the other side of the Atlantic," she says. "She can't get into trouble all the time."

"She'll find a way," Ty says.

"And I love that you want to protect her, I do. But she's my sister. It's my job," Indie says.

He shakes his head. "She's my sister too now." He turns to me. "You are, Sienna. You're not like a sister to me. You are my sister."

"And you wouldn't kill your sister's boyfriend," I say. "Because she'd never forgive you."

"Apparently, it wouldn't be good for my marriage." Ty squeezes my sister's hand. Then he releases it, turns to Cam. "But I'll take the risk if you hurt her. If you break her heart, I'll destroy you."

It's what I told him about Indie. I can't really object.

It's almost sweet.

Way too much. But that's Ty.

She whispers something in his ear.

He actually… smiles.

And Cam nods. "Of course."

And they… shake.

Okay…

Men are weird.

Indie shoots me one more *I can't believe you kept this from me for half a year* look then she says good night and drags her husband to the elevator.

I close the door.

For a minute, I stand there, shell-shocked, confused.

Ty was angry. And now he's… not angry.

My sister can talk him down.

Even if she doesn't, he won't kill Cam. He might kick his ass. Or throw a punch Cam won't dodge.

I didn't think Ty followed the bro code, but hey…

422

Male ego and paternalism and all that bullshit.

Ty means well. He's trying to protect me. He won't kill my boyfriend.

He won't kill his own cousin.

Hopefully.

And—

Cam closes the distance between us. "I do, Sienna." His fingers brush my cheek. "I can't say it yet, but I do."

He loves me.

He's not saying it to avoid Ty's rage.

Cam loves me.

He pulls me into a slow deep kiss.

And it's there.

All his love pours into me. And all my love pours into him.

This is weird and complicated and messy.

And I wouldn't have it any other way.

Epilogue

SIENNA

W hen I was a kid, family dinners were my favorite part of the week. When Dad died, and the tradition ended, I missed the togetherness as much as I missed the ice cream sundaes.

Even when Indie brought back weekly dinners, when it was just the two of us on a Monday night, eating pasta and going out for gelato—

It was great, but it wasn't the same. I missed those dinners for a long time.

I never thought I'd say enough with the family dinners already.

But oh my fucking god, enough with the family dinners already.

This is Hunt family dinner four in as many weeks. All six of us. Me and Cam, Indigo and Ty, Ian and Eve.

Cam's been here for an entire month.

And Ty's been torturing us with togetherness and expensive wine.

We do it at his apartment. I don't *have* to dress up, even if all three Hunt men wear suits to the occasion (as if they ever wear anything else).

When Cam's in London, I show up in jeans, sweats even. Not as a *fuck you* to Ty, because I'm not saying *fuck you*. It's more playful. More *you're you and I'm me and let's keep it that way*.

See, this tradition didn't start four weeks ago, when Cam arrived to celebrate the end of my first year of school.

It started the Friday after we were, uh, discovered. (I didn't see Ty and Cam duke it out, but Indie says both of them walked out of the room like they'd been throwing verbal punches. I think actual punches would have been easier. I would have rather Indie tackled me than looked me in the eyes and said *I'm not mad you lied, I understand why you did, but I'm disappointed you didn't feel you could be honest with me.* That was agony. And it did take a while to win her trust back. We're good now, but she was concerned all winter).

Supposedly, these dinners are about trust and family time. And they are. And I love the trust and family time, but...

Well, Ty scares me. He shifts into *I'll destroy the bastard* whenever Indie or I mention a perceived slight. And it's not even in an angry way. It's more a quiet intensity. Like of course Ty will destroy anyone who hurts his wife or his sister-in-law.

It's his duty, and he does it proudly.

Which is sweet.

But intense.

(I guess that's a good description of Ty. Only the sweetness is more under wraps).

Ty's not quite as grr when Ian and Eve join us. They're here half the time and I don't really mind being a fifth wheel now that Eve and I are friends. I enjoy watching Ian bait Ty. It's so strange and delightful seeing Ty's younger brother side come out.

And whenever Cam's in town, he joins us too.

Now that Cam's visit is almost over, and he's about to go back to London—

Ty really is torturing us on purpose, I swear. We sit through five courses. Five freaking courses.

Ty tells a million stories over dessert.

It's a good thing he's an excellent cook. This chocolate torte is perfect. Rich and gooey and covered in fresh raspberries.

Finally, after Ian takes over *embarrass the younger family member* duties, and tells his fiftieth story about trying to teach Ty how to flirt (he was hopeless, truly hopeless. It's a good thing he was a handsome football player, because otherwise... no chance).

Finally, after a billion hours not fucking my boyfriend, we say goodbye and head to the elevator.

And take it to the lobby.

Huh?

"We're going to your place?" I ask.

Cam's palm skims my bare back.

Since he's been here, I've been dressing up. Not because I like looking fancy, exactly. More because I love the way he looks at me when I'm wearing something short and low-cut.

"You don't want to?" He pulls me into a tight embrace.

"It's far."

"Six blocks?"

I nod. "Mine is right there. We could be naked already."

"We could be naked right now."

"We're almost to the lobby."

"So?" He raises a brow, daring me.

"You wouldn't."

"You wouldn't either." His fingers skim the hem of my dress. Then they dip under it.

He runs his hand up my thigh. Higher, higher, higher—

There—

"Fuck, sweetness." He presses his palm against me. "You're not wearing anything under this."

"I know."

"You didn't tell me."

"It's supposed to be a surprise."

He pulls me into a slow, deep kiss as he draws circles on my clit.

Again and again and—

Ding.

Fuck.

He pulls his hand back as the doors slide open.

My body whines. Six blocks is too far. Upstairs is too far. Everything is too far.

He smiles, completely aware I'm in agony and savoring every minute, then he slips his jacket over my shoulders and he leads me outside.

Summer wool.

It really is comfortable. Perfect for the weather. The late June sky is dark and gloomy. The air is cool but humid.

If circumstances were different, I'd appreciate the layer.

Right now?

I'm already on fire. I need less fabric, not more.

"It's only six blocks," he says.

My lips part with a sigh.

His smile widens. "You can make it."

"I'm not sure that's true. I might die of sexual frustration."

"Ten hours since your last orgasm and you're going to die of sexual frustration?"

I nod.

He pulls me into a hard, deep kiss.

Fuck.

My entire body is humming. There's only one thing in my head. *Need Cam now. Need Cam now.*

And I feel it from him too. He needs me; he wants me; he loves me.

He hasn't said it yet, but I know.

Maybe I should be more concerned. It's been six months since we officially deemed ourselves boyfriend and girlfriend. That's a long time to wait for those three little words.

But it's nothing compared to waiting four months to fuck him.

After that...

Six months is child's play.

Besides, I'm not waiting, really. I'm with him. Yes, he's in London most of the time, but we text every day, we talk twice a week; he stays here for a four-day weekend once a month.

And this. He's been here since I finished the school year. For an entire month, we've been tangled in his sheets (he bought an apartment in January) or exploring the city or daring each other to run further, farther.

It's true. He fucked me in the shower this morning (after we ran a five-mile race; which he just barely won), but that was ten hours ago.

Practically an eternity.

"It's definitely fatal." My fingers curl into his neck. "I'm not sure I'll make it all the way."

"You're losing your strength?"

I nod.

"I'll have to work with that." He leans down, lifts me into his arms, holds me to his chest.

I hook my arms around his neck instantly. "Are you really doing this?"

"Unless you want to admit you're full of shite."

"I would never."

"Uh-huh." He carries me down the street.

I hold him tightly the entire walk. It's Friday night. The Financial District is quiet. Mostly drinkers breaking from hotel bars to smoke or business people leaving work late.

But every single person we pass looks at us like we're crazy.

We are.

Love does that to you. It makes you crazy.

I expect him to release me when we move into his building, but he doesn't. He carries me into the elevator, turns so I'm facing the buttons.

"Hit my floor, sweetness," he says.

"You can set me down."

"No. You're going to need that strength."

Mmm. Yes. I free one of my hands long enough to tap the penthouse button. Then I look up at him. "Hey."

"Hey."

I curl my fingers into the back of his head, pull him into a soft, slow kiss.

My lips part.

His tongue slides into my mouth.

The elevator dings.

I nearly jump out of his arms, but he holds me tightly as me moves down the hallway. He even asks me to unlock the door.

When I do, he kicks it open, carries me into the big, airy room.

The red couch is the same. The clean hardwood is the same. The oak dining table is the same.

But the balloons are new.

Big, gold letters spelling *I love you, Sienna.*

I'm glad I'm in his arms, because I'm pretty sure I've lost the use of my limbs.

He carries me all the way to the couch. Lays me on the supple red leather.

I need to touch him.

I need to fuck him.

I need to kiss him.

Did I mention I need to fuck him?

"Cam…" Words refuse to form on my lips. There's too much I want to say. I love him, I want him, I need him.

He smiles, sits next to me, pulls me into his lap. "I do, Sienna." He cups my cheek with his palm. "I love you."

"Yeah?"

"Yeah."

He pulls me into a slow, deep kiss. "I have, for a long time."

"I know."

"I wish I could have said it sooner."

"I know, but this is—" My fingers curl into his neck. "It will be perfect after you fuck me."

He smiles.

Oh god, I know that smile. That's *Sienna is adorable and I'm going to savor that instead of fucking her this instant.* "What? What's funny?"

"I love you so fucking much, Sienna."

"Yes, yes, you love me. Sex now. Talk later."

He laughs.

"No, no, no laughing. Fucking."

"Stop making me laugh then."

"I'm not trying."

"That's what makes it funny."

"I hate you."

"Sex soon," he says.

"Yeah?" My voice perks.

He chuckles. "This first." He motions to a gift on the coffee table. A tiny white box wrapped in gold ribbon.

When did he put that there?

"Are you waiting to open a present?" he teases.

"I have to move off your lap to reach it."

"You can come back to it."

"But I don't want to leave it."

Again, he laughs.

This time, I don't mind so much. Well, I never mind. It's kind of sweet, how much he enjoys my quirkiness. And I love his laugh. It lights up the room.

Just…

I also want him to fuck me immediately.

Greedy, I know, but I'm always greedy when it comes to Cam.

I unwrap the present to find a key on a sleek gold chain. It's marked with my initials. *SS.* Like the key I gave him last year.

Like the key he gave me when he bought this place.

So, what is this?

"Look under the key," he says.

It's not just white gauze. It's a folded paper. A plane ticket.

First class to London, Monday. The seat next to his.

"Come with me," he says. "Stay for the summer."

"All summer?"

"Until pre-season."

Until soccer pre-season. That starts in August, which only leaves us five weeks. But five weeks? That's the most time I've ever had with him.

"I'll have to work a few days a week. The rest of the time, I'm yours."

Five entire weeks with him. Where he's mine and mine alone. "Cam." My heart rises in my throat. "I… Yes. Of course."

"Yeah?" He runs his thumb over my temple.

"Yeah." I lean into the touch. For a moment, I savor the

sweetness of the gesture, then I bring my hand to his tie and I look him in the eyes. "But sex now."

"Right now?"

"Yes, right now."

"Here?"

"Unless you can teleport."

He smiles as he pulls me into position, so I'm straddling him. "I love you so much, sweetness."

"I love you too." I tug at his tie. "Now, less sweet talk. More dirty talk."

His smile widens. "Come here."

He pulls me into his arms, carries me to the bed, lays me on the smooth sheets.

And then he shifts into that other version of Cam. The dirty, demanding man who makes me come.

The dirty, demanding man who's mine and mine alone.

Want More?

Sign up for my mailing list for the exclusive extended epilogue to *Dirty Secret* for another taste of Cam and Sienna.

In the mean time, read the entire Hunt family saga, starting with *Dirty Desires*, Ian and Eve's book.

College student Eve is broke and out of options. Tech mogul Ian Hunt offers her a lifeline: six figures for every one of her firsts.

Turn the page for a sample.

All caught up on the Hunt family? Go back to the beginning of the Dirty-verse with *Dirty Deal*, a fake marriage romance.

Or, if you've already ready every book in the Dirty-verse, check out *Tempting*, a best friend's brother romance.

Dirty Desires - Excerpt

EVE

"Is it really true?" A man with grey hair leans across the bar. Lowers his voice to a stage whisper. "Are you really a virgin?"

I press my lips together. No need to smile. As the owner put it, I'm not here for my charming personality. I'm here because the club is light on girls with a "punk bitch" aesthetic. "What was that? Appletini?" I pretend as if I can't hear the man. "Or was it chocolate martini?"

He looks me up and down. "You."

Is there a drink that sounds like *you?* Something bright pink. With a raunchy name. The kind of drink college girls order on spring break. I don't have a problem with grown men ordering a *blow job* but this guy—

No, that's only going to give him ideas.

Forget it. "Is the well vodka okay?"

He reaches for my hand. Wraps his greedy fingers around my wrist. "Eve, isn't it?"

"The apple martini—"

"Sure. Give me the best you've got."

I guess that answers that question. Is inappropriate question guy embarrassed by a bright green drink? No. He wants the best. The very best vodka. The very best apple liqueur. The very best... shit, what else is in this drink?

The owner didn't hire me for my expertise. He hired me because a) I begged, b) a friend from high school vouched for me, and c) I could start work on my eighteenth birthday.

I guess there's also d) a lack of girls with teal hair and tattoos. I am the only "punk bitch" who works at Devil's Point.

It's a dive and the customers are assholes, but the tips are good. Besides, there's something satisfying about mixing drinks, learning formulas, perfecting recipes.

After six months, I know cocktails pretty well. But this is the first Appletini.

I improvise. Vodka, apple liqueur, lemon.

I shake the drink with ice, strain it into a martini glass, slide it across the bar.

To his credit, Drunk McHandsy offers his credit card without provocation.

I file the card. There's no space for Drunk McHandsy, but it's Tuesday evening. Quiet. Except for the bachelor party by the stage, the club is empty. I need to make this guy feel important if I want to go home with enough tip money to cover rent. "What did you say you do?"

"A doctor. I know the female anatomy well." He winks. Takes a long sip of his apple martini. "Shit, this is good." He turns to the stage for a moment. Watches a lean blond dancer undo the buttons of her blouse one at a time.

Yes, this isn't *just* a dive bar. It's a strip club. That's the other reason why the owner hired me. He was sure I'd "get dollar signs in my eyes as soon as I saw what the dancers were pulling in."

I understand his point.

Between rent, tuition, and Addie's medical expenses, I need money.

On a good night, I go home with a few hundred dollars.

On a good night, the woman working the stage—she goes by Britney—goes home with a few thousand.

Only she has to touch all these strange men. She has to let them touch her.

I see the way men reach for dancers. They think twenty dollars buys them carte blanche.

"Is that why you don't dance?" Drunk McHandsy turns to me with wide eyes. "Because you've never been with a man?"

"I like making drinks." I strain the extra liquor into a martini glass.

"Are you saving yourself for a good man?"

"Why? Do you know one?"

His laugh echoes around the room. "So it is true?"

"That I need a good man?" Let's face it, I need a man like I need another bill to pay. Eighteen years full of disappointing men. My father, my bosses, even the senior year English teacher who refused to let me pick Margaret Atwood for my final project.

"That you're a virgin?"

There's no way I'm getting out of this question with a good tip. Either I lie and say no. Claim an interest in women (if only). Or I tell him the truth.

Well, some of it.

"I am." I finish the green drink. Let it warm my cheeks and throat. Let it sweeten the music and soften the air.

"Really?"

"Really."

"You just…" He glances at Britney as the song shifts to *Hit Me Baby, One More Time*. Dancers work a three-song set. Clothed, topless, nude. This is number three. Of course, she interprets nude in her way. The panties come off. The schoolgirl skirt stays on.

The frat bros celebrating a friend's wedding go wild.

It's an apt choice. Britney. Apparently, her virginity was *the* gossip of the day. Everyone was obsessed with the pop star maintaining her innocence.

This male obsession with virginity... I don't get it. Yes, I'm a virgin. Yes, I like men. Yes, I've had boyfriends. Two. In high school.

Yes, we did all the normal things.

We kissed, held hands, watched movies. Boyfriend number two even got to second base. His hands were too cold. His touch was too blunt. But I still enjoyed it. I still wanted more.

There was something stopping me. Fear. Nerves. An inability to trust him with my body. I'm not sure. I lost my chance.

Dad left and life got way too complicated for boyfriends.

"You don't look like a virgin." He studies my teal hair. My thick eyeliner. My black mini-dress. "You look like... a sex kitten."

Gross.

"Like you know how to please a strong man."

Even more gross. I reach for the drink, but it's empty. For the best. I need to stay focused. So I make rent. "It's the makeup."

Addie says I look like a punk rock princess.

I prefer to think of my attire as a shield. The eyeliner says *I don't give a fuck what you think.* The dark lipstick says *leave me alone.* The combat boots say *I will kick you in the head if you fuck with me.*

That's probably why this guy is asking. He can't see my combat boots. He doesn't know I'm at the end of my rope. He doesn't know I'm completely out of patience.

He leans back to finish his Appletini. Then he sets the glass on the bar. Motions for another.

It's hard to keep a poker face with him watching me, but I manage.

There. I tap the order into the machine. Pour. Slide the glass to him.

"Guys must ask all the time." He holds up the drink as if to toast. "If you're a virgin."

"Word gets around."

His eyes fix on my breasts. He watches my chest rise and fall with my exhale. He watches like he's picturing me in his bed. Like he's sure he has me where he wants me. "Do you want them to stop asking?"

Why? Does he have a button that will change the culture. Swap gender roles, so we obsess over male virginity and shrug at the thought of women who sleep around. *Girls will be girls.*

"I have a solution." He holds up his drink. "A proposition, actually."

"Shoot."

"You don't work here for your health."

What gave that away?

"You must need money. I have money. A lot of it. But I don't have you. What do you say, Eve? What do you say we make a trade? Something I want for something you want."

Author's Note

Much like Indigo, I'm a music lover and a "lyrics person." As a teenager, I obsessed over two albums in particular (by two different beautifully broken lyricists. Was I in love with them? Oh yeah, but that's a story for another time and another series. If this paragraph calls to you, check out *Sing Your Heart Out*).

One of these albums featured a man with an extremely tortured, breathy voice. He spilled his guts exclusively for my ears. And the first song of his album was something shocking to my teenage sensibility:

A boy not ready for sex.

The narrator is at a party, feeling self-destructive and depressed. An aggressive woman propositions him. He's not ready, but he goes upstairs with her anyway. It's part of becoming a man. What choice does he have, if he wants to be a man?

So he sleeps with her, even though he feels sick the entire time.

Is it sexual assault? Is it consensual? He's not sure. He

never says no. He never says yes. He's not sure what to call it, but he knows men are supposed to want sex, regardless of the other details.

As an adult, I can put the song into context:

We still expect men to want sex, any sex, all sex, period, end of sentence.

As a teenager, the song blew my freaking mind. A guy not ready to have sex? Was that really possible?

Even then, I knew his confession was rare.

Men didn't admit fear or inexperience or inability. Certainly not in the realm of sexual desire.

Fifteen years later (give or take), people are more able to see boys, and men, as potential victims. But the view of men as sex seekers and women as gatekeepers is strong, especially in romance.

Have you ever seen this joke on social media?

What's one thing an alpha hero would never say? "Not tonight, babe, I have a headache."

But why not?

Why can't an alpha hero say no?

Are these men immune from headaches? What about other physical maladies?

Emotional ones? Sure, some people use sex as a coping mechanism, but plenty don't. And, let's face it, the favorite coping mechanism of many a broken bad boy--alcohol, as much as possible--is known for its dick disabling effects.

What about people who's sex drives shut down when they're in pain or under stress? Or people who are just tired or in a bad mood or in need of alone time?

Why can't those people include men?

Why can't alpha heroes say no?

I get it. These are sexy books. We want them to be sexy.

But can't a man who says no be sexy?

The bossy heroes we adore say no everywhere outside the bedroom. Why not in the bedroom too?

And not just in a "you'll come when I say you come" kind of way.

In a "not right now baby. I have a lot to think about" kind of way.

Or "I'm not in the right headspace" kind of way.

Isn't a man who knows how to tend to his own emotions sexy?

I don't know what your answer is. But, for me, that's an obvious yes. And, even if it wasn't, I'm an extremely skilled writer (if I say so myself). I can make anything sexy.

I can certainly make a man who says no sexy.

I can make mutual respect sexy. (Well, I don't really know how to find anything else sexy. What's hotter than a man who respects you as a woman, a professional, and a sexual being?)

I hope I've brought you that with *Dirty Secret*. I hope I brought you a hero who isn't any less sexy because of his hang ups or his status as a victim.

And I hope you love Cam and Sienna as much as I do, because I really fucking love this book.

It's strange calling *Dirty Secret* fun because of the subject matter, but it's really fucking fun. I'm most known for writing about found families of bad boys, both ridiculous rapscallions and brooding grumps, and I loved bringing that energy into *Dirty Secret*.

I hope to write a series like *Dirty Secret* next, a world of rich, powerful men with secrets and senses of humor, who are all part of one big dysfunctional family, found or otherwise.

And I hope to see you there.

Until then, if you loved this book, you'll love *Dirty Desires* and *Dirty Wedding*. If you've read those already, try *Tempting*, for another forbidden romance with a brooding hero and light BDSM themes.

Whatever you do, keep reading.

Love,

Crystal

Acknowledgments

My first thanks goes to my husband, for his support when I'm lost in bookland and for generally being the sun in my sky. Sweetheart, you're better than all the broken bad boys in the world.

The second goes to my father, for insisting I go to the best film school in the country, everything else be damned. I wouldn't love movies, writing, or storytelling half as much if not for all our afternoon trips to the bookstore and weekends at the movies. You've always been supportive of my goals, and that means the world to me.

A big shout out to all my beta readers. And also to my ARC readers for helping spread the word to everyone else in the world.

To all my writer friends who talk me down from the ledge, hold my hand, and tell me when my ideas are terrible and when they're brilliant, thank you.

Thanks so much to my editor Marla, and to Hang Le for the cover design.

As always, my biggest thanks goes to my readers. Thank

you for picking up *Dirty Secret*. I hope you'll be back for my next book, *Broken Beast*, a sexy, moody Beauty and the Beast story (and maybe my most damaged hero EVER!!!). Exact details & dates to be announced. (Title may be changed).

Also by Crystal Kaswell

Sinful Serenade

Sing Your Heart Out - Miles

Strum Your Heart Out - Drew

Rock Your Heart Out - Tom

Play Your Heart Out - Pete

Sinful Ever After – series sequel

Just a Taste - Miles's POV

Dangerous Noise

Dangerous Kiss - Ethan

Dangerous Crush – Kit

Dangerous Rock – Joel

Dangerous Fling – Mal

Dangerous Encore - series sequel

Standalones

Broken - Trent & Delilah

Come Undone Trilogy

Come Undone

Come Apart

Come To Me

Sign up for the Crystal Kaswell mailing list

Printed in Great Britain
by Amazon

25637639R00260